Dear Reader,

I really can't express how flattered I am and also how grateful I am to Harlequin Books for releasing this collection of my published works. It came as a great surprise. I never think of myself as writing books that are collectible. In fact, there are days when I forget that writing is work at all. What I do for a living is so much fun that it never seems like a job. And since I reside in a small community, and my daily life is confined to such mundane things as feeding the wild birds and looking after my herb patch in the backyard, I feel rather unconnected from what many would think of as a glamorous profession.

But when I read my email, or when I get letters from readers, or when I go on signing trips to bookstores to meet all of you, I feel truly blessed. Over the past thirty years, I have made lasting friendships with many of you. And quite frankly, most of you are like part of my family. You can't imagine how much you enrich my life. Thank you so much.

I also need to extend thanks to my family (my husband, James, son, Blayne, daughter-in-law, Christina, and granddaughter, Selena Marie), to my best friend, Ann, to my readers, booksellers and the wonderful people at Harlequin Books—from my editor of many years, Tara, to all the other fine and talented people who make up our publishing house. Thanks to all of you for making this job and my private life so worth livi

Thank you for this trib
for putting up with me
Love to all of you.

Diana Palmer

D0711531

DIANA PALMER

The prolific author of more than one hundred books, Diana Palmer got her start as a newspaper reporter. A multi–*New York Times* bestselling author and one of the top ten romance writers in America, she has a gift for telling the most sensual tales with charm and humor. Diana lives with her family in Cornelia, Georgia.

Visit her website at www.DianaPalmer.com.

THE Essential COLLECTION

DIANA

New York Times and *USA TODAY* Bestselling Author

PALMER

TRILBY

TORONTO NEW YORK LONDON
AMSTERDAM PARIS SYDNEY HAMBURG
STOCKHOLM ATHENS TOKYO MILAN MADRID
PRAGUE WARSAW BUDAPEST AUCKLAND

Recycling programs
for this product may
not exist in your area.

ISBN-13: 978-0-373-36401-5

TRILBY

Copyright © 1992 by Susan Kyle

First Published by Ivy Books

This edition published by arrangement with Harlequin Books S.A.

For questions and comments about the quality of this book
please contact us at Customer_eCare@Harlequin.ca.

www.Harlequin.com

Printed in U.S.A.

Chapter One

There was a yellow dust cloud on the horizon. Trilby stared at it with subdued excitement. In the months she'd spent on the ranch, in this vast territory of Arizona, even a dust cloud had the potential to lift her boredom. Compared to the social whirl of New Orleans and Baton Rouge, this country was uncivilized. October was almost over, but the heat hadn't lifted. If anything, it was worse. To a genteel young woman of impeccable Eastern breeding, the living conditions were trying. It was a long way from the family mansion in Louisiana to this isolated wooden frame house near Douglas, Arizona. And the men who inhabited this wasteland were as near to barbarians as a red Indian. There were plenty of those around, too. An old Apache and a young Yaqui worked for her father. They never spoke, but they stared. So did the dusty, unbathed cowboys.

Trilby spent a great deal of time inside, except on wash days. One day a week, she had to go outside, where she and her mother dealt with a big black cast-iron pot in which white things—like her father's shirts—were boiled, and two Number Two tin washtubs in which the remainder of the clothes were, respectively, washed by hand against a scrub board and rinsed.

"Is it going to be dust or rain?" her little brother Teddy asked from behind, scattering her thoughts.

She glanced at him over her thin shoulder and smiled gently. "Dust, I expect. What they call the monsoon season has passed and it is dry again. What else could it be?" she asked.

"Well, it could be Colonel Blanco and some of the *insurrectos,* the Mexican rebels fighting Díaz's government," he suggested. "Gosh, remember the day that cavalry patrol rode onto the ranch and asked for water and I got them a bucket?"

Ted was only twelve, and the memory was the high point of his young life. Their family's ranch was near the Mexican border, and on October 10, Porfirio Díaz had been reelected president of Mexico. But the strongman was under attack from Francisco Madero, who had campaigned against him and lost. Now Mexico was in a state of violent unrest. Sometimes the rebels—who might or might not belong to a band of *insurrectos*—raided local ranches. The cavalry watched over the border. The situation in Mexico was becoming even more explosive than it usually was.

It had already been an interesting year up until that point, too, with Halley's Comet terrorizing the world in May and the sad event of King Edward's death on its heels. In the months that followed, there had been a volcanic eruption in Alaska and a devastating earthquake in Costa Rica. Now there was this border trouble, which made life interesting for Teddy, but deeply upset ranchers and private citizens. Everyone knew people who were connected with mining down in Sonora, because six Sonoran mining companies had their headquarters in Douglas. And plenty of local ranchers also owned land over in Mexico; foreign ownership of Mexican land to exploit mining interests and ranching was one of the root causes of the growing unrest over the border.

A detachment of khaki-clad U.S. Cavalry soldiers from the encampment at Fort Huachuca had come riding through only today, their officers in a snappy touring car with mounted troops behind them, scouting for trouble and looking so attractive that Trilby had to choke down a wildly uncharacteristic impulse to smile and wave at them. Teddy had no such inhibitions. He almost fell off the porch waving as they filed by. This column didn't stop to ask for water, which had disappointed her young brother.

Teddy was so unlike her. She had blond hair and gray eyes; he had red hair and blue eyes. She smiled as she remembered the grandfather for whom he was a dead ringer.

"Two of our Mexican cowboys admire Mr. Madero very much. They say Díaz is a dictator and that he should be thrown out," he told her.

"I do hope the matter is settled before it ends in a total war," she said worriedly, "so that we don't get caught in the middle of any fighting. It worries Mama, too, so don't talk about it much, will you?"

"All right," he said reluctantly. Airplanes, baseball, Mexican unrest, and the often related memories of his elderly friend, Mosby Torrance, were his biggest thrill at the moment, but he didn't want to worry Trilby with just how serious the situation down in Mexico was becoming. She had no idea what the cowboys talked about. Teddy wasn't supposed to know, either, but he'd overheard a good deal. It was frightening to him; it would be more frightening to his sheltered older sister.

Trilby had always been protected from rough language and rough people. Being in Arizona, around Westerners who had to cope with the desert and livestock and the weather—and the threat of rustling to stay alive—had changed her. She didn't smile as often as she had back in Louisiana, and there was less mischief about her. Teddy missed the Trilby of years past. This new older sister was so reserved and quiet that sometimes he wasn't sure she was even in the house.

Even now she was staring out over the barren landscape, into the distance, with that faraway look in her eyes. "I expect Richard is back from Europe by now," she murmured. "I wish he could have come out to see us. Perhaps in a month or so, when he's settled at home, he can. It will be pleasant to be in the company of a gentleman again."

Richard Bates had been Trilby's big love interest back home, but Teddy had never liked the man. He might be a gentleman, but compared to these Arizona men, he seemed pretty anemic and silly.

He didn't say so, though. Even at his age, he was learning diplomacy. It wouldn't do to antagonize poor Trilby. She was having a hard enough time adjusting to Arizona as it was.

"I love the desert," Teddy said. "Don't you like it, just the least bit?"

"Well, I suppose I'm getting used to it," she said quietly. "But I haven't yet developed a taste for this horrible yellow dust. It gets into everything I cook," she said, "as well as into our clothes."

"It's better to do girl stuff than brand cattle, I tell you," he said, sounding just like their father. "All that blood and dust and noise. The cowboys curse, too."

Trilby smiled at him. "I expect they do; Papa, too. But never around us. Only when it's an accident."

"There's lots of accidents when you're branding cattle, Trilby," he drawled dryly, imitating his hero Mosby Torrance. He was a retired Texas Ranger and the ranch's oldest hand. Teddy looked at her, frowning. "Trilby, are you ever going to marry? You're old."

"I'm only twenty-four," she said self-consciously. Most of her girlfriends back home in Louisiana were married and had babies. Trilby had been waiting patiently for five years for Richard to propose. So far, he was no more than a friend, and her heart was heavy.

She might have been swayed if other young men had come courting, but Trilby wasn't beautiful on the outside, even if she did have a warm, gentle heart and a sweet nature. She didn't have the kind of face that set male hearts quivering, even back home. Here on a cattle ranch there weren't many eligible men who were marriage worthy. Not that she wanted to marry anyone she'd met in Arizona. She thought of cowboys as a lazy lot, and many of them drank, and used tobacco and alcohol, and never bathed.

Her heart ached as she thought about how fastidious Richard always was. She wished they'd never left Louisiana. Her father had inherited the ranch from his late brother. He and her mother had sunk every dime they had into the place, and it took all the family, plus the hired help, to run it. It had been a dry year, despite the floods, and ranchers were losing cattle across the border. All this trouble, Trilby thought, when Arizona was on its way to becoming a state. So uncivilized.

The desert was a drastic change for people more used to swamps and bayous and humidity. Trilby and her mother and father, too, had come from money, which was the only reason Jack Lang had enough to stock the ranch. But their finances had suffered over the past few months, and things were no better now than they had been. But they'd all adapted amazingly well—even Trilby, who'd hated it on sight and swore she'd never be happy on a ranch in the middle of a desert with only two lone paloverde trees for shade.

"Look, isn't that Mr. Vance?" Ted asked, shading his eyes as he spotted a solitary rider on a big buckskin horse.

Trilby ground her perfect teeth at the sight of him. Yes, it was Thornton Vance, all right. Nobody else around Blackwater Springs rode a horse with that kind of lithe, superior arrogance, or tilted his Stetson at just that slant across his tanned brow.

"I do wish his saddle would fall out from under him," she muttered wickedly.

"I don't know why you don't like him, Trilby," Ted said sadly. "He's very nice to me."

"I suppose he is, Teddy." But he and Trilby were enemies. Mr. Vance had seemed to take an instant dislike to Trilby the day they were introduced.

The Langs had lived in Blackwater Springs for almost three weeks by the time they made Thornton Vance's acquaintance. Trilby remembered his delicate, faintly haughty wife holding carelessly to his arm as the introductions were made at a church social. Thornton Vance's

cold, dark eyes had narrowed with unexpected antagonism the minute they'd spotted Trilby.

She'd never understood that animosity. His wife had
been faintly condescending when they were introduced.
Mrs. Vance was beautiful and knew it. Her dress was
ready-made and expensive, like her purse and lace-up
shoes. She had blond hair and blue eyes—and her well-
bred contempt for Trilby's inexpensive clothing had been
infuriating. Her little girl looked subdued. No wonder.

Back in Louisiana, Trilby had worn good clothes herself. But now there was no money for frivolities, and
she had to make do with what she had. The implied
insult in Mrs. Vance's cold eyes had gone straight to her
heart. Perhaps unconsciously she'd extended her hostility
toward the woman to include Thornton Vance himself.

Thornton Vance had frightened Trilby from the beginning. He was a tall, rough, fiery sort of man who said
exactly what he thought and didn't have any of the usual
social graces. He was an outlaw in a land of outlaws, for
all his wealth, and Trilby had no use for him. He was as
different from her Richard as night was from day. Not exactly her Richard, she had to admit, not yet. But if she'd
been able to stay in Louisiana for just a little longer, if
she'd been a little older… She groaned inwardly as she
tried to understand why fate had cast her into Thornton
Vance's path.

Vance's cousin Curt had been totally different from
Thorn, and Trilby had warmed to him at once. She liked
Curt Vance because he was cultured and gentlemanly,
and he somehow reminded her of Richard. She didn't
see him often, but she was fond of him.

Curt had seemed fond of Mr. Vance's wife, too. Sally
Vance had managed to interfere every time Trilby had

spoken to Curt, holding his arm with a faintly proprietorial air. Her antagonism for Trilby had been more evident every time they met, so that finally Trilby managed not to attend any function where she was likely to see the other woman.

Sally had died in a very suspicious accident just two months after the Langs arrived in Blackwater Springs. Mr. Vance had accepted the routine condolences from her family, but when Trilby offered hers, he actually turned on his booted heel and walked away in what was a visible and very public snub, motioning his little girl along with him.

Trilby had never had the nerve to ask how she'd managed to offend a man she'd only just met. She hadn't even looked at him properly. He'd avoided her like the plague, even when they met socially and he had his little girl with him. The little girl had seemed to like Trilby, but she couldn't get near her because of the icy Mr. Vance. She seemed uncomfortable in her father's company, and Trilby could understand that. He intimidated people.

He'd mellowed in the past two months, though, because he often came to the ranch to see her father. He always talked about water rights and how the drought was affecting his great herds of cattle. Mr. Vance owned an enormous tract of land, thousands of acres of it, with part in the United States and part in Mexico, in the state of Sonora. Apparently Blackwater Springs Ranch sat smack-dab in the middle of the only reliable water source nearby, and Mr. Vance wanted it. Her father wouldn't discuss selling any land. That was like him. He wouldn't give up those water rights, either.

Trilby's busy mind coasted when Thornton Vance reined in just in front of the steps and crossed his tanned wrists over the pommel. Though a wealthy man, he dressed like one of his cowboys. He wore old denim jeans with worn leather bat-wing chaps. His shirt was checked and old, too, with scratched leather wristbands over the cuffs. A huge red bandanna drooped around his strong neck. It was stained and dusty now, and wrinkled. His tan hat wasn't in much better shape, looking as if it had been twisted, rained on, and stomped a few times. His boots were disreputable, like Teddy's after he'd been working cattle, the toes curled up from too much dampness and the heels worn down on either side in back. Mr. Vance didn't look very elegant, she decided, and her distaste for him showed in her face.

"Good morning, Mr. Vance," Trilby said quietly, remembering her manners, belatedly and reluctantly.

He stared at her without speaking. "Is your father at home?"

She shook her head. He had the kind of voice that was soft as velvet and deep as night, but it could cut like a whip when he wanted it to. He did now.

"Your mother?" he tried again.

"They're off with Mr. Torrance at the store," Teddy volunteered. "He drove them in on the buckboard. Dad says Mr. Torrance is used up, but it isn't true, Mr. Vance. He isn't at all used up. He was once a Texas Ranger, did you know?"

"Yes, I knew, Ted." Mr. Vance let his dark eyes slide back to Trilby. They were set in a keen, sharply defined face with a straight nose and darkly tanned skin, black eyebrows matching the equally thick, straight black hair under his hat.

Trilby felt inadequately covered for some reason, even though her neat calico dress was very demure.

She wiped her hands unnecessarily on her apron. "I should get back to the kitchen before I burn my apple pie," she began, hoping he might take the hint and go.

"Am I being offered a slice of it?" he drawled instead.

She almost panicked. Teddy answered for her, his young voice excited. "Surely!" he said enthusiastically. "Trilby bakes the best pie, Mr. Vance! I like it with cream, but our cow's gone dry just lately and we've had to do without."

"Your father didn't mention the cow," Vance said as he swung lithely out of the saddle and tied the reins to the porch post. He came up onto the porch with a bound, his long, lithe body as graceful out of the saddle as in it. He towered over Teddy and Trilby, too tall and forceful.

She turned quickly and went back into the house. At least her blond hair was up in its neat braid, not loose and uninhibited as she usually wore it around the house. She looked much more cool and collected than she felt. She wished she had some red cayenne pepper; she'd fill Mr. Vance's pie full of it. He probably thrived on hot peppers and arsenic, she thought wickedly.

"We got another cow yesterday, from Mr. Barnes down the road," Teddy volunteered. "But sis got busy baking and hasn't milked her. I'll go and do it for you, Trilby, while you check the pie. It will only take a little while."

She tried to protest, but Teddy had grabbed the tin milking pail and rushed out the back door before she could stop him. She was left alone, and frightened, with the hostile Mr. Vance.

He wasn't bothering to camouflage his hostility now, either, with Teddy out of the way. He pulled a Bull Durham pouch out of his pocket, along with a small folder of tissue papers, and proceeded to roll a cigarette with quick, deft movements of his long-fingered hands.

Trilby busied herself checking inside the wood stove to see if her pie was finished. Back home, there had been a gas stove. Trilby had been secretly afraid of it, but she sometimes missed it now that she had to cook on the wood-burning one, the best they could afford. Stocking the ranch had been expensive. Keeping it going was getting harder by the day. Teddy should never have mentioned the cow going dry.

She saw the brown crust even as she smelled the mingled cinnamon and sugar and butter smell of baking apples. Just right. She took her cloths and got it quickly out of the oven and onto the long cooking table that ran almost from wall to wall. Her hands shook, but thank heaven, she didn't drop the pie.

"Do I make you nervous, Miss Lang?" he asked, pulling up a chair. He straddled it, his powerful body coiled like a snake's as he folded it down onto the chair and rested his forearms over its back. He looked very masculine, and the very set of his muscular body, with the chaps and jeans drawn tight over long, powerful legs, made Trilby feel awkward and shy. She'd never noticed Richard's legs at all. Her sudden interest in Thorn's unsettled her, made her defensive.

"Oh, no, Mr. Vance," she replied, with a vacant smile. "I find hostility *so* invigorating."

His eyebrows lifted and he had to stifle a smile. "Do you? Yet, your hands shake."

"I have little experience of men…except for my father and brother. Perhaps I'm ill at ease."

He watched her push back a wisp of blond hair with eyes that held nothing but contempt. "I thought you found my cousin quite irresistible at that social gathering last month."

"Curt?" She nodded, missing the look that flared in his dark eyes. "I like him very much. He has a pleasant manner and a nice smile. He gave Teddy a peppermint stick." She smiled at the memory. "My brother never forgets a kindness." She glanced at him warily. "Your cousin reminds me of someone back home. He's a kind man. And a gentleman," she added pointedly, her eyes making her opinion of his garb, and himself, perfectly plain without a word being spoken.

He wanted to laugh out loud. Sally had told him about seeing Curt and Miss Lang here in a passionate embrace. She wasn't the first to mention the relationship, either. A lady from the church—a notorious gossip—had mentioned seeing Curt and a blond woman in an embrace at a gathering. He'd taken the gossip home to Sally, who'd told him about Trilby. She'd done it quickly, but almost reluctantly, too. Thorn remembered that she'd gone quite pale at the time.

The revelation had left him with a fine contempt for Trilby. His cousin Curt was a married man, but Miss Lang didn't seem to mind shattering convention. Funny, a woman who acted as ladylike as she did, behaving like that. But then, he knew too well what deceivers women were. Sally had pretended to love him, when she'd only wanted a life of wealth and comfort.

"Curt's wife also admires him," he said pointedly.

When she didn't react, he sighed roughly and took a long draw from the cigarette, his eyes never leaving hers. "The wrong type of woman can ruin a good man and his life."

"I have found very few good men out here," she said

flatly. She busied herself slicing the pie. Her hands shook and she hated the fact that he watched them, his smile mocking and unkind.

"You don't seem to find the desert too hot, Miss Lang. Most Easterners detest it."

"I'm a Southerner, Mr. Vance," she reminded him. "Louisiana is hot in the summer."

"Arizona is hot year-round. But you won't find an overabundance of mosquitoes. We don't have swamps here."

She glared at him. "The yellow dust makes up for it."

"Does it, truly?" he asked, mocking that very correct Southern accent that brought to mind cotillions and masked balls and mansions.

She wiped her hands and put the knife aside. She wouldn't throw it at him, she wouldn't!

"I suppose so." She went to get the dishes for the pie from the china cabinet, praying silently that she wouldn't drop any of them. "Do you care for iced tea, Mr. Vance?" And if I only had some hemlock…

"Yes, thank you."

She opened the small icebox and with an ice pick chipped off several pieces of ice to go in the tall plain glasses. She covered the small block of ice with its cloth again and closed the door. "Ice is wonderful in this heat. I wish I had a houseful of it."

He didn't reply. She took the ceramic jug of tea she'd made for dinner and poured some of the sweetened amber liquid into the glasses. She'd fixed three, because surely Teddy would be back soon. She'd skin him if he wasn't! Her nerves were strung like barbed wire.

She put a perfect slice of pie on a saucer and placed it before him at the table with one of the old silver forks her grandmother had given them before they'd left Baton Rouge. She placed a linen napkin with it and put the glass of tea on it. The ice shook and made a noise like tiny bells against the glass.

His lean hand shot out as she withdrew hers and caught her small wrist in a hot, strong grasp. She caught her breath audibly and stared at him with wide, wary eyes.

He scowled faintly at her reaction. His gaze went to her hand as he turned it in his and rubbed the soft palm gently with his big callused thumb. "Red and worn, but a lady's hand, just the same. Why did you come out here with your family, Trilby?"

The unfamiliar sound of her name on his lips, in that deep, soft tone, made her knees weak. She stared at his work-toughened hand, at the darkness of his skin against the paleness of her fingers. His touch excited her.

"I had nowhere else to go. Besides, Mama needed me. She isn't that well."

"A fragile woman, your mother. A real Southern lady. Just like you," he added contemptuously.

She lifted her eyes to his. "What do you mean?"

"Don't you know?" he replied coldly, and the dark eyes that met hers were full of distaste. "You won't find much polite society out West, my girl. It's a hard life, and we're hard people. When you live on the fringe of the desert, you get tough or you get dead. A little bit of fluff like you won't last long. If the political situation here gets much worse, you'll wish you'd never left Louisiana."

"I'm hardly a bit of fluff," she said angrily, thinking that his late wife fit that description far more than she did, although she was too polite to say it. "Why do you dislike me so?"

He grew more somber as he looked at her. He wanted to throw his contempt in her face, but he didn't speak. A minute later, Teddy came in the back door with half a pail of milk, and Thornton Vance slowly released Trilby's hand. She rubbed it instinctively, thinking that she'd surely have a bruise on the back of it by morning. She had delicate, thin skin, and his grip hadn't been gentle.

"Here's the milk. Did you cut me a slice of that pie, Trilby?"

"Yes, Teddy. Sit down and I'll get it."

Teddy pretended not to notice Trilby's unease, putting it down to the presence of Mr. Vance....

"There, wasn't that good?" Teddy asked the visitor when they'd finished the delicious pie. Thorn had wolfed his down with delight.

"Not bad," Thorn agreed. His dark eyes narrowed on Trilby's pale face. "I think your sister finds me hard going, Ted."

"Not at all," Trilby said, denying it. "One learns to take headaches in one's stride." She got up abruptly and gathered the dishes, taking them quickly to the sink with the iron pump attached. She pumped it to get water into a pan and then poured water into the kettle and set it on the wood stove to boil.

"The stove sure does make it uncomfortable in the summer, doesn't it, Mr. Vance?" Teddy asked.

Thorn had smothered a grin at Trilby's last riposte. "You get used to things when you have to, Ted," Thorn said.

Trilby felt a twinge of sympathy for him. He'd lost his wife, and he had probably cared about her a great deal. He couldn't help being rough and uncivilized. He hadn't had the advantages of an Eastern man.

"That was good pie," Thorn said directly, and sounded surprised.

"Thank you," she said. "Grandmother taught me how to cook when I was just a little girl."

"You're not a little girl now, are you?" Vance asked curtly.

"That's right," Teddy agreed, not realizing that the question was more mockery than query. "Trilby's old. She's twenty-four."

Trilby could have gone right through the floor. "Ted!"

Thorn stared at her for a long moment. "I thought you were much younger."

She flushed. "How you do go on, Mr. Vance," she said stiffly. "Speaking of going on…"

Vance smiled at her. It changed his face, made it less formidable, charming as his black eyes sparkled. "Yes?" he prodded.

"How old are you, Mr. Vance?" Teddy interrupted.

"I'm thirty-two," he told the boy. "I suppose that puts me in the class with your grandparents?"

Teddy laughed. "Right into the rocking chair."

Vance laughed, too. He got up from the table and pulled his pocket watch out of the slit above the pocket of his jeans. He opened it and grimaced. "I've got an Eastern visitor arriving on the train this afternoon. I must go."

"Come again," Teddy invited.

"I will, when your father's home." He glanced at Trilby speculatively. "I'm having a party Friday evening, a get-together for my Eastern visitor. He was a relation of my wife's, and he's somewhat famous in academic circles. He's an anthropologist. I'd like you all to come."

"Me, too?" Teddy asked excitedly.

Vance nodded. "There'll be other youngsters around. And Curt will be there, with his wife," he added, with a pointed glance at Trilby.

Trilby didn't know what to say. She hadn't attended an evening party since they'd been in Arizona, although they'd been invited to several. Her mother didn't like social gatherings. She might agree to this one, because it wouldn't do to offend someone as wealthy and powerful as Thornton Vance, even if he did look and act like some sort of desperado.

"I'll mention it to Mama and Papa," she told him.

"You do that." He took his hat in hand and walked with easy strides to the front door with Trilby and Teddy behind him.

It was tilted at the usual rakish angle when he swung lazily into the saddle. "Thanks for the pie," he told Trilby.

She tilted her chin at just the right angle and smiled at him coldly. "Oh, it was no trouble at all. I'm sorry I couldn't offer you some cream with it."

"Had you lapped it up already?" he tormented.

She glared at him. "No. I expect you curdled it."

He chuckled with reluctant pleasure. He tipped his hat, wheeled the horse gently, and eased him into a nice trot. Trilby and Teddy watched him until he was out of sight.

"He likes you," he teased her.

She lifted an eyebrow. "I'm not at all the kind of woman he'd be interested in."

"Why not?"

She glared at Thorn's back with mingled excitement and resentment. "I expect he likes his women with their necks on the ground under his boot."

"Oh, Trilby, you're silly! Do you like Mr. Vance?" he persisted.

"No, I do not," she said tersely, and turned back into the house. "I have a lot of things to do, Teddy."

"If that's a hint, sis, I'll go find something to do myself. But I still say Mr. Vance is sweet on you!"

He ran off, down the long porch. Trilby stood with the screen door open watching after him, worried. She didn't think Mr. Vance was sweet on her. She thought he was up to something, and she didn't know what. But she was worried.

When her mother and father came home, Teddy related Mr. Vance's visit to them, and they smiled in that same knowing way. Trilby flushed like a beet.

"He isn't interested in me, I tell you. He wanted to see the both of you," she told her parents.

"Why?" her father asked.

"He's having a party Friday night," Teddy said excitedly. "He said we're all invited, and I can come, too. Can't we go? It's been ever so long since we've been to a party." He glowered at them. "And you won't let me go to see Mr. Cody's show Thursday afternoon. They said it will be his very last show—and he's got Pawnee Bill's Far East Show on the same bill, with real elephants!"

"I'm sorry, Teddy," his father said, "but we really can't spare the time, I'm afraid. We're shipping cattle to California this week, and we're still behind some of the other cattle companies getting ours en route."

"Buffalo Bill's last show and I'll miss it," Teddy groaned.

"Perhaps he isn't really retiring. Besides," Mary Lang said gently, "there's sure to be one of those new Boy Scout troops starting up soon in Douglas, what with all the publicity the movement is getting. You could join that, perhaps."

"I suppose. Can we go to the party? It's at night. You can't work at night," he added.

"I agree," Mrs. Lang said. "Besides, dear, it really wouldn't do to offend Mr. Vance when we're neighbors."

"And I suppose," her husband said mischievously as he looked at his daughter, "there won't be anyone for Thorn to dance with if Trilby doesn't go."

Which called to Trilby's mind an image of the reprehensible Mr. Vance dancing by himself. She had to smother a grin.

"Trilby calls him Mr. Vance," Teddy pointed out.

"Trilby is being respectful, as she should be," Mr. Lang replied. "But Thorn and I are cattlemen. We use first names."

Thorn suits him, Trilby thought to herself. He was just as sharp as one, and could draw blood as easily.

She didn't say it. Her father wouldn't approve of blatant rudeness.

"We're going, then?" Trilby asked.

"Yes," Mrs. Lang replied, smiling at her daughter. She was a pretty woman. She was almost forty, but she looked ten years younger. "You still have a nice dress that you haven't worn since we've been out here," she reminded Trilby.

"I wish I still had my lovely silk ensemble," Trilby replied, smiling back. "It was lost on the way here."

"Why is it called such a silly thing?" Teddy muttered.

"Well, I never!" Trilby laughed. "And don't you think

naming a stuffed bear for Teddy Roosevelt is silly?" Trilby asked absently.

"Of course not! Hoorah for Teddy!" Teddy chuckled. "His birthday is Thursday, the same day as Buffalo Bill's show; I read it in the paper. He'll be fifty-two. I was named for him, wasn't I, Dad?"

"Indeed you were. He's a hero of mine. He was a sickly, weak child, but he built himself up and became a rugged soldier, a cowboy, a politician… I suppose Colonel Teddy Roosevelt has been everything, including president."

"I'm sorry he wasn't reelected," Mrs. Lang replied. "I would have voted for him," she added, with a meaningful look at her husband. "If women could vote."

"A wrong that will one day soon be righted, you mark my words," Mr. Lang said affectionately, and put his arm around his wife's thin shoulders. "President Taft signed the Arizona statehood bill in June, praise God, and many changes will now occur as they work to get the constitution ready for ratification. But whatever happens, you're still my best girl."

She laughed and nuzzled her cheek against his shoulder. "And you're my best boy."

Trilby smiled and left with Teddy, leaving her parents to themselves. Years and years of marriage, and they were still like newlyweds. She hoped that someday she would be as fortunate in her marriage.

Chapter Two

Thorn was halfway back to the ranch when a cloud of dust caught up to him. He turned his head in time to see Naki, one of the two Apache men who worked for him, rein in to match his speed. The other man was tall and had long, shoulder-length black hair. He wore a breechclout and high-topped buckskin moccasins with a red-checked shirt and a thick, red-patterned cotton band tied around his forehead to keep his hair out of his eyes.

"Been hunting?" Thorn asked him.

The other man nodded.

"Find anything?"

The Apache didn't even glance at him. He held up one hand, displaying a thick, bound book. "I've been looking for it everywhere."

"I mean, did you shoot anything that we could eat for supper?" he said, glowering.

Naki's eyebrows lifted. "Me? Shoot something?" He sounded horrified. "Kill a helpless animal?"

"You're an Apache Indian," Thorn reminded him,

with exaggerated patience. "A hunter. Master of the bow and arrow."

"Not me. I prefer a Remington repeater rifle," he said in perfect English.

"I thought you were going to get us something in buckskin."

"I did." He held up the book again. "*Leatherstocking Tales,* by James Fenimore Cooper."

"Oh, my God!" Thorn groaned. "What kind of Apache are you?"

"An educated one, of course," Naki replied pleasantly. "You're going to have to do something about Jorge's cousin," he added, the lightness gone from his tone and the smile from his deep-set black eyes as he stopped and faced the other man. "You lost five head of cattle this morning, and not to drought and lack of water. Ricardo confiscated them."

"Damn the luck!" Thorn cursed. "Again?"

"Again. He's feeding some revolutionary comrades hidden out in the hills. I can't fault his loyalty to his family, but he's carrying it to extremes and on stolen beef."

"I'll have it out with him." He glared at the horizon. "This damned war is coming too close."

"I won't argue." Naki tucked the book in his saddlebags. He produced two rabbits on a tether and tossed them to Thorn. "Supper," he announced.

"Are you coming down to share it?"

"Share it?" Naki looked horrified. "Eat a rabbit? I'd rather starve!"

"What did you have in mind, or dare I ask?"

Naki's white teeth gleamed in a face like sculpted bronze. "Fried rattler," he said, his eyes glittering.

"Snob," Thorn accused.

Naki shrugged. "One can hardly expect a man of European ancestry to measure up to a culture as ancient and sophisticated as mine," he said, eyes sparkling with humor. "Meanwhile, I'll track Jorge's cousin down for you and bring him along."

"Don't, please, do anything nasty to him."

"I?"

"No need to look so innocent, if you please. Or wasn't it you who staked out that drummer on an anthill with wet rawhide when he sold you some snakebite medicine that didn't work?"

"A doctor should stand behind his cures."

"He didn't know you were a Latin scholar," Thorn reminded him. "Much less that you knew more about herbal medicine than he'd ever learned."

"He won't forget."

"I daresay he won't," Thorn agreed. "And I believe he led a lynch mob after you...?"

"From which you were kind enough to save me," Naki recalled. It had been the beginning of their friendship, and it went back a long, long way. Naki had reformed a little. Not much.

"Bring your snake and I'll have Tiza cook it for us."

"He cooks like he rides," Naki muttered.

"I'll cook it, then."

"I'll bring Ricardo along directly."

He turned his paint pony and rode leisurely away.

The rest of the week passed all too quickly. Trilby dressed for Thornton Vance's party with fingers that were all thumbs. She didn't want to go to Thorn's house.

She dreaded the evening as she'd never dreaded anything else.

The only expensive gown she owned that had made it out from Louisiana with her was a lacy beige one. A vicious dust storm had destroyed most of their possessions on the drive from the train to their new home on Blackwater Springs Ranch. Even now, Trilby could feel the smothering sting of yellow sand as it had blanketed them, almost buried them, on the way from Douglas. One of their acquaintances had only smiled when he was told of their ordeal, remarking that they'd best get used to dust storms out here.

They had, after a fashion. But Trilby sometimes longed for the cool green bayous of her youth and the sound of Cajun patois being spoken on the streets as she went to the bakery each Saturday for a sack of *beignets* and to shop for new dresses.

With a full purse, it had been fun to go to town in the chauffeured T-model that Rene Marquis drove for the family. Her cousins had always been her friends as well, and there were parties and afternoon teas and picnics…and then, so suddenly, there had been Richard. But before he'd done more than hold her hand in his, her uncle had died, and her father had announced that the family was moving to Arizona.

Trilby had cried for days, but it hadn't swayed her parents. Richard had gone off to Europe with his own family, with flattering reluctance and a promise to write. But to date, Trilby had written dozens of letters and she had only a card from Richard, from England. It wasn't even remotely loving. Only a friendly note. Sometimes she despaired of ever gaining his love.

She pulled herself up short. It really wouldn't do to

let herself look back. This was home now. She had to adjust to being an Arizonan, to a different kind of life. But Richard might still come to stay; he might discover passionate feelings for her. She sighed dreamily.

She put on the gown, longing for the old days when she'd had plenty of fine clothes to wear. Money was no longer plentiful. She wanted to leave her hair loose around her shoulders, but Mr. Vance being Mr. Vance, it was better, she supposed, to appear dignified and conservative, so that she didn't give him any special reasons for mocking her. He sometimes looked at her as if he actually considered her in the same light as a lady of the evening. It puzzled and hurt her. Not that she ever let it show.

She braided her soft blond hair with a blue ribbon and piled it on top of her head, grimacing at the severe thinness of her face. The heat had worn her down just lately. She had little appetite, and her slenderness had exaggerated itself.

When she finished dressing, she pinched her cheeks and lips to put a little color in them and picked up the lacy black shawl the Mexican ladies called a "mantilla." Her father had brought it to her from Mexico the last time he'd been down there to buy cattle.

"You look lovely, Trilby," her mother said warmly.

"So do you." She hugged the older woman, approving the neat, elegant black dress her mother was wearing.

Her father, in his black suit, and Teddy, in his short pants and jacket, looked uncomfortable but fashionable. They climbed into the Model-T and waited while the man of the house fiddled around until it finally cranked. Then Trilby prayed all the way to Mr. Vance's ranch that it wouldn't snap a band, or break down, or have a flat tire on the deeply rutted road. It was drizzling rain, and it would be terrible to have to get wet waiting and hoping to be rescued.

Fortunately everything went without a hitch. They pulled up in the long dirt driveway that led to Los Santos Ranch. It was an adobe structure, two stories high, with balconies all around the upper level and patios and gardens surrounding the lower one. Every plant near it seemed to be blooming, even the tall, thin ocotillo that made a natural fence near the front. It was the first time Trilby had seen it, and she was enchanted. Most of the structures she'd seen in Arizona were made of adobe, but they were usually simple and very small. This showplace was something out of a slick Eastern magazine, elegant and expensive.

Thornton Vance was waiting for them on the front porch, which was long and cool-looking with its hammock on one end and comfortable chairs on the other. Light blazed out of the glass windows, spilling in patterns on the sandy, cactus-studded front yard. There was a breeze, but it was a warm night despite the faint mist of rain. The house looked warm and inviting. Incredible, Trilby thought, considering how uninviting its master looked when his dark eyes rested on her. In his dark suit and white shirt, he looked a little severe. His black hair was neatly combed. He looked as elegant as any New Orleans gentleman. Trilby was surprised at how handsome he was when he dressed up.

"Nice of you to invite us, Thorn," her father said, with easy courtesy, as he helped first Trilby's mother, then Trilby, out of the car.

"My pleasure. Watch your step, Trilby. You're headed for a mudhole," he said abruptly. "Here, Ted, hold this."

He handed Teddy his glass and abruptly swung Trilby up in his arms—to her shock and her parents' quickly concealed delight.

He turned, carrying her up onto the porch as if she weighed nothing at all. It didn't seem to affect him, either, having her so close. But it affected her. She could barely breathe. His cologne was faint and barely detectable, but she seemed to be engulfed in its manly scent. His arms were strong and warm around her. She could feel the muscles in them despite the covering of his long-sleeved shirt and dark jacket. He wasn't breathing hard at all, as if her weight was unnoticeable.

"Better hold on," he murmured, with faint amusement. She was holding herself so stiffly that she felt brittle, and he knew she was barely breathing. It puzzled him that a woman of her character should be so nervous in a man's arms. He didn't imagine she'd been nervous in Curt's! "It's a bit of a steep climb up this porch."

That slow drawl was seductive. The pitch of his voice had dropped, just enough to stroke her ears like velvet. She'd never been so close to a man before, and the steely Mr. Vance was devastating even at a distance. This was hardly conventional behavior, and she wanted to protest, but her parents were chiding her for being so wary.

"Relax, girl," her father said, chuckling. "Thorn won't drop you."

Defeated, her thin arms climbed jerkily until they rested on his broad shoulders.

His head turned. His eyes met hers in the faint light from the windows, and the sounds of music and laughter and talking died suddenly as she was caught and held in their dark glitter.

His step didn't falter, but he wasn't watching as he

carried her slowly up onto the porch. And before he stopped to put her down, his arm contracted very slowly, very deliberately, to bring her breasts hard against his chest.

She shivered at the unexpectedly stirring contact, so vulnerable that she was unable to conceal the reaction of her body to the faint caress.

He didn't speak. Slowly he let her feet down on the floor. As he bent to release her, his mouth was only scant inches from her lips. He searched her eyes, and she felt her body grow warm at the look on his face. It was expressionless, except for the explicit longing in his eyes, the single-minded intent. He stood straight, releasing her, and she stood before him helpless, unable to move, to speak, to act.

Thorn watched her curiously. For a woman of her type, she was amazingly sensitive to his touch. Not that he found it strange that the apparently very correct and puritan Miss Lang should fall apart because of the attentions of a rough cattleman. She was obviously putting on a good act. And why not? She knew he was rich.

"Would you care for some punch, Trilby?" he asked, but his eyes had dropped to her mouth—and he looked as if he might bend and take it under his any second.

Trilby could hardly find her voice. She was so shaken that her purse almost fell from her fingers. "Yes," she choked. "I would."

If only he would stop staring at her lips! He made her trembly with an emotion she didn't understand at all. Her legs would hardly support her. It was difficult to breathe. Her heart was beating like a hummingbird's wings against her rib cage. All because Thornton Vance was looking at her mouth!

He took her arm, aware of her parents' exchanged smiles. So they were thinking along *those* lines. He smiled faintly to himself. He was glad that Trilby was vulnerable to him. He found her very attractive, and he'd been a long time without a woman. He hadn't wandered up to the wrong side of Tucson for entertainment, or anywhere else since his wife's death. He was beginning to feel that abstinence. He knew what Trilby was. He wouldn't need to worry about her reputation.

And if she fell in love with him a little, that wouldn't hurt, either. He might enjoy having her become serious about him just before he cut it off. Trilby had all but destroyed his cousin's marriage. The gossip hadn't been lost on him, and Curt's wife, Lou, had cried on his shoulder more than once. Lou didn't know the identity of Curt's clandestine lover, but she did know that the woman was a blonde. Vance had never doubted that it was Trilby. After all, Sally had seen her with Curt.

It was too bad about Jack Lang inheriting that ranch, he thought bitterly. If it hadn't been for the Langs coming here to claim Blackwater Springs Ranch, Thorn would have been able to buy it. Then he wouldn't be losing cattle right and left to drought. He had water on his Mexican property, but it was getting too dangerous to try to run cattle down there. He'd had one raid after another on his stock since the fighting had begun after Díaz's reelection. Here, water was running out.

Thorn had to find a way to save Los Santos from ruin. The land came first. His father and his grandfather had instilled in him a terrible sense of responsibility for the land, for the heritage it represented, for the need to preserve it at any cost.

For just a moment, it flashed through his mind that

he could solve all his problems by marrying Trilby.
But he dismissed it at once. She wasn't the sort of
woman he wanted in his home. He wasn't sure he
ever wanted another woman that close.

Sally had sworn eternal love until he'd married her
and taken her to bed. Afterward, she'd been a bubbling
caldron of excuses. She enjoyed her wealthy way of
life, but not her ardent husband. After a few weeks
of her utter coldness, he lost most of his feeling for
her. Her pregnancy had been the last straw. She hadn't
wanted a child, and she never fully adjusted to moth-
erhood. For the few months before her death, she'd
been different. There had been a new light in her eyes,
a new radiance to her face. But not when her husband
was near. She hated him, and never lost a chance to
tell him so. Even Samantha suffered her hostility. At
the last, Sally had seemed to resent her family bitterly.

The accident that had claimed her life had been in
a buggy one rainy night. She'd gone to sit with a sick
neighbor. When she hadn't come home the next morning, he'd gone looking for her. He'd found her body in
the wreckage of the buggy, half lying in a creek. It was
on an out-of-the-way road, though, and nowhere near
the sick neighbor. He'd assumed that she'd gotten lost
in the dark, and his conscience had hurt him for letting
her go alone. There was little love in their marriage, but
he had loved her until her selfishness and greed killed
his feelings for her.

He glanced toward his daughter Samantha, who was
standing against the wall just inside the house, looking
hunted. She was so fragile-looking, he thought. Odd,
she'd been less high-strung since her mother's death,
but she was sad and shy, and, odd thing, she was very

nervous around Curt and Lou. He did care for his child, but there was little love left in him. What was love, after all, he thought bitterly, but an illusion. A marriage for practical reasons had a better chance of success. As for the bedroom, there was no shortage of willing women to satisfy his hunger. He didn't need a wife for that. His eyes sought Trilby, dark with masculine appreciation of her slenderness and grace.

Samantha approached the adults warily, managing a shy smile for Trilby. "Hello," she said.

"Hello. It's Samantha, isn't it? You look very pretty," Trilby said gently.

Samantha looked surprised at the compliment. "Thank you," she mumbled self-consciously. "May I go to bed, now, Father?" she asked, with painful shyness.

"Certainly," he said. He sounded very stiff and uncomfortable. Not like Trilby's loving, affectionate father. "Maria will go with you." He motioned to his housekeeper, who nodded and came forward quickly to herd the child upstairs.

"Don't you tuck her in at night?" she asked, without thinking.

"I do not," he answered, his voice hardly inviting further questions. "Will you have lime or fruit punch?"

"Lime, please."

He filled a cup for her and placed it in a saucer. Her hands shook, though, and he had to hold them to help steady it. His eyes met hers again, narrow this time, and probing.

"Your hands are like ice. You can't be cold?"

"Why can't I?" she said defensively. "I'm thin. I feel chill more than most people."

"Is it that, Trilby?" He lowered his voice, and his head, so that his eyes were very close to hers. His lean hands smoothed over the backs of hers. "Or is it this?" His thumb found the damp palm of one and drew over it in what was a blatantly sensual gesture, while his eyes kindled panic in her bosom.

The punch overflowed, fortunately missing her dress and his trousers.

"Oh, I'm—I'm so sorry!" she stammered, flushing.

"No harm done." He motioned for one of the waiters and drew her out of the way while the man cleaned it up. Her parents and Ted were already mixing with the huge crowd, and no one seemed to have noticed the accident.

"I never used to be so clumsy," she said nervously.

He drew her back into a small alcove that led to the lighted patio, its paper lanterns making artificial moons in the darkness. His hands framed her face and tilted it up to his dark eyes. "I don't think it was clumsiness."

He bent then, and she felt the warm, slow brush of a man's mouth for the first time in her life. Even Richard had never once tried to kiss her. She'd had only dreams… She stiffened helplessly at the intimacy and a faint gasp passed her dry lips.

Thorn lifted his head. The expression on her face, in her eyes, was one she couldn't have pretended. It was genuine surprise, mingled with awe, fascination. He had more than enough experience to recognize what she was feeling—and to know that it was new to her. Incredible, he thought, a woman of her experience being so stunned. Unless it was a pretense…

He bent again to make sure, but she jerked away from him, one slender hand going to her mouth. Above it, her gray eyes were like saucers in a delicately etched face blanched with uncertainty.

Thorn grew irritated with her for that dramatic facade. His face hardened; his eyes went cold. He stood watching Trilby, contempt in his very posture as he stared at her slender body.

"Don't tell me you usually react that way to a man's caress?" he asked, with smiling mockery. "There's no need to pretend for me, Trilby. We both know that you aren't unfamiliar with the feel of a man's mouth on yours—even on your body."

The sheer effrontery of the remark made her hand twitch. Her eyes flashed at him and she straightened. "If I had a gun, I'd shoot you, I swear I would! How dare you make such a statement to me!"

He raised his eyebrows. "What kind of treatment did you expect, Miss Lang? Do you think that prim act fooled me?"

She stared at him blankly. "What prim act?"

He looked vaguely mocking. "It's not very effective coming from your sort of woman," he drawled. "We both know you want a hell of a lot more from me than kisses."

She gasped with furious indignation and gave him a fierce glare before she abruptly moved away from him, almost running. He poured himself a cup of punch and wandered off to mingle with his guests. But even as he smiled and wound through the crowd, he was thinking about Trilby. He really shouldn't have baited her like that. Even if she'd been having a blatant affair with Curt, it didn't make her a prostitute. She might actually love the man.

He didn't understand why he'd said the things he had,

except that thinking of her with his cousin made him angry.

His eyes finally found her, dancing with, of all people, Curt. The other man was about his height but much heavier and less abrasive. Curt had a ready smile and he liked women. They liked him, too, with his city manners and gentlemanly ways.

Thorn had been fond of him until his wife had thrown Curt up to him as an example of what she called a "civilized man." He was tired of coming off second when compared to a dandy. Seeing Trilby in his arms made something explode inside him, especially when an icy, resentful Lou, Curt's wife, sat seething as she watched them dance.

"How's the Mexican problem?" Jack Lang asked, pausing beside him long enough to divert his attention.

"Getting worse, I think," Thorn replied. He glanced at Trilby and away again. It was all he could do not to throw a punch at Curt for his duplicity. "Don't let the women stray far from the house. We've had a few cattle stolen. One of my men tracked them down into Mexico. We never did catch the thieves."

"You can't fault the peons for taking the side of the insurgents," Jack said patiently. "Conditions under Díaz are intolerable for the Mexican people, from what we hear from our vaqueros."

"They've always been intolerable. They always will be," Thorn said impatiently. "The average Mexican peasant has centuries of oppression behind him, from the Aztecs all the way up through Cortés and the Spanish and French, and, eventually, Díaz. These are a perennially oppressed people. They've been forced to knuckle under to everyone, especially the Spanish.

It takes generations to overcome a suppressed attitude. They haven't had enough time yet to break the pattern."

"Madero seems to be doing it."

"Madero is a little rooster," Thorn mused. "His heart's in the right place. I think he may surprise the *Federales*. They underestimate him. They'll regret it."

"His army is ragtag," Jack protested.

"You need to read history," came the dry reply. "It's chock-full of ragtag armies taking over continents."

Jack pursed his lips. "You're amazingly astute."

"Why, because I live on a ranch and spend my life around cattle and dust? I'm well read, and I have a friend who knows more about the past than he knows about the present. Did you meet my Eastern guest over there? McCollum's an anthropologist, although he also teaches archaeology. He comes out with his students every spring to interview people from local Indian tribes and look for evidence of ancient cultures."

"You don't say! He never told me any of that," Jack murmured, eyeing the tall, rough-looking blond man who was talking to an area businessman.

"McCollum won't talk about his work. He's opinionated enough about everything else," Thorn said, with an amused smile.

McCollum glanced at Thorn and glowered. A minute later, he excused himself to the man with whom he was speaking and joined his host. "You're talking about me, aren't you?" McCollum demanded bluntly. "Behind my back, too."

"I was telling my neighbor how much you know about the past," he said, smiling. "This is Jack Lang.

He owns Blackwater Springs Ranch. Jack, this is *Dr.* Craig McCollum."

"Glad to know you," Jack said. "Are you here to dig around?"

"No, more's the pity. I'm in town on business, so I stopped in to see Thorn. What do you think about the Mexican situation?"

Jack told him. McCollum, a tall, dignified man, pursed his lips and his dark eyes narrowed. "You think the peons have a chance?"

"Yes," Jack said. "Do you?"

McCollum shrugged. "I don't know," he said. "Thorn has probably mentioned that he has several Mexican cowboys who work for him. Their fathers worked for his father. To them, being dominated by foreigners is a bitter way of life. Change takes time."

"Is Madero going to win?"

"Yes, I think so," Thorn said after a minute. "He genuinely cares about his people and he wants something better than they have for them. He's managed to win the support of most of his people, and they'll fight. Yes, I imagine he'll win. But before he does, a lot of good blood is going to be spilled. What concerns me is that some of it may be ours. We're in a sticky position here, on the border."

"We don't have to get involved," Jack said stubbornly.

Thorn smiled indulgently. "We're already involved. Or haven't you noticed that some of your vaqueros disappear for a day or two at a time?"

Jack cocked his head and shrugged. "Yes. They go to see their families."

Thorn chuckled and drained his punch glass. "They go to ride with the Maderistas and help raid neighboring ranches. Be careful they don't raid your yours. You've lost some cattle recently, too, I believe?"

"A few head. Nothing serious."

"Perhaps those few were to see if you'd give chase," Thorn cautioned. "Keep a close watch on your herd."

"Yes. I'll do that." Jack sighed heavily, his eyes going to his wife, who was talking animatedly to some neighbors. "I dragged my family out here without realizing the gravity of the situation, you know. I had no idea the Mexicans would revolt. I put every dime we had into this operation, but it isn't going as I thought it would. I'm losing my shirt, Vance."

"Give it time," Thorn said, mentally weighing his own chances to latch on to the ranch if Jack looked like he was losing it. "Things generally work out by themselves."

"Yes, if I have anything left by then."

"No need to sound so pessimistic," Thorn reminded him. "If things heat up, there are plenty of U.S. troops ready to combat any threat. And besides the local militia, there's support from Fort Huachuca if it's needed. Buck up. Come on, I'll introduce you to a couple of my bankers. You may need a friend in commerce one day. Craig, you can keep us company."

From her position with Curt, talking to two unmarried young women talking about the upcoming marriage of a third, Trilby watched Thorn Vance and Craig McCollum with her father. Dr. McCollum wasn't at all bad-looking, but it was Thorn who caught her eye. He was nice-looking when he made the effort, she thought reluctantly. Black suited him; it made him look more muscular, even taller than he was.

While she stared at him, he suddenly turned his head

and caught her staring in his direction. A cold anger contracted his brows, and she flushed and looked quickly away. Her heartbeat was unusually fast and she wished she didn't feel or look quite so breathless. It hadn't been like this with Richard. She'd been so fond of him, but he hadn't made her knees go weak. For heaven's sake, all she'd thought about since she'd arrived was how it would feel if Thorn kissed her with real passion—not that faint brushing contact that had unnerved her. She almost wished that she'd given in to him, but that was unseemly, unladylike, and totally impossible. She couldn't encourage him. A widower like Thorn Vance would certainly want more than she was prepared to offer, and he was hardly likely to offer her marriage. He was something of a ladies' man, she gathered from their conversation, and he seemed already to think her a woman of loose morals. She had no thought of ending up a scarlet woman because of her body's helpless reaction to him. She'd simply have to keep her distance from now on.

"Look at her," Lou bristled minutes later when Thorn took her onto the dance floor. She was glaring toward Trilby, who was still standing beside Curt. "Has she no shame?"

"I'll take care of it," he told the woman, who was dark and much older than Trilby. "Don't worry."

"So blatant," she choked. "He's got two children, and he doesn't care how much gossip he stirs up. It isn't only her. Now there's some woman down in Del Rio." She dabbed at her eyes miserably. "I wish I'd never met him."

"What do you mean, some woman in Del Rio?"

"A pretty little Mexican peasant girl whose father

owns a taverna," she said huskily. "He spends all his time down there."

That struck Thorn as odd. If Curt were having a mad affair with Trilby, why was he seeing another woman as well? And a poor Mexican girl, at that?

"He likes to see me humiliated," she whispered, glaring at her husband's back. "He enjoys hurting me."

"Why should he want to do that?" Thorn asked gently.

Lou blushed. "I was…in the family way when we married," she said, faintly resentful. "He's never let me forget it. He didn't want to marry me."

It began to make sense. "Are you certain that he's seeing Trilby?" he asked her.

She shrugged. "He disappears every other night. Maybe he's seeing them both. How should I know? I hate him!"

"No, you don't."

She sniffed. "No, I don't. I wish I could." She leaned her head against him. "Why couldn't I have loved you, Thorn? You'd never cheat on your wife."

"It's not my way," he agreed.

"Look at her," she muttered, glaring at Trilby. "So cultured and citified and elegant. She's nothing to look at, though. All bones and a face that no man could call pretty. I'm much better to look at than she is!"

"Now, Lou," he said gently.

She stumbled and had to regain her balance. "I'm being spiteful, I know. Why don't her people control her? If she'd been raised right, she wouldn't be carousing around with my husband!"

The question made Thorn thoughtful. Mary and Jack Lang were moral people. They hadn't raised Trilby to be licentious. Surely if they knew she was seeing Curt they'd stop her. Of course, he rationalized, they might not know about it.

Minutes later he approached her where she stood with Curt and slid his hand down to capture hers.

"Excuse us, won't you?" he told Curt, and he didn't smile. His cousin's eyebrows arched in surprise.

Thorn led her onto the floor, where several people were doing a lazy waltz to the music of the live band he'd hired.

"I think it's time Curt spent just a little time with his wife," he said icily.

Trilby flushed with anger. She smiled coolly. "How kind of you to sacrifice yourself on her behalf."

He shifted his eyes to where Lou was coaxing a reluctant Curt to dance with her. The whole situation made him angry.

His arms contracted around Trilby, and she stiffened. "I might as well dance with a slab of lumber," he remarked as they went around the floor for the second time. His hand gripped her slender waist hard and he shook her gently. "Will you *relax?*"

She was stiff in his arms, because she was angry at the remarks he'd made and frightened of how he made her feel. Her hand in his was cold and nervous, more so when his fingers began sliding in and out between her own, making her knees wobbly. He'd been so antagonistic, and now he was acting as if—as if he wanted to seduce her!

"Please stop doing that," she said irritably, tugging at her hand.

"Doing what, Miss Lang?" he asked, with every evidence of innocence.

She glared up into his dancing dark eyes and then down again. "You know what."

"You relax and I'll stop doing...that."

Her teeth clenched. "Have you no knowledge of civilized behavior at all?" she asked haughtily.

His dark eyes glittered at her. "I'm a man," he said quietly. "Perhaps you aren't used to the breed?"

Her gray eyes flashed at him. "I do most certainly know a few men!"

"Pretty city boys," he shot back. "With nice manners and manicured nails and slicked-back hair."

"There's nothing wrong with manners, Mr. Vance," she told him. "In fact, they rate rather high on my list of priorities."

"You sound very indignant. I've seen a setting hen less ruffled than you look right now," he said mockingly. "All feathers and fury because I've insulted your background." The smile faded as he looked at her. "I buried my parents with my own two hands," he said, shocking her into lifting her eyes. "They were killed by Mexican bandits raiding up into Arizona. I have no love for outlaws, and less for Eastern tenderfeet who think a man is measured by his vocabulary. Out here, Miss Lang, a man is measured by his ability to hold on to what's his, by his ability to protect his loved ones and insure their survival. Pretty talk doesn't stop bullets or build empires."

"You sound very critical of city folk," she began.

"I am critical of them. We had two Washington big shots out here after my parents were gunned down. We tried to explain the situation brewing in Mexico and the need for some protection for settlers here, and we got nothing but promises of 'looking into the situation.'"

"Washington is quite far away," she reminded him.

"Not far enough away for me," he said shortly. "I couldn't get any cooperation from Washington or the army, so I handled the problem myself."

"The problem?"

"I tracked my parents' murderers down across the border," he explained.

"Did you find them?"

"Yes." He glanced toward the band and motioned to them. They'd been winding down, but they began the song again.

She didn't pursue the question. The look in his dark eyes had been fairly explicit. She had a terrible vision of men being gunned down.

He felt the quiver against his hand at her back and he nodded. "You're going to have to get a little tougher if you want to live in this country."

"Did I ever say that I wanted to live here, Mr. Vance?" she asked with soft hauteur. "I came because I had no choice."

"You seem to like some things about it," he continued, with faint sarcasm.

"That's right, I do love the dust! I'm thinking of starting an export business so that I can share it with the world." She couldn't face another argument. "Can we stop dancing?"

"Why?" Her attitude put his back up. She was making his desert sound like some alien and unwanted land. She made him feel like some uncivilized savage. Well, perhaps he was, but he didn't like her so superior attitude. She was hardly fit to judge him, considering her behavior with his married cousin.

His hand contracted, bringing her close against him

so that she could feel his chest warm and hard against her breasts, even through several layers of cloth. "Don't you like being held close to my body like this, Trilby?" he asked, with deliberate mockery, holding her shocked eyes.

"Of all the insufferable things to say!" She stiffened and stopped dancing. No man had ever talked to her like this. She stared at him as if she wasn't sure she'd heard him correctly.

"You do that so well," he remarked cynically. "You almost convince me that I've shocked you."

She was out of her depth, and disturbed. He made her feel things she didn't want to feel. "*Shock* is hardly the right word. Please let me go," she said tersely.

"Very well," he replied, loosening his hold. "But don't think you'll escape me completely," he added mockingly. "I don't give up when something, or someone, interests me."

The words had an ominous ring.

"I should prefer to become an object of interest to a fat sidewinder!" she returned.

Her analogy amused him. He smiled, which made it even worse. Trilby turned away and muttered to herself all the way back to her parents and Teddy.

It was one thing to be faced with a head-on accusation and reply to it. But Thorn Vance was only making nebulous innuendos, and she didn't know how to handle them. She couldn't imagine why he thought so badly of her.

If it had mattered, she might have pressed him for an answer. As it was, she told herself, Richard was the only man in her life. That being the case, what did Mr. Vance's opinion matter?

Chapter Three

After Thorn's contempt the night before, it was doubly shocking to Trilby when he suddenly appeared at the ranch the next morning and invited her to go for a ride in the desert.

He looked as if he expected her to refuse, and his smile was mocking. "Not on a horse, Trilby," he drawled. "I've brought the touring car, as you can see."

She glanced doubtfully at the big, open car. "I don't like automobiles," Trilby said. "We had one back in Louisiana and our chauffeur was forever snapping bands, and having flat tires, and skidding into the ditch on muddy roads. Even the one we have now is too fast," she added, with an accusing glance at her grinning father.

"The buckboard would be less comfortable, I assure you."

"Do go, Trilby," her mother said gently. "It will do you good."

"Indeed," Jack Lang agreed.

Trilby could hardly tell them what Thorn had said to her the night before, or accuse him publicly of treating her like a loose woman. Her pride wouldn't let her advertise his opinion of her.

"What about Dr. McCollum? Aren't you neglecting him?" she asked, grasping at straws.

"Craig left on the El Paso train," he said simply. Then he simply stared at her, his mocking smile daring her to produce another excuse.

She was no coward. "All right," she said composedly. "I'll go with you, Mr. Vance."

She dressed in a long blue dress with lace-up shoes and a frilly hat. Then she wrapped a shawl around her shoulders—just in case the weather changed—and went out to Thorn.

He'd certainly impressed her parents with his apparent pursuit of Trilby. And the dignified gray suit he was wearing only added to the image he was projecting of a pillar of the community. Jack and Mary were beaming at him, their approval so obvious that it was embarrassing. Only Trilby knew that whatever Thornton Vance's intentions were, they certainly weren't as respectable as he looked.

"I'll have her back before dark," he assured them. "Don't worry, I'll take care of her."

"Why, of course you will, dear boy," Jack Lang replied, as if it were a foregone conclusion and needed no emphasis.

Trilby sat quietly while Thorn cranked the car and came back to sit beside her. Naturally, she thought bitterly, it wouldn't take him a half hour of sweat and muttered swear words to get it running, as it had Richard when he'd taken her and Teddy out riding. She held that competence against Thorn. It was just one more thing that set him apart from most men.

She waved as they sped off down the wide dirt road
that led toward the mountains. She held her hat on, glad
of the windscreen that kept the thick dust out of her face.
The car her father drove was missing its windscreen.
Teddy had accidentally knocked a baseball through it.

"Too fast?" Thorn asked, glancing ruefully at Trilby.
"I'll slow down a bit."

He did, lifting his booted foot from the accelerator
pedal. The car chugged along, so loud that conversation was next to impossible even if he'd been a talk-
ative sort. He glanced out at the brownish hue of the
land, where the grasses were dormant in autumn. The
paloverde trees that dotted the landscape were glorious.
He glanced at Trilby, wondering if she knew what they
were. He pulled off the main road onto a smaller dirt one
that led back to a secluded box canyon. As they drove,
Trilby noticed that trees became more plentiful and the
mountains loomed large and ghostly.

"Oh!" she exclaimed, delighted with the wooded
canyon.

He pulled over, onto the side of the road, and cut off
the engine. "Do you like it?"

"Why, it's lovely," she exclaimed. Her wide eyes were
expressive. "I had no idea there were places like this in
Arizona. I thought it was all cactus and sand."

"You'd have known sooner if you'd ever agreed to
come out with your father and brother," he chided.

"I eat enough dust in the house, thank you, without
going out in search of more during roundup," she replied.

"Dust won't melt you, sugar plum," he said, with faint
sarcasm.

"I hardly expected that it would, and please, could
you refrain from calling me pet names?"

He turned in the seat to face her, idly rolling a cigarette while he stared at her. There were only the two of them in the world, in this beautiful wild place. Trilby was intensely aware of him as a man and was fighting not to respond to him. It was very easy to remember how it had been when he'd kissed her the night before. She was much too vulnerable to him, and he had a bad opinion of her. She must remember that, somehow. Her posture straightened as she fought not to betray the tingling excitement he engendered in her.

But he saw her discomfort and understood it very well. "You're very stiff and formal with me, Trilby. Why?"

She met his searching gaze bravely. "It isn't me that you're interested in, Mr. Vance," she said shortly. "I'm not completely stupid."

She surprised him. That didn't often happen with women. Sally had been pretty, but not particularly intelligent. Trilby was. "Then if I'm not interested in you, what am I interested in?"

"The water on my father's property," she said, without backing down.

He smiled appreciatively. "Well, well. And what makes you think that?"

"You need water. You don't have enough, and we do, and my father won't sell or lease any to you. That's why," she replied. "My father doesn't even suspect that you might be playing up to me for ulterior motives. He thinks the sun rises and sets on you. So does the rest of my family." She glared at him. "For myself, Mr. Vance, I think you're a shipless pirate."

He chuckled softly. "Well, that's honest, at least." He

stuck the rolled cigarette in his thin mouth and produced a match to light it. Pungent smoke filled the air.

"I don't really blame you," she said after a minute. She fumbled with her cloth drawstring purse. "I suppose water is life itself out here."

"Indeed it is." He took another draw from the cigarette. "Are you up to a little walking?"

"Of course," she said, glad to escape the confined space.

He came around and opened her door, carefully helping her out. The touch of his fingers made her heart jump. She moved quickly away from him and began to walk down the road. It was so peaceful. The wind blew noisily and there was a smell, a crisp, earthy smell, in the air. Her eyes found rock formations in the hills beyond. The trees were golden and magnificent against the faint reddish yellow of the maple leaves.

"What sort of trees are those?" she asked curiously.

"The golden ones? They're paloverde trees. They have long strands of golden blossoms in the spring, and in the autumn they go glorious. I like them better than the maples."

"Those others are oaks, aren't they?"

"Some of them. That—" he indicated an enormous tree with a bent trunk "—is a cottonwood. A few decades ago, people used to strip off the bark and scrape the tree for sap. It's sweet, you see, like a confection."

"Oh," she cried delightedly, "how clever!"

"And those are willows," he added, gesturing toward a stand of sapling-type trees along the banks of the stream.

She looked around suddenly. "Is it safe here?" she asked quickly. "I mean, are there Indians near here?"

He smiled. "Plenty of them. Mostly Mescalero and Mimbrenos Apaches. There used to be a wealth of Chiricahuas, but when Geronimo was captured, the government shipped his whole band back East to Florida and kept them in a fort on the bay at St. Augustine for a long time. They finally moved them back out to New Mexico. Geronimo killed a lot of white people, but then, the white people killed a lot of Apaches, too. Gen. George Crook finally got him to surrender. Quite a fellow, old *Nantan Lupan.*"

"What?"

"Grey Wolf. It's what the Apaches called Crook. They respected him. When he gave his word, he kept it. Odd for a white man. He did all he could to help the Apaches for the rest of his life, after Geronimo's surrender. Geronimo died February of last year."

"I didn't know that."

He glanced at her. "You Easterners don't know much about Indians, do you? Apaches are interesting. They called the old Chiricahua chief Cochise, but his Apache name was *Cheis.* It means oak. God only knows how it got altered to Cochise. He was a wily old devil, smart as a fox. He led the U.S. Cavalry on a merry chase until the peace came. But Geronimo refused to give up and live at the white man's mercy on a reservation. There were times, not so long ago, when just the name Apache could make a grown man tremble out here."

She kept quiet, waiting for him to go on. She was fascinated with his knowledge of the Indians.

He smiled, sensing her interest. That pleased him. "Indians are not ignorant. I have two Apache men who work for me. One of them is Chiricahua. And he is," he added dryly, "hardly the Eastern image of an Indian.

You'll see what I mean when you meet him. His name
is Naki."

"What does it mean?" she asked curiously.

"He's actually called Two Fists, but Apache has glottal stops and nasalizations and high tones... I can't pronounce his second name. Naki means 'two.'"

"Are you...do you have any Indian blood?"

He shook his head. "My grandmother was a pretty
little Spanish lady. They had a little girl. My grandfather got tired of the responsibility and deserted her." He
let that slip. He'd never told anyone else.

"Didn't he love her enough to stay?"

He grew stiff. "Apparently not. My grandmother
starved to death. If it hadn't been for my great-uncle,
the one who owned Los Santos, my mother would have
starved, too. She and my father inherited Los Santos
when my great-uncle died. I was eighteen when Mexicans raided up here and killed them."

"Did you have brothers or sisters?"

"I was one of three kids; I had two sisters," he said.
"They both died of cholera."

"I'm sorry."

"I was just a kid at the time. I don't remember much
about them." He smoked his cigarette as they walked,
his head high. He walked without stooping, his posture
perfect, like his clothing. For a cowboy, he wore the suit
very well.

"You said your grandmother was Spanish..."

"And you wonder why Mexicans attacked her daughter and son-in-law," he guessed.

"Yes."

"Don't you know yet that most Mexicans hate the
Spanish? It's one of the reasons they're fighting now.

They've had Spanish domination since Cortés. They've had enough," he replied simply. "But the people who killed my parents weren't revolutionaries. They were just bandits."

"I'm sorry. About your parents, I mean."

"So was I."

There was a wealth of pain in the words, and she remembered reluctantly how his expression had told her he dealt with the murderers. She turned her attention to the ground, looking at the sandy soil. "Does much grow out here?" she asked idly.

"The Hohokam, the Indian people who once inhabited this land before the time of Christ, were an agricultural people. They learned to grow corn in clumps, and to irrigate the land. They had a system of government and a religion that was far ahead of their time. They may have existed as a culture for thousands of years."

She stared at him with renewed respect. "How do you know all that?"

He chuckled. "McCollum," he said simply. "It pays to have an anthropology professor for a friend. He's very good at his job. He stays with me when he's exploring ruins in the area. He comes several times a year when he's teaching."

"I like him. I didn't realize he was an educator," she said.

"Yes. He teaches anthropology and archaeology at one of the big colleges up North."

"It must be interesting. Do you go with him when he looks for ruins?"

"When time allows." He shoved one hand in the pocket of his slacks and slanted a look down at her from under the wide brim of his hat. "Do you like archaeology?"

"I know very little about it," she admitted. "But it's interesting, isn't it?"

"Very." He put out a lean, tanned hand suddenly and stopped her in her tracks. "Be still a minute. Don't talk. Look there." He pointed toward the bushes, and she felt her heart racing. Was it a rattlesnake? She wanted to run, but just as her feet got the message from her brain, a funny, long brown bird went scampering from under the bush to dart across the road.

She laughed. "What is it?" she exclaimed.

"A roadrunner," he told her. "They hunt and kill snakes."

"Well, bully for him." She chuckled.

"Snakes are beneficial, you silly child," he chided. "Bull snakes and rat snakes and black snakes don't hurt anything. They eat rats and mice. And a king snake will kill and eat a rattler."

"I don't want to look at one long enough to identify it," she informed him.

He shook his head. "Come on."

He led her off the trail eventually, and into a shady area where a stream cut through the forest floor. Huge, smooth boulders ran up from the stream toward the mountains.

"This is an old Apache camp," he told her. "It isn't on the reservation, of course, but they still come here sometimes. Naki likes to camp here when he's rounding up strays. He's marvelous with horses."

"Does he wear war paint and headdresses?" she asked innocently.

He glared at her. "He's Apache," he said. "Apaches

don't wear feathered headdresses like the Plains Indians. They wear a colored cloth band around their foreheads and wear their hair shoulder length. They don't live in tepees like the Plains Indians, either. They live in a sort of round or oblong lodge called a wickiup."

"Do people out here hate the Indians?" she asked.

"Some do. There have been times when we were allies with them, and even with the Mexicans, to fight off the Comanches when they tried to come south and conquer us."

"Oh, my!"

"And the Confederate flag flew over Tucson once, during the Civil War," he said, chuckling at her. "A lot of Southerners settled out here in Arizona. You should feel right at home."

"I wish I did," she replied quietly, and meant it. She stared down at the soil. "There aren't any cacti right here."

"Plenty out on the desert, mostly saguaro," he told her, "and organ pipe. Those saguaro are huge and heavy. They have a sort of woody skeleton inside. One can kill a man if it falls on him."

"What are the tall, thin ones?"

"Ocotillo," he said. "Mexicans use it to build thorny fences."

"We have prickly pear cactus in Louisiana," she said. "Do you?"

"Not in Baton Rouge," she said, grinning.

He stopped walking and turned to look at her. "Do you speak any French?"

"Just a little," she said. "Mama is fluent." She searched his dark eyes. "Do you?"

"I speak Spanish fluently," he said. "And a smattering of German."

He didn't look away, and neither did she. For moments that stretched with sweet tension, he looked down at her. Her lips parted as her heart began to race. He had the most decadent effect on her, she thought.

His dark eyes dropped, as no gentleman's would, to her bosom. She caught her breath.

"Limits," he murmured. "You Eastern women can't live without them. Out here, a man sees something he wants and he just takes it."

"Including women?" she asked huskily.

"It depends on the woman," he replied. "My wife was like you, Trilby," he added bitterly. "A hothouse orchid transplanted into hot, sandy soil. She hated it, hated me. She should never have married me. She wouldn't have," he added, with a cynical smile, "but she did like my money."

The thought irritated him. He didn't like remembering Sally. Trilby brought it all back.

"You...loved her?" she asked.

"Yes," he said harshly. "I loved her. But she wanted poetry and roses every morning and maids to wait on her. She wanted a gentleman to escort her to social functions. She hated my roughness, hated the loneliness. She grew to hate me. Everything about me," he added, averting his eyes. "I don't need telling that I'm a savage. Sally told me twice a day."

Incredible that she should pity him, she thought, watching his rigid features grow even harder. How terrible, to love someone who hated you...

He looked down and caught her compassionate stare. It made him furious that she should feel sorry for him.

It made him more furious that he'd begun to like her, to enjoy her company. She was a tramp, and he was letting himself be drawn into her sticky web. He was a fool!

He threw the cigarette down in the dirt and reached for her.

"I don't need your pity," he said curtly, staring at her mouth. "Not when you're more contemptible than I'll ever be!"

His mouth bit into hers, twisting, hurting her. She gasped and tried to fight him, but he was much too strong. His arms were like vises, his mouth tasting of tobacco and pure man. He used his body like a weapon to humiliate her. His lean hands slid quickly to her hips and ground them against his thighs.

The intimacy was staggering to a woman who'd barely been kissed before. Her body seemed to flush all over at the shock of feeling the changed contours of his body against her stomach. She cried out, furiously outraged and embarrassed by the unspeakable liberties he was taking, beating at him with her fists and trying to kick him.

Surprised at her show of fury, he let her go. She stood glaring at him with a red face, her hair escaping from its tidy bun, her gray eyes blazing. She reached up and struck him across the mouth as hard as she could.

"You savage!" she cried, shaking all over. "I knew… you were…no gentleman!" she raged.

"And you're no lady, you Louisiana tramp," he said, without flinching from the blow. His eyes were like death as he looked at her. "If I were a little less civilized than I am, I'd throw you down in the dusty road and ravish you where you lay."

Her face went even redder. Her mouth trembled, tears

formed in her eyes at the blatant insult. To think that dear, courtly Richard had never done more than touch her hand, and this savage had—had…

"You lay one hand…on me…and I'll hit you with a tree limb! How…dare you?" she choked, almost sobbing with rage. "I shall…tell my father!"

"Do that," he replied calmly, "and I'll tell him about the affair you're having with my married cousin!"

She stared at him as if he'd gone mad. "What are you talking about?"

"It's too late to lie about it," he told her, his voice cold with contempt. "Sally saw you and Curt kissing each other. She told me, several weeks before she died."

Her face went from red to deathly white. She faltered and almost fell. His hand shot out to steady her, but she threw it off, hating him.

"That is a lie," she whispered, shaking. "It is a vicious, unfounded lie!"

"Why would my wife lie to me?" he drawled. "And she's dead now. How convenient for you. She can hardly contradict you, can she?"

She swallowed, and then swallowed again. She thought she might faint. She knew there wasn't a drop of blood in her face. His expression told her that arguing with him wasn't going to change his mind. He'd decided that his wife's lie was gospel. Nothing she said was going to convince him that she'd done no more than talk to his cousin Curt.

She lifted her hobble skirt with trembling cold hands and started unsteadily back toward the car.

He followed her, opening her door with overblown courtesy.

She didn't look at him as she got in. She couldn't

bear to. She sat like a statue as he cranked the car and turned it back toward home.

It wasn't until he pulled up in her front yard that he spoke again. "There's no use playing the martyr with me," he said carelessly. "I know what you are."

"If I were a man, I would shoot you through the heart," she said, choking. She was shaking with outrage and temper. "When I tell my father what you've accused me of, *he* probably will shoot you! I hope he does!"

He raised both eyebrows. "You can't possibly mean to actually confess to him?" he asked insolently. "You'll destroy his illusions."

She controlled her urge to slap him again, but barely. "Mr. Vance," she said, with cold indignation, "in order to conduct a clandestine relationship with your cousin, I should be obliged to leave the house after dark."

"That would be no problem. You have an automobile," he reminded her.

"I can neither drive nor ride a horse," she said stiffly.

He hesitated. "Then someone could have driven you."

She nodded. "Oh, of course. My parents would understand that I wanted to leave the house at night, alone, something I've never done in my life!"

She was blowing holes in his theory. He frowned. He didn't like the cold facts she was putting to him.

"The incident Sally told me about was at a party that your parents attended," he said, averting his eyes with growing unease.

"I see. I've been prejudged, without even the chance to defend myself." She stared straight ahead, shivering as a distasteful thought came to her. Her hands gripped her purse. "I suppose…your wife didn't confine her confession to you."

"She told Lou, Curt's wife," he replied.

Her eyes closed. So that explained why Curt's wife had been glaring at her so furiously. Probably the vicious gossip had gone the rounds of the entire community. And all because she'd liked Curt and enjoyed talking to him. It had been perfectly innocent.

"Why don't you ask your cousin if I've been having an affair with him?" she asked weakly.

"And have him lie to save your good name?" He laughed. "That would be intelligent, wouldn't it?"

"Mr. Vance, I should never think to accuse you of any intelligent act," she said in a harsh tone. "As for your disgusting slander, it is unfounded and grossly unfair. Yes, I shall tell my parents." She turned and looked at him fully. "The truth is the best weapon I know. And you, sir, will live to regret having accepted a lie without question—even from your late wife."

Her indignation registered then, and later. She got out of the car, avoiding his assistance, and marched toward the house. He went after her.

Her parents and Teddy were not inside, so there was no necessity for him to explain Trilby's hostility. Trilby went straight into her bedroom and slammed and locked the door with an audible click, without a single word to Thorn.

He stood outside the closed door and his tall body went rigid. Why had she acted as if he'd done something unspeakable to her, when he was only telling the truth?

"Oh, damn women!" he cursed violently, and went back out the door.

When Jack and Mary came back, Trilby had just

bathed her face and hands in cold water. But her eyes were obviously red, and so was her pert nose.

"Why, my dear," Mary exclaimed, "what's happened?"

"Your hero has shown his true colors," Trilby told her father, with trembling dignity. "His wife told him that she saw me kissing his married cousin Curt. He believes that I am involved in a clandestine affair with the man."

Mary gasped. Jack's face went hard with contained rage. "How dare he!" he raged. "How dare he make such an accusation to you!"

"I do not want to see Mr. Vance again," she said pointedly, folding her hands tightly in front of her. "I told you from the beginning that I considered him an uncivilized savage. Perhaps now you'll understand why."

"I'm shocked," Mary said heavily. She took Trilby's hand and tugged her into the living room, to pull her down gently on the sofa. "Thank goodness Teddy is still mending harnesses with Mr. Torrance. I would hate for him to hear this."

"Yes," Jack said, his voice curt. "He idolizes Thorn."

"Mr. Vance is a good businessman," Trilby said, choking. "He's very wealthy and you cannot afford to antagonize him. But now, will you both please stop pushing me at him? He believed that I am—that I am a woman of easy virtue, and when he was alone with me, he behaved in a very…ungentlemanly fashion." She gripped her hands tightly together. It was painful to have to say these things to her parents. "I do not wish to be forced into his company again."

"And certainly you will not be!" Mary said shortly, daring her husband to argue.

"Indeed not," Jack murmured. He sighed heavily and

ran a hand through his gray-sprinkled hair. "Trilby, I misjudged the man. I'm very sorry."

"So am I, Father, because you admire him."

"How can he believe such a thing of you?" Mary groaned. "And why did his wife tell such an obvious lie? It makes no sense."

"It makes a great deal of sense if she told the lie to avert suspicion from herself," Jack said tautly. "That's something we can never repeat outside this house," he cautioned the women. "I do not want an action for slander against us when we're already in financial woe."

"I don't want to make any trouble for Mr. Vance," Trilby said, with dignity. "I only want him kept away from me."

"You can be certain of that," Jack assured her. "If any business crops up that requires his presence here, I'll give you ample warning, my dear. I'm very sorry to have placed you in such an awkward position."

"You weren't to know how he dislikes me," she told her father bitterly. "Oh, I do wish we'd never left Louisiana! Richard will be home soon…"

"And you want to see him?" Mary said. She smiled and patted Trilby's hand. "Well, he can come out to us for a visit. Would you like that? He can stay as long as he likes."

"Do you mean it?" Trilby asked enthusiastically. "Truly?"

"Truly." Mary laughed and hugged her daughter. "It will make a nice change to have young male company in the house."

"Could he bring Sissy and Ben with him?" she asked, mentioning his sister and brother. "And perhaps his cousin Julie?"

"Certainly."

"Just a minute." Jack laughed. "How am I to feed these pilgrims?"

"We can butcher a steer, of course," Mary replied. "And there are plenty of vegetables."

"I give up. Go ahead, have him out."

"You're a dear, Father," Trilby said, her harsh experience of the morning already forgotten in the joy of having her heart's dearest wish granted. She would see Richard again! It was almost worth the anguish of the day.

Chapter Four

Trilby sent a letter to Richard's sister, Sissy Bates, inviting the four of them out to the ranch. Then she went home with her father and went on with her everyday chores while the days passed and she waited impatiently for a reply.

Thorn Vance had been pushed firmly to the back of her mind. She no longer cared about his opinion, and her father had called on Curt and Lou Vance the day after Thorn's insulting behavior toward his daughter.

He came home furious. He and Lou had exchanged harsh words until Curt came in and asked what the fuss was about. When Jack told the man what Thorn had said, Curt was appalled.

Although to Jack, Curt had looked frankly guilty, he had denied immediately any involvement whatsoever with Trilby. He apologized for his cousin Thorn's suspicions and for any embarrassment Trilby might have suffered. He gave his wife a vicious tongue-lashing and promised to speak to his cousin and correct the undeserved blemish on Trilby's name with anyone who might have been misled by the gossip. Jack left somewhat placated but still seething about the insult to his daughter's good name. It was beyond him why a man like Thorn Vance should have so easily accepted Trilby's guilt. Most men, himself included, had instincts about women. Trilby kept close to home and she was never blatant in her dress or speech. Of all the things he prized, his good name and that of his family was his greatest treasure. He hoped that the damage could be corrected. In Baton Rouge, no one who knew the Lang family would ever question the good name of his daughter or his wife. But here in Arizona, that was not the case.

Trilby had worried herself sick about public opinion. She wasn't a coward, but Blackwater Springs was a small community. Doors closed when malicious gossip got around. She hated the gossip much more for her mother's sake than for her own. She didn't know how they could face their neighbors ever again.

They had to, however. Jack Lang insisted on taking his family to church the following Sunday. He set them down in a prominent pew, glancing around as if ready to do battle on his daughter's behalf. Hiding at home, he told his family, was more or less tantamount to admitting guilt. Since Trilby had nothing to be guilty about, there was no reason not to let the neighbors see them holding their heads up.

It wasn't until after the ceremony that two of the more socially prominent matrons came forward to pass the time of day with the Lang family. One of them mentioned that some malicious gossip about Trilby had been scotched by Curt Vance himself. They were certain that his wife had been instrumental in spreading it.

Trilby was somewhat placated. She noticed that Thorn Vance wasn't among the worshipers. No, Mr. Vance didn't come to church since his wife's death, one of the women offered. Pity, too, she added, when his little girl could certainly use the benefit of the gospel.

Trilby murmured suitably. But she was relieved that Curt had apparently made an attempt to put an end to the nasty gossip. She only hoped it would stop. She was certain that she'd never forgive Thorn Vance as long as she lived for what he'd said and done to her.

Days went by without Thorn stopping by, and she actually began to relax and try to put the incident into perspective. Best of all, a cable arrived from Louisiana. Richard and his brother and sister and cousin would leave the following week for Blackwater Springs. Trilby let out a whoop that could be heard halfway down the block and danced a jig on the way back to the runabout.

"Good news, I assume?" Her father chuckled.

"Yes! Oh, Father, he's coming, he's actually coming!"

"It's good to see you smile again, daughter," he said gently. He pressed her hand warmly. "It will be worth the trouble to have you happy."

"I can hardly wait!"

"I am not surprised."

He drove her back home. There was a celebration that night for Trilby's good fortune. Then, just as they began to prepare for bed, loud gunshots echoed through the desert, accompanied by the sound of bellowing, stampeding cattle.

Jack and Teddy rushed into their clothing and out onto the front porch. Old Mosby Torrance was already there, tall and stiff-necked, his watery blue eyes blazing out of a face like honed leather.

"Ten of them," he panted, having run from the bunkhouse. "Vasquez and Moreno saw them. Mexicans, they think, after the cattle."

"We'll give chase," Jack said coldly. "I'll have Mary fetch some rations. Roust the men and I'll break out some extra ammunition for the rifles."

"No sooner said than done, boss. I'll get my Winchester—"

"Oh, not you, Torrance," Jack said abruptly, staring at him as if he thought the old Texas Ranger was off his bean. "No, you have to look after the women. You, too, Teddy," he told his son, who looked shocked. "This isn't a job for either of you. I'll get my guns."

Torrance looked violent. Teddy moved forward. "It's okay, Mr. Torrance," he said miserably. "I guess we're both out of it."

The old man swallowed. "Damnedest thing about getting old, boy," he said huskily, "is that everybody thinks you're no account anymore."

"I think you're magnificent, sir!"

Torrance felt the sting go out of Jack's words as he looked down into the hero-worshiping face of the youngster. He had a son of his own somewhere. But his wife had died of pneumonia one winter while he was out chasing outlaws; he didn't know where the boy had been sent. By the time he got home, it was all over and his only child had vanished without a trace. He'd searched, but to no avail. He looked at Teddy and hoped that his child was as sturdy and brave as this one.

"Can you shoot?" he asked Teddy.

"I sure can," Teddy replied. He grimaced as he glanced after his father. "He doesn't think so, though.

Gosh, Mr. Torrance, nobody thinks we're any good for a fight, do they?"

"I reckon not. Well, I'll go get my gun anyway, in case they make a play for the house. You can help me keep watch outside." He glared toward the hall. "I don't guess he'll mind that."

"Not if we don't tell him," Teddy said, and grinned conspiratorially.

Torrance chuckled. Teddy really was one hell of a boy.

He went back to the bunkhouse and took out his nickle-plated, mother-of-pearl-handled .44 Colt revolver. The gun had been in a lot of battles with him over the years. It was still a respectable weapon, despite the .45 that most everyone carried these days. Like himself, the gun was out of place in a century that boasted machines that went as fast as a horse on the land and in the air. He was like a prehistoric man, he sometimes thought. Someone who'd lost the world he belonged in, and who couldn't quite fit into the new one.

It was a different story just after the Civil War when he became a Texas Ranger and wrote his own history as he went. Along with men like Bigfoot Wallace, he was a legend among Texas peacemakers. He'd backed down outlaws and gunfighters; he'd once backed down a whole damned lynch mob after a prisoner. But none of that was known out here, and nobody cared what he'd been fifty years ago.

Maybe he should be grateful that he even had a job, he supposed. Not that Jack Lang had had much choice about hiring him. He was foreman until Lang had inherited the place. Now he was the cattle foreman. Lang was his own boss.

He stuck the gun in its gunbelt and picked up his Remington, checking the action before he strode back out the door. He was tall and lithe. Except for his white hair, he looked much the same as he had when he was in his thirties, his step sure and firm on the wooden floor of the porch, his carriage erect and proud. What a hell of a shame, he thought, with faint amusement, that a man had to go and get old. There had been a time when he was sure he was going to be young forever.

Jack Lang came out the door buckling on his gun belt with fingers that just barely managed it. He was dressed in an exaggerated Western style, with woolly shotgun chaps and leather wristbands, new boots with heavy rowels on the spurs, and a pair of pearl-handled six-guns that looked like something out of a dime novel.

The Easterner always dressed like that when they went out to hunt rustlers. They never found any, because Lang didn't trust the Apache boy who scouted for them, and he didn't believe that anyone could track a man through a stream.

Torrance shook his head. Somebody ought to tell that dude that woolly shotgun chaps were suited to Northern winters and were worn by Montana and Wyoming cowboys, not Arizona ones. Those heavy rowels were Mexican—no self-respecting, civilized man would think of using them on his horse. The pistols were pretty, but they'd never been fired. And those wristbands would come in handy for a roper, but Jack Lang couldn't throw a rope.

Torrance kept his thoughts to himself, though, and just nodded when the boss told him to watch the women. He could track as well as that Mexican, Vasquez, whom Lang had given scouting chores to. Better. And he could

still outshoot any one of Lang's other cowboys. He knew
Mexicans because he'd trailed so many of them in his
Ranger days. But Lang would never know that, because
he didn't think a man Torrance's age was fit for cowboy
work.

He sighed more wistfully than he knew when the outfit
rode off without him. Teddy came to stand beside him.

"It's all right, Mr. Torrance," Teddy said. "I know
that you could do a better job of it than any one of Dad's
men. Even if he doesn't."

Torrance looked down at him with pure delight.
"You're a wonder, Teddy."

"So are you, Mr. Torrance."

Inside, Trilby watched the men ride away and worried. One of the hands had mentioned going by Los
Santos to pick up Thorn Vance. Her father had argued
with the man, and Trilby knew why he didn't want Thorn
involved. But then she'd heard the telephone being rung,
and her father muttering because it took the operator so
long to wake up and put his call through.

He had the operator ring Los Santos and presumably
spoke to Thorn, quite curtly. There was a pause, and her
father muttered his agreement to stop by Los Santos on
his way after the bandits. She hoped Thorn wouldn't
lead her vulnerable father into any gunplay. Jack Lang
posed very well, but he knew next to nothing about violent men....

When the makeshift posse got to Los Santos, Thorn
was already waiting for them. His rifle was in its sheath
and he was wearing a sidearm, a black-handled Colt .45
that had belonged to his great-uncle.

He'd had to browbeat Jack Lang into letting him join

the party. The Easterner had been hell-bent on going alone with his few men, and Thorn had a sudden mental image of the older man lying dead in the Arizona dust.

His conscience had burned him raw over his assumptions about Trilby. He'd done enough damage to her reputation that he hadn't felt right about going back over to the Lang place. He knew Jack and the rest of the family despised him for what he'd said to Trilby, although, miraculously, she seemed not to have told anyone what really happened during that ride on the desert. It was better than he deserved, he admitted. Now at least he could help keep her father alive. Perhaps that would atone a little for his actions.

Samantha had been asleep, and he hadn't woken her. The child was so withdrawn and quiet lately that he worried about her. She was thin and pale as well, not a healthy child in any way. He wished that his emotions weren't locked in steel so that he could communicate with her on some level. But since Sally's death, Samantha had drawn into her own mind. He didn't know how to reach her anymore.

He watched Jack Lang ride up, his expression preoccupied.

Jack, in turn, studied the Westerner, feeling suddenly overdressed and out of place. Thorn looked grim, Jack thought, and even under the circumstances, he was able to appreciate how very Western and dangerous the other man looked in his jeans and blue-checked Western shirt and red bandanna. He had on wristbands, as Jack did, but Vance's were scarred and worn dark with age. His boots had small rowels on the spurs and he was wearing wide, bat-wing leather chaps. His hat wasn't a new one like Jack's. It was weather-beaten and warped, but it

suited him somehow. A rope was looped over his saddle
horn and he was carrying the usual saddle roll that most
of his men's gear sported. A colorful Mexican poncho
was thrown over one broad shoulder and he was smok-
ing a cigarette with lazy disinterest. For a man going to
war, he looked magnificently unaffected.

Jack had to bite back angry words. He hadn't really
spoken to Thorn since his conversation with Curt Vance.
It was difficult to have to deal with a man who'd been
instrumental in very nearly ruining his daughter's reputation.

"Ready to go?" Thorn drawled when Jack reached
him. "I can add ten men to the party."

"I'm sure we have enough," Jack replied stiffly. "I
brought six."

Six men, plus himself and Vance, to hunt down a party
of bandits. Thorn could have chuckled at the man's innocence. The Mexican revolutionaries probably boasted fifty
men. Fighting across the border was growing stronger by
the day as the resistance to Díaz's rule mounted. Several
different small bands of insurrectionists were raiding local
stock from the northern Sonoran province of Mexico—and
they weren't averse to taking local cattle over the border
to sell as well as feed hungry men. Of course, they didn't
exactly pay for the local cattle they took. Things in Mexico
were definitely building to war, Thorn thought privately,
and he was worried more by the day about the grim possibility of American intervention if fighting migrated over
the border. Intervention would mean war with Mexico,
and no one wanted that.

"I'd feel more comfortable with my men along,"
Thorn said. He looked straight at Jack as he spoke and
he didn't blink. The look was as vivid as a curse.

"As you wish, of course," Jack said austerely. He hadn't mentioned Trilby, and neither had Thorn. But both men were having trouble acting naturally.

Thorn had heard about Jack's visit to his cousin and what had been said. He and Curt had argued for the first time in memory. But at last, Curt had convinced him that his shadowy paramour was not Trilby. The revelation had left Thorn confused and brutally ashamed. He'd savaged Trilby, all because Sally had accused her. But why had Sally lied? That was the only piece of the puzzle he couldn't fit in.

However, there was no time for it now. Thorn put his hand to his mouth and let out a fierce, piercing whistle. Immediately ten mounted men rode out and joined the small party.

They looked a lot like their boss, Jack thought. Most of them wore weather-beaten clothing and they were armed to the teeth. One or two of them looked absolutely roguish. There were two Apaches in the group; one short, aging one and another who was tall and well built with oddly intelligent black eyes. He looked positively grim.

"You're not taking the Indians?" Jack asked under his breath.

Thorn mentally counted to ten. "Naki and Tiza are my trackers," he told Lang. "The best in my outfit. I can't even find the signs they can."

"Look here, I don't trust Indians," Jack snapped. "The stories I've heard about them…"

"I don't imagine you've heard that in the old days some whites kept the Apaches as slaves?" he asked quietly. "Or that soldiers often attacked Indian villages and killed women and children?"

Lang cleared his throat. "Well…"

"I'll vouch for my men. All of my men," Thorn said quietly. "Let's ride."

"Yes, of course." Jack raised his arm and motioned for his men to follow. He tried to fall in alongside Vance, but the man put his spurs gently to his horse's flank and went like the wind. Jack Lang knew for a fact that he couldn't have managed to even stay on the horse at the speed Vance was going. He fell back, riding with his own group as Vance and his men outdistanced them. Jack refused to let himself ask who was leading the party. It was apparent that Vance was.

Despite the faint color breaking over the mountains, it was mostly dark. But the Apaches dismounted from time to time and stared around at things like boulders and stony ground. Lang was certain no man could track over rock, but the Apaches were able to. They led the men across the broad, white river that separated Jack's land from Vance's, and off to the west of Douglas.

"Vance, this is near the border. Damned near the border," Jack said, voicing his concern. "We can't go over into Mexico without permission."

Thorn leaned his wrists over his pommel and gazed at Jack Lang. "Listen, there's no question that the raiders have crossed the border. We only needed to know where, not if. They'll be down below Agua Prieta, and we can find them if we're quick. If we wait until we get permission, you'll lose half your herd. Besides that, we can't risk the army coming down here after us."

"But, man, if we're caught…"

"We won't be." He signaled to his men and rode forward at a quick clip.

Jack hesitated, but in a minute, he followed.

They trailed the Mexicans to a valley just below the San Bernadino Valley, careful to keep plenty of distance between them and the U.S. Army troops that were bivouacked there along the border. The bandits were so confident that they'd settled down to a nice, leisurely breakfast with one of Jack Lang's steers being butchered as the main course.

There were only six of them. That convinced Thorn that they were only renegades, not part of any Maderista forces. These men were acting on their own, he was pretty sure, but they didn't look quite smart enough to be acting without guidance. He wanted to know whom they were working for.

He signaled to his men, forgetting that it was Jack Lang's party, and rode into the camp, unfurling his lasso at the same time. He threw a loop over the man who looked like the leader and jerked him down. The others had drawn their weapons, but finding themselves outnumbered and outgunned, they quickly threw up their hands, crying out in garbled Spanish.

A rapid monologue of Spanish exploded from Thorn, who stepped gracefully out of the saddle to hog-tie the leader. But as he began to question the man, one of the Apaches, the tall one, approached him and, with a cold look at Jack Lang, began to speak in his own tongue.

"We're not alone here."

"Speak English," Thorn snapped.

"Not in front of him," Naki replied, indicating Jack Lang. "I've heard what he's been saying. If he insults me once more I'll tie him bare-legged to a cactus. You tell him that," he added, with a cold scowl in Jack Lang's direction that made the older man look uncomfortable.

"Will you tell me what you found out?"

"When you tell this stage cowboy that he's headed for a stake and some firewood, I will."

Thorn glared at him. "It was the Iroquois in the Northeast, not the Apaches, who burned people at the stake!"

Naki glowered as he eyed Jack. "Are you sure?"

"Damn it!"

"Oh, very well! There are about a hundred *Federales* headed this way."

"Why didn't you say so?!" He turned in the saddle. *"Federales,"* Thorn said sharply. "We'll have to clear out. Get those cattle moving!" he called to his men.

They fired into the air to stampede the milling cattle, and Thorn quickly threw his roped quarry across his own saddle before he mounted and lit out for the border.

"Don't spare the horses!" he called to Jack Lang. "We can't let ourselves be caught on this side of the border!"

"As I said myself before we sashayed down here," Jack muttered to himself, but not so that Thorn could hear him.

They made it across the border just minutes ahead of the Mexican soldiers, cattle and all. In the ensuing rout, all but the Mexican thrown across Vance's saddle managed to escape while the cowboys tried to salvage the cattle. They did lose a few head in the process, but not enough to make any great difference in Jack Lang's fortunes.

With Thorn in the lead, they rode hell-for-leather for Blackwater Springs Ranch. Trilby heard them come up and ran to the window. Jack Lang and Thorn were just riding up to the front of the house. She was so relieved to see her father that she instinctively ran out onto the porch.

Thorn saw her just as he tossed the trussed Mexican to the ground and loosened his rope, leaving the freed man lying there. He looked utterly ruthless as he turned to her.

"Get in the house and stay there," he said, with icy command.

She began to disobey just as the Mexican looked at her and laughed. He said something in Spanish to Thorn.

It was obviously something insulting, and about her, because Thorn went for him on the spot. The Mexican pulled a knife, which Thorn was too furious to notice. But Naki saw it. As the smaller man raised it to strike, Naki's hand flashed down to the big hunting knife he carried in a sheath on his belt. He whipped it out and flung it, handle first, with frightening speed and accuracy, knocking the Mexican's knife right out of his hand.

"I say!" Jack Lang exclaimed from where he was sitting beside Naki.

The Apache slipped out of the saddle gracefully and retrieved his knife. Thorn and the Mexican were mixing it up roughly now, knocking each other about with little care for which bystanders they knocked over.

"Heathen savages," Naki remarked as he swung back into his saddle.

Jack Lang stared at him incredulously, diverted from the fight.

"That!" Naki emphasized, waving one arm toward Thorn. "God in heaven, man, don't you even care that they're in danger of bashing each other's brains out? I thought you white people were civilized!" He managed to sound disgusted and superior.

"You speak English!" Jack gasped.

"Yes, but it leaves a foul taste in my mouth. Mixed metaphors, double negatives, alliteration…"

He turned his horse and rode off, still muttering to himself. He could barely contain his laughter as Jack Lang sat with his mouth open, gaping after him.

Thorn and the Mexican were drenched in sweat and covered with dust and blood. Thorn was tall, but the Mexican was broader, and his pride had been damaged by the indignity of his treatment.

But Thorn eventually beat him into a dazed submission and, dragging him up, began to question him in curt Spanish. The man answered reluctantly, but he did finally answer. Thorn let him go with a shove.

"Give him a horse," he told Jack Lang. "I'll reimburse you."

"We're letting him go?" Jack gasped. "But he should be arrested, tried for his crime!"

"I said, let him go," Thorn told the older man in a way that defied protest.

Jack motioned to one of his men and sent him after a suitable mount. Trilby had gone back into the house at the beginning of the unpleasantness, but she was hopelessly drawn to the window as she heard the sickening thuds abate. What she saw made her run for the back porch, where she was violently sick.

While she was sitting at the kitchen table, sipping hot, sweet tea to calm her nerves, Thorn came in with her father. He was bare-headed, his face cut and badly bleeding, like his knuckles.

"Can you do something for Vance, Trilby?" her father asked curtly. "Your mother is in the bedroom and she won't come out."

Trilby didn't blame her. "Of course," she said, bucking

up. She could hardly contain her nausea. The smell of blood was overwhelming. She got a pan and went to the sink, adding a clean cloth to the water she pumped into it. She sat down at the table beside a weary Thorn and slowly began to clean his cuts. She didn't look into his eyes. In fact, he didn't lift them; he acted oddly subdued. Perhaps, she thought bitterly, he was in pain. She had to fight the urge to leave the room and let him stay that way, but her soft heart outweighed her outrage for the moment.

"I don't understand why you wanted the Mexican turned loose," Jack said irritably.

"Keeping him would cause his men to come after him," Thorn explained, wincing when Trilby wiped his cut cheek. "Some Mexicans are like Apaches when they want revenge."

Jack was beginning to get the picture. "I see."

"I doubt it, but you'll just have to take my word for it. They make a habit of raiding north of the border for cattle and selling them to a big landowner in the southern province of Sonora. I told them if I caught them on this side of the border again, I'd have a little talk with their benefactor. I don't think we'll see them again anytime soon. But there are other raiders. This isn't the end of it."

"I was afraid you'd say that." He grimaced as he saw Thorn's face. The man had helped him, despite the damage he'd done. "You look terrible."

"Fighting isn't pretty. Is it, Trilby?" he asked her, with a glint in his dark eyes as he suddenly looked up, full at her.

She averted her eyes. "No." She had to choke the word out. "What did he say that made you attack him?"

"I'll never tell you that," he said solemnly. "He did it to provoke me, hoping he could catch me off-guard and put that knife into my belly."

"Your Indian friend," Jack said uneasily. "He's not what I expected."

"He's not what anyone expects," Thorn replied. "Thank God for his skill with a knife. I'd have been gutted but for him."

"How fortunate for you that you weren't," Trilby said. Her eyes looked into his. "Am I to understand that you were actually defending me?" she asked, with quiet hauteur.

He caught his temper as it started to flare. When he spoke, his deep voice was soft. "Yes. No murderous bandit should be allowed to talk that way about a decent woman," he said shortly.

She dipped the bloodstained cloth back in the water, noticing how pinkish the once clear water had become. She lifted it back to Thorn's face. "But then, I'm not a decent woman, according to you," she replied bitterly.

He caught her wrist tightly. His eyes were frankly apologetic. "Curt told me the truth. I'm sorry. More sorry than you realize."

"Don't ruin your image, Mr. Vance," she said as she tugged her hand out of his grasp and continued her ministrations. "I hardly think apologies are part of your repertoire."

Her father was hovering nearby. Thorn wished him in Montezuma. He needed to see Trilby alone, to see if he could mend the distance he'd put between them. She acted as if she despised him and he'd given her good reason. Even a blind man should have realized that her innocence was no pretense.

"Your man, the Apache," Jack persisted. "He speaks English."

"Does he, really?" Thorn asked, managing to look surprised.

Jack cleared his throat and walked out.

His absence gave Thorn the opportunity he'd wanted to patch things up with Trilby, if he could.

"Look at me," Thorn said quietly. "Trilby...look at me."

She forced her eyes down to his.

"I'm sorry," he said softly. "Did I frighten you that day?"

She flushed and turned away.

He got up, standing behind her. His lean hands caught her shoulders gently. "You're upset. You'd never even been kissed, had you?" he said regretfully.

"No," she said through her teeth. "And what you did..."

He let out a heavy breath. "Yes. What I did is something that belongs in a relationship between married people. You learned things about me that you'd never have known in the normal course of things."

She flushed and was glad that he couldn't see her face. "I'd better finish cleaning your face, Mr. Vance," she said stiffly.

He turned her toward him, bending so that he could see her eyes. "Don't hate me," he said, his voice surprisingly soft. "I was wrong. I want to make amends."

"Do you? Then please stay out of my way." She laughed uneasily. "I want nothing to do with you."

His face stiffened. He'd frightened and shocked her. She made him feel inadequate somehow. His hands fell from her shoulders and he sat back down again.

His attitude made her feel guilty. "You have my forgiveness if you think you need it, Mr. Vance. I'll thank you for defending me, regardless. I'm sorry you were hurt on my behalf."

"These little cuts?" he said heavily. "They sting, but they're not much. I've had bullet wounds hurt worse. They tear the flesh when they penetrate."

Her hand paused in midair. "Bullet...wounds?" She swayed and her knees turned to jelly.

He caught her as she went down, holding her propped against his strong body. "Trilby, for the love of God..."

She drew a slow breath and the nausea and the faintness began to dissipate. "I'm sorry," she said weakly. "It's just...there was so much violence!"

She felt fragile. So fragile. He bent suddenly and swept her up completely off the floor in his arms, turning into the living room, where her father had just reappeared from outside.

"Trilby, what's wrong?" Jack asked.

"She fainted. I shouldn't have mentioned bullet wounds," Thorn said ruefully. "She needs to lie down."

"Yes. Of course. This way."

Her father led the way to her neat bedroom, standing aside to let Thorn carry her in and place her delicately on the white embroidered bedspread.

"Jack?" Mary Lang called suddenly, her voice almost hysterical. "Jack, where's Teddy?"

"I think he's out back with Torrance," Thorn said over his shoulder.

"Oh, bother," Jack muttered. "Trilby, dear. Are you all right?"

"Yes, Father," she whispered. "I'm just a bit sick. And glad that you're all right."

He nodded. "I'll be right back."

Left briefly alone with Thorn, Trilby tried not to meet his eyes. He looked terribly cut up, and she wondered if that cut on his cheek would heal without leaving a scar.

"I'm sorry about all this," he told her stiffly. "I guess you've never seen a fistfight before, either."

"Hearing it was bad enough." Her eyes glanced off his face. "You should bathe your face again tonight," she murmured.

"I'll do that. Naki has some kind of herbs he uses on cuts. I'll let him doctor me."

"Are you sure he won't poison you?" she asked, with faint humor.

"He's my friend," he said simply. "Friends don't poison each other. If you're sure you're all right, I'll be on my way."

"Thank you for looking after my father," she said, with stiff pride.

"He needed looking after," he said shortly. "My God, he'll lose everything if he doesn't toughen up."

"It's so brutal out here," she said suddenly, her wide eyes expressive.

"Of course it is. It's no place for lilies."

She blanched. Her hands dovetailed on her waist as she lay there looking up at him from her pillow. She felt vulnerable with a man in her bedroom. He seemed to fill it, dominate it. He looked at her as if she were hopeless. Perhaps she was.

His dark eyes slid down her body to her slim ankles and back up again. She was slender and well made, and he ached thinking about how her mouth felt under his.

But she was looking at him as if he frightened her. Probably he did, he thought bitterly. He'd been antagonistic toward her from the very beginning; he'd insulted her, been roughly physical with her, and then he'd savaged her reputation. How could he expect her to trust him?

That was a pity, when she'd begun to appeal to him in a totally new way, he thought ironically. She'd been scared to death and sick while he fought the Mexican, but she was game! White in the face and shaking, she'd still had the nerve to doctor his wounds. He admired her. He'd admired her when she fought with him verbally, and she'd done that from the first time they'd met. He couldn't remember one time when he'd ever admired his late wife—except in the very beginning of their relationship.

"I won't let anything happen to your father, Trilby," he said quietly. "To any of you."

She swallowed down a bout of nausea and closed her eyes. "This terrible country," she whispered. "I wish we'd never come."

He hated the way she said that. "Listen, it's not as bad as you're making it out. Trilby, I'd like to show you my desert…."

Her eyes flew open and began to glitter with feeling. "The way you showed me last time?" she asked accusingly.

He muttered under his breath and stood up. He swept off his hat and wiped the sweat from under it with the long sleeve of his shirt. "You won't see my side of it, will you?" he asked quietly. "I acted on what I believed to be the truth."

"God sitting in judgment? Your opinion of me makes me sicker than your wounds, Mr. Vance," she said huskily, her gray eyes wide and unblinking in a face like paper. "I have no use for a man who can jump to a conclusion and refuse to let go of it, even when all the evidence contradicts it."

"Sally lied to me," he repeated.

"Yes."

"I didn't know you," he persisted. "I had no idea what kind of person you really were."

"You might have given me the benefit of the doubt," she said coldly. "As it happens, my father was able to undo the damage you did to my reputation. That is fortunate, because a beau of mine is coming out to stay very shortly. I should hate him to get a bad opinion of me from local gossip."

He went very still. "A beau?" he asked.

She smiled haughtily. "Apparently you think my lack of beauty precludes me from having gentleman callers. It might interest you to know that not all men judge a woman by her face or form. Richard admires me for my intellect."

"Richard who?" he shot at her.

"Richard Bates. We grew up together in Baton Rouge. His family and mine would very much like for us to marry," she added deliberately. "And so would I. I've loved Richard half my life!"

He felt tight as a drawn cord. Her dislike and contempt for him were as tangible as his had once been for her. He felt small and mean, and because his guilt made him raw inside, he lashed out.

"He's a city boy, I gather? One of those dandies with no brain or guts?"

"Richard is a gentleman, Mr. Vance," she said, with faint hauteur. "Which is something no woman could ever accuse you of being. Certainly not if she'd ever had the misfortune to be alone with you!"

He flushed. His hand crushed the brim of his hat and his wounded face went livid. "You don't pull your punches, do you?"

"I wish I could punch you, Mr. Vance," she said fervently. "I wish I were a man for just five minutes. I'd do you more damage than that Mexican managed!"

He drew himself up to his full height. "I've apologized," he said shortly.

"And you think that wipes out months of harsh treatment and contempt and insults." She nodded.

Put that way, no, he didn't. He let his eyes wander over her face for one long moment as he began to realize just how much he'd made her hate him. He was going to lose her and her father's water rights in one fell swoop, and this Eastern dude she loved was going to waltz in and scoop her right out of his life. He felt sick right where he lived.

He didn't say another word. He turned abruptly, slammed his hat back on his head, and walked out of the room.

Trilby closed her eyes. Let him go, she thought angrily. She certainly didn't want him. She never had! She thought about Richard instead, and the tenseness left her face all at once. Richard was coming, at last! For once, her dreams seemed to be coming true. When Richard arrived, the vicious Mr. Vance would become nothing more than a bad memory.

Bad, like the events of the day. Trilby refused to think of the danger her father had been in. She wanted nothing to spoil the joyous time ahead.

Chapter Five

When Trilby got up, minutes later, Mary Lang was still sick and faint from what she'd seen outside her window. The whole unpleasant episode had pointed out what was worst about their new home.

"I had no idea men fought like that," Mary told her daughter later when they were sitting quietly together after putting out a meal for Jack. "I'd never seen men fight."

"Neither had I. The Mexican said something about me. Mr. Vance wouldn't tell me what it was, but it was why he hit him."

"Thank you for taking care of his wounds, Trilby," Mary said. "I just couldn't!"

For the first time, Trilby felt older than her mother. It was not to be the last time she felt that way.

The idea of Thorn fighting for her was surprising. Of course, he had sworn that he'd changed his mind about her. But it didn't wipe away the damaging things he'd said.

He came visiting late one afternoon at the end of the

week, after Jack Lang had come in from checking his
line riders. The sun was going down and the sunset,
always spectacular, had brought Trilby onto the darkened front porch steps to watch. She was sitting there,
alone, while her family talked around the kitchen table,
when Thorn rode up.

Her heart raced as he swung lithely out of the saddle
and tied his mount to the post. Fear, she supposed, had
to be responsible for that reaction. Or anger, perhaps.
She noticed that he was still wearing working garb.

Her innate sense of courtesy wouldn't let her be deliberately rude to a visitor, in spite of the hostility he
kindled in her. "You usually ride a horse when you come
to visit, Mr. Vance," she commented politely from her
perch on the top step. "I thought you liked automobiles."

"I don't. Not particularly." He sat down beside her, a
lighted cigarette in his hand, and he didn't remove his
wide-brimmed hat. He smelled of leather and tobacco
and dust and sweat, but Trilby didn't find him in the least
offensive. That reaction puzzled her. Since she didn't
like him, shouldn't she find his nearness unpleasant?

"Father is in the kitchen with Mother and Teddy—"
she began.

"I won't accost you, Trilby," he said quietly. "Not this
time. Talk to me."

"Why, about—about what?" she faltered.

"I've had a difference of opinion with my daughter on
the subject of school," he said. "I've been trying to help
her do her lessons, but she refuses to cooperate. She's
so withdrawn that I can't seem to reach her at all."

The child interested her, despite her resentment of
Thorn. "Doesn't she go to school?"

"She did. The school closed when the schoolteacher

went back East to get married. Sally was teaching her. Now there's no one to do it anymore, except me. The only alternative is to take a house in Douglas and send her to school there, as some other married ranchers have done."

"Does she learn easily?"

"Easily enough, when she wants to. But she's not been the same since her mother died. I've arranged to spend more time with her. Perhaps I can encourage her to learn if I work with her myself. I've neglected her, I suppose. I've had a lot on my mind."

"I'm sure you have. The Mexicans are closer to you than to us. I suppose the revolution worries you."

"It worries everyone who lives on the border," he said flatly. "Each side thinks we're supporting the other, when we're doing our best to stay neutral. It causes difficulties."

"There was something in the paper about an anti-American riot in Mexico City," she said. "And there are rumors that Madero and his followers are planning an all-out attack."

"The signs point to it." His eyes were quietly appreciative of her pretty, blue-checked gingham dress with white rickrack around the square collar. Her hair was long and loose, and Thorn was aroused by it. Suddenly, violently aroused.

His lean hand speared into the thick waves gently, lifting them so that her head was tugged back, her face uplifted at a very intimate angle.

"Please, don't," she said stiffly. She pulled angrily at his wrist.

"I have ears like a fox," he said. His voice was quiet, soft. "And we're in the dark here." He leaned closer, his smoky breath on her lips, making her weak, making her want his mouth on hers again. Her own reaction made her angry and she pushed at his chest.

"There's no need to fight me," he said irritably. "I'm not going to hurt you."

"Of course not," she agreed, her eyes furious. "You're only going to force your attentions on me and then say that I tempted you!"

He let her go at once. "My God," he said heavily. "You won't forget, will you?"

She straightened her hair and her skirts with trembling hands, averting her gaze from his hard face. "I don't want your attentions, Mr. Vance. I thought I'd already made that quite clear to you."

"I'm wealthy—" he began.

"And you think that matters to me?" she asked harshly. "I would not sell myself to the richest man on earth if I did not love him. I would love my Richard if he were a poet, with no income to speak of. It isn't for his station in life that I yearn."

"I thought you were a grown woman," he said curtly. "You speak like a schoolgirl in the throes of calf love!"

Her chin went up and her gray eyes kindled with temper. "You have no right to make light of my feelings! You know nothing about me."

He searched her thin, pale face. "That's true enough," he said, his voice deep in the hush of evening. "I've assumed a great deal, but I've never sought to know you."

She turned her face toward the horizon, with its thin streak of color. Fiesta colors, she thought absently. The sunset had a Mexican flavor tonight.

"You don't approve of me, do you, Trilby?" he asked easily, lounging back against one of the square wooden columns to roll another cigarette. "I'm neither civilized nor safe, like your dude from back East."

"A civilized man treats a woman like a lady."

"You sound like a well-brought-up Spanish girl," he said, amused. "Very correct, helpless without her duenna."

"No duenna in her right mind would allow you within a mile of her charge," she said bluntly, glaring at him as she remembered the vicious pain of his kiss when he'd taken her for that ride in the desert.

"I hurt you, didn't I?" he asked quietly. He stared at the tip of his cigarette. "You aren't going to forgive what happened."

"I have forgiven you, Mr. Vance. It's simply that friendship is all I have to offer you," she added.

He glared at her. "What can an Eastern man give you that a Western man can't?" he demanded.

"Civilized behavior!" she returned. "Decent treatment. Tenderness. Things you know nothing about."

He laughed without humor. "I guess it must seem like that to you. You're a game girl, Trilby. Sick to death of violence, but you still had nerve enough to doctor me. I won't forget that. You've got grit."

"I don't imagine many people who associate with you can manage without it," she muttered.

"I'll take that as a compliment," he told her.

The screen door banged as her father walked onto the porch. "Thorn, isn't it?" Jack Lang welcomed him, extending a hand as Thorn got lazily to his feet. His enmity for Vance had been forgotten after the other man had saved his cattle. Apparently Vance and Trilby were back on speaking terms, too, which boded well for everyone. "Good to see you. Come in and have coffee with us."

"Thanks. I stopped by to ask you if you'd like to come to a fiesta tomorrow evening."

"A fiesta?"

"Down at Maladora. It's a saint's day celebration. Music and dancing and food. I think you might like it. It's only about an hour away and we can take the car."

"That would be fun," Jack said. "I'm sure Mary and Teddy and Trilby would enjoy it."

Trilby had no interest in fiestas or Thorn Vance's company. But her father was so enthusiastic that she would have felt very mean indeed to have refused. "I like music," she said.

"So does Samantha," he replied. "She'll be with me, of course. It's her birthday."

He smiled at Trilby, and she felt something incredible happening to her. She didn't know whether or not to trust the awkward, disturbing emotions he kindled. She had to remember her beloved Richard, who was coming in only a few days to see her.

Thorn Vance was untamed, untamable. He wasn't safe to flirt with or make love with. He was hardly the sort of man she'd ever want to end up marrying, even if he was exciting to be with. That being the case, she simply had to keep her wits about her.

"Thank you," Jack replied, with a smile. "We'd be delighted."

"Fine. I'll come by for you around four tomorrow afternoon. Good night." He smiled down at Trilby. "I'll look forward to it."

She watched him ride off with a frown on her face. She wondered why he'd decided to take her family to the fiesta. Perhaps he was simply trying to make amends, she told herself, and went back to daydreaming about Richard.

Col. David Morris hung up his telephone at Fort Huachuca and a frown appeared on his handsome face. More trouble on the border, and once again he was going to dispatch another troop down the border to keep watch on the situation. Skirmishes had mounted daily since the outbreak of insurrection in Mexico. He might as well go with Captain Bell this time, he thought with resignation, and talk to the rancher who'd had cattle run off. It wasn't going to do any good. He had no authority to cross the border; God knew, it would probably lead to war if any of his men so much as stepped over the line. Even if he did have authority, Mexico was a big country. God alone knew who'd taken the cattle. He could hardly round up citizens of another sovereign nation and search them for woolly longhorns.

The thought amused him. He smiled, his high-cheekboned face less severe than usual. He got up from his desk, running a hand through his thick blond hair. It had been light brown before he'd been sent out here to command his troops, but the Arizona sun had bleached it blond. He glanced at himself in the blemished looking glass on his wall and pursed his lips. For a man of thirty-six, he wasn't too bad-looking, he thought with faint sarcasm. Selina seemed to think he was a figure from Greek mythology. Especially without his clothes.

His wife, Lisa, never looked at him. She'd grown broody and morose since the death of their baby earlier in the year. She had never enjoyed him in bed, even when they first married. That was mutual. He found

her passable, but she'd never stirred him. He knew she'd
loved him at first. But he'd married her only because of
her father, who had been a very influential general. Once
she found out, it had killed all her feelings for him. Then
he'd started straying to other women's beds.

She hadn't said anything about his amours lately.
She'd been oddly secretive. She was so reclusive that
he hardly knew she was in his quarters at all. He really
must speak to her, he thought as he called in his adju-
tant. But it would have to wait. As usual, military business took precedence.

He was saluted by members of his black 9th cavalry
on the way to his car. The 9th and 10th were the famous
"Buffalo soldiers," whose proud history gave him no
cause for regret at being commandant here.

All the long drive to Douglas, he thought about seeing
Selina again. She was proprietress of a hotel on the small
town's notorious Sixth Street. It was more a bawdy house
than a hotel, but Selina had a voluptuous body and the
gift of making a man feel like a conqueror.

Lisa was quiet and shy and not very much to look at.
But Selina…ah, she appealed to parts of him that were
far removed from his heart. Her exquisite body could
arouse him even in memory. He gave her expensive gifts,
sent her flowers, doted on her. Thank God Douglas was
a good ride from the fort, so there was little danger of
Lisa finding out about her. These days, Selina was the
only recreation he had.

His driver sped the big touring car past the small
complement of troops stationed at the Douglas fair-
grounds, and David saluted its officers as he rode past.
This small garrison was hardly a threat to the Maderistas, but it boasted some brave men and would do in a

pinch. In times of real danger, troops from Fort Huachuca and other posts could be quickly dispatched to any trouble points. There had been some incidents just lately, and David was worried about the future. Things would surely get worse before they got better, here on the border.

The Gadsden Hotel was, he considered, the ideal place to get local gossip about the border situation. The hotel was majestic, a meeting place for the rich and powerful, not to mention a gracious lodging. He found the information he sought within minutes of entering, from the good-natured desk clerk, and was soon on his way out of town.

It was one of the dustiest days in recent memory. His men wore their bandannas pulled snugly over their mouths and noses to keep from choking on the yellow grains. Douglas frequently sprinkled her streets with water to try and keep the dust down, but it only made matters worse. Each porch boasted a feather duster, which was used by guests to brush themselves down before entering the house. Like the sprinkling, it really did very little good.

It was a pleasant day, just cool enough to feel good as they rode down the long road toward the ranch. Morris's eyes darted from right to left, searching for signs of invaders. Inevitably, he thought, Mexicans were going to boil over that border and start trouble. He hoped the military would be able to cope with it.

Blackwater Springs Ranch was hardly impressive, he thought as they neared the frame ranch house. The fences were sagging from their posts and in obvious need of repair. The scattered herds of cattle were emaciated, and there wasn't much feed. If there was an operation in trouble in Arizona, this was it.

Easterners, he thought, were so sure of themselves until they knew the reality of ranching here in the desert. It was no place for tenderfeet, but they all had to learn the hard way.

He had his driver pull up at the house. He halted his small mounted column and waited for someone to come out on the porch.

Jack Lang was pleased and somewhat shocked to find a troop of cavalry on his doorstep, but he introduced himself and invited the colonel inside with his usual exquisite manners.

"No time, thanks all the same," Morris said curtly. "Listen, I want to know about the trouble you had."

Jack flushed a little at the abrupt tone, but he told the officer what had happened. He didn't mention that they'd crossed the border to apprehend the raider; only that they'd questioned him and released him.

"He said he wasn't part of Madero's force?"

"That's right."

Morris looked thoughtful. "There are always men on the fringe of armies who commit crimes on their own, but this bears watching, Mr. Lang. We can't allow Mexican patriots to defend their cause on United States money."

"I agree. The problem is trying to prevent it. I have a limited number of hands."

"This is usually the case in outlying areas. We will, of course, increase our patrols. I will also alert the troops in Douglas and those in the San Bernardino Valley near the Slaughter Ranch—assuming that you have not."

"But I have," Jack protested. "At least, my neighbor, Thorn Vance, has."

"Vance." He said the man's name with a little apprehension. "Yes, I know of him. Well, that's good, then. We'll step up our patrols and hopefully prevent a repetition. I'm sorry to hear of your trouble."

"We recovered most of the stolen cattle," Jack told him.

"The prisoner?"

"We let him go," Jack said.

"Wise of you," Morris agreed. "Mexicans are vengeful. You wouldn't want them down on your head for holding one of their own against his will."

"That's what Vance said."

"He's lived out here all his life. Not a bad idea to take his advice. It's sound." He touched his hand to his hat. "I'll say good day."

"Good day, Colonel."

Jack watched him speed away and wondered why he'd come. There was so little the military could do about his situation. It was a big country—with plenty of hiding places for men and cattle. He sighed and went back into the house.

David went back through Douglas and ordered his men to proceed back to the fort while he conducted some private business in town. There were no comments, but two of the men snickered as they rode out of town. It was an open secret that the colonel had a kept woman.

After sending his driver off on a few errands, for appearances' sake, David made his way to the small boardinghouse where Selina worked.

She was sitting at one of the tables, very correctly dressed, her black hair in a soft bun, wearing a pretty pink dress that covered most of her body. She glanced up with a pert smile when she saw Morris sweep off his hat and approach her.

"David, how lovely to see you!" she said in her softly accented Spanish, her eyes lighting up just at the sight of him.

She got up from her chair and took his hand, lowering her eyes demurely in case anyone was watching them. The house was mostly empty this time of day, though, and no one was.

"Do come and see the new sofa the owners have put in the library," she coaxed.

He went with her, his heart pounding madly in his chest. She led him into a small reading room and closed the single door. She leaned back against it, and there was a click as she locked it.

"You're covered with dust," she complained as she went into his arms.

"Never mind the dust. Kiss me!"

He found her mouth and kissed her with unbridled hunger. He moaned sharply as he felt her hips lift and thrust violently against his.

"It's been two weeks," she moaned.

"I know!"

His trembling hands bunched the skirt of her dress up until he could find her dark, soft thighs. He stroked them while his mouth devoured hers, delighting in her whispery moans and the fury of her small hands at the front of his tunic.

He backed her up to the door and lowered himself. His hand found the fastenings that separated them. He lifted his head and looked into her flushed face as he suddenly caught her hips and lifted her into the hard, urgent thrust of his aroused body.

She caught her breath. "Da...vid! We can't!"

His mouth covered the laughing protest, holding her still as his body ground into her rhythmically. The door made faint clicking noises as the pitch increased, and then began to slam as his hips drove for fulfillment in a mindless oblivion.

Selina smiled sadly as she felt him convulse. She'd never wanted anyone so much, but like most men, he wanted his own pleasure more than he wanted hers.

He leaned his forearm against the door while he shuddered, barely able to breathe. He relaxed then, his body heavy and throbbing on hers. "I'm glad the house was deserted," he whispered ruefully.

"Yes. Let me go, David," she said quietly.

He lifted his head then and looked at her with lazily sated eyes. "You never look as if we've made love," he speculated. "It's just for my sake that you allow this, isn't it? You love me, but you have no interest in sex."

She shrugged. "It does not matter."

His lips pursed. "Perhaps it's time I thought more of your pleasure, little one."

He lifted away from her and proceeded to remove his clothes. It was broad daylight. She'd never seen a man naked. She was faintly shocked to see that David was still erect, capable, when he stood in front of her. He had a good body, very muscular and lean.

"This is the library—" she began.

"So it is. We've never made love on the floor, have we?"

She blushed. His big hands went to her clothing and began to remove it with deft skill. She didn't protest

once, not even when she was nude and his eyes were
making a meal of her full breasts and long, elegant legs.

"What an expression." He laughed softly. Then he
bent and took her breast into his mouth and began to
suckle it. At the same time, he lifted her in his arms and
carried her to the huge Persian rug that lay between the
chairs and the velvet-covered sofa. He laid her down on it
and knelt between her thighs. For minutes that stretched
like hours he simply looked at her, touched her lightly.
Then his head went down against her stomach and he
began to caress her with his mouth in ways that no man
in her life had ever touched her.

She gasped when he clenched both thighs in his hands
and bent his head hungrily to her core. She struggled, but
the heat of his mouth was so sweet, so incredibly plea-
surable, that she couldn't hold out against it. He drew
her through layers of exquisite sensation to a place that
pulled her into a thread of pure aching tension.

When she was sobbing, clutching at him, begging, he
drew into a kneeling position and jerked her body up to
encompass the swelling need of his. She convulsed at the
first hard, violent thrust. The spasms went on and on as
he pushed inside her taut body. She laughed, and cried,
and clung to him as he took her all the way to paradise
before he finally shuddered and collapsed on her.

Much later, she sat dazed in a chair, fully dressed,
and couldn't even look at him.

"It was like taking a virgin," he said with satisfaction, standing over her in his uniform once more. "Like
our first time together, except that you were nervous and
shy and afraid then."

She stared at her fingers. "Do you do that…with your
wife?"

"I've never done that with anyone," he said curtly. "And I never will. Only you. I love you. Hasn't that occurred to you?"

Her face lifted, white and strained. Her dark eyes met his. "Love...me?"

"Love you," he agreed.

"But I'm—I'm not a lady, or anything," she blurted out.

"You are to me," he said firmly.

"How can you care for me? For a lowborn woman like me?" She wept.

He framed her face in his hands, smiling with faint triumph at the unexpected vulnerability he found there. "You're quite a woman, Selina."

He kissed her, and then she clung to him, her cheek on his chest. "Please tell me that I'm the only one, even if it isn't true," she whispered.

"You are the only woman," he said honestly. "And you'll be the last in my life." He bent and kissed her with slow tenderness. "I'll be back."

She watched him leave, her mind whirling with the experience he'd just given her. The days were going to be very long before she saw him again.

She thought of his wife and her blood ran hot. That was a situation she'd have to do something about eventually. She didn't want to share him with another woman. But for now, she'd bide her time. If he really loved her, and she was almost certain that he did, he wouldn't ask her to share him. He must not love his wife, she decided. He must not care about her at all. She began to hum as she went about her chores.

Chapter Six

Trilby watched the colorfully garbed Mexicans dance to the throbbing rhythm with a sense of pleased detachment. In all the long months they'd been in Arizona, this was the first celebration of its kind that she'd seen. Despite her natural reticence, she found the blurs of color and the festive atmosphere beckoning.

Beside her, Thorn leaned idly against an adobe wall, twisting a piece of rawhide in his lean fingers. He hadn't dressed up for the occasion. Neither had Jack. Trilby and her mother were the only people who looked Eastern in the entire crowd. Most of the Mexican women wore white blouses with colorful skirts and the men wore white trousers and bright ponchos. Trilby grimaced at her neat navy blue dress with white lacy trim and buttoned-up high heels. She tugged nervously at the high collar of her dress.

"Don't fidget," Thorn chided softly. "You look fine."

"I didn't realize how overdressed I would be," she protested. "It's so—so casual."

"These people don't have the kind of money they'd

need for fancy duds," he said simply. "But they're happy, for all that."

"They seem to be that," she agreed, somehow envying them their exuberance. Her own was always tightly contained, held back. "It isn't dangerous to be here—with the Mexican trouble, I mean?"

"Even if some of these people are sympathizers, we're in no danger," he consoled her. "I know most of the villagers here. Some of their relatives work for me."

"Oh." But she wasn't relaxed. Even now her fingers were clenched tightly together. Thorn glanced down and saw them. With a faint smile, he put the rawhide into the pocket of his long-sleeved white shirt and reached down to take Trilby's soft hands in his.

"Relax," he told her, his eyes quiet and steady on hers. "You're always so tense, little one, so brittle."

"It's—it's difficult for me," she faltered, while the music played loudly around them, interspersed with the laughter and noise of happy people. Odd sensations were winding around inside her as the look lasted just a little too long for conventional politeness. She felt as if he were seeing right inside her.

"What is? Enjoying yourself?"

"I suppose so. We're much more subdued back home."

His eyebrows lifted. "Is that so? I thought that the Cajuns at least were wild."

"But I'm not a Cajun," she said. "Not really. My people were originally from Virginia. They came to Baton Rouge after the Civil War and settled there. My family has been there ever since."

His grip on her hands became gentler, caressing. "Don't you ever wear your hair down?"

"I...well, no, I don't," she murmured. "You always

thought of me as a—a loose woman. It seemed to me that wearing my hair down was somehow bad…"

He grimaced. "I don't know why Sally said what she did," he told her, his eyes narrow with regret. "If I'd known you even a little better, I'd never have believed her."

"Your cousin was only being friendly," she said defensively. "He was kind to me. That's all he ever was. Only kind."

He brought her palm to his lips and kissed it slowly, making her body tingle. "I'll be kind to you, if you'll let me, Trilby," he said softly, looking up into her eyes. "I'm genuinely sorry for the way I squared off with you. Nothing I've ever done in my life disturbs me more."

She fought the delicious pleasure his level stare kindled in her. She felt drawn to him despite her resolve, and she didn't like it. He was a ruffian, nothing like her Richard.

"I don't hold it against you," she said slowly. "You didn't know me."

"I want to," he said huskily. His eyes seemed to darken—and they held a wisdom and certainty that made her more uneasy than she already was.

The band was now playing a slow, sultry tune. He drew her among the throng of dancers and brought her very correctly into his arms. "Dance with me, Trilby."

He began to move to the rhythm. He didn't do anything to offend her, but the feel of his warm, strong hand at her waist and the faintly caressing grip of his fingers around her own made her feel weak-kneed. She looked into his eyes and was lost, caught there.

"Am I beginning to seem less a savage to you,

Trilby?" he asked quietly. "Or can't you forget what you saw when I brought the Mexican back to the ranch?"

She colored delicately. "I suppose one does get used to such things, eventually."

"One has to," he said, mocking her gently. "Toughen up, little one. You've got nerve. You only need to develop it."

"I've thought about going back home," she said abruptly.

His tall frame stiffened. "Why?"

"I—I miss it. I miss Richard," she blurted out in a vain attempt to stop her heart from beating so madly as he held her.

"You'll forget him, in time," he said curtly. Suddenly his hand slid completely around her and brought her close to him, his cheek resting against her hair.

"Don't!" she pleaded breathlessly. His broad chest was crushing her soft breasts, and in the intimacy of the embrace, the enveloping warmth of his strong body, she felt her heart run wild. "Thorn!"

The sound of his name on her lips thrilled him. His hand caressed her back slowly. "I won't let you go," he said under his breath.

"I'm not...suited to this life," she managed. Her eyes closed helplessly as the feel and scent of him got through her defences, making her vulnerable. "To this place. I'm a city girl."

"You can learn to be a country girl."

"It isn't your decision."

"Don't bet on it," he said grimly.

She started to protest, but just as she formed the words, Samantha tugged at her father's sleeve and stopped them.

"Papa, may I have a fried pie?" she asked. "They're called tamales."

"They'll burn your tongue." He chuckled, letting Trilby go so that he could kneel in front of his daughter. "This is pure Mexican fare, child, not the watered-down version Maria makes us at home."

Samantha warmed to the unfamiliar affectionate smile he was giving her. "For certain sure?" she asked, big eyed.

He nodded.

She grimaced. "Oh, very well." She glanced up at Trilby shyly. "You look very nice, Miss Lang," she added.

"So do you, Miss Vance," Trilby replied, with a gentle smile.

Samantha smiled back and shot off toward the vendors.

"She'll do it in spite of me, and she'll have a belly-ache all night long," he groaned.

"She's very like you, isn't she?" she asked.

He looked down into her eyes. "In some ways, yes." He touched her soft mouth with his fingertip. She jumped at the sensation it produced and stepped back. He smiled, because he knew why. "You're very flushed. Dancing with me makes your heat beat like a drum. I could feel it while I held you."

She colored. "You don't talk like a gentleman."

"I'm not a gentleman," he reminded her. His dark, intent gaze fell to her mouth. "I'd like to drag you behind a building and kiss you until you couldn't stand up. I'd like to make your mouth as red as the bandanna on that Mexican over there."

"Mr. Vance!" she protested.

He looked around for her people. They were talking to some other people, and he chuckled softly as he suddenly clasped Trilby's hand and tugged her along with him down a narrow, dark alley.

"What are you doing?" she whispered frantically. "What will people think—?"

He stopped the question with his mouth. His arms lifted her against him. He kissed her slowly, with exquisite tenderness, and he felt as if he could fly. She tasted of coffee, and his head spun as he drew her even closer and parted her lips under the pressure of his warm, questing mouth.

Trilby resisted, but only for an instant. The feel of his warm strength, the intimacy of his mouth on hers relaxed her until her bones seemed to melt in her body. She gave in all at once and slid her arms around him, shaky and trembling with sensations that made her body throb. It was impossible to resist the pleasure he offered. She closed her mind to all the reasons she should protest and simply gave herself to his ardent skill.

The kiss lengthened. Her body began to pulse with heat as she lifted closer to him, thrilling to the powerful chest so close that she could feel it flattening her breasts. But she was enthralled, helpless to resist. She could only move closer, seeking to prolong the delight, the hunger that grew even as she fed it.

Her reaction quickly went to his head. He'd been without a woman since his wife's death, and she made magic in his starved body. He groaned, and she felt his hand suddenly shift to her breast, the thumb rubbing softly over her nipple, making it hard. This wasn't decent, she thought hysterically. She should make him stop!

But she was drowning in the new experience. The

dark, forbidden pleasure he was giving her was exquisite. She felt him turn her slightly, just enough to give that maddening hand better access to the soft swell of her body.

"Sweet," he whispered unsteadily into her mouth. "You're… the sweetest honey I've ever had, Trilby." He groaned, shifting. "Let me touch you under your bodice."

His hand worked at fastenings. And he'd said that he no longer thought badly of her. The stark intimacy of what he was doing suddenly penetrated the fever in her mind and body. She pushed at his chest frantically, shocked at what she was doing. She jerked away from him, her face furiously red as she panted for breath.

"What is it?" he asked, a little dazed.

"You said that you didn't believe what your wife said about me, but you do! You must, to insult me so!" she whispered in shaken anguish. "Oh, let me go!" she cried, pushing at him when he tried to restrain her.

His face contorted. "It wasn't an insult. Trilby, be still and listen to me!" he groaned, tightening his grip.

But she tore loose with sudden determination, running back to the music and the dancing. Tears stung her eyes. He still thought she was a loose woman. He'd touched her in that indecent way. And she'd let him! She'd…encouraged him!

He caught her arm just as she reached the milling dancers and pulled her gently into the dance.

"It wasn't an insult," he said doggedly, looking into her anguished eyes. "Damn it, you're a woman, aren't you? Hasn't your mother told you anything about how it is between a man and a woman?"

"Decent men don't touch decent women the way you just touched me," she whispered tearfully.

He drew in a slow breath and rested his eyes on her soft blond hair. And he'd thought her experienced! He didn't quite know how to handle this latest emotional crisis.

"Will you listen, at least, and let me try to explain?"

"I want to go home," she said in a choked whisper. Her eyes bit into his. "I hate you!"

Sally had said the same thing to him so many times. After she'd found herself pregnant with Samantha, she'd said it almost daily. Trilby had the same contemptuous look in her eyes that his wife had once had, and it made him sick to his stomach. His temper overcame his compassion.

He let go of her abruptly. "By all means, Miss Lang. We'll leave as soon as your people are ready. Perhaps you're not woman enough for me after all!"

With that cold insult, he left her.

She watched him stalk away with wounded pride. She didn't want to ruin the fun for the rest of them, but she couldn't bear to stay after what had happened. She didn't know why she'd allowed him to drag her off like that, why she'd allowed him to touch her in such an indecent manner.

Her face flamed as she had to ask herself if she really was a woman without morals, and if it showed to an experienced man. Perhaps Thorn had only seen what she really was. She fought tears as she rushed back to her parents.

"You're so flushed, Trilby," Mary exclaimed, laughing. "Are you all right?"

"I feel sick," Trilby said, without preamble, pressing a thin hand to her stomach. "I'm sorry, but could we leave?"

"Darling, certainly we may." Mary put a protective arm around her and went to find Jack. Minutes later they were on their way down the long dirt road that eventually led to Blackwater Springs.

Trilby sat in back with Mary and Teddy. Her little brother kept up a nonstop flow of excited chatter about the piñatas, while Jack Lang shouted comments about the fiesta to Thorn over the roar of the engine.

She was glad that it was over. She could go home and try to get her scattered nerves back together before Richard came. She had to remember that she loved Richard. She might be vulnerable to that savage in the front seat, but Richard was her whole heart. She leaned her head back and closed her eyes. What if Richard guessed that she was a loose woman? What if it showed? Even worse, how could she have allowed Thorn to touch her in such a way when she loved Richard—if she wasn't a woman of easy morals?

She worried herself with that question long after a taciturn Thorn had left them at their door and wound on toward home with his little daughter beside him.

Lisa Morris heard the door to the officers' quarters slam shut. She turned as her husband took off his hat and jacket, tossing them idly onto a chair. Without thinking, she picked them up and brushed them off. The dust was so thick that she never seemed able to keep clothes clean.

A long black hair caught her attention, and the scent of perfume. Cheap perfume. She stiffened. Her hair was blond, not black, and she never wore perfume.

She didn't look at him as she put the jacket back down with concealed distaste. "You've been away from the post."

"Yes. Scouting around for lost Mexicans," he said, and yawned. "I'm tired."

"Down near the border?" she asked pleasantly.

"Around Douglas," he said, glancing at her curiously. "Why?"

"I wondered if you'd seen anything of the *insurrectos,*" she asked, hedging.

He laughed. And he'd thought she was suspicious of him! How could she know about Selina, anyway?

"I never see them. They're ghosts. Fox fire. Smoke in the wind. Ask anyone."

"Yes, I see." She was sick all over. She knew about his kept woman in Douglas. Another officer's catty, spoiled wife had taken great delight in telling her about Selina. She couldn't know that Lisa had long since stopped caring whose bed her husband warmed. She was tired of him, tired of life itself.

Her straying husband didn't know that she'd secretly filed for divorce. The papers were soon to be served, and she had no idea how he was going to react. She was afraid of his temper, but she couldn't stomach any more humiliation. She just wanted her freedom.

"David," she began quietly, "I should like to go back East."

He whirled, shocked. "What?"

She folded her hands in front of her, pale but composed, her plain face giving away nothing of her inner turmoil. She looked at him with soft blue eyes that were haunted and hurt.

"I said I should like to go back to Baltimore," she replied. "I have a cousin there who would let me live with her."

"Cousin Hetty," he spat out, "who would make a slave of you!"

She lifted her face proudly. "Am I more than that here?" she asked huskily. "Keeping house for you while you visit your kept woman and come to my arms reeking of cheap perfume?"

If she'd raged at him, or screamed, or acted in any way haughty, he could have dealt with the accusation. But she did none of those things. She spoke calmly and almost indifferently, her eyes devoid of emotion.

His cheekbones went ruddy with shame as he looked at her. "You turned me out of your bed when you lost the baby, madam," he reminded her tersely. "A man gets hungry."

"But you never wanted me, David. Not really," she said, with lowered eyes.

That was true, and it hurt. "Perhaps I grew tired of making love to a wax effigy!"

She didn't flinch. She had no nerves left. She'd worn them out on this harsh country years ago. It had taken her youth and her baby. She didn't want David, but she had wanted the child.

"You married me because my father was your commanding officer," she said accusingly. "We both know it. You didn't love me. You pretended to, until your promotion came through. You kept pretending while you rose in rank. After my father died, you no longer needed to pretend. But an officer doesn't desert his wife, does he, David? Not if he wants to continue to rise in rank. You see," she said, with faint amusement, when he flushed, "I know you very well. My father did, too, but I wouldn't listen to him."

He couldn't deny what she was saying. It was the

truth. He hadn't loved her. She'd been cold and unwelcoming in bed, and even her pregnancy hadn't prompted any tender feelings in him. He didn't love her. He had been guilty of pretending to, because he was poor and ambitious. Her father was rich and high in rank. He'd seen marriage to Lisa as a quick way to climb the military ladder. But after a while, the misery of being married to a woman he didn't love overshadowed the triumph of his military success.

"You didn't have to marry me," he said.

"I realize that." She studied his handsome face with more wistfulness than she knew. "I knew no man would ever marry me for myself," she said, shocking him. "My father's rank was the only asset I had. It's all right," she said. "I haven't been completely unhappy. In fact, there were—there were times when I thought I cared for you. But it's best that we part. I can't live with you anymore, David, knowing about—about her."

He took a long, slow breath. "You won't leave," he said coldly. "I'll be damned if you'll leave! You belong to me," he added.

"I'm not property."

"You are if I say you are," he replied. "You have no money of your own, and I won't give you any. How do you expect to get passage back to Maryland?"

"Why won't you let me go?" she cried. "You don't want me!"

"You're my wife," he said stiffly. "And I am commanding officer of this post. I won't have the men gossiping about me."

"So that's it. You don't mind if I run away, so long as it doesn't reflect on you!"

His jaw tautened. "You have nothing to complain about.

You have a roof over your head, a fine reputation, and nice dresses to wear."

"I suppose you think those things will make my life bearable while you carouse with your loose woman."

Her wounded expression irritated him. "If you want another child, I'll give you one," he said shortly.

"David, how very generous of you," she said, with the first hauteur he'd ever known from her. "And what an ordeal it would be, I'm sure."

Her antagonism was surprising. He looked at her and realized suddenly that he'd never taken the time to get to know her in the two years they'd been married. She was like a shadow, keeping house, cooking, cleaning. They never spoke. He'd made love to her when he needed to, and she'd become pregnant and lost the baby.

Afterward, there had been Selina. His interest in his wife had never been more than curiosity. He hadn't given her any of the tender passion he'd shown Selina today. He'd never made an attempt to arouse Lisa. Now he wondered why. She had small breasts, but she was sweetly made, and her body had a pretty curve to it. He'd kissed her once or twice, finding it not at all unpleasant. But it was Selina who made him wild, who fired his blood. He loved Selina.

"I don't want to stay here, David," Lisa persisted.

He moved closer to her, his hand tilting her chin. "I'd like some coffee." She flushed with resentment and anger as his fingers caressed her. He mistook her color for shyness and he smiled with faint conceit as he bent and started to kiss her.

But at the first touch of his lips, she twisted away from him, her eyes blazing. "Don't you touch me!" she spat unsteadily. "Don't you dare come hotfoot from that woman's bed and try to manhandle me!"

She wiped her hand over her mouth as if the touch of him had made her sick, as if he disgusted her.

"You flatter yourself," he said tautly, deeply insulted. "Selina is twice the woman you are."

"Save your caresses for her, then," she replied proudly. "You may force me to stay here, sir, but you will never force me to enjoy it."

She went into the kitchen, and he stared after her with mingled surprise and shock.

Thorn Vance was kneeling at a water hole when his vaquero on horseback came to a halt beside him. Nearby, two cows lay dead in the sun.

"It is poisoned, señor, yes?" Jorge asked him.

Thorn cursed. "Yes, it's poisoned. Alkali, damn the luck!" He got to his feet. "I thought it might be arsenic. I do own land in Mexico."

"It is known that you allow the Maderistas to water their horses here, señor, that you are sympathetic to the cause," the smaller man said solemnly, and with a smile. "No true revolutionary would harm you."

"They won't have to, it seems. This was the last good water I had," Thorn said roughly. He stared at the water hole furiously. "Thirsty cattle who can't get water will die in droves. They drilled for water in the San Bernardino Valley and found underground springs," he said almost to himself. "I may be forced to do the same."

"There is water in the river."

"Sure, but it's on Blackwater Springs Ranch, and Lang won't sell to me. He won't even lease me water."

"In the old days, señor, your father would have used

the water even without permission," Jorge reminded him grimly.

"I'm not my father." He swung back onto the saddle gracefully. He didn't want his cowhand to know that if it hadn't been for Trilby, he might have gone that route. She already thought he was an uncivilized savage. He couldn't bear to have her think worse of him than she already did.

He hated the way she'd run from him the night of the fiesta. He'd wanted to tell her that it was passion, not an insult, that had prompted him to touch her that way. He'd wanted her badly, and he had lost control. But he hadn't meant to upset her.

It was his own fault, and he owned it. If he hadn't entertained such stupid misconceptions about her, he'd never have given her reason to doubt his intentions. He'd lost all the ground he could have gained, and this Richard was coming to the ranch soon to see her.

The thought of the man made him gag. He knew the Easterner was his total opposite, and Trilby fancied herself in love with the prissy dude.

Jack Lang had mentioned Trilby's suitor only once, and not in a disparaging way. The unknown Richard came from their world, from parlor manners and easy living. He wouldn't smell of cattle and smoke, he wouldn't be covered with dust in old clothes, he wouldn't know one end of a gun from the other. Trilby would see those as advantages. Thorn saw them as competition.

"We'll try further afield," Thorn said, easing his mount into motion.

"The Apache can find water, señor," the Mexican told him. "You know the truth of this. Naki has the gift."

"I may let him try. I have enormous respect for the

talents of these desert-bred Apaches, Jorge. They have knowledge the white men have never gained."

"Ah, señor, you are not like these newcomer gringos who look down their oh-so-straight noses at the dark-skinned people," he said wistfully. "You are like the *patrõn,* your father. You know the way of things, señor."

"I respect knowledge, in all its various forms," Thorn replied. He laughed bitterly. "Which makes me a savage to certain Easterners."

Jorge knew of whom he spoke, but it would not be politic to mention it. "Many say the same of Madero. But whatever he may be, he is the liberator of an oppressed people."

"You sound like a fight promoter."

"Señor!"

He chuckled at Jorge's outrage. "I know how your people feel about Madero, and why."

"*Sí,* señor," Jorge agreed, a little less ruffled. "He is a saint to my people—he and the others who fight for our freedom."

"I'll cheer him on, but I won't fight for him," he told the smaller man, his dark eyes glittering. "Mexico's internal affairs are no concern of mine, unless Madero or any of his men make them so. In which case," he added softly, "he will wish he had not."

The Mexican sensed the tall man's anger. "Should oppression not be the business of every free man, señor?" he asked, with quiet pride.

Thorn glanced at him. "Oh, hell, maybe so," he said angrily. "But I've got enough problems of my own without adding yours to them. Come on. Water, Jorge, not civil war. Not today, at any rate."

Jorge chuckled. "If you say so, *patrón.* Certainly,

the *insurrectos* mean no harm to you. It is with Díaz that they quarrel. These foreigners who mine our land, they have so much," Jorge remarked thoughtfully. "And yet, in Mexico, little children go hungry. It is the way of the world, and yet, it should not be, *patrón*."

"Are you showing signs of becoming a socialist, *compadre?*" he asked the small man.

Jorge laughed, his white teeth flashing in a face like polished bronze. "Not I, señor. A Maderista, perhaps?"

Thorn swept off his hat and made a long swipe at the Mexican with it. Jorge laughed and spurred his mount ahead.

Later, at the ranch, Thorn considered what Jorge had said about water. Perhaps it was a last-ditch stand, but it might be worth some conversation.

He approached Naki. His name consisted of two Apache words, but Naki was the only one most people could pronounce, so around Los Santos, the Apache became known as Naki. In his polite fashion, he answered to the name as if it had been given to him at birth.

Naki was tall for his race, very taciturn and quiet. He had no wife, no family. He wasn't an old man, yet there was something ancient in his black eyes. He kept much to himself. Only to Thorn Vance did he warm, and that was because Vance had taken the time to learn his language. He was the only white man who had ever done that in Naki's memory, except for the archaeologist, McCollum. Not that Naki understood only Apache. He spoke several languages, but when he was brooding he would only answer to Apache. This was one of those times.

Having tried English and failed, Thorn queried in

Apache, "Where is Tiza?" referring to the man's Mimbreños Apache friend who usually tracked with him.

"Oyaa. Naghaa," Naki replied in his slow, deep voice, adding another few words behind them and drawling out the long vowels, punctuating the syllables with glottal stops, nasalized consonants, and high tones as necessary to make the meanings clear. "He has gone. He is walking around."

Thorn looked off toward the horizon and chuckled. *"Nakwii,"* he corrected, glancing wickedly toward Naki. "He is vomiting."

The Apache shrugged. "White man's liquor. I did not give it to him."

Thorn went down on one knee, meeting the quiet eyes of the other man. Naki was in his middle thirties, barely older than Thorn's thirty-two years. "I've humored you. Now speak English."

"If you wish. But it leaves a bad taste in my mouth," Naki replied dryly—in barely accented, almost perfect English, a legacy from his years in hiding with the priests when his Chiricahua relatives had been sent off to a Florida prison after Geronimo's capture. "Your use of Apache is not practiced."

"I haven't got time to practice it. I need to find water. A lot of water."

"Is that all?" Naki waved his arm. "There's a river a few miles away," he said helpfully.

Thorn glared at the Indian. "I need water right here for my cattle," he emphasized. "I can't move the river."

Naki shrugged. "Move the cattle."

"You can be so damned maddening," he said irritably. "Why don't I fire you?"

"Who else could read Herodotus to you in the original

Greek?" came the sardonic reply. "Not to mention leading your archaeologist friend to the best digs. Without me to guide him, McCollum would pitch headfirst into a mine shaft and never be seen again."

Thorn threw up his hands. "All right, I concede that you're a miracle of education. Now how about telling me where to look for water?"

Naki leaned toward Thorn conspiratorially, his straight black hair falling around his handsome, high-cheekboned face. "Try Blackwater Springs Ranch."

The Apache got to his feet and walked off, leaving Thorn in a raging fury. Thorn was certain that the Chinese had nothing on his friend when it came to being inscrutable.

Chapter Seven

Naki mounted his horse with consummate ease and rode back to where Thorn was still standing, glaring at him.

"No need to glower at me," he said imperturbably. "We Apaches wrote the book on being taciturn. When I find water, I'll come back," he said. "If I don't find it, I'll send you a note before I throw myself off a cliff."

"Apaches don't have a sense of humor," Thorn reminded him. "Every book I've ever read says so."

"You've been reading the wrong books. Ask your archeologist friend McCollum. He spent a month with us. We gave him some very interesting information about our people." He grinned.

"Craig McCollum isn't an archaeologist, he's an anthropologist who also teaches a course in archaeology. And future historians will curse you if you confused him about your culture," Thorn pointed out.

"He did at least have the decency to learn our language, as you have. Most of your people are too arrogant to feel the need."

"It's a hell of a language to learn."

"So the *anthropologist*—" he stressed the word "—said. He was required to take notes in Apache and even to do a life history of the elders he interviewed for information. However, white man, our language is still simpler than yours," Naki retorted. "See you in a few days." He turned his paint pony and trotted off toward the sunset.

Tiza waved to him. He paused and told the old man where he was going but declined company. There were times when he craved solitude. This was one of them.

The railway station on Railroad Avenue in Douglas was crowded for a Saturday. Trilby was all but dancing on the platform, her blue gingham dress swirling around her ankles as she walked, her pert bonnet crowning her upswept blond hair. She looked young and attractive with her radiant face, and Mary Lang smiled at her impatience.

"Gosh, sis, can't you sit down?" Teddy muttered impatiently. "You're wearing a hole in the wood!"

"I can't wait! Oh, what if he isn't on the train?" Trilby wailed. "I can't bear it if he isn't on the train!"

"He telegraphed us that he would be. Julie and Ben and Sissy are with him, too. We'll have a grand time, girl." Jack chuckled. "It will be nice to see familiar faces from home."

"Especially one face, Trilby's thinking," Mary said, with an indulgent smile.

"Oh, Richard, take me away with you!" Teddy said in a theatrical voice, sweeping an arm over his eyes.

Trilby hit him with her parasol. "You stop that!"

He stuck his tongue out at her. "Richard and Trilby, Richard and Trilby— Ouch!"

"Stop that, young man," Jack admonished. "That will be quite enough misbehaving for one day."

Teddy rubbed his sore posterior and glared at his father. "You're horrible to me, Father."

"Remind me of that again when you buy a peppermint stick at the drugstore."

Teddy's eyes lit up. "How about an ice cream instead?"

"Not today. Our guests will be tired and want to go straight to the ranch. But next time we come to town, I promise you an ice cream. Will that do?"

"Yes, sir!"

Trilby barely heard the byplay. Her eyes were riveted to the horizon, where the train was puffing furiously toward the station, thick smoke rising and drifting behind it in the wind.

"Sets fires all along its path, damned thing," an oldtimer was muttering nearby. "I hate trains. I hate civilization. When I came here in '52, 'tweren't even a road. Or a town, for that matter. 'Twere only Apaches and a few Mexicans. 'Twas a better place without all these tearooms and ice-cream parlors and women's betterment leagues!"

"They closed down the only saloon out of twenty that would give him credit last week," Jack whispered to Mary, and chuckled. "He hasn't had a drink since."

Mary choked back a laugh. She glanced back at the runabout, which would only hold three people unless they packed in like sardines. Richard was bringing Ben and Sissy and Julie with him; that made four. Trilby, her father, mother, and Teddy made another four. They'd never have managed to stuff them into the car, so they'd hired a second one, complete with driver, from the local livery. It had been Trilby's idea, and she'd paid for it with the money she made from selling eggs and butter. Mary had felt sad that the small fee had come so hard. She, like Trilby and the others, was used to a much richer standard of living than they'd been able to enjoy since moving here.

Mary was distracted by the arrival of the train. Its puffing approach brought more people onto the platform, straining to see through the smoke. Several were coughing when the iron horse pulled to a stop, finally, and passengers began to climb down the steps onto the siding.

"Look!" Trilby exclaimed as a tall, sandy-haired man with a valise stepped nattily from the train. "It's Richard!"

Richard Bates heard her and looked in her direction. He was a tall, blond man with a faint mustache and a pale complexion, dressed in a natty gray suit and matching bowler hat. A smile broke out on his handsome face as he spotted her. "Trilby!"

She wanted to run into his arms, but his stance wasn't that welcoming. He moved toward her with his usual lazy grace and took her hand. He kissed it warmly, but with no more than gentle amusement and some affection. His eyes took in her family before they came back to her.

"How nice of you to invite us," he said. "We've all looked forward to this visit. Sissy, come on!" he called irritably over his shoulder. "She's so maddening," he groaned. "She can't seem to walk two steps without falling over her feet. That's what comes of spending your life with your nose stuck in a book!"

Sissy was his sister, one of Trilby's oldest friends. "You mustn't be unkind, Richard," she chided. "Sissy's very intelligent."

"She's a trial. You don't know!" he moaned. He glanced back and smiled in a different way at the striking blonde just leaving the train before Sissy. "There's my best girl. Come here, Cousin Julie, and meet the Langs. Everyone, this is my cousin, Julie Moureaux, from New Orleans. You remember my sister Sissy, of course, she's just coming down the steps. And my brother—Ben, where are you?"

A young, dark-haired man who was just a little too thin was escorting Sissy off the train. They made an interesting pair, the slight, brown-headed girl in spectacles beside the lanky, clumsy youth. They favored each other far more than they favored their older brother.

"They're so fascinated by thoughts of wild Indians that they've embarrassed me every step of the way, staring out the train windows looking for them," Richard said disgustedly. "They've been certain that we were all going to be scalped the minute we crossed the border into Arizona. I'd never have brought them with me if I'd had any idea how they'd behave on this trip." He turned back to his cousin while Sissy and Ben were busy staring around in absorbed fascination with their new surroundings. "Julie," he continued, with a smile, holding her hand warmly, "you remember Trilby, don't you?"

"It's been years since we've seen each other, but of course I do," Julie said politely, her blue eyes twinkling. She extended her hand with a friendly smile. "It's so nice of you to invite us all. I hope we won't be a trial to you."

"How silly, of course you won't!" Mary Lang replied, coming forward to greet them. Trilby was at a loss for words as she saw with sinking heart the way Richard and Julie were behaving toward each other. "You must think of the ranch as your home, for as long as you like."

Richard looked around at the desolate landscape and the sand and grimaced. "I should think that won't be long, Mrs. Lang. How does one survive in a horrible place like this?"

"It isn't easy, I promise you," Trilby said, refusing to allow Richard's perfectly normal response to the desert to unsettle her. It was horrible, after all. Hadn't she said so time and time again?

"Why, it isn't horrible at all, my lad," Jack Lang said indignantly. "You'll see. It has a great deal to offer."

Richard merely shrugged and smiled at Julie.

Sissy came forward to be soundly hugged by Trilby, along with Ben. "Oh, it's so good to see you again!" Trilby told the other girl. "I haven't any women friends out here. Except for Mama, there's been no other woman to talk to."

"I'd hardly call Sissy a woman," Richard said, with brotherly candor. "She's straight as a stick and she actually goes to college!" he added, as if his sister's interest in higher education was an aberration. "She's twenty-three and she's never had a beau—"

"Shut up, Richard," Sissy muttered, pushing her glasses back on her prim nose with a vicious jab of her finger. Through the lenses, her green eyes glittered at him. "A lot you know about me!"

"You're unkind, Dick," Ben said, and turned red at his own audacity. "You're always picking on Sissy."

"Now, both of you stop," Cousin Julie chided. "We're guests here, remember, and you're acting like babies."

Sissy and Ben glared at her. She was younger than they were, at nineteen, and they didn't like her, either.

She seemed to realize that she'd overstepped her bounds, because she smiled languidly and laughed a little nervously. "Do let's go. It's so *hot* here!" She fanned herself.

"I do second that idea." Richard sighed, taking Julie's arm. "I detest this place already!" he said disparagingly as he stared around them.

Trilby was feeling sicker by the second. She clung to her friend Sissy's arm. Sissy looked at her with vague sympathy, but there was no time to talk now.

Ben helped Sissy and Julie into the rented touring car while Jack Lang struggled with the luggage. Neither of the visiting young men seemed willing to put themselves out in any way. As Trilby watched, she tried to imagine Thorn letting her father shoulder that weighty burden. It irritated her that she couldn't.

The last straw came when Richard elected to ride not with Trilby but with his cousin and sister and brother. Trilby was heartbroken, and tried not to show it. Mary knew. Her smile was meant to be reassuring, but Trilby only felt like crying. All her hopes had been pinned on this visit. Nothing had changed at all. Only the scenery in which Richard smiled politely and looked right through her.

The ride back to the ranch was long and tiresome. Trilby sat rigidly beside her mother and father while Teddy sprawled in the backseat. Richard had put a leisurely arm around Julie when they got into the rental car. It was still there, Trilby noticed as she looked back through the thick dust at the other car.

She'd looked forward to this visit for so long…and now she wondered if it wasn't going to turn into a nightmare. Richard had been polite but nothing more. He certainly didn't act as if he'd missed her in the months she'd been away.

They stopped at a crossroads when they were nearing the ranch, and a party of mounted men rode up around them. Trilby thrilled at the display of horsemanship. But it irritated her to realize that these were Los Santos riders—and their mocking, handsome boss was riding at their head.

"Thorn, how good to see you," Jack Lang greeted him. "What brings you out this way?"

"We're acting as escort," Thorn said evasively. His eyes drifted from Trilby to the front seat to the tall, handsome young man and other passengers in the car behind them and his eyes twinkled. He was getting a picture that relieved all his fears, even if Trilby did look as if her favorite dog had just died.

"There have been a few incidents on the border just recently," Thorn added, "and news has gotten around about your Eastern visitors. I thought you might feel more comfortable if we were riding close by."

"Indeed we will, and thanks." Mary laughed. "Thorn, let me introduce you to our guests." The cars stopped and she got out with Trilby. Thorn dismounted, and they walked back to the second car to make the introductions.

Trilby watched their reactions with interest. Sissy's eyes were wide and curious as they darted around the dangerous-looking group of men. She saw the Apaches with Thorn and her eyes widened.

Sissy was fascinated with anthropology. She'd enrolled at a college up North where it was taught, and she was staying with a great-aunt and going to class. She was between quarters now and delighted to renew her old acquaintance with her friend Trilby.

It had fascinated her to learn about other cultures, but her primary interest was in Apaches. Her professor knew a great deal about them and had loaned her books and articles about them. She'd read every scrap of information she could find in the library, as well, but here was a live specimen at hand. Not only alive—but so masculinely beautiful to look at that she felt her heart turn over.

The man was tall. You could tell, she thought, by the length of his stirrups and the size of his horse. He had long black hair down to his shoulders, straight hair with the sheen of a blackbird's plumage, thick and faintly windblown, with a thick, colorful band of cloth around his forehead holding it in place. He was well made, very strong-looking—from his broad chest in its blue-checked shirt to his long, powerful legs in high-topped moccasins that came to the knee. He was wearing leggings, but his bronzed, muscular thighs were bare under them. His hands were crossed over the pommel of his saddle and they were beautiful. Her eyes lingered on the long, tanned fingers.

But his face was the real work of art. He had high cheekbones and an arrow-straight nose. His eyes were large and deep-set and very brown. His mouth was oddly thin for an Indian's, and he had a square jaw and a high forehead. She thought as she studied him that she could have spent the rest of her life just looking at him.

Naki was all too aware of the white woman's fierce

regard, but he pretended not to notice it or her. Apaches considered it very bad form to pay too much attention to women in public. Their rigid code of morals had many taboos in that respect. Despite his education and the time he spent in the company of whites, he was very Apache in his attitudes.

But he noticed the white woman, all right. She was slender and tall and not too bad to look at. She wore glasses. He wondered if that meant she was intelligent. He sometimes felt starved for a little educated conversation. He'd loved his late Mexican wife, but her vocabulary was limited to simple talk about themselves and the world around them. She had no education at all. He wondered what it would be like to sit and talk with a woman about the writings of Poe or Thoreau. He laughed inwardly. This woman was probably as frightened as she was fascinated. She probably thought of him in the white man's usual stereotype: the poor, pitiful, ignorant savage. He enjoyed playing that role, for no other reason than to see the look on the faces of his victims when he began quoting Thucydides or Herodotus, or spouting nineteenth-century British poetry.

"Excuse me, Mr. Vance," Sissy interrupted softly, her green eyes huge behind her small wire-rimmed spectacles. "But...is he Apache?" she asked, nodding toward Naki.

"Yes, he is. Don't worry, the Apaches aren't hostile these days, despite the horror stories they may have told you on the train coming out here," Thorn said reassuringly. He motioned to Naki, who rode forward. The Apache looked regal somehow with his bronzed, handsome face like a death mask. But the dark eyes that glanced off Thorn's twinkled with unholy mischief.

"This is Naki." Thorn introduced the man to the slender, blue-dressed girl from back East. "Naki, this is Miss Sissy Bates. She's from Louisiana."

Naki didn't like the way those green eyes made him feel. He was properly dead inside since Conchita's death and he wanted to remain that way. So he hammed it up for all he was worth. He touched his hand to his breast. "Ugh!" he said, nodding shortly. "Me heap good Injun!"

Thorn raised his eyebrows, and one of the cowboys buried his face in his hand. Jack Lang himself was hard-pressed not to give the show away, having heard Naki speak perfect English, but if the Indian wanted it kept secret, that was his business.

Sissy, having taken the Apache's magnificent performance to heart, was disappointed. She'd expected more than that from such an elegant man. She might as well live down to what was probably the usual white woman's role. It might pique his interest, and she wanted to stick in his mind. She wanted him to remember her, although for the life of her she couldn't say why. There was no future in getting interested in a man like that. Even if she was, suddenly and totally.

"Uh…he, Mr. Naki, doesn't scalp people, does he?" she asked Thorn in a loud whisper. Odd, how the Indian's eyes suddenly glittered, almost as if he were amused. Such intelligent eyes, too.

Thorn had to fight down laughter. He frowned thoughtfully. "Well, I don't believe he's scalped anyone this month." He turned and asked Naki, in Apache, if he was enjoying himself.

Naki nodded and replied in his native tongue, "Is this woman a mental patient?"

"It makes you wonder, doesn't it? They must have told her about Apaches on the train."

"Tell her I've got a scalp in my pocket," Naki murmured. "I dare you."

"Shut up," Thorn muttered.

"What is he saying to you?" Ben asked, curious.

"He's saying that the white woman looks strong and has good teeth," Thorn answered, smothering a grin. "He wants to know how many horses you want for her."

Sissy and Ben gaped, Richard made an indignant noise, and the Langs hesitated, trying to decide how to answer the insolent affront to their guests.

"You liar," Naki told Thorn in Apache, insulted. "I wouldn't take that one if they offered me a hundred horses for her! She has no meat on her bones." That wasn't quite true, but he wasn't admitting to his boss that he found the woman fascinating.

"You're making them suspicious," Thorn told him, still speaking Apache. He smiled. "Can't you smile?"

Naki pulled his lips back from his teeth and looked straight at Sissy in the most menacing way. She cocked her head and stared at him. Oh, well, if he wanted her to pretend, she could. She put a hand to her breast and caught her breath audibly, moving almost into Ben's lap trying to back away.

"You go now," Thorn told Naki in English, nodding curtly.

"I could tell you where to go, all right," came the taunting reply in Apache. He rode away without looking back.

"Isn't he majestic?" Julie enthused. "Oh, Sissy, do stop acting so terrified. He looked quite nice."

"Savages," Richard said uncomfortably. "How do you bear to live near them?"

Thorn gave him a measured look. "We manage to survive all sorts of varmints out here," he told Richard, with pure malice. "Even Eastern tenderfeet."

Jack Lang took that for a joke and laughed. So did Richard, so thick that the insult didn't even register. It did to Trilby, however. She gave Thorn a glare that might have stopped a truck. He only smiled.

"We'll be getting on," he told Jack, swinging gracefully back into his saddle. "Nice to have met you folks."

Thorn tipped his hat, but he didn't take it off.

"We appreciate the escort, Thorn," Jack Lang said warmly.

Richard leaned forward. "I say, is there any chance of making up a hunting party while we're out here in the wilds?" he asked. "I'm something of a sportsman, old chap. I've been boar hunting in Africa just recently."

"We have wild pigs here," Jack Lang interceded. "And white-tailed deer, too. I expect Thorn wouldn't mind taking you all out on an overnight camp, if you're game."

"Certainly!" Richard enthused. "I've packed my camp tent…."

"We have plenty of tents," Thorn replied in a slow, level drawl. This was working very much to his advantage. "How long are you staying?"

"Quite some time, I imagine—" Trilby began angrily.

"Only a week or so, dear old thing." Richard sighed. "Sorry, but I've been invited to stay with my cousin— the Duke of Lancaster—at his estate in Scotland."

"Oh, Richard, what a snob you sound!" Julie chided. "It's hardly gentlemanly to mention such a thing when you're barely off the train."

"Sorry," he said, with a sheepish smile at her.

Trilby didn't miss the sparkle in Julie's eyes. Neither did Thorn.

He straightened in the saddle, tall and elegant-looking even in his working garb. The bat-wing chaps he was wearing did nothing to disguise the hard, powerful muscles of his legs. Julie was looking at them under her lashes. Trilby noticed and felt an odd pang of irritation. "I'll be in touch, then. Keep to the main road, Jack," he cautioned her father. "We'll be somewhere nearby until you get home. Sing out if you need us."

"I've got the rifle here in the floorboard," Jack said.

Thorn nodded. His own sidearm was worn on his hip and was prominently displayed in a disreputable old black holster.

"Is it really necessary to wear a pistol like that in public, Mr. Vance?" Julie asked curiously.

His lean, beautifully masculine hand touched the worn butt. He had long fingers with immaculate flat nails. "Yes, ma'am, it is," he told her. "We've had a lot of trouble down here since the Mexican Revolution began. We have an army post here in Douglas, but we're pretty far out of town. Sometimes we have to depend on ourselves."

"You don't mean Mexicans actually shoot at you?" Julie gasped.

Thorn cocked an eyebrow. "That's exactly what I mean. Jack will tell you that it isn't safe to ride around without an escort right now, or to go very far from the house unless one of the men goes with you. A few precautions won't hurt."

"We'll make sure the girls stay close. Thanks, Thorn," Jack told him.

"My pleasure." He touched his fingers to the wide

brim of his hat. Under it his dark eyes were shadowed. "Good day. Nice to have met you."

He nodded curtly to his men, spurred his horse, and rode out in front of them down the trail that paralleled the road. He rode as he did everything else, with grace and style. Trilby's eyes reluctantly followed the long line of his body.

"My, can't he ride!" Julie said enthusiastically. "He's very handsome, this neighbor."

"He's a widower," Jack told her.

"Yes, and he's sweet on our Trilby." Teddy chuckled.

Trilby flushed. "Be quiet, Teddy, do!" she cried.

"He looks quite rough," Richard remarked coolly. "And those men...some of them were Mexican, and I shiver to think of those Apaches loose on the territory at night. He lives with savages, doesn't he?"

"Yes... Well," Jack said stiffly, feeling driven to defend Thorn, "it *was* their country first."

"They did nothing with it to speak of," Richard remarked haughtily. "Such a backward people! How do you bear it out here, Trilby?" he asked.

It was the first question he'd addressed specifically to her, and her face grew radiant. "It's very different from back home," she agreed. "I miss it terribly."

"I don't wonder," Richard said.

Sissy and Ben were standing a little apart while the others talked.

"Why were you shivering?" her brother asked under his breath. "You and I both know that you're fascinated with the noble red man."

"That particular red man is a conundrum," she replied quietly. "Did you see the way his eyes twinkled when

Mr. Vance spoke to him? I'd bet money that it was all an act. I don't think he's stupid. I think he was playing."

"Sissy, most Indians aren't on a par with college professors," her brother said gently.

"Most, yes. But that one…" She gnawed on her lower lip. "Ben, wasn't he magnificent?" she asked softly. "I've never seen anyone like him."

"Watch it," he cautioned. "There are racial lines out here. Don't start crossing them. You know how Richard is."

"Richard can crawl under a can," she replied. "I want to know more about Mr. Vance's hired hand."

"Just be careful, won't you?"

"Did you hear what that red fellow said about Sissy?" Richard muttered suddenly. He glanced at her. "Of all the insults!"

"Oh, yes." She straightened her pert straw hat and smiled at her brother. "He was measuring my scalp, I'm sure."

"You spend half your life in museums looking at old photographs and paintings of Indians," Richard muttered. "Well, I'm glad you've finally seen the light. Indians aren't at all romantic, they're unclean and ignorant and impertinent."

"And you're a snob," Sissy said haughtily. "I'm an anthropology student. Other cultures interest me."

"Really? You should talk to Thorn," Jack Lang said seriously. "He has a friend who's an anthropologist."

"Does he?" Sissy enthused.

"Yes. A man named McCollum. He comes out every summer to go on digs around the local sites. Thorn knows them all."

"I don't believe it!" Sissy gasped. "That's my anthropology professor! Dr. McCollum!"

Trilby laughed. "And you never said! Not in one of your letters!"

"I was saving it all up for when I visited you," Sissy said smugly. "It's so good to be here!"

"And so good to have you," Trilby added. She glanced at Richard, but he was busy pointing out local color to Julie.

"Mr. Vance is quite good-looking, isn't he?" Sissy asked Trilby.

"Better look out, Trilby, or Sissy will be stalking your local beau." Julie laughed pleasantly, deliberately slanting a pretty glance up at Richard, who was frowning. "He's rather a savage, isn't he? I suppose living with Mexicans and Indians would make a man rough."

Trilby looked—and felt—sick to her stomach. Julie was making her point very well; Richard was hers, and she wasn't going to let Trilby near him. If Richard noticed her possessive attitude, he didn't seem to mind it. He smiled at her indulgently.

Trilby started back toward the car without another word. She had no idea what to say, at any rate. Richard noticed her quiet withdrawal with sudden consternation. He started to say something else, but Jack Lang prevented him by hustling Ted and Mary, along with Trilby, into his car. He started off again. The noise of the engine drowned out any further conversation.

A few miles from Los Santos, a small family of Mexican peons was entertaining one of Madero's officers. The small thatched adobe hut was barren, except for a few chickens scratching around on its packed-dirt floor. A small fire lit the dismal interior, where the peon's woman cooked tortillas with the meager amount of flour the Maderisto had brought them.

"Muchas gracias," the tall, young man murmured when he was served the tablespoon of beans on the tortilla. He was careful not to offend these people by refusing their hospitality. They had nothing, but they were proud. To deign not to accept the offering of this precious food was to offend beyond repair.

"It is our pleasure to serve you," the peon said earnestly. "It is for people like us that you ride against the *Federales.*"

"We will win one day, amigo," Madero's man said fervently. "Our cause is just. We will win back the land that was taken from our people by these filthy Spaniards. We will make these dogs pay for what they have done to Mexico."

"Sí," came the fiery reply.

"Now, tell me what news there is."

"A party of gringos has come to Blackwater Springs Ranch, it is said. Wealthy ones from the rich cities of the East."

The officer nodded and frowned thoughtfully. "They are not like the gringo who recently visited with the *patrón* of Los Santos? A learned man with no wealth?"

"No, señor," the peon protested vehemently. "These gringos have much money. *Mucho dinero.* My friend Juan works for Blackwater Springs Ranch. He says that he saw with his own eyes many bank notes and gold coins."

"Now that is interesting," the younger man said. "I will take this news back to Mexico with me. And next time," he added, smiling as he got to his feet, "there will be more flour. Perhaps even some coffee."

"Señor—" the woman of the house wept, kneeling to kiss his hand "—we thank you in the name of the Blessed Virgin for your kindness. In my prayers each night I will ask the Virgin to intercede for you and keep you safe."

"And I for all of our people," the man said solemnly. "It is not right that we have so little when the *patróns* have so much and are ever greedy for more. And what the *Federales* have done to the villagers—¡ay de mi!— we will take our land back. We will feed the hungry and take back what the invaders have stolen. We will make them pay for their crimes against us, I swear it!" he said hoarsely.

He was remembering sights that made him sick, atrocities he had seen at the hands of the *Federales* who rode for Díaz's government against the revolutionaries. The reputation of the men was terrifying to the peons. They tortured these innocents, killed women and children, all in the name of the government of Mexico. Government, he thought angrily, his compassionate eyes sweeping the pitiful interior of this hut. It was no government of the people that allowed the poor to starve and tried to take even what little they had. Something must be done. Madero was the man to do it. *"Vayan con Dios, mis amigos,"* he said, sweeping off his hat. "I will take this news you have given me to our friend Francisco Madero. Adios!"

Richard walked around the Lang house stiffly, trying to get his sore limbs to work properly. Julie was lying down, along with Sissy, because they found the heat

Trilby

unpleasant. Ben was out at the barn with an old Texas Ranger named Torrance and young Ted, listening to hair-raising tales of the old West.

He had no interest in such things. He hunted, but he had no time for the fairy tales of useless old men.

Trilby was in the kitchen with her mother, making biscuits. He propped his shoulder against the doorjamb and watched them, his blue eyes quiet and curious on Trilby. She'd changed since he'd seen her. She was still plain, of course, but he hadn't remembered how sweet she was. Julie could be a pain sometimes with her sharp tongue and outspoken nature. Trilby was her exact opposite. She made a man feel taller, somehow. He liked the way her silent adulation made him feel. He'd missed it.

"Busy, busy, aren't we?" he teased.

Trilby reddened and her hands fumbled as he walked into the room. She laughed nervously. "You gave me a start. I thought you were resting."

"Resting is for ladies. I'm quite recovered from the trip, except for a bit of soreness. Some of the passengers thought the Mexicans might actually rob the train, can you imagine?"

"It isn't so farfetched as you might think," Mary interrupted, and proceeded to tell him about a recent incident in Mexico, during which shots had been fired into a train on the Mexican Northwestern Railroad and several passengers killed.

"Killed?" Richard gasped.

"Yes, indeed," Mary replied. "There have been riots and shooting all over Mexico, especially in Chihuahua. American troops have been sent to Texas to patrol the border, and it's said that thousands of insurgents are massing near Chihuahua ready to attack."

"And Madero's ranch near Laredo was raided," Trilby added. "He escaped, but they got a lot of his horses."

"There's war talk everywhere," Mary said worriedly. "I do hope we won't end up at war with Mexico over this." She shook her head as she poured canned beans into a pot and poured water from the kettle into them. She placed the pot on the wood stove gingerly and put the lid on it, wiping her face with her apron when she finished. "Honestly, the heat in this kitchen is crippling. Trilby, why don't you take Richard out onto the porch and introduce him to the swing? I do declare, the heat never lets up, even in the autumn."

"It's rather dusty out," Richard said. "I'd prefer the living room. Is there any tea going? It's been a long day."

"Certainly," Mary said, smiling wanly.

Trilby didn't miss the disapproval, quickly erased, in her mother's eyes. Richard wasn't going to like it here. That was made more apparent by the minute.

They went into the living room. Richard made a distasteful face at the sofa. It was dusty.

"It's impossible to keep all the dust out," Trilby felt compelled to tell him. "I'm sorry…."

"This damnable desert," he said, shaking his head. "How did you end up here, Trilby? You'll grow old before your time. And the company around here… That Vance man and his uncivilized companions. My God!"

Trilby couldn't manage to defend Thorn Vance, although she really did have to resist the urge. Odd, how it wounded her to hear him maligned, when he'd done so much damage to her own reputation. Lately, though, he'd been different. Almost…tender.

She watched Richard as he flopped down on the sofa with a grimace. He propped his neatly clad foot on it without regard for its age or fabric.

She fiddled with the skirt of the plain brown-and-white-checked gingham dress she'd changed into when they'd arrived back from the station. Her blond hair was long, about her shoulders, and she'd pinched her cheeks and lips to make them red. But she was still, unfortunately, plain. Richard would compare her to Julie and she'd be found lacking.

"Julie hates it here," he said, stifling a yawn. "And I don't think Sissy's going to last much longer. Did you *see* her face when the Indian smiled at her?"

"I think you underestimate Sissy," she replied, feeling a sudden surge of indignation. "She isn't a coward. And if she's studying Indians in anthropology…"

"She's a silly little chick with no brain."

Trilby's eyes flashed. "She's quite educated, actually—and in her own element, she's very composed. The wild West isn't everyone's favorite place."

"You poor darling, it certainly isn't yours. You look drab, Trilby," he said thoughtfully. "Wan and thin and all bones. You should come back East with us, I think."

She brightened. "Do you think so?"

"Certainly! You could find someone to stay with, couldn't you?"

He acted as if it was of supreme indifference to him whether she did or not. Her face fell. She'd hoped for so much. And she had so little. She smiled, as if it didn't matter, and went back into the kitchen to help Mary. Her dream visit was becoming nightmarish, and he'd only been in residence for a day.

She'd thought it couldn't be any worse, but it

progressed downhill from that day. Richard found everything irritating, from his bedroom, to the lack of indoor facilities, to the well-drawn water that had to be heated on the stove for baths. He simply had to have a bath daily, and when Jack mentioned that water was a valuable commodity, he only laughed.

Ben was less abrasive. He spent most of his time with Teddy and Mosby Torrance and the cowboys, learning about cowboying. To everyone's amazement, he took to horses like ducks to a pond and within two days was riding like a native. He even donned cowboy regalia and wore it so naturally that one of the Mexicans remarked that he belonged to the ranch already. When he wasn't riding, he was sitting with Teddy, listening to Torrance's tales about the wild old days with flattering interest. Torrance took a shine to him at once, and it seemed a mutual thing.

Sissy stuck to Trilby like glue, which made any conversations with Richard awkward. It didn't matter much, because Julie, when she wasn't sleeping, was clinging to Richard's arm.

"The Indians aren't going to attack, really they aren't," Trilby assured Sissy. "You simply have to relax and stop looking for war parties."

Sissy sighed and grimaced. "Is that how I look? I'm not afraid of war parties," she said, although she couldn't admit that what she was looking for was one particular Apache whom she found fascinating. Silly to think he might seek her out.

With her dark hair in a bun, wearing a middy blouse with her long skirt and lace-up high heels, Sissy looked very ladylike. Even her spectacles didn't detract from her pretty face and big green eyes. And when she smiled,

she was lovely. But she'd been oddly silent since she'd
been here. She wasn't the bubbly, enthusiastic companion Trilby had known in childhood. She seemed preoccupied.

"Julie seems to be enjoying herself," Trilby ventured,
watching Julie and Richard through the hall doorway as
they played checkers in the living room.

"She's crazy mad for Richard," Sissy said sadly. "I'm
sorry. I know you were sweet on him. But they're very
much alike, don't you see?"

"I suppose." She didn't want to; she felt miserable.

Sissy hugged her impulsively. "Don't worry so, you'll
get lines in your face. It will all work out as it's meant
to, you know," she added gently.

Trilby hugged her back. "I'm so miserable. Does it
show? I thought he'd missed me, but he hasn't really.
Nothing's changed—except that I've daydreamed too
much. He's wild about Julie."

"I know. I wanted to write and tell you, but I couldn't.
Perhaps this visit is really a good thing. I love my
brother, but he doesn't deserve someone as sweet as
you, my friend," Sissy said solemnly. "He's not half the
man Ben is."

Trilby laughed softly. "My head knows that, but my
heart won't listen. I've loved him forever."

"I don't know very much about love," Sissy murmured, her eyes on the horizon. "I don't suppose any
man will ever love me. It's just as well," she said quickly
when Trilby started to protest. "I don't really think I'm
suited to the life of a housewife and mother. I'm too
odd. Trilby, do you think we might go exploring in the
mountains?" Sissy asked suddenly. "I'd simply love to

look for old ruins. The Hohokam Indians lived in this area long ago, Dr. McCollum said."

"Imagine your Dr. McCollum being Thorn Vance's friend. I suppose he knows a lot about this area," Trilby said.

"Indeed, yes, but he tells us very little about the Apaches," Sissy added, with a curious frown. "I do remember some of the other students talking about a particular Apache that McCollum mentioned in a lecture, but I was out sick that day and the notes I borrowed didn't include a reference to it." She glanced at Trilby. "There must be artifacts in this area; it's so historically rich."

"Yes, I think we might be able to go fossicking. I'll ask Papa."

"Thank you," Sissy said. "That would be so lovely. And are we really going hunting? I don't want to shoot anything…."

"We won't have to. That's something the men enjoy. But camping out would be fun, wouldn't it?" Trilby asked. "I've often wondered what it would be like. I've never had the opportunity. But with all of you along, I don't imagine it would be very fraught."

"No, indeed," the younger woman said, smiling. "What a grand idea, Trilby! I'm so glad I didn't decide to take classes this quarter so that I could come."

"I'm glad you didn't, too," she told her friend. But her sad eyes never left Julie and Richard. "College will still be there in January when the next quarter begins."

Richard heard Trilby's soft voice and sensed her scrutiny. He was enjoying being the center of attention in a tug-of-war between shy little Trilby and sophisticated Julie. He glanced up and caught Trilby's eyes and smiled slowly. She blushed, and he laughed.

"Something amuses you?" Julie asked him curiously.

"Why, I find the game invigorating," he replied. But it wasn't checkers he was really talking about.

Chapter Eight

Lisa Morris was chafing under the knowing glances and pitying looks from the other officers' wives. She was used to army life, having grown up in barracks. She was even used to her husband's affairs. But she'd never before had him flaunt one of them so that his behavior became common knowledge.

The only excuse she could find was that he might be genuinely in love this time. If so, surely he would be pleased to let the divorce go through. She had to tell him, and soon.

She was so lost in her thoughts that she walked straight into a tall, khaki-clad man without seeing him.

"Steady on there, Mrs. Morris," a gruff, curt voice sounded over her head. Strong, firm hands grasped her shoulders…and as quickly let them go when she was steadied.

She looked up into the incredibly blue eyes of the post physician, Dr. Todd Powell. He was a captain, and a totally different sort of man from her husband. He was so fierce that none of the soldiers on the post ever pretended to be ill to get out of unpleasant details. He had a vicious temper when he was pushed, and he occasionally drank to excess.

But to Lisa, he'd been kind. When she lost the baby, and her husband was gone on maneuvers, it was Todd Powell who sat beside her bed all night long while she cried and slept. It was Todd who'd buried the tiny infant. It was Todd who'd talked to her, and listened to her, and finally forced her back to life again. He might frighten everyone else, but Lisa felt a strange and curious tenderness for him.

It reflected in her soft eyes when she smiled up at him. "Thank you, Captain Powell," she said gently. "I had my mind on other things, I'm sorry."

He drew in a rough breath. "Other things being your husband's latest paramour, I gather?" he asked bluntly.

She flushed. "You should not say such a thing to me."

"Someone must talk some sense into you, madam. How long do you intend to put up with your husband's outrageous behavior? You must have heard the gossip."

"I have, of course." She hesitated, glancing around to make sure nobody was within earshot. "I…have instigated divorce proceedings. I have no idea where I shall go…."

His face softened. So did his eyes. "I have." He took her arm and led her back the way she'd come, toward a car. "You come with me."

"Captain Powell!" she protested.

"Just to meet someone," he said. He put her inside and got in next to her, cranking the car with some difficulty before he got it into gear, muttering impatiently all the while.

The wind felt good in her face. She stopped worrying

about more gossip. Dr. Powell had a take-charge manner that made her feel as if she were being swept along on a comfortable breeze. She smiled at the irony of being looked after. She'd spent most of her life looking after her father and then David. It was rather nice to have someone treat her with such care.

He didn't go far, just to a small settlement beyond the post, near the small town of Courtland. "Here it is," he said, and led her to neat white house among several that flanked the tiny post office. He knocked on a door—and smiled, doffing his hat, when a thin, elderly woman answered it.

"Hello, Todd," she said in welcome. "Who's this?"

"A young woman who'll be needing a place to stay very soon," Todd said. "Do you still have a spare room to let?"

"Of course I do," the woman said kindly. "I'm Mrs. Moye. And you can trade chores for your keep, if you need to."

"You don't know me—" Lisa began.

"I know Todd," Mrs. Moye said. "His opinion of you is enough for me."

"I'm not quite ready—" Lisa began again.

"Whenever you are, the room will be free," Mrs. Moye said. "Won't you come in and have a nice glass of tea?"

"I wish we had time," Todd said courteously. "Perhaps next time."

"I'll look forward to it. Goodbye, my dear."

"You didn't introduce us," Lisa remarked as Todd opened the passenger door for her.

"It wouldn't have been wise." His blue eyes stabbed

down into hers for a long, intent moment. "You're too thin," he said shortly. "But you're still lovely."

She felt giddy. No man had ever looked at her as Captain Powell did. He made her feel odd sensations stabbing into her thighs, her lower belly. She seemed to tingle all over. Even at his most intimate, David had never provoked such pleasure.

Todd cleared his throat. "I suppose we had better make haste back to the post."

"Yes. Yes, certainly."

She got in. His hand on her wrist was meant to assist, but it lingered just for a moment. She looked up at him and her whole body felt on fire. He was tall and big but not fat. He had hands the size of hams and a face that was craggy and rough and not at all handsome. His thick black hair was straight and unruly, falling over his broad, sweaty brow. He had thick eyebrows and a huge nose. He wasn't handsome. But he had a mouth that she wanted to kiss, and her eyes fell away from it in something like panic.

"Watch your skirt," he said curtly.

He closed the door and went around the car. She watched him with uncertainty and longing. She couldn't afford to let herself care about him. He was only being kind.

He knew what it was to hurt. His wife and son had been killed many years ago. He drank sometimes when he remembered. He'd told her about it while she lay sore and anguished, after the loss of her baby. He knew how it felt to lose a child, he'd said. He'd told her about the Apache uprising that had caused the death of his family, about his own anguish. He had, he told her, spoken of it to no one else.

It had been a moment out of time, one that had embarrassed them both a little afterward. They'd skirted around the faint intimacy and never mentioned the incident. But ever since, there had been an affinity between them that grew stronger by the day. He watched her when she was out of her husband's barracks, just as she watched him when he wasn't looking. She tried not to. She was an honorable woman, and Captain Powell was an honorable man. But if she hadn't been married... Oh, if only!

They arrived back at the post without any prying eyes watching.

"Thank you," she told him hesitantly. "It's very nice to know that I'll have a roof over my head, if I should need it."

"He will not stop, you know," he said quietly. "If anything, you can expect the affair to worsen with time. He is reckless, and she is deeply in love with him. She isn't a bad sort," he added gruffly. "She's a rather nice woman, and not the kind to chase after a married man. The advances were his, not hers."

"I see," she replied. She searched his eyes. "You know her?"

He looked uncomfortable. "I know of her. Her family is poor, but honest and honorable. They do not approve, but she is young."

She shifted a little. "Perhaps he, too, is in love," she said quietly. "It would explain his most recent behavior." She lifted her eyes. "Thank you for helping me."

His jaw clenched. "It is no hardship to help someone in need. Good day, Mrs. Morris."

She watched him walk away, his hands clasped behind him in his own characteristic posture as he strode back toward his dispensary. He looked sad and lonely, and she was sorry that he was alone. In a very real way, so was she. Tonight she had to tell David about the divorce, she decided. Putting it off would serve no purpose....

She'd only just put supper on the table when the front door slammed and heavy footsteps echoed into the kitchen, where she was lifting the coffeepot from the stove.

"Captain Arthur said that you'd gone riding with Captain Powell," David raged, red-faced.

She turned to him very calmly. "Why, yes, I did," she said. "Your supper is on the table."

He didn't speak for a minute. She could almost see his brain working, trying to decide how to deal with this new, odd behavior.

"Why were you riding around with the post physician?"

"Because he knew of a room to let," she said, her eyes very steady and unblinking, like those of a snake poised to strike. The difference it made in her appearance was uncanny. From a mousy, quiet girl, she'd suddenly transformed into a stubborn, independent woman. Even her posture was different.

"It looks bad for you to be seen in the company of another man—" he began.

"Does it look better for you to be seen with another woman?" she asked quietly.

He flushed. "Selina is none of your business," he said tautly.

"It's the entire post's business, or didn't you know that the wives of your officers take great delight in pointing it out to me?" she asked.

He ran an irritated hand through his thick blond hair

and looked uncomfortable. "I didn't realize that," he said slowly.

"It doesn't matter, David. Not anymore. I've seen a lawyer," she said, taking a deep breath. "I'm divorcing you."

He looked absolutely stunned. He gaped at her. "You are…*what?*" he burst out. "How dare you!"

She clasped her hands tightly in front of her. "It is for the best… Surely you realize that? If you truly love this girl, and she loves you…"

He was stunned speechless. His career was his first thought. A divorce would be a reflection on his manhood, especially if his wife left him, instead of the reverse.

"You have to stop the proceeding," he said icily, his eyes dangerous.

"I will not! David, we both know that you only married me for position. For years, you've disgraced me with every woman who took your fancy. But this latest affront is unbearable. You have made me a laughingstock. I am divorcing you. And there is nothing you can say or do that will stop me!"

He lost his head. Without a thought beyond revenge for the humiliation she intended, he lifted his hand and struck her full across the cheek, the blow hard enough to knock her back into the hot woodstove.

She screamed and jerked away as a white-hot lick of pain burned along her hip where the fabric touched. It burst into flames quite suddenly. She beat at it with her hands, the fear and pain taking the sting out of her cheek as she desperately tried to put out the fire.

David was stunned for a moment. Then he reacted quickly. He grabbed the bucket of water on the cooking table and flung the contents at her skirts. The fire went out, but she'd been badly burned. He could see the blistered red flesh of her hip and side through the blackened hole.

"Lisa, forgive me, I never meant to…" he began hoarsely.

She slapped at his hands, weeping in pain, and got a chair between them. She felt sick all over. The pain was terrible. He suddenly blurred in her sight and a black oblivion washed coldly over her.

Todd Powell was bending over her in the post dispensary when she awoke. He had a coldly cynical look in his blue eyes and a blunt way of speaking that managed to offend almost everyone. The men were as afraid of him as they were of the Indians, which amused him no end.

He narrowed one eye as he studied the unkempt hair and bruised cheek of the woman on the cot. Behind him, David Morris looked wan and sick.

"I've given you a little morphia for the pain, Mrs. Morris," Powell told her curtly. "You'll have a bad burn, and probably a scar, but you'll live."

"Thank you," she said drowsily.

"May I take her home now?" David asked.

Powell turned and looked at the younger man. "No."

"I am your commanding officer," David pointed out.

"I am neither blind nor ignorant," the physician replied, undaunted. "One look at her cheek explained this…accident…to my satisfaction, Colonel Morris. Your illicit activities are known to all of us. And I know that your wife has instigated divorce proceedings. She will not return to your barracks. Unless you relish the thought of a court-martial for conduct unbecoming an officer and a gentleman, I advise you not to press the issue."

"You take a great deal on yourself," David said angrily, but he wasn't pushing.

"I've been out here a long time, Colonel," Powell said easily, his eyes measuring the other man. "While you were back East situated in Washington society, I was out on the desert digging arrowheads out of troopers while we tracked Geronimo across this godforsaken wilderness."

David colored. "Dr. Powell…"

"Go home, Colonel," Powell said gruffly. "You are excess baggage here."

David hesitated. After a long, regretful look at Lisa's averted face, he went out and slammed the door.

"Thank you," she said sleepily.

A big, callused hand touched her forehead. "Go to sleep, Mrs. Morris. No thanks are necessary."

She drifted off, feeling safe for the first time in recent memory, despite the lingering pain and fear. When she was asleep, a somber man with a big nose and weary blue eyes sat beside her and held her hand. He didn't let go until morning.

Thanksgiving Day had been quiet and uneventful. The women had spent the day cooking and the evening cleaning up. It had been a congenial gathering, but Trilby's heart wasn't in it. Richard's attentiveness to an increasingly flirtatious Julie had ruined the holiday for her.

Sissy persuaded a depressed Trilby to go with her into the desert, only a little way, where there were a few scattered ruins.

"Are these Hohokam ruins?" Trilby asked when the

two women had climbed out of the buggy and were wandering around a site with broken pottery on a plain near the close mountain chain.

"I don't know." Sissy knelt down and picked up a piece of pottery. "Isn't it incredible?" she said, with reverence. "Trilby, do you realize that this little piece of pottery was made by human beings perhaps a thousand years ago?"

Trilby fanned herself with the broad-brimmed hat she was wearing with her long riding skirt and middy blouse. Sissy was similarly dressed, and it was hot in the desert. The dry air made little difference.

"I do wish we'd brought the car," Sissy was murmuring.

"The horse and buggy are much less trouble, believe me, but I'm glad you drove it on the way down."

"I think you're doing very well as a pupil," Sissy remarked.

Trilby smiled. It amazed her that she'd felt brave enough to come out with Sissy, but the horse pulling the buggy was a gentle one and didn't frighten her, and she hadn't had to drive. Yet. She looked up, frowning. "Sissy, there are clouds on the horizon. Remember what I told you—about the danger of dry washes even if the rain is miles away, and about the terrible flood back during the summer?"

"Yes, I remember," Sissy murmured, but her mind wasn't really on it.

"We'd better go back."

"But we just got here!"

"Sissy!"

"Now, Trilby. I just want to poke around a bit. This isn't a dry wash, after all. Why don't you pick up Richard at the corral?" she added, with a sly grin. "I can't be bothered to move right now." She sighed theatrically. "You shall have to go alone." She peered up at Trilby and grinned. "I'm sure you'll be heartbroken about having to pick me up on your way back."

Trilby's heart leaped. It was an opportunity to be alone with Richard, who'd ridden with them as far as the corrals to watch the men brand cattle. The girls had left him there with a promise to be back in a few minutes to pick him up. Sissy was playing Cupid, and Trilby blessed her for it. Except that she'd have to drive the buggy alone. She studied the quiet horse nervously; he was tethered by having his reins trail on the ground, a miracle of training, she sometimes thought.

"I'm still a bit nervous about that horse," Trilby said worriedly.

"He likes you. Just snap the reins to make him go and pull back on them to make him stop. He'll follow the road, and Richard will drive on the way back."

"Well…all right. But I shouldn't leave you alone out here—" Trilby began.

"Don't be silly. I'm perfectly safe. I even have this ugly thing your father insisted we carry." She picked up the pistol gingerly by the handle as if it were a snake. "Ugh!"

"I'll only be a minute or so," Trilby promised, her eyes brightening with delight at the thought of being alone with Richard. "You are such a lovely person!"

"I know it." Sissy chuckled. "Go on. Give Julie something to worry about."

"She could have come with us," Trilby muttered.

"And ruined her complexion in the sun? Horrors!"

Trilby laughed. She climbed into the buggy. "I won't be long."

"It's all right if you are," Sissy murmured, lost already in her pottery hunting.

Trilby made it to the corral in one piece, but she gratefully gave the reins to Richard on the way back. She and Richard bumped along the road with a lengthy silence between them. He was hot and half out of humor from the heat and the smell of branding. He'd gotten sick, actually sick, at the corrals, and some of the cowboys had laughed at him. His pride was stinging.

"I detest this place," he said irritably. "I'm sorry I came."

Trilby shifted uneasily. "I'd hoped you might enjoy your visit, Richard," she said. "It's not so bad once you get used to it."

"I can't agree." His eyes scanned the horizon. "It's like hell, pardon the expression. It really is a wasteland."

Trilby lowered her eyes to the floorboard as he touched the reins gently to the horse's rump, forcing him to go faster. "Are you going to marry Julie, Richard?"

"I don't know," he said. "She's pretty and sweet and her people have money. She certainly isn't content to live in the middle of the damned desert!"

Trilby's eyes brightened and overflowed with tears.

"Oh, damn! Here, Trilby, I didn't mean that." Richard pulled back on the reins and stopped the horse. His hand touched her pitiful face. "I'm sorry, little one. Really, really sorry. Trilby…"

He tilted her chin up and looked at her soft, trembling mouth. He'd only kissed it once, long ago, but it looked very tempting with her gray eyes full of tears. Smiling ruefully, he bent and brushed his mouth slowly over her lips before he settled it between them and pulled her close.

Trilby had expected stars to shatter if Richard kissed her like this. She was surprised to find that it was nothing like the explosive pleasure Thorn had kindled in her body. That wounded her, and she reached up to kiss him back, trying to force herself to feel what she must feel. She loved him! Of course she did!

The man on horseback close by was certain of it when he saw them kissing. He was bristling with fury, feeling betrayed and murderous.

"Stop," Naki said quietly, reaching out a firm, strong hand. "That isn't the way."

"You're one to talk about restraint," Thorn said brutally, jerking his arm away.

"Oh, but restraint and the courts make a good combination for my people," he told Thorn. "One day we'll throw you white eyes out on your ears, just as the Mexicans are determined to do with their Spanish overlords in this revolution they've started. Except that we'll do it legally—and beat you at your own game."

"Good luck to you."

"Women are fickle," he added, watching as the woman disengaged herself from the man. "That one is out of place here."

"She wouldn't be if she tried to fit," Thorn said through his teeth. With his broad-brimmed hat pulled low over his lean face, he looked menacing. "Damn that Eastern dandy! Why did he have to come out here now? He isn't even a man! My God, he was vomiting at the sight of cattle being branded!"

Naki chuckled softly. "I noticed."

"So did everyone else. What does she see in him?"

"The past," Naki said wisely. "Memories that live in him." He looked at his friend. "If you want her, take her."

"That's your philosophy, is it?"

Naki shrugged. "Women among my people are strong and independent and fiery, much like Mexican women. They laugh at weakness in a man. That one might be the same. You might show her the blond man's weaknesses and your strengths."

"Sometimes you amaze me with your insight," Thorn said thoughtfully. "Let's go down and break up that touching tryst."

Naki's eyes turned skyward. "Rain's coming. Wasn't that skinny woman in glasses with her when they came out?"

Thorn frowned, wondering how Naki knew that. Thorn had seen them go bumping by in the buggy, but Naki hadn't been around. "So she was. They were going to look for pottery, her younger brother said."

"I'd better find her. The ruins are near a dry wash."

"She seemed pretty frightened of you when we were introduced. I'd better go."

"No. I will," Naki replied, smiling mischievously. "I'll take her back to the ranch for you."

"Don't enjoy it too much."

Naki raised his eyebrows. "Would I enjoy the terror of a naive young woman?"

"You sure as hell would! Just remember that they're Jack Lang's guests, and I want his water."

"You want his daughter just as much, unless I miss my guess."

"Get out of here," Thorn muttered.

Naki chuckled. He wheeled his pinto and rode away toward the ruins.

Trilby had pulled away from Richard when she spotted the riders in the distance. Angrily she realized at once who they were.

"What is it?" Richard asked, smiling. He thought she was shy and it touched him. She wasn't as exciting as Julie, but her soft mouth was sweet and he liked kissing her. Having Trilby under his spell was too flattering to miss.

"It's Thorn Vance and one of his men—the Apache, I think," Trilby said nervously.

Richard turned his eyes toward the rise where they were sitting. As he watched, the Indian turned his pony and rode away. Vance moved toward them, as at home in the saddle as any of the cowboys. Richard was irritated by the way he looked, so damned arrogant and confident, when he rode up beside the buggy.

"Good day," he said, touching his fingers to his hat. "Having trouble with the horse, or are you lost?"

Trilby flushed. "Neither. We only stopped to talk," she choked. The way Thorn was looking at her made her uncomfortable. He brought back vivid memories of the fiesta and the feel of his long, powerful body against her own while his mouth made magic against hers. Kissing him had been as explosive as touching fire, while the same caress with Richard was oddly unsatisfying.

"Surely you must have something better to do?" Richard seconded, with angry eyes.

Thorn pushed back his hat. "Oh, I do," he agreed, with amusement. "But there's a flash flood looming. I think you'd better get home while you can."

Trilby suddenly remembered her friend. "Sissy! I left her at the ruins!"

"Naki's gone to fetch her," Thorn said. "She'll be all right."

"The Apache?" Trilby was horrified. "She'll faint dead away! She's afraid of him!"

"She'd better get used to him," Thorn said. "He's going camping with us. You do still want to go?" he asked Richard.

The young man brightened. "I say, of course I do. It's been dead boring, just sitting around the house."

"You're certain you like to hunt?" Thorn asked, with a veiled reference to the man's unsettled stomach at the branding.

Richard's cheekbones flushed. "There is a substantial difference between hunting and tormenting cattle."

"Rustling is a real threat out here, son," Thorn said condescendingly. "Cattle we don't brand, we don't keep."

"I'm certain that Richard knows that, Mr. Vance," Trilby said pointedly.

He met her eyes levelly, leaning over the pommel of his saddle. His dark eyes twinkled with humor and traces of desire. They dropped to her soft mouth and lingered there so long that her pulse began to race. She fingered the reins nervously, afraid that Richard might notice Thorn's interest.

He did. It amused him that the older man found Trilby attractive when Trilby obviously didn't share that interest. He slid a possessive arm over her shoulders and drew her close, feeling her go soft.

"This hunting trip, when will we go?" Richard asked Thorn.

He straightened in the saddle, his fascination with

Trilby's mouth turning to frank dislike of the dandy sitting so close beside her.

"In two or three days," he said. "I'll make arrangements with Jack Lang and lay in some supplies. You have your own rifles with you?"

"Yes, indeed," Richard replied. "I never travel without my hunting and camping gear."

"Naturally not."

"I'm sorry that you're in such a hurry, Mr. Vance," Trilby said meaningfully, "because of the rain."

"Is that why I'm in such a hurry?" he asked. "Very well. I must be, I suppose. Be careful and don't linger in any dips in the road. It could be fatal. I could escort you, if you like."

"We can get home all by ourselves," she muttered. "You're sure your Indian cowboy will see about Sissy?"

"I'm sure," he assured her.

Richard frowned. "You'll see about Sissy yourself, I hope," he told Thorn. "I don't like the idea of my sister alone with an Indian."

"Your sister will be perfectly safe, I assure you."

Richard took that to mean that Thorn would go along after her and he relaxed.

"Very well then. Good day." Richard twitched the reins and urged the horse into a trot, leaving a smug, amused Thorn behind.

"He does have a way of making one bristle, doesn't he?" Richard said as he removed his arm and stretched lazily. "Still, it will be pleasant to do a spot of hunting. Here you go—" he handed her the reins "—you drive for a while. I'm simply exhausted. Try not to hit too many bumps, won't you, lovely?"

He leaned back, crossed his arms, and closed his

eyes—and Trilby could have screamed. She realized only then that Richard had been paying her attention to get at Thorn. It hadn't even been real, only pretended. She wanted to cry.

As they wound down the road toward the ranch, the clouds moved closer. She hoped Sissy would forgive her.

Chapter Nine

Sissy was getting more nervous by the minute.

There was thunder in the distance and Trilby still hadn't come back. She remembered the terrifying story Trilby had told her about the floods that had killed several people a few months back. She wrapped her arms tight around herself, clutching her precious pieces of pottery in the handkerchief where she'd tied them. She hoped her passion for the past wasn't going to be her downfall.

The sound of a horse's hooves diverted her. Odd, she thought, there wasn't the usual metallic noise that accompanied the approach of Mr. Lang's horses. Her heart began to race. Unshod ponies were usually ridden by Apaches, she seemed to recall.

Even as the thought occurred to her, the tall Apache Mr. Vance had called Naki came into view over the ridge. She could hardly believe it! Her eyes widened and her heart leaped. He did look so majestic against the clouds. But she didn't dare let him see her interest.

He rode straight down to her and reined in, sitting high in his saddle to look down his arrogant nose at her. He didn't smile menacingly this time. He simply stared. His dark eyes gave away nothing as they registered her poise and composure. This was a far cry from her most recent behavior when they'd met.

She really was thin, he thought, and much too pale. But even if she was afraid of him and hiding it, she wasn't running. That intrigued him.

"Rain," he said, pointing toward the horizon and then to the dry wash nearby. "White woman drown in wash when rain come," he said stoically.

She stared up at him with a mischievous gleam in her green eyes. She was sure there was much more to this man than what he showed. He was very handsome, she thought, the kind of man who'd never give a plain-Jane like her a second thought. She sighed as she realized that her lack of looks was just as much a handicap out here as it had been back home. Nothing changed except the location in which you were miserable, she thought.

"You don't have to look as if you find the prospect of my imminent demise so delightful," she said, with droll humor.

Both his eyebrows arched. "Perhaps you sink like rock in that rig." He nodded toward her long, thick skirt.

His sarcasm unseated her temper. "Perhaps you fall off that high horse and break your arrogant neck." She mimicked his accent.

He chuckled and crossed his wrists over the pommel of his saddle, leaning over it to study her. He liked her. He couldn't remember feeling such warm thoughts about a woman since Conchita. Conchita had been beautiful. This woman wasn't. Yet there was something about her that touched him. "Heap plenty rattlesnakes out here."

"Sorry to bash your hopes, but I don't mind rattly

snakes. We have them back East, and bigger than the ones I've seen in Arizona so far." She looked past him. "I'd just love to stand and talk to you, dear man, but I don't relish drowning out here. My friend should be along soon to pick me up."

"Not soon." He shook his head. "Too busy kissing white man in buggy."

"Oh, bother!" she said worriedly. "She'll forget me and I'll drown!"

"Injun save white woman. I carry you away from here."

She eyed him warily. This didn't sound real. Apaches lived in a modern age, but she knew for a fact that some of them still lived free in the Sierra Madre and raided Mexican villages even now. If he was having a silent laugh at her expense, and she thought he was, it was time to make him show his true colors.

"In a pig's eye," she said smartly. "I'm not going to be carried off to your tepee and made to chew your moccasins. I haven't forgotten that you asked Mr. Vance how many horses my brother wanted for me. I wouldn't go to the nearest rock with you!"

His dark eyes twinkled. "Chili pepper," he murmured.

"Red-hot chili pepper," she agreed. "Watch out I don't burn you, red man."

So much for subterfuge. He wouldn't mind giving himself away to this spicy Easterner. "You're an interesting proposition, Miss Bates," he replied in perfect English. "But we can discuss your appalling metaphors later. I don't like the look of that cloud. Climb up, before we both drown here."

Both eyebrows arched as she realized that her hunch

about him was right. She laughed and pursed her lips. "It's the sun," she said. "I've been out here too long. You make big joke, huh?"

"I speak English rather well, as it happens, and drowning is nothing to joke about," he replied easily, moving the horse closer. He reached down a big, lean hand. "Come on. We haven't much time. Distance is deceptive out here, and floods can be upon you before you realize it. Two of Vance's acquaintances drowned in the summer flood, and they knew the land."

"You really do speak English quite well," she said shyly.

"I speak English, Spanish, and Latin. Even some Greek. But English is adequate for the time being."

The sound of rain prompted her to action. She reached up and found herself jerked into the saddle in front of him. His strength fascinated her. She was used to rather academic men, not men of action. He controlled the nervous pinto expertly with only the pressure of his knees while he settled her against him and turned the horse back toward the Lang ranch. He smelled of wind and piñon pine and desert. He wasn't at all dirty, although a bit of the yellow dust feathered his clothing. It feathered her own as well.

"Why?" she asked, staring at the handsome bronze face that was much too close for comfort.

"Why the deception?" He smiled with faint arrogance. "I enjoy living down to the opinion most of you whites have of the poor ignorant savage."

She flushed. "Ouch."

"I suppose it never occurs to any of you that there were great civilizations in this country when your European ancestors were knocking one another over the head with sticks."

"The Hohokam were very civilized," she had to agree. "Their society was structured around peaceful cohabitation and sharing, and their purification rites for killing an enemy lasted so long that they were hardly ever able to go to war," she added.

"You're educated," he said, smiling with pleased surprise. He glanced down at her as the horse eased its way over the rutted dirt road. "Yes. The Hohokam lived here perhaps thousands of years ago. They irrigated the land and cultivated it, planted crops, built cities. They were intelligent and peaceful."

"Not *your* ancestors…?"

He burst out laughing.

"No," she exclaimed, thinking she'd insulted him, "I didn't mean it like that. I meant they weren't the forebears of the Apache, were they?"

"No one knows. Archaeologists believe they may be the ancestors of the Pima and Papago," he said. "Do you even know what the word *Apache* means?"

"No."

"It's a Zuñi word. It means *enemy.*"

"What do the Apache call themselves?"

"The People."

"I knew a Cherokee girl just briefly back home," Sissy said excitedly. "She said the Cherokee word for themselves means *Principal People.*"

"Sioux also means *people.* Most Indians call themselves that. How did you manage to learn so much about us through all that fear?"

"It wasn't fear. I was living down to your image of white women," she teased. "Apaches carry off women captives…."

He looked down at her and pursed his lips. "So we

do," he said, amused. His eyes fell to her bodice. "And just imagine what we do to them. My, my."

She colored a little and glared at him. "Mr. Naki—"

"I'm called Two Fists in my own language," he said, correcting her. "Doesn't that sound properly Indian, as names go?"

"If you could stop looking at me like that…"

His dark eyes looked directly into hers. "You do blush beautifully," he remarked. "I don't rape white women, Miss Bates. In fact, I prefer darker skin and more of it. We won't mention that what you're thinking is impossible on horseback."

She went scarlet then. "I wasn't thinking a single thing!"

"I suppose I should apologize for making an indecent remark like that, but you know how we savages are."

"Of all the audacious, outrageous—"

"They even call us that in books," he added, ignoring her adjectives. "Noble savages. As if we don't have brains at all."

She laughed finally. He was outrageous, all right. "How did you learn all those languages you said you speak?" she asked, diverted.

"The priests hid me when the U.S. Government moved Geronimo's whole Apache tribe out to Florida after Geronimo surrendered. Eventually they got as far back as Fort Sill, Oklahoma, but I was keen to stay in my mountains here. The priests discovered that I could be taught. So they taught me."

"Your parents?"

"My mother died when I was born. My father was killed trying to escape the cavalry when they rounded us up," he said bitterly.

"I'm sorry...."

"Your people always are, aren't they?" he asked as the past came searing through him. He looked at her without seeing her. "They took everything we had and killed and enslaved us in the process. They virtually destroyed the Chiricahua Apache. I have more in common with the Mexican peasants than I have with the whites, Miss Bates. I know what it is to be an oppressed race without the means to rebel."

"Your people did fight," she argued, "just as the Mexicans are fighting now."

"Perhaps the Mexicans will win. There are enough of them—and God knows, their cause is a just one," he said, with fervor. "But my people were few and scattered. And do you know what separates us from the whites, Miss Bates? Do you know the difference between your people and mine? It's greed. The white man wants to own or control everything around him. The Apache wants only to live at peace with the world and his people. Greed is as alien to most of us as honor is to most whites."

She was shocked. It had been a morning for revelations, but this was an especially unexpected one. He was more learned than she, and probably more intelligent. How terrible to have such a mind and be treated like a monkey.

"It must be very painful to have people misjudge you so badly," she said after a minute.

He searched her quiet, soft eyes. "Thorn said that I frightened you. He didn't want me to come and fetch you."

"I'm not afraid of you at all," she said ruefully. "You aren't the only one who can act. I don't suppose you might be willing to teach me about your culture?" she asked.

He chuckled dryly as they approached the Lang ranch. "I might be persuaded."

"Why are you called Two Fists?" she wondered out loud.

He reined in the pony and shifted her, his eyes level and steady on hers. "When the cavalry came for us, I went for one of the soldiers with both fists."

"Oh."

"I was five years old," he murmured, smiling. "The priests begged me away from the officer I attacked, and he let me go with them. I've never forgotten. He was a doctor. He's stationed at Fort Huachuca and he visits me from time to time."

"He must be a kind man."

"In his case, it was a great kindness. Apaches had killed his wife and young son the month before."

"He must be a very special man."

"Yes. There's been enough killing on both sides to make for uneasy acquaintanceship between my people and yours."

"I suppose so." She moved her hand and it encountered his long, thick black hair. She started to remove her fingers, but then she impulsively touched the sleek thickness of the long black strands. "I've never seen a man with long hair before."

The touch of her fingers in his hair was starkly disturbing. He caught them and pushed them away, his eyes suddenly cold and unapproachable.

"Excuse—excuse me," she stammered, averting her eyes.

He felt guilty for his brutal rejection, but he had no

place in his life for her. White and red never mixed. They could become each other's worst liability.

"Hopeless situations are best avoided," he said icily.

When she realized what he was admitting, her heart raced like a wild thing. Slowly, so slowly, she lifted her eyes to his and found something in them that she'd been searching for all her life.

"No," she whispered in protest as the sensation of being snared formed in her body.

"No," he agreed. But the hand at her back moved up into the thick bun that held it at her nape. He arched her upward so that her body touched his, so that her face was close enough to let his eyes fill the world. She trembled with a surge of sudden, shocking pleasure.

His fingers contracted and something purely male and conquering filled his face and eyes as he read her submission and reacted to it.

"Confine your relic hunts to the land around the house as long as you stay here," he said huskily. "Because this," he emphasized, his hand reinforcing his mastery, "is a high wind with no shelter. Do you understand?"

"I think so." She shivered with something approaching pleasure. It was a sensation she'd never experienced.

He nodded and his hand slowly released its grasp. His eyes searched hers. "I had a woman," he said huskily. "She was young and Mexican and very, very pretty. We lived just over the border in Mexico. Her brother was a dissident who hated the government and was friends with a man named Blanco, who is becoming well known today as a revolutionary. One day an officer in the Mexican government came by our house with his company and Conchita's brother, Luis, was there. They had been hunting him. They shot Luis and accused us of being revolutionaries." His eyes darkened with pain. "The officer grabbed Conchita and I went for him. Two of his men helped knock me out. I won't tell you what was done to Conchita. Fortunately, somewhere in the middle of it, she died." His face hardened. "I want no more of what I felt for her. I work for Thorn Vance and I live alone. I will live alone for the rest of my life."

Tears stung her eyes hotly and overflowed, fogging her lenses. She wept for him and the woman he'd loved. She wept for herself for having the misfortune to feel something so suddenly for a man who didn't want anyone's affection. She wept for the world.

"I abhor tears," he said through his teeth.

She took off her glasses and wiped her eyes with the back of her dust-sprinkled hand. "Oh, so do I," she whispered brokenly. "So please don't ever cry in front of me. I'll just go to pieces if you do."

He found himself smiling a minute later. Smiling, when the pain had been at its worst just seconds before. With a rough sound, he traced the tears down her cheeks and looked into her wet eyes with a kind of inner knowledge of her that shocked him. She didn't usually cry. He knew that, somehow; knew that she didn't show weakness or pain or grief in front of others.

"You said it was a pretense, your fear of me when we first met," he said suddenly. "Why?"

She grimaced. "Men don't notice me. I'm plain and thin and educated...I wanted you to notice me," she choked, dropping her eyes.

And he had. Looked and remembered and longed for her. He looked out over the horizon to the house where people were now standing on the front porch. He and

Sissy were out of the way among the rocks, just out of sight. But soon they'd be missed and looked for. He had to take her down there.

"I'm sorry," she said, replacing her glasses. "I shouldn't have pretended."

"I was doing the same thing," he replied solemnly. "I enjoy the reaction I get from whites when they discover that I'm not totally stupid."

"Women are stupid, too, didn't you know? We're made for scrubbing floors and having children. God gave us minds, but we keep them in the pantry so they won't rot," she said dryly.

He burst out laughing. She made his heart lift. "I see that you have had your portion of bad treatment."

"That is an understatement, sir. I mentioned going to a university and half the people in my family fainted. Nice girls do not get educated; they get married." She pushed back a strand of hair that had come loose from her neat bun as he urged the horse forward. "I want to know about the ancient peoples who lived here. I want to know what they did, what their culture was like. Aren't you curious?"

"Yes," he replied. "I wish I knew more."

"You could go to school, too."

"An Indian at a university?" He looked properly horrified.

"Well, I suppose several people in your family would faint, too."

"I have no family left," he said matter-of-factly.

"I'm sorry. Family is nice, even if it does get on your nerves from time to time."

"So I'm told. I must get you home," he said, glancing up at the sky. "Rain is very dangerous here."

"You told me that."

He chuckled. "So I did." He shifted her more comfortably as the horse ambled along the road. "Have you a Christian name?"

She nodded. "Alexandra. My family calls me Sissy. When Ben, my brother, was young, it was the closest he could come to my given name."

"Alexandra." He smiled faintly. "It suits you."

"Did you have a Christian name?"

"The priests called me *Hierro*. It means 'iron' in Spanish. They said I had a head like it."

"I can believe that."

"A woman's place is to agree," he chided.

"All Indians are savages," she joked.

He smiled. So did she. The horse began the slow decline down from the rocky ridge toward the house. The rain was starting to fall already.

"I can't believe you actually allowed him to bring you home in that fashion," Richard told Sissy with icy hauteur. "An Indian, putting hands on my sister!"

"Would you rather he'd left me out in the desert to be washed away in a flood?" Sissy raged at him. She'd been astonished at the attack over the supper table. Mary and Trilby had been on the porch when Naki brought her home. They hadn't said anything, although Mary had looked numb. The men had been out with the cattle, and were only told about Naki's intervention when they came home at suppertime. The fur had begun to fly at once.

"The lack of convention—" he began furiously.

"I have to agree," Jack Lang intervened, his face stiff. "I'll speak to Thorn about his man."

"Why don't you speak to *him* about it?" Sissy demanded. "He isn't an ignorant savage."

Richard scoffed. "He doesn't even understand English."

"He speaks three languages," Sissy said shortly. "English is one of them. He's much better educated than you are, brother, dear, and he's much less of a snob."

She walked off, ending the argument. Behind her, she heard Jack Lang and her brother still deploring Naki's actions. Julie's trill voice joined in, deploring Sissy's outlandish behavior. Naturally, she thought, Julie would love taking Richard's part against her!

If Sissy had hoped a good night's sleep would stop any further discussion of her adventure, she was doomed to disappointment. Richard and Jack were fuming about the incident all through breakfast, and Sissy was alternately berated and talked about.

"Men!" she said, exasperated, as a fascinated Trilby joined her in the living room after they'd put away the dishes.

"Did you say yesterday that Naki speaks several languages?" Trilby asked curiously.

"Yes. He was educated by the priests. He's very interesting," the other girl said hesitantly, and blushed.

Trilby didn't know what to say. She knew that Sissy's brother Richard was shocked at her behavior. So was Trilby's family, and she, herself. Sissy was her best friend, but part of her knew that Richard was right about the hopelessness of any relationship between a white woman and a man of another race. "Sissy, he's an Indian," she said. "Despite his education, he's a man of another race."

"Not you, too," Sissy said sadly. She sat down on

the worn sofa wearily. "Ben is the only member of my family who didn't find my attitude shocking. He's young, of course. It seems I shall have to fight the whole world and my best friend in order to be Naki's friend."

"No, of course you shan't," Trilby said at once, loyalty breaking through her disapproval. "I'm sorry."

"He said you were kissing Richard," Sissy murmured dryly.

Trilby hesitated. She nodded. "Yes, I suppose I was. But it wasn't what I expected," she said involuntarily.

"You're in love with him. Surely it should have been everything you wanted it to be."

"It wasn't." Trilby sat down beside her and folded her hands in her lap. "I don't understand."

"Neither do I, unless those pointed references Julie's been making to your tough neighbor really do make sense. Thorn Vance is very attractive, Trilby. And he doesn't look at you in the way most men look at neighbors."

Trilby flushed. "Well, we got off to a bad start. He thought I was something I wasn't, and he treated me in an ungentlemanly fashion."

"Oh?"

Trilby glanced up and down. "He's…very experienced. I saw a side of him that I shouldn't have seen at all. Now he's sorry about it, but I don't trust him anymore." She grimaced. "Sissy, I've loved Richard for years. But when he kissed me, I—I felt nothing!"

Sissy caught her hand and pressed it. "And when the very handsome Mr. Vance kissed you, you did?"

"Yes." She put her face in her hands. "I'm so ashamed. To feel…like that…about a ruffian!"

"How do you think I feel? I'm attracted to a savage red man."

Trilby made a face. "And I was no help at all. I'm…" She hesitated and stared at Sissy. "But I thought you were terrified of him!"

"I always wanted to go on the stage," Sissy replied mischievously. "He was very attractive and I wanted to make him notice me. Now, I'm not sure I should have. He isn't at all what I expected."

"That seems to work both ways."

"Trilby!"

She got up as her father came into the room. "Get your hat and jacket on, please," he said haughtily. "We're going to pay a call on Thorn Vance. I must make certain that he deals with this problem. Sissy, I shall have to ask you to accompany us."

"But—" Sissy began.

"Please do as I ask," he said curtly. "I shall be standing in for your brother, since I know Mr. Vance better."

Which, translated, Trilby thought wickedly, meant that Richard didn't relish having his back teeth knocked out by Mr. Vance for challenging his employee.

"I wouldn't miss it for the world," Trilby murmured, smiling at Sissy as she got her things together.

Thorn gaped at his visitors. "You want me to what?"

"Fire that ruffian Apache, of course," Jack Lang said huffily. "I really can't have him treating a female guest of mine in this fashion, even if he does have a vocabulary like an Oxford scholar."

"He didn't treat me in any fashion, Mr. Lang," Sissy groaned. "Why won't you listen? He saved me from a flood!" She turned to Thorn, exasperated. "Mr. Vance, can't you make him understand? I was not insulted."

"But you were, my dear," Jack argued. "To have a savage like that actually touching you…"

"Since I seem to be the cause of this tempest, perhaps I should participate in the debate?"

The object of the discussion walked in the door, tall and very composed, having been forewarned of this visit by Thorn after Jack Lang had telephoned that he was coming over.

Naki looked taciturn and very Apache in his characteristic clothing with his long black hair loose around his broad shoulders. But he smiled at Sissy. She smiled back.

"I say…" Jack Lang began hesitantly. Naki was tall and fit, and Jack was too aware of his own physical limitations.

Naki came closer, towering over Jack. "You find me objectionable, Mr. Lang. May I know why?" he asked quietly.

Jack's face went scarlet. "You're very direct."

"I find that it saves argument," Naki replied. He didn't lower his eyes or retreat an inch. If anything, he looked more belligerent than Jack did. "I want to know why you find it objectionable that I saw Miss Bates home."

"It—it wasn't that," Jack faltered. "Of course we're grateful for your intervention."

"But you would have preferred that a white man save her. Unfortunately, they were in short supply at the time."

Jack had the grace to lower his eyes. This man was as well educated as Sissy had intimated he was, and Jack felt like a cad.

"I expect such prejudices from Arizonans, Mr. Lang," Naki replied. "Sadly, I do not expect them from Easterners, who are supposedly more sophisticated and better educated than rural settlers."

Jack grimaced as he met the Apache's eyes. "Prejudice doesn't have a permanent address, sir, I'm sorry to say."

"Back East, it is people with black skin, not red, who are objects of scorn, is it not?" Naki asked coldly. "People who were, in their native lands, warriors."

"You phrase things in an unusual way."

"Before the Spanish came, the Indians in Mexico were Aztecs and Mayas," Naki continued. "They were a proud and intelligent race with their own system of government and worship and economic structure. Cortés and the Spanish, or course, destroyed them. The Aztecs and Mayas were 'savages.' Now it is the intelligent people, the Spanish conquerors, who take land from the peons and give it to wealthy foreign landowners and enslave the native people by working and taxing them to death. This is civilized behavior, I take it?"

Jack cleared his throat. "Sir, you have an odd grasp of the reality of things."

"I have an honest and unprejudiced view of the world around me," Naki replied. "I base my opinion of people on character, not color."

"Naki spends his summers leading Craig McCollum around the desert," Thorn said. "He's quite knowledgeable, as you see." His dark eyes glittered. "And out here, we don't consider it an insult for a man to save someone's life."

"But it isn't done!" Jack argued.

"I think it is for me to say if there was an insult," Sissy

insisted. "And I assure you that there was not. This gentleman saved my life. How can you condemn him for it?" she asked Jack. "Would you rather, if it had been Trilby, that she die in a flood rather than accept help from a man whose skin color was different than hers?"

Put like that, Jack could find no further argument. He subsided. "I must concede that I should rather have my daughter than my prejudices," Jack said. "But your brother—"

"My brother is a prejudiced, foppish snob," Sissy said icily, ignoring Trilby's start. "Like his contemporaries, his outlook on the world is as narrow as a beam."

Jack cleared his throat while Trilby flushed; Thorn's eyes began to glitter with amusement.

"I apologize for my behavior," Jack said to Thorn, and reluctantly included Naki in his apology. "I am grateful for what you did."

"De nada," Naki said in careless Spanish. "I daresay the contempt of my people was worth a life."

"Sir?" Jack asked.

"My people find whites distasteful, Mr. Lang," Naki took pleasure in pointing out. "They will disapprove of my contact with a white woman, regardless of the reason."

"Of all the impertinent…!" Jack gasped.

Naki chuckled softly. After a minute, the Easterner grasped the analogy and a smile touched his mouth.

"Yes, I do see your point," Jack replied.

"Let me walk you out," Thorn offered. He took Trilby's arm, his touch triggering a mild shock to her system. Incredible that Richard, whom she loved, couldn't cause this kind of reaction. It was only provoked by a man whom she detested. Or…did she?

"Close call, white eyes," Naki said under his breath to Sissy.

"Not my idea to come raging over here, either."

"I knew that."

She studied him covetously, seeking his dark eyes. "We've already agreed that it would be a bad thing to try and become friends, under the circumstances."

"A very bad thing," he agreed.

"Too much opposition."

He nodded.

She smiled wistfully. "I hate people telling me who I can choose for friends."

He smiled back. "So do I."

It was like having the sun come out of a cloud. Her heart lifted and began to shine through her green eyes.

He wanted far more from her than friendship, but it was all they could have. He knew it, even if she didn't. "They won't make it easy for you," he said, nodding toward the others who were walking toward the car.

She stared at him levelly. "I don't care," she said huskily, without realizing what she was telling him until it was too late.

His eyes splintered with feeling. His jaw tautened as he recognized the emotion for what it was. His fists clenched by his side.

"Sissy!" Trilby called in a curt whisper.

Sissy moved quickly onto the porch ahead of Naki. She looked unsettled, so Trilby maneuvered just in front of her while they made their goodbyes.

She hadn't known if Thorn was aware of the undercurrents until he darted a glance back at Naki and then at Sissy before he met Trilby's worried eyes.

"Don't worry," he said under his breath. "I'll handle it."

"You don't understand," she said quickly, mindful of being overheard while Sissy was asking Jack to help her into the car.

"Yes, I do," Thorn said. "It's all right."

Oddly that pacified her. He lifted her hand to his mouth and kissed the warm, moist palm hungrily. Her face colored, and he held her eyes for a long, taut moment.

"I know exactly how he feels!" he whispered fiercely, his eyes as stormy as Naki's had been. He abruptly let go of her hand. Then he led her to the car and helped her in with a stony face and without another word. All the way home, Trilby heard nothing that was said. Her palm still tingled.

Chapter Ten

Lisa Morris was drifting between reality and consciousness. She smiled as she remembered the swing in her backyard when she'd been a little girl. Her father had been away on maneuvers, and she and her mother had stayed with her maternal grandmother in Maryland. There had been a huge Victorian house and a big yard with a swing hanging from the branches of the trees.

"I do so love to swing," she whispered dimly.

"What a hell of a thing to be dreaming about," came a disgusted, sarcastic voice.

She forced her eyes open. A man was standing over her, a tall, lean man in a soiled officer's uniform with the tunic open. He was unshaven and his thick black hair was lying rumpled on his broad forehead. There was no male beauty in that rugged countenance, and he had lips that seemed set in a permanent sneer. In his big hand was a thick shot glass that looked recently drained.

"Captain Powell?" she asked huskily.

"Himself." He nodded. He set the shot glass down

with a thud. His bloodshot eyes looked down into hers. "How do you feel?"

"Sore." She grimaced as she moved, and then flushed as she realized that she was wearing nothing under the sheet that covered her. She was horrified.

"Oh, for God's sake, I'm a physician," he said icily. "Do you really think that at my age a woman's body is any mystery?"

She swallowed and clutched the sheet. She was woozy from the drugs and her hip and side were stinging from the bad burn, but she had a little modesty left. "You're a man," she began, trying to explain her embarrassment.

"And you're a married woman," he added. "Moreover, a married woman who's lost a child."

Her face clouded. Yes, he would have reason to know. The night she lost the baby, he'd stayed by her bedside all night long. He'd held her hand and talked to her in a voice so soft that it hadn't seemed like this cynical man's at all. David, she recalled, had been away on maneuvers. She hadn't known at the time, but he'd been in Douglas with Selina that particular night.

"You stayed with me," she said drowsily, and smiled. "Did I ever thank you?"

"I'm a doctor," he reminded her. "It's my job."

God forbid, in other words, that anyone should accuse him of tender feelings or compassion, she thought suddenly. He was very soft under that nasty veneer. No wonder he did his best to terrorize the people around him.

She lay back against the pillow with a shaky sigh. Her hair was loose around her white shoulders. She looked drawn and wan, but the man looking at her found her beautiful.

"He hasn't left a mark on you, except that one on your cheek," he said unexpectedly.

She touched the bruised place. "He hasn't ever hit me before."

"That wasn't what I meant, although I hold him in contempt for it, just the same. I meant," he added slowly, searching her eyes, "that you seem untouched."

She lowered her eyes to his tunic. Under it, thick black hair was visible where his red long johns were unbuttoned. She averted her gaze quickly. That evidence of his masculinity seemed indecent in this room, despite his profession.

"Do I embarrass you?" He laughed. He sat down beside her on the bed and turned her face back to his taunting eyes. They were a vivid, bright blue and they seemed to see right through her. "You don't like looking at me, do you? I'm ugly and hairy, and the kind of ruffian a woman like you wouldn't give a second look, even if you weren't married and decent."

She caught her breath at his plain speaking. "Captain Powell, please!"

"He hit you," he said harshly. "I could have killed him for it! My God, he never deserved you!"

It was beginning to dawn on her that he cared about her predicament. She looked up at him with shy curiosity. "You're very blunt, sir."

"Yes, I am. Blunt. And a little drunk. I drink to forget what the Apaches did to my wife and son, Mrs. Morris. They tied me to a post and made me watch it."

Her hand went up to his face and she touched his cheek with shy compassion. "I'm sorry," she whispered. "Oh, I'm so sorry!"

His voice broke. He lay his unshaven cheek against

her breasts over the sheet and began to weep. Hot tears fell on her. She felt them even through the fabric, and she hesitated for only an instant before she cradled his face to her. Déjà vu, she thought. He drank to numb his pain, but he wasn't proof against it. How often did he feel this torment—and have no one to share it with, no one to hold him? What a travesty life was, she thought miserably. Was anyone free from suffering in all the world? Her arms tightened around him and she cradled his head to her, whispering soft words of comfort.

A long time later, he lifted his head and moved away from her, his face quiet and faintly shamed.

"I have felt so sorry for myself," she said quietly. "You make me ashamed. I have so little to mourn, compared to you."

His back stiffened. "I drink too much," he said abruptly. "Do you need something to help you sleep?"

"No, thank you. The pain is—is not so bad."

He nodded and started out.

"Captain...Powell?"

He turned, hesitant after his loss of control. "Yes, madam?"

"Please. Do you have a—a shirt or something that I could put on?" She flushed and dropped her eyes.

"Forgive me. It's been a very long time since I've been around a decent woman." He moved into the other room and came back with a white dress shirt, a very long one. He laid it beside her on the cot. "You are in no condition to put it on."

She went scarlet. "Sir..."

"Doctor."

After a minute she gave in to the offer of help. He was

a doctor, and she was too dazed and in too much pain to manage alone.

He slid an arm behind her, helping her into a sitting position. She groaned, because every movement was painful. He'd put salve on the burns and lightly bandaged them, but any motion that pulled the skin was excruciating.

"Just sit still and let me get you into it," he said stiffly.

He pulled the sheet down. In the faint light of the lamp, he looked at her small, pert breasts. His expression changed. She felt his professional interest change to a very personal one, and her body reacted to his intense scrutiny in a way she didn't understand. David had never looked at her. He'd taken her, very roughly, but not in love. He'd never wanted to look at her nude body. But this man was not only looking, he was telling her with his eyes that he found her exquisite.

I must not enjoy this, she told herself. Only a kept woman would allow a man to look at her nudity so openly and not protest.

"Captain Powell," she said, shaking, then drew an arm up over her breasts with flushed embarrassment.

His vivid blue eyes searched hers. "Forgive me," he whispered. "Forgive me. I…" He fumbled with the shirt and eased her arm into it, gently putting it in place before he moved it around her and helped her put the other arm in. He buttoned it with big fingers that barely managed the task before them they were shaking so badly.

He helped her back down and drew the sheet over her again. "It will be sore for several days. If you are determined to return to your barracks, your—your husband will need to help you dress until the healing process has time to take hold."

"I have no intention of going back to the barracks. And even if I did, sir, my husband cannot bear the sight of me," she said through her teeth, her eyes staring straight up at the ceiling. "I could expect more help from a passing stranger than from him."

He looked down at her wan face for a long, long time. "I cannot imagine a man so blind, madam, that he could resist the sight of you unclothed. And if saying that to you is indecent, then I am indeed a sinner in need of salvation."

He turned and left the room, a little unsteadily. Lisa stared after him in mute surprise. Her body tingled with new sensations, ones that her neglectful husband had never been able to arouse in her. She clutched at the sheet and closed her eyes. She prayed for a long time, confessing her pleasure in Dr. Powell's eyes and her need for forgiveness. She was a married woman to whom infidelity was unthinkable. Even if her husband had indulged in a sinful affair, she was a different kind of person. She was not free to enjoy any sort of relationship, even an innocent one, with another man. Not until her divorce was final. All the same, the doctor's eyes had provoked a sensation she'd never known in her life. She hoped that by morning he might think it had been a dream. Perhaps in time, she could even convince herself that it had been.

Col. David Morris was off post, as he had no right to be, spending the night in Selina's arms. It was the first time, and it wouldn't be the last, he thought. He did love this woman.

He rolled over, his face stark in the moonlight that came in through the window. His behavior had shocked him. He hadn't meant to hit Lisa. God knew, she was entitled to be outraged at the way he'd treated her. He'd married her to advance his career; he'd dragged her out here to a life for which she was unsuited; he'd made her pregnant and then ignored her when she miscarried; he'd been having a passionate affair with another woman. When Lisa had announced that she was leaving him, he'd hit her. He groaned aloud. He hadn't meant to strike her. He certainly hadn't meant her to catch on fire and be so badly burned.

"What's the matter?" Selina drawled sleepily.

"My wife is divorcing me," he said.

Selina sat up, no longer sleepy. "Divorcing you?" Her face beamed.

"Yes," he said, with a rough laugh. "You can marry me, if you like, when the divorce is final."

She wept for joy. It was the end of her particular rainbow, more than she'd ever dared to hope for. "Oh, David, I'll be so good to you," she whispered fervently. "So good."

She pulled him down beside her and began to prove it, the best way she knew. Long before his mind gave in to her, his body did. It was just as well to let Lisa have her divorce, he thought as his body began to surge. Just as well, indeed.

Later that day, as he rode back toward the post, he heard sounds that alarmed him. Carefully, cautiously, he eased his automobile into the shade of some paloverde trees and cut the engine. Ordinarily he rode his horse down here, disgusted with the infernal machine that broke down more often than it served him. But he'd been in a hurry to get to Selina.

He listened. Horses. Many horses. As he watched from his concealment, a party of men—Mexicans, judging from their huge sombreros—cautiously worked their way toward Douglas.

He didn't recognize them, but he knew they weren't locals. There was something about them that fairly screamed of revolutionaries. They would bear watching. When he got to Fort Huachuca, he could phone the garrison in Douglas and report this troop movement. If they were operating on American territory, all hell was going to break loose soon. Perhaps there was something to those rumors of smuggling and a local junta that he'd been hearing lately.

Thorn Vance rode over to the Lang ranch with plenty on his mind. He couldn't get Naki to talk to him for the first time in memory. He knew the Apache was fascinated by the Langs' bespectacled female guest, but he didn't know what to do about it. If the man's emotions were involved, it could be a sticky situation, especially given her brother's opinion of Indians. He didn't know what might come of the ill-fated relationship, and he had no authority to keep Naki away from Sissy Bates.

On the other hand, he might be able to talk to the girl if he could find an opportunity. Perhaps that would be possible on a hunting expedition, so he'd made preparations to take the Langs' guests up into the mountains for a camping party.

Jack Lang was less than enthusiastic, but Richard showed the first real interest of his trip.

"Jolly good!" he exclaimed, aping his idol, Theodore Roosevelt. "When can we leave?"

"At first light," Thorn told him. "I don't want to be

out after dark unless we're encamped, given the Mexican situation."

"Certainly. But won't we be near the border?" Richard persisted.

"No," Thorn assured him. "Farther away from it, if anything."

"In that case, I'm game. How about you, sweetness?" he teased Cousin Julie, who leaned against his shoulder with pure coquetry.

"I can hardly wait," she said huskily.

Trilby should have been jealous. She wanted to be. But when her eyes met Thorn's curious ones, she felt her insides caving in. Her gaze lowered to his hard mouth and she wanted it with such an unexpectedly fierce need that her nails dug into her palms. She turned away to straighten a doily on the table, and all the while she felt Thorn's eyes on her back.

"Are you bringing Samantha?" Mary Lang asked Thorn.

"Not on this trip," he said, his voice oddly deep. "She's staying with my cousin Curt and his wife in town." He didn't add that Samantha had begged to go with her father. She didn't seem to enjoy staying with Curt and Lou. Why hadn't he ever noticed that before? He'd have to talk with her about it sometime soon.

"How nice for her. She'll miss you, of course," Mary said.

Thorn didn't agree, but he was too polite to say so. "I'll be by at first light to pick you all up," he said.

"Thorn, you're welcome to take my car, too, if you need it," Jack began.

"We'll go up on horses. It's the only way to get there,

I'm afraid," Thorn said. "If any of your party can't ride…"

"Don't be silly." Richard chuckled. "Ben and Sissy and I grew up on horses, and Julie rides like a native."

"Trilby doesn't, though," Thorn observed.

"I can learn," she said curtly.

"Indeed you can," he replied, watching her. "I'll teach you."

She had visions of that, of Thorn's hands on her arms, on her body as he sat behind her and held her on the horse. She felt hot. Her hand went automatically to a fan and she began to move it against the stifling heat.

"I tried to teach her," Richard said, stung by Thorn's attention to Trilby. "She's very slow—"

"That's unfair, Richard," Sissy cut in. "You were impatient and you shouted at her. You aren't a good instructor. I expect Thorn will be more patient."

"As patient as I need to be," he said, and his eyes punctuated the words, making Trilby even more self-conscious than she had been. She flushed as he stared at her.

Richard watched the byplay and was determined to throw a stick into the spokes for the manly Mr. Vance. He didn't want Trilby falling hard for that rustic rancher. He meant to make certain nothing came of the man's regard.

"Richard, you look very pensive," Julie murmured.

"Do I? I wonder why." He looked down at her and smiled. She almost purred. He was going to do something about her outrageous flirting one day, he promised himself, and see if she could make good on all those commitments her eyes were making.

* * *

They started off early the next morning, a small caravan going down the dusty road. Trilby sat uneasily in the saddle, so nervous that her horse almost bolted as the others became smaller and smaller in the distance.

"Here, this won't do, little one," Thorn said gently. He dismounted, reached up, and plucked Trilby from the saddle. He carried her to his own horse while she clung to him, oblivious to the faint curiosity in the eyes of his men as they rode past.

"What—what are you doing?" she faltered.

"I'm going to take you up in front of me. Don't fidget. You'll upset Randy."

"Who's Randy?"

"My horse." He eased her up into the saddle and quickly mounted behind her. His lean arms came around to take the reins, and she felt the immense power of his whipcord body behind her as he guided the big bay gelding onto the trail that led to the mountains. His arm contracted around her waist to hold her securely. "All right?" he asked in her ear.

She felt her heart beating and wondered if he could. "Yes," she whispered.

His mouth eased just under her ear and against her neck where the pulse beat wildly. "You smell of flowers, Trilby," he breathed. "Sweet and fragrant."

Her body trembled in his embrace as she struggled with incredibly powerful longings. "Thorn," was all she could manage.

His lean hand opened and pressed deeply into her stomach, pulling her back against him in an intimacy she should have railed against. But all she could do was moan and shiver a little at the feel of his body.

"My God!" he ground out. He sucked in his breath, maddened by the submission. "What a time to give in to me, Trilby!"

"I'm not…giving in," she managed huskily. But her eyes were closed and she was throbbing all over.

He spurred his mount and dashed up to the rest of the party, a man driven by desires he could neither satisfy nor indulge.

Julie and Richard were trotting side by side, talking all the way. Sissy was riding, very sedately, next to Ben.

"Naki didn't come with you?" Trilby asked when she trusted her voice again.

"He's already at the camp, scouting around. You do know that he's infatuated with Sissy?"

"And she with him," she agreed. "But it's all right. Sissy is a good girl."

"Sure she is. But Naki is a man. All man. And he isn't more than human. He wants her. Make sure you keep her with you as much as possible. I don't know if either of them realizes it yet, but there's a very powerful physical chemistry growing there. Alone in the woods, nothing would stop them."

"They're adults," she said slowly.

"So are we," he whispered, and pulled her closer to him. "And do you want to pretend that you aren't hot and cold all over with my body this close to yours?"

She swallowed, her eyes closing as he drew her back against him yet again. "You…mustn't," she choked.

"I must," he said through his teeth. "God, Trilby, I'm in agony, can't you tell?"

"It isn't…me," she said, wounded. "You think I'm something I'm not. You—you still don't believe that I haven't been a loose woman."

"That has nothing to do with what I feel," he denied. "Trilby, I know you aren't what I first suspected. I've told you that a dozen times!"

"But you treat me that way!"

"I treat you as if I want you," he said, his breath hot and unsteady. "I do. It's not because I think of you as a loose woman. It's because I want you with every part of me. I dream about being with you, completely with you. You're in my very blood, Trilby."

The arm holding her was faintly unsteady, and she was frightened of the emotion it betrayed. She wanted to kiss him so much that it was almost painful, but she couldn't—didn't dare—give in to it. It was sinful to want this sort of thing outside marriage. "It's wrong to feel like this," she said tautly. "It's bad, Thorn."

"It is not," he replied, his voice as strained as her own. "I've tried to tell you ever since the fiesta that it's not wrong. What we feel for each other is rare. Why can't you accept it?"

"I...love Richard," she whispered.

"Richard is a habit," he said coldly. "One you're about to lose your taste for, once you discover that he belongs to his cousin."

"He doesn't!"

"Open your eyes and see. They're inseparable. He'd die if she asked him to. Perhaps he doesn't realize it yet, but she has him in her dainty little hands."

He was right. She knew that he was, but Richard was her only protection against what she was feeling for Thorn.

"But they're cousins," she reasoned.

"And surely you know that cousins can marry," he replied.

"I don't want to discuss it."

"That's right, Trilby, bury your head in the sand. But what is building between us won't be denied much longer. I know it. And so do you."

She did know, but she wouldn't admit it. She held her body stiffly and didn't give an inch all the way up into the mountains.

It was cool and dark and tree-studded near the stream where they pitched camp. It was high enough, too, to be defensible if they needed to defend it. Trilby wasn't supposed to know that. She'd overheard Thorn discussing it with Mosby Torrance, who'd gone along despite Jack Lang's protests that he was too old.

The tents for the women were pitched near the fire, while the men put theirs up in a ring around the inner circle. It would afford more protection if they got in a tight spot.

"You didn't want to bring us," Trilby remarked to Thorn after the cowboys had prepared a wonderfully filling meal of beef stew and biscuits over the open campfire.

Thorn was sprawled on the blanket that covered his saddle, his hat off, his spurs and chaps tossed beside him. But he was still wearing his sidearm.

"Damned right, I didn't want to come up here with Mexico seething to blow apart just down the road," he agreed, half listening to the Mexican with the guitar who was serenading the rest of the party. Naki wouldn't come into the camp at all, and Sissy had noticed and been hurt by it. Not only that, he ignored her completely around the others and acted as if he'd been insulted when she spoke to him once. Since then, her friend had been withdrawn and morose.

"Then why did you agree to bring us here?" Trilby asked.

He turned his head to where she sat perched on a small boulder, watching him. "Because I didn't like the way you were looking at Bates," he said bluntly. "He's a city boy. A fop. You think you want him because he's the only single man you've known. But I'm here now, and I want you."

She flushed. "I don't want you, Mr. Vance," she said.

His dark eyes glittered into hers and there was a faint, mocking smile on his lean face. "The hell you don't," he said softly.

She averted her eyes with a shocked, heated gasp and then refused to look at him again. She wandered back to the rest of the group on shaky legs and sat beside a subdued Sissy while the Mexican sang of broken hearts and wistful dreams.

Chapter Eleven

Sissy went to the creek to get water for more coffee, her mind not quite on what she was doing. It was cold at night, this late in November, and there were thick clouds drifting overhead. More than likely it was going to rain. Somehow, it seemed appropriate for that to happen. She felt like a rainy day inside.

As she bent to rinse the dark blue–speckled metal pot in the swift-running water and then fill it, she heard something. It was a musical sound, haunting and lovely in the stillness. The Mexican with the guitar was still playing in the distance, but this was close. Very close.

She got to her feet and listened. The sound came closer. She lifted the pot and moved down the wooded path away from the stream. As she approached a spreading paloverde tree, she made out a tall human form leaning against it.

Naki had a colorful blanket around his shoulders and he was playing, of all things, a flute. He was playing it quite well, too.

She was stung by his earlier behavior and started to march right past him, but he moved into her path.

"Am I supposed to be flattered that, having ignored me completely all day, you've decided to play a flute for me tonight?" she asked stiffly.

He smiled faintly. "It is our way not to notice women when others are present. Didn't you know?"

She held the coffeepot tighter. It was cold against her breasts. "A—a custom?"

"That's right. Men and women don't even look at one another in camp. Any display of affection or attention toward the opposite sex is considered bad manners."

"Oh."

"You didn't know." He nodded. "You have a great deal to learn." He moved toward her, his steps faintly menacing. He looked very alien in the fading light, tall and powerful and overwhelming. "Apache men stop bathing together when they leave boyhood behind. Even when we go swimming, we always wear a breechclout. Modesty, shyness, these are Apache."

She looked up as he reached her. "And…the flute?"

"Lovemaking," he said softly.

She flushed. Her skin seemed to go hot. The hands holding the coffeepot were numb.

He handed her the flute and took the coffeepot away, setting it gently on the ground. He opened one side of his blanket.

"Is that…meaningful?" she asked hesitantly. "That gesture?"

"Very," he replied.

She stepped under his arm without further prompting, and he enclosed his arm, and the blanket, around her shoulders.

"Now what?" she whispered, thrilling to the warm strength of his body so close. She felt safe and secure and adored.

"Now we can talk, until we're discovered," he answered. "Or I can play for you."

She handed him the flute and smiled.

The music was soft and slow, and she knew that she'd remember it all her life. There should have been stars or at least a full moon, but there was only the cloudy night and the faint mist of rain that began to fall.

She didn't care if she drowned. She'd been transported to another place, another time. She closed her eyes and laid her cheek on his shoulder.

"Alexandra."

"Yes?" she whispered.

"Take your hair down."

She fumbled with hairpins until the wealth of her dark hair was tumbling in waves down over her shoulders and back. It fell to her waist.

"Yes," he said softly, touching it with the hand that held the flute. "Yes, it's lovely. You never wear it like this?"

"It…wouldn't be proper," she said hesitantly.

"Cultural taboos?"

"Perhaps."

His lean hand smoothed over it. Bravely she lifted her own fingers to his thick hair and touched it, fascinated with its cool cleanness, its length. He bent and brushed his cheek over hers.

"Apaches…don't kiss, do they?" she whispered.

"Never after marriage. Rarely before." His mouth eased toward hers. "But I was married to a Mexican woman, and she loved to kiss me. She taught me how."

The last words went into her mouth. His hard lips had covered hers and his arms folded her completely against his broad chest. She stiffened a little and caught her breath.

He lifted his head. "You haven't done this before?"

She swallowed. "Well…no, actually," she confessed. Her big eyes met his. "You see, I'm not pretty, and I'm educated."

He smiled gently. "Is it offensive to you, to have my mouth on yours?"

Her body tingled. "Oh, no. No."

His hand found her face and his thumb tilted her small chin. "If I kiss you softly, will it make you less afraid?"

"I'm…not afraid," she said unsteadily. "Really, I'm not."

"Apache women are chaste," he whispered. "Like you…"

She welcomed him this time. His mouth was hard and warm and moist, and she very much liked the way it felt when he increased its slow, deep pressure on her lips. Her hands clutched at his shirt and she made a tiny sound.

His hands tangled in her hair even as her own were burrowing up through his to the strong nape of his neck. Her body began to tremble with a strange, throbbing sort of pleasure. She wanted to get closer to him, but he was already holding her so firmly that she could feel his chest flattening her soft breasts.

He lifted his head quite suddenly. The feel of her body weakened him. His legs were trembling because he wanted her so badly. But this couldn't happen. He could no sooner dishonor her than he could fly.

He moved her chastely back to his side and pulled

that blanket back around them. His breath was unsteady as he began to play the flute again, but in a little bit it calmed. Sissy trembled as she clung to him. It took a long time until her heartbeat calmed.

"What is this called?" she asked finally, indicating the way they were standing.

He gave it an Apache sound. "Courting, you whites call it," he translated. "It's very circumspect. Usually."

"As I said, I haven't kissed anyone before."

"Yes. I noticed," he replied dryly.

"I'll be better once I learn how," she replied, her tone faintly wounded and defensive.

"You're quite good at it already, but in the interest of your continued purity, we have to stop doing it now."

"Oh!"

He looked down at her. "Have I shocked you? These things aren't usually discussed. Do you understand what can happen when a man and woman who find each other attractive spend too much time alone?"

"I'm not that stupid," she said, swallowing.

He sighed wearily. "We find ourselves in an impossible situation, as it is. I don't want to increase the burden by doing something unconscionable." He tilted her face up. "Alexandra, no matter what happens, there can never be a child… There must never be one."

She winced because the thought hurt her, but she nodded bleakly.

"It is not my wish," he added. "But a child who belongs to both cultures belongs to neither. This mixing of races is not a good thing."

"Then why did you gather me into your blanket?"

"I meant the mixing that produces children," he specified. He searched her eyes, trying to see them in the darkness. "I find you unbearably attractive."

"I feel the same," she whispered.

He groaned softly and laid his cheek atop her dark hair. "It is hopeless."

"I know." But she didn't move away, and he didn't let go. She clung to him, safe in his arms, while the mist feathered her skin.

The heavy rain came later, after Sissy had reluctantly left Naki and gone to bed. Trilby was almost asleep when the tent where she slept alone suddenly began to leak on the side where she was lying. She and Sissy had been supposed to share a tent, when at the last minute Julie threw a fit and insisted that Sissy share with her. Trilby was left alone, which she began to think was part of Julie's strategy to unnerve her.

She was soaked. She'd slept in her long split skirt and middy blouse, and she couldn't face the thought of staying in wet clothes for the rest of the night. She opened her case and took out fresh things, but she had no place to change. The water was pouring in.

Thinking that she might make her way to Sissy and Julie's tent to change, she blundered out in the dark. A tall shadow loomed up, and she almost shrieked in fear.

"What the hell are you doing out here?" Thorn demanded. "Why aren't you asleep?"

"I'm soaking wet, that's why," Trilby muttered. "I must have accidentally rolled into the side."

"I hardly think so," he said tautly. "Come with me. I seem to have inadvertently become part of the plan. That being the case, I'll help things along."

"I don't understand…." She panted as he dragged her along with him through the rain.

"You will."

She expected him to stop at Sissy's tent, but he didn't. He continued to the outer rim, where Richard's was pitched, and stopped. There was a lamp on inside it, with two shadows close together and murmurs becoming louder by the minute.

It was Richard's tent. There were only three women in camp. Sissy was his sister and Trilby was here with Thorn, which meant that it could only be Julie in there with him.

She was so miserable that she didn't realize where Thorn was taking her until they were warmly cocooned in his tent.

She stood clutching her dry clothes, slightly damp by now, her big gray eyes wide with what felt like betrayal.

Thorn took off his hat and slicker and tossed them aside. His dark eyes bit into Trilby's in the darkness of the tent as he lit a match and looked at her face.

"The tragedy queen," he scoffed. "Now you know, don't you? I'm certain you were meant to. I saw someone moving around, which is why I got up. Obviously your friend Julie started your tent leaking to bring you outside, so that you'd catch her with Richard. By now, of course," he added bluntly, "I'm certain she's back in her own tent laughing her head off."

She felt her face grow hot with muted anger. "Oh!"

He blew out the match. "Are you shocked that she's fighting so hard to keep him? Don't you know how painful it can be to want someone the way she wants your languid beau?"

"I don't know what you mean—!"

He reached for her, covering her mouth with his even as the words started to escape.

She gasped, but he paid no attention to her struggles. They grew quickly weaker as the powerful arms closed around her, riveting her to the length of him. He was warm and strong, and the mouth devouring hers was expert. She made a sound.

"You want this as much as I do. Stand still, Trilby. Don't make noise," he whispered unsteadily, his mouth teasing hungrily at her soft lips. "Don't make a sound, or someone might hear us even above the rain."

He lifted her closer and began to kiss her again. The pleasure he gave her was much too thorough and drugging to leave any room for argument. She went soft in his arms and began to kiss him back. Somewhere in the middle of the endless pressure against her mouth, she felt him ease her to the ground. She didn't protest. What he was doing to her was much too sweet. She loved the way he was kissing her. He was slow and tender and very thorough, and she ached for more.

Even when she felt his body move over hers, she didn't make a sound. He was heavy, but the weight of him in some strange way eased the throbbing ache of her body. She shifted a little to bring him against her where she hurt the most and she gasped at the unfamiliar feel of a totally aroused male body.

She hadn't known that men changed like this, or how it happened. She felt the hardness of his body without really understanding what it meant. But it threatened her and she stiffened a little.

His only reply to that telling gesture was to kiss her again and very slowly ease one of his long, jean-clad legs between hers, imprisoned in the long split skirt.

The faint rhythm of it made her feel oddly tense, but it was a warm, sweet, addictive kind of tension that she quickly began to enjoy. She caught her breath and her hands clutched at him, telling him without words that she didn't want him to stop.

He smiled against her mouth and kissed her again. His mouth was slow now, without any urgency. But it was a terrible kind of tenderness that he was giving her, and his body began to tremble as time stretched by. His hands were gentle on her slender body, not offering to become invasive just yet. But the way he touched her made her want them to.

As his lean fingers played around her rib cage, her body arched up to them in a slow, helpless rhythm. She knew what the touch of them would do to her breasts, and she wanted it. She wanted him to feel the softly mounded flesh, to touch it. She wanted him to peel away her bodice and touch her hot skin, so that it might cool. She wanted him to open his mouth and place it over her nipple....

Even as she thought it, she felt the air on her skin as his warm mouth found its way to the place she wanted it. She shivered and clung to him. The rain beat down on the tent and made a noise that drowned out her helpless cries of passion.

He was whispering something, his voice heated and urgent. She felt his hands on her skin, making the ache go away. His chest was cool against her hot breasts, and it was hairy. The hair tickled, but she didn't mind because he was kissing her in a new way, deeply and hotly so that she shivered with sensation.

His body was against hers, too, but something was different....

Seconds later, she realized what it was. But by then, it was too late. His hands held her firmly while his bare legs suddenly went between her own and he pushed down. He went inside her body, actually inside it, in a stark invasion of herself that she'd never even imagined! All her reading hadn't prepared her for the intimacy of a man's naked body over her own, for the reality of sexual possession.

She cried out against his hard mouth in shock and amazement, and then in pain, as the rhythm made him groan and whisper ardently against her ear while his body tore away the protective barrier of her maidenhead and possessed her utterly.

Chapter Twelve

"Thorn! You...can't!" she gasped.

But he could, and did. He was helplessly driving for satisfaction, blind with need and beyond words. He groaned and his body clenched as he felt the petal-soft envelopment of himself trigger an explosive urgency. He held her under him and pushed blindly, rhythmically, over her until he was able to satisfy his agonizing need of climax.

When he felt it, his mind went completely blank except for a blinding white pleasure that lifted him, arched him, into the cradle of Trilby's softness.

"Oh...my...God!" His voice shivered reverently.

He held it, only for a second, and collapsed, devastated, onto her.

She wept hotly, because she knew, couldn't help but know, that he'd achieved paradise. But for her, the climb had been painful and unfulfilling. She felt cold, with the sweat on his chest cold against her breasts in the night air...while his body still throbbed in the aftermath of satisfaction and he gasped for air to breathe. Her secret places hurt, felt as if they'd been torn. He was heavy on her and his body was cold, and there was an uncomfortable wetness…there.

He felt the tears as he turned his head and began to kiss her face with lazy tenderness.

"Please," she whispered miserably. "Let me go."

"No, little one," he murmured gently. "Not yet."

His lean hand slid up her bare thigh and between their bodies. His mouth slowly found hers, tenderly parting it while his fingers moved down and began to touch open nerves.

She gasped and pushed at him. But even as she feverishly protested the stark intimacy, he touched her body in a way that made it suddenly his. Her fingers curled into his hard arms as the sweet, dark pleasure washed over her body. She gasped again, but this time she didn't push.

"I know," he whispered. "It hurt and you're disappointed. But this time, I promise, it won't hurt. See how this feels, sweetheart?" he asked huskily, as his hand moved on her and she moaned and shivered. "Isn't it good, Trilby? Doesn't it make you want more? And I can give you that…."

Seconds spun into minutes; she began to bite at his mouth, pulsating with the rhythm and the sharp pleasure and the building tension that was magical and hellishly, shamefully, satisfying.

Her fingernails bit into his arms. She couldn't see his face, but she could hear his breathing. Like hers, it was ragged and quick. She knew that as long as she lived, she'd remember the sound of his breathing mingling with hers while the rain beat down on the thick canvas

over them in a tattoo no softer than her whispered cries
of pleasure.

"Oh…please, Thorn," she choked, her voice a thin
whimper as she writhed against the fabric beneath them.
Wanton sensations weakened her, held her at a peak of
tension that was devastating. "Please…please…make
me…whole…"

"Soon." He breathed the word into her mouth. "We
mustn't go too fast. It must be slow and take a long time,
so that your body will be ready to accept mine when I
take you again."

The words went through her like ecstasy. She dug
her fingers into his back, wanting him. She whispered
it into his ear, barely able to get the words out through
her thick tongue.

His mouth moved down to her breasts. He nibbled at
them, suckled and touched them with his tongue while
he pleasured her. It would almost have been enough
with the sudden urgency that made her guide his hand
in a wanton demand that would shock her afterward.
But now it was only important to end the torment and
the tension, to get past the barrier that blocked her surrender to pleasure. Only a little…more. A little… more.
She shivered suddenly and harsh little cries pulsed out
of her throat as the ecstasy overwhelmed her and she
went rigid.

At that instant, he went into her, and she saw stars
behind her open eyes. There was no pain, no future, no
past, only the invasion of this man's body into hers and
the convulsive passion that left her totally at his mercy
while he buffeted her welcoming hips until she shuddered and lost consciousness.

He held her for a long time afterward, gently

smoothing her hair, her yielded, soft body in his arms while the rain saturated the earth around the tent. He made no move to dress, nor did she. The reality of their loving was too astonishing.

"I…must go back…to my tent, Thorn," she whimpered. Tears rolled down her cheeks.

He kissed away the tears. "You mustn't cry, sweetheart," he whispered. "You gave me your virginity." His voice was deep against her ear. "I felt you give it to me, Trilby," he moaned. "I felt it."

She gasped. His mouth covered hers, and she wanted him again. It was incredible. Her body was sore, but it demanded. She shivered and pulled at him, her hands urgent as they smoothed with helpless need over his slender flanks.

"No," he whispered. "No, Trilby. Not again. We dare not. It would hurt you now."

She sobbed, but he held her and rocked her, cradling her in his arms until she quieted.

"You must marry me," he said finally. "You realize that, don't you?"

"Thorn…"

"I may have given you a baby, Trilby," he whispered into her ear.

Her breathing stopped. She lay in the darkness, in his arms, and tried to imagine how it would feel to bear his child.

She laid her cheek against the hard throb of his hair-matted chest and realized only then just how badly she'd burned her bridges. Yes, there could be a child. And they were not married.

"Oh…oh, dear," she began unsteadily.

"Trust me," he whispered roughly. "Stop fighting me.

I want you more than my own life. I can give you everything you want, everything you need. Marriage isn't the end of the world—and now we have no choice," he said solemnly.

"No choice," she repeated, sick at heart. Now there was no hope of finding happiness with Richard, even if she had fooled herself into believing he might notice her with Julie around. She could never have Richard now. Thorn had made her into something not quite ladylike. He'd shown her a dark side of herself that shocked her.

Thorn was having his own thoughts. He had Trilby now—*and* access to the water on her father's land. And with it, he had the most incredibly sensual experience of his life. Imagine feeling like that with a virgin! All his plans had worked themselves out, with no conscious effort on his part. But he'd taken Trilby's choices away, and she was crying. He didn't feel very proud of himself.

"Samantha can be your flower girl," he began. "And if Sissy would like to stay for the wedding, she can be maid of honor. Would you like that?"

She bit her lip with nervous fear. Samantha. Marriage. Babies. But Thorn hadn't once mentioned love. He'd only said that he wanted her. And like an idiot, she'd let her emotions run away with her. She'd...lain with him!

"It must be soon," he added quietly. "Very soon."

She flushed. "Oh...my," she whispered unsteadily.

He kissed her forehead with breathless tenderness. "Stop trying to sound like a fallen woman. We're going to be married, Trilby. We made love to each other, but the world isn't going to end. All right?"

"All right," she echoed dully. He meant to be comforting, but he wasn't. She felt like a fallen woman. The things he'd said to her…and she'd said them back! She flushed and scrambled out of his arms to dress.

After a minute, he followed suit. When they were clothed again, she felt even more ashamed of her lack of principles. He escorted her out of the tent, her arm clasped tightly in his lean hand. He lit a lamp for her and took her to the spare tent they'd fixed for the equipment.

"It will be dry, at least," he said.

She looked up at him for the first time since they'd been together. He looked different. Younger. More vital. Without the hardness, the stoic expression she'd grown used to. He looked uncomfortable. She grimaced inwardly as she wondered if perhaps he was regretting their abandonment as much as she was. He didn't look happy, certainly. Perhaps he hadn't really wanted to marry her. But he was an honorable man, and they'd let their emotions carry them to the point of no return.

He had her promise to marry him, despite what she thought she felt for Richard. Now he was sorry that he hadn't proposed honorably. She'd always feel trapped. And what if she really did love Richard? He'd have robbed her of any chance for happiness. It had seemed so right. Now it was anything but right. He could have cursed his impetuousness, his selfishness.

"Try not to worry," he said quietly. "We'll have a good life together, Trilby. I'll take care of you and your family. I swear, you'll have no cause for regret."

But she would, she thought miserably. Because there was only desire between them. He didn't love her. And there was still Richard. Even if he'd betrayed her with Julie, he'd been her world for such a long time. She was sick with confused emotions—and guilt and shame.

He read the worry in her face. "Try not to hate me," he said quietly.

"It was my fault, too, Thorn," she said hesitantly. She didn't know what she felt. She'd been raised to believe that women endured the foul lusts of men only to get children. Now she knew that it was only a myth, that women could have pleasure, too. It shocked her.

His hands contracted around hers as he searched her eyes. "You can't back out," he cautioned. "We can't let our people suffer for our error, if there are consequences."

"You already have Samantha," she began, seeing a whole new set of complications developing.

"I won't mind more than one child," he said. "I don't think you will, either. Once this camping trip is over, we must apply for a license and find a minister."

"Samantha may not like me," she persisted.

"Samantha adores you. Don't look for trouble," he added stiffly. He averted his eyes. It was difficult to face her now, with the passion that had exploded between them abruptly cooled. He'd never touched Sally like that. He'd never once wanted her so badly that he couldn't stop. But Trilby had almost demanded him. He still tingled from the ecstasy he'd known with her.

"I'll go in now," she said shyly. Her body was sore. She felt ashamed. She searched his face and let her eyes stray to his shirt. He hadn't quite buttoned it all the way, and a goodly part of his broad, hair-roughened chest was visible. She averted her eyes quickly when she realized how it was affecting her to look at him. It disturbed her that she was so receptive to him physically. She'd always thought that she was rather cold. Now she discovered the buried sexuality in her body and was frightened and repelled by it.

"I must go in," she repeated nervously.

"You'll be comfortable and dry in here," he said. "Sleep well, Trilby. If it helps, I'm sorry I let things go so far."

He sounded as troubled as she felt, and he looked unapproachable.

"So am I," she said stiffly. "Good night."

He nodded curtly and left her without even looking back.

She went into her tent, weary with pleasure and sadness, and closed the flap.

Thorn stood outside for a long moment, wavering. He should never have let it happen. The look on her face was going to haunt him. He'd done nothing but hurt her since the day they'd met. He wished he knew why he reacted as he did to her. His behavior with Trilby was inexplicable. Almost as if he loved her. He scoffed at that. He was growing fanciful in his old age, he thought as he went back to his own tent.

Trilby hardly slept. When morning came, she felt dragged out and guilt-ridden. Julie looked wounded, and Richard was morose and unapproachable. When Julie went toward him, he actually walked away, leaving his pretty cousin in tears.

Julie didn't know that he'd lost his respect and affection for her in one night. By offering to give in to him, she'd given him the impression that she was any man's for the taking. And a man of the world, of his social class, certainly didn't marry a woman who was experienced or easy.

He glanced at Trilby and felt sorry for the way he'd

ignored her in Julie's favor since he'd come out here. Trilby was the kind of girl a man married and cherished. You wouldn't find her rooting around a man's tent in the middle of the night asking to be taken. Yes, Trilby was just his sort, and it wasn't too late to put things right. Julie could rant and rave if she liked, but no one would pay her much attention. He no longer wanted her. And he didn't particularly care if she knew it.

When they gathered around the campfire for breakfast, Richard seated himself next to Trilby and addressed himself to caring for her needs.

"I've been rotten to you, haven't I?" he said quietly. "I'm sorry, Trilby. I was infatuated with Julie, but I've had my eyes opened," he added, with a vicious glare in Julie's direction.

Julie flushed and looked away. She'd never dreamed that Richard would react as he had to her impulsive gesture. All she'd meant to do was let Trilby hear them together. And it had been so sweet to kiss him, too. But he'd actually thrown her away once Trilby was past and ordered her out of his tent. Such cheap behavior told him what Julie truly was, he spat at her, and he wanted no part of a hussy.

She'd gone back to the tent she shared with Sissy and cried herself to sleep. At least Sissy didn't know what was going on. She'd been soundly asleep. But Trilby knew, she had to, and Julie hated the pity in the other girl's eyes as much as she hated Richard's sudden attention to her.

Trilby could guess how he'd had his eyes opened, but it wasn't the sort of thing a woman could say to a man. She directed her attention to her plate and forked scrambled eggs into her mouth. Everything she thought she'd felt for Richard had died a quick death.

Thorn had gone to help attend to the horses. When he came back and found Richard sitting beside Trilby and apparently on good terms with her, he could have cursed.

With a savage anger, he cleaned and loaded his rifle, keeping well away from the rest of the group. Trilby noticed his absence and began to feel that their intimacy had completely killed his interest. He might have decided that he didn't even want to marry her, and that was terrifying. If she became pregnant what would she do? She would be ruined.

As the day progressed, Thorn continued to ignore her, except for a glare now and again. She didn't credit Thorn with jealousy of Richard's sudden interest in her. She assumed because he was glaring at her that he held her in contempt now for her behavior of the night before. Her own guilt compounded the situation, and she began to avoid him, too. Which, of course, made a bad situation worse.

The men went off by themselves to hunt in the afternoon. Sissy and Trilby were left with a subdued, wounded Julie, who wouldn't speak and kept to herself in her tent.

Trilby reluctantly told Sissy what had happened.

"They were together all night?" Sissy asked.

"I don't know if they were or not, honestly. I'm almost certain that Julie did something to my tent to make it leak. Thorn came to see about me and we both heard her with your brother. I don't know if anything happened, but Richard seems very angry with her this morning."

"Now you see what my dear brother is really like, don't you?"

Trilby nodded. "I'm afraid so."

"Finally," Sissy said.

"I'm going to marry Thorn. At least, I think I am. He asked me."

"Congratulations! Thorn will take care of you."

Trilby shrugged. "He doesn't love me. Thorn, I mean. I don't think any man I've ever known has loved me. But Thorn is well-to-do and we get along. I expect we'll settle."

"Do you love him?" Sissy asked gently.

Trilby looked at her bleakly. "That doesn't matter."

"But of course it does."

She studied the other woman. "Where did you vanish to last night after supper?"

"I was being serenaded. Didn't you hear the flute?" Sissy asked, with forced cheer.

"The flute?"

She nodded. "It's an Apache custom." Her face fell and all her pretended gaiety dropped away. "I don't know what we're going to do. He feels just as I do, but we live in a world that doesn't encourage people from different races to fall in love."

"You poor dear."

Sissy sighed. "I have the worst luck, don't I?"

"But he was ignoring you yesterday."

Sissy smiled at her. "Another custom. They're a fascinating people. I told him that Dr. McCollum was one of my professors. He was impressed. I'm going to take another archaeology course in the spring, and if I do, I can come back out here with my class. We solicited pledges from our families to pay for the trip. We'll get to stay for a whole two weeks. I'll get to see him again," she said huskily, already feeling the pain of parting.

"See?" Trilby asked gently. "You have something to look forward to."

"Oh, yes. Except that I have to say goodbye first," the other girl said, subdued. "I don't know how I can. I love him," she whispered fiercely. "Trilby, I love him so much!"

Trilby didn't know what to tell her. She hugged the other girl warmly, comfortingly, but her concern about Sissy showed in her troubled eyes.

"Here, now," Trilby said after a minute, diverted from her own woes by Sissy's. "Let's clear away the dishes. I'll get some water from the stream."

Sissy dried her eyes and forced herself to smile. "Okay."

Richard was as wild a man with a hunting rifle as Thorn had ever seen. Even Ben was nervous of his brother, dodging as the older man shot haphazardly into the brush.

Thorn caught the barrel and threw it up just in time to spare one of the men a bad wound as Richard's unplaced shot was aimed at him.

"Watch yourself," Thorn said shortly. "If you continue this carelessness, I'll relieve you of that rifle."

Richard was indignant. "Like hell you will, sir!"

Thorn didn't blink. "I won't have my men shot. If you don't secure that rifle, I'll secure you." His hand dropped menacingly to the butt of his handgun. He didn't say another word. He didn't have to. The gesture was explicit.

Richard laughed nervously. "You're joking, of course."

"No."

"I wouldn't have shot anyone, for God's sake!"

"I'm glad to hear it. Shall we get on?"

The Westerner moved away with his own rifle in his free hand, his easy stride as menacing as that sidearm. Naki, who was standing nearby, gave Richard a cold stare before he turned and went along with Thorn to continue tracking their quarry.

"Surely to God, he wouldn't have shot me!" Richard whispered to Ben.

Ben wasn't certain of that. "You'd better be careful where you point that thing next time," he said quietly. "Mr. Torrance told me about Thorn Vance. Yes, he'll use the gun if he's pushed, I think. He's killed men, you know."

The older man's face went even paler. "A savage like that shouldn't be allowed loose!"

"He's a rich savage," Ben replied. "And a bad enemy. If you accidentally shoot anyone, there's no telling what he might do."

Richard got the point. He was intimidated by Thorn Vance. The older man had a sharp edge that he didn't really want to test. For the rest of the day, he was a model guest, even disguising his contempt for the Indian fellow. He wouldn't turn his back on that Apache, either, he thought angrily. He might have an enormous vocabulary, but that look in his eyes was as savage as the desert.

Only Ben got a white-tail deer that day. He threw it over his saddle and proudly rode into camp with it. The men exclaimed over its beauty and the delicious meal that it would provide. Richard drawled that the head, mounted, would look nice over the mantel back home.

Trilby didn't look at it. She was too squeamish, and she loved animals.

Sissy hugged her brother warmly and praised his skill. Julie was still in her tent. Sissy took her a plate at supper, but she wouldn't eat.

Richard knew what was wrong with her. He didn't care if she was broody. She was a grown woman and it was she who'd come to him the night before. If she wanted to play the wanton, she was welcome to the consequences. He felt no guilt.

He sat down beside Trilby and began to talk animatedly, not even sore about Thorn's treatment of him earlier. He bragged about his other hunting expeditions and the big game he'd killed, hoping to impress the men.

He didn't impress Thorn, who sat a little away with a cup of black coffee cupped in his lean hands. The rancher was as morose as Trilby. He didn't look at her or even speak to her. Eventually he went to bed after a walk about the perimeter of the camp. He didn't say good night to Trilby, a noticeable omission.

She stayed beside Richard, easing the ache in her heart with his gentle interest. Odd, she thought, that Richard had been her whole world just months before. And now he was nothing except camouflage to keep Thorn from seeing how miserable she was from his rejection.

Just as the camp settled down that night, something disrupted the peace. The rain had long since ended. Trilby had gone back to her own tent and was almost asleep when sounds of movement disturbed her.

A tall figure moved into the tent and knelt beside her. She jerked up, and a hand went gently over her mouth.

"Be quiet," Thorn said sharply, his deep voice urgent.

"Get dressed as quickly as you can. Do you know how to fire a gun?"

She shivered. "N-no," she stammered, frightened by the urgency of his tone. Light glinted from the lamp outside the tent flap and in it she spotted Mosby Torrance.

"Torrance, get the others," Thorn called over his shoulder.

"Yes, sir."

The older man moved away, but before he had she saw the glint of the steel-barreled Colt .45 in Thorn's lean hand.

"What's wrong?" she asked at once.

"Mexicans," he replied tersely. "Naki was scouting down the mountain and ran into a party of them creeping up on us. We may have to make a run for it. I hope your friends have nerve, Trilby. Everything depends on it."

"Sissy and Ben will stand fast," she said quietly. "I... don't know about the rest."

"You don't know if your beloved has nerve, is that it?" he asked coldly. "I think he'll drop to his knees and beg if he's overwhelmed, for what it's worth, but I won't let anything happen to him."

"What about Sissy?"

"Naki will protect her with his life. I think you know that already," he added.

"Richard won't like that."

"Damn Richard!" he said coldly. "Get up."

She did, still dressed, and fumbled for her shoes. She put them on quickly and wrapped up in her jacket. She was almost shaking when Thorn herded her out of the tent and into the shadows of the trees, where Mosby Torrance and a taciturn Naki had gathered the others.

"I say, this is damned inconvenient," Richard was muttering. "I don't hear a thing."

"You won't, until your throat's been cut," Thorn assured him. "These men are revolutionaries and they're desperate. They have nothing. If they can capture one of you and hold you for ransom, believe me, they'll do it."

"Can't the army do something?" Ben asked.

"There isn't enough of it to cope with the numbers of revolutionaries," Thorn told them. "It's a long border. Come on. Move quickly and as quietly as you can. We'll go down the back side of the mountain and hope that we can avoid them. If we can't, it will mean a shooting scrape, I'm afraid."

"I'll see to the women," Mosby Torrance said, gathering Julie and Sissy and Trilby together. "Don't worry," he told Thorn as he leveled his six-shooter in a steady hand. "Nothing will get past me."

"I believe it, sir," Ben said, and smiled.

"Thank God we left Teddy at home," Trilby said softly. "I'd hate him to be here."

"He'll curse because he isn't." Torrance chuckled. "Come on, ladies."

Sissy threw one worried, distraught glance at Naki, but she knew he wouldn't return it. Custom was too deeply ingrained in him. With a silent prayer for his safety, she followed the others.

Naki had a huge knife in a belt around his narrow waist and a rifle in one lean hand. Looking at him, Thorn thought that it was easy to see why early settlers grew nervous at the mention of the word *Apache*. In his high-topped fringed moccasins and breechclout, his was a savage appearance. He was wearing a shirt, but it hardly detracted from his fearsome countenance. When they'd known it was going to come down to a fight, he'd dipped a finger into a pouch at his belt and brought it out with a smear of red color, so that now his face was painted with a red jagged lightning bolt, the red matching the color of the band of cloth around his head. He was as disturbing as the situation.

"How many?" Thorn asked the Apache.

"At least ten," Naki replied quietly. "All mounted."

"You came back into camp alone, didn't you? Maybe you led them here!" Richard accused wildly.

Naki turned to the blond man with resigned irritation. "Mr. Bates, even an ignorant savage would be hard-pressed to justify helping his employer into the hereafter."

Richard flushed. It was disconcerting to hear an Indian using such precise English. The man didn't even have an accent!

"Can we outrun them?" Ben asked.

"On these swaybacked, glorified packmules you're riding?" Naki asked disbelievingly.

Thorn glared at him. "Go ahead. Insult my horses."

"I thought I just did," Naki replied. "Despite the… ah…inexperience of your guests, proper mounts would have been wiser."

"Is it my fault that some of them would have fallen off proper mounts in less than five minutes?" the rancher growled. He popped his sidearm back into his holster with unnerving precision. "Let's get going. Ben, you and Richard catch up with Torrance, please, and cover his retreat."

"And where will you be?" Richard drawled sarcastically.

Thorn smiled. It wasn't a pleasant smile, either. "Naki and I will welcome the visitors into camp."

Richard scoffed at that, but he went with the others. When they caught up with Torrance, he moved beside Trilby and took her arm, for all appearances her sole protector. Thorn glared down at him, but this was no time for jealousy. He motioned to Naki and they vanished back into the trees.

"Are they really going to welcome the Mexicans, Mr. Torrance?" Sissy asked as they quickly made their way down to where the horses were tethered in a makeshift corral.

Torrance glanced at her. She was closest to him, and the others were talking among themselves. This one thought like a man, he mused, and she showed no fear. He could tell her the truth, because she could take it.

"No, ma'am, they aren't," he replied. "They'll kill as many as they can and pin down the others to give us a chance to get away."

Sissy caught her breath. She looked back up the hill, grimacing. Naki could take care of himself, she knew, but to think of him being killed was insupportable.

"The Apache is not careless, Miss Bates," Torrance said perceptively.

She turned back, flushing. "I was worried about both of them," she argued.

"Yes, ma'am. This way."

She followed him, unnerved by his quickness. Some of the people at the ranch seemed to feel that Mr. Torrance was too old to matter, but she wouldn't have written him off at all; there was more to him than what showed.

Trilby didn't look back. She was afraid that her face

would give her away. Thorn had cared enough to come and get her first, so that had to mean something. But for now, she was too worried about him to think.

"You'll be all right," Richard said, smiling. "I'll take care of you."

"You're fickle, Richard," Julie said brokenly. She didn't look pretty. She looked worn and upset.

He turned and stared into her red face. "Most men take a woman at her own valuation," he said shortly. "Women who behave cheaply demean themselves."

Julie gasped and went scarlet. "How could you! How could you say such a thing? I love you. I only wanted you to know that I love you. It isn't as if anything even happened!"

"Your behavior was intolerable," he said bluntly, and didn't back down. "You demeaned yourself, whatever your motive."

Julie buried her face in her hands and began to weep.

"That was cruel," Sissy told her brother. "You are no gentleman!"

"Who are you to discuss morals with me, when you permitted a red Indian to put his filthy hands on you?" Richard returned.

Sissy's eyes flashed furiously. "You mangy cur!" she raged.

"Please," Trilby interrupted shortly. "We're in a very dangerous situation. This is not the time to fight among ourselves."

"Trilby's right," Richard said, smiling at her to disguise the upset his sister's unexpected temper had dealt him. "Let's get back to the ranch while we can."

"I hope Thorn and Naki will be all right," Sissy said in a subdued tone.

"So do I," Trilby agreed.

With a brokenhearted Julie trailing behind, they made it to the horses—and Trilby had an anxious moment when her gentle mount almost deposited her back on the ground. But in minutes they were riding back along the dirt trail down the mountain. In the distance there was a sudden, sharp report, followed by many more. The fighting had begun. Trilby began to pray as she thought of Thorn wounded and in pain, with enemies all around him and no one to take care of him.

He has to be all right, she thought, her troubled eyes looking back the way they'd come. Please, God, he has to be all right!

Chapter Thirteen

The first shot came from behind a tree. Thorn whirled with his pistol out even as he heard it. He fired, catching a badly concealed man in ragged clothes and a faded, colorful serape in the shoulder.

"Look there!" Naki called quickly.

Three more Mexicans were rushing over the brief clearing between the rocks and the trees, their rifles firing sporadically.

Naki's rifle spoke, dropping one of the men. Thorn accounted for another. The two men dived for cover as the third Mexican began fanning his pistol.

There was a rapid-fire burst of Spanish and the sound of many more footsteps.

"Damn!" Thorn muttered, glaring at Naki. "Now see what you've done!"

"Me?" the Apache asked.

"That's right, act innocent." He reloaded his gun quickly.

"If you trip over a rock, it's my fault," Naki muttered as he peered around his boulder.

"Well, usually it is," the other man said.

A bullet *whanged* nearby and took off a shard of the boulder behind which they were crouching.

"Damned greasers," Thorn raged.

"Shame on you for resorting to racial insults."

He glared at Naki. "Bloodthirsty savage."

Naki looked skyward. "And I thought I might reform you— Look out!" He flashed the rifle around and shot over Thorn's shoulders, just in time to stop his friend from being killed by a shadowy figure in a homespun poncho. There was a groan and a thud.

"Thanks," Thorn said huskily. He was breathing hard, like Naki, adrenaline raging through his system as he spared a thought to Trilby and the others. He couldn't afford to worry about that. He had to keep his mind on what he was doing to protect them.

Naki echoed his thoughts. "We're going to be pinned down if we don't do something, and there's no guarantee they won't go after the others. Where's that cocky white Eastern peacock?"

"Now who's using racial insults?"

"Well, he is cocky," Naki said, defending himself. "I'll circle around and get behind them."

"Be quiet about it."

"I'm an Apache," Naki pointed out. "Who do you think invented being quiet?"

He was gone seconds later, vanished like a wraith in the darkness, and so quietly that not one footfall could be heard.

Naki eased through the undergrowth, using trees and boulders for shelter....

Three Mexicans were crouching behind two large boulders, trying to peer through the darkness. They gabbled among themselves and began to argue about tactics, which worked to Naki's advantage. While they were shouting at one another, they couldn't hear him.

He eased the knife from his sheath and waited, all his senses alert. His body tensed as he poised to do what was necessary to save the lives of his friend and the woman who was rapidly becoming everything to him.

One of the party threw his hand downward at the others in disgust and said that he was going to go it alone, damn them.

It would be the last thing he ever said. He reached the trees where Naki was waiting—and was quickly and efficiently sent to join his ancestors.

Naki cleaned his knife on the Mexican's pants leg and quickly donned his sombrero and poncho. He kept his head down and eased out into the open, the rifle held in his right hand as he approached the other two. They were discussing the ransom they hoped to get for the gringos they meant to kidnap, and as Naki listened stealthily it became quite clear that saving poor Mexican comrades was less important to them than stuffing their own pockets with American currency.

They wheeled and started to shoot.

"*¡Chihuahua!* It is only Juan!" one of them growled. They turned away.

"*Lo siento, compadres,*" Naki said, throwing off the sombrero, "*pero, no me llamo Juan.*"

They reacted to the voice telling them his name wasn't Juan, but too late. Naki swung the rifle into position and fired from the hip, quickly dropping both men. He hated killing, but these men would have had no hesitation whatsoever about killing his party. They were desperate.

In some way, he could understand their desperation, but he couldn't allow them to harm Sissy. His blood boiled when he thought of the Mexicans who had killed his brother-in-law Luis and his wife Conchita. Those had been *Federales,* and these were not. He had to remember that. He knew very well the plight of the poor Mexican peons, and he could sympathize with them. But these men would have taken Sissy's life. Some of the revolutionaries, as he knew, were less than honorable and not above making a profit in the cause of liberty. The thought made him vaguely nauseous.

Thorn called to him suddenly as he came into the clearing.

Naki looked up, once again the calm and educated friend of years, not the ancient Apache with his prey.

"I see you found them," Thorn said.

"Fortunately, I found them in time," he answered. He stood up and sheathed the knife.

"There were two others, but they made a run for it," Thorn told him. "I let them go."

Naki exchanged a knowing look with the other man. "It was Mexicans who killed your parents."

"Yes. But I'm no more a cold-blooded killer than you are. I'll shoot only in self-defense."

Before Naki could respond, noisy movements fell on the silence, and both whirled with their rifles leveled as Richard came panting into view with the others behind him.

"For God's sake, keep the women back!" Thorn yelled.

"Did the Apache scalp anyone?" one of the women exclaimed. Julie, of course.

"No, the Apache didn't scalp anyone," Naki said

angrily. "Apaches don't scalp people or raid wagon trains. This is 1910, for God's sake."

Trilby looked past Richard and her supper made a repeat performance. She rushed into the bushes and vomited, the sight of the dead men even in the dim light so graphic and violent that she couldn't bear it.

Sissy darted around Richard and went forward, her eyes wide and curious.

"No!" Naki said firmly, his stance as fierce as the dark eyes that found her face. "Get back."

"Don't you order my sister around," Richard growled. "Come here, Sissy," he added for good measure.

"He can't order me around, but you can?" Sissy asked haughtily, glaring at her brother. "I'm not squeamish. If they aren't dead, I know a bit of first aid."

"They're dead, all right," Naki said coldly.

Sissy knew, because he'd told her, why he had reason to hate some Mexicans. But he didn't look triumphant; he looked drawn. She wanted to go to him, but the circumstances made that impossible—and so did his unapproachable demeanor.

Her eyes ran over the ground one last time before she turned and went back to the others. Death held no fear for her; she believed in an afterlife. But she was sorry for the dead Mexicans, just the same. This wasn't the time to mention it, she decided.

"How could you look at that?" Julie choked when she rejoined the small group. "It's savage."

"I must agree," Richard said haughtily. "Was it necessary to—to butcher them?"

"They had an equal opportunity to butcher us," Naki said, without preamble, standing taller as he stared at the white man. "Would you like to know what they would have done to the women?" he added, with a cold smile.

Sissy knew already. "Richard, that's enough," she told him when he seemed disposed to argue.

"Aren't you forgetting your place?" her brother demanded.

"My place," she told him, "is wherever I choose to be. You have no rights over me and no authority. And don't you forget it."

"I shall certainly have something to say to Mother about your behavior," Richard promised her.

Her eyes flashed at him. "Do you think I care?"

"You must not," he returned, "considering the company you keep!"

Her hand flashed at his cheek, connecting with a loud crack. He touched his face and stared at her in patient astonishment.

"You hit me!" he gasped.

"I certainly did, and I enjoyed every second of it," she replied. "Now shall we go, brother, dear?"

He didn't say another word. Sissy didn't look at Naki as she walked past her brother, back the way they'd come. She was observing the Apache custom, and he had to know it. He did. He smiled secretly to himself as he joined Thorn to bury the dead Mexicans.

The men were left in shallow graves and covered with rocks. It was arduous work in the rocky ground, but no trace of them could be left for the others to find.

"We'll have to notify the army," Thorn said afterward. "This could be the start of something very unpleasant. I don't like the idea of Mexican revolutionists dancing across the border like this, despite my sympathy for their

cause. I'll bet you ten dollars to a tin bucket that they
had kidnapping on their minds."

"Yes, they did, but they weren't part of the revolutionary force. I overheard them talking," Naki said. He
told Thorn the rest of it. The other man glanced toward
Trilby, who was just getting herself back together, and
he thought vaguely that his world might have ended if
the renegades had succeeded in harming her.

They gathered the others and packed up their camp.
The hunting trip was definitely over. Fortunately it hadn't
ended in tragedy.

Trilby found herself riding beside Thorn as they
left the mountain trail and started back down the long,
winding dirt road toward the ranch. She was no better
a horsewoman now than she had been in the past, but
she couldn't bear to share Thorn's mount. He seemed to
know it, because he didn't insist.

"Are you all right now?" he asked quietly.

She was still a bit green, but as he'd once said, she
was game. "Yes," she said.

He glanced toward her with open interest. She looked
younger somehow, very fragile and vulnerable. He
wanted to scoop her up in his arms and carry her down
the mountain and keep her forever. His sense of possession was disturbing.

"I meant it about getting married," he said slowly.

"I know. But—but you don't have to—" she began.

"Don't be ridiculous. I want to." He shifted the reins
in his lean hand, his tall body rocking gracefully with
the motion of the horse. He seemed almost part of it.
Trilby, on the other hand, was bouncing all over her
saddle and barely staying on. "It's Christmas in a little

less than three weeks. We could be married before then, if you like."

"That…would be all right," she agreed finally. "Would we live at Los Santos?"

His heart lifted at her agreement. "Where else?" he asked reasonably. "It's my home; mine and Samantha's."

She felt walls closing in on her. There really was no way out. But even now, she couldn't bring herself to meet his eyes. She was shy and nervous with him, as she had been in the very early days of their turbulent relationship.

"I could go back East…." she began.

His dark eyes pierced hers. "And do what? Pretend to adopt a child, if I have really given you one? And where would you live, Trilby?"

She grimaced. "It's so difficult," she managed to say.

His face hardened as he watched her gaze ricochet off Richard, who was riding with Julie again. They hardly spoke, but he did glance at her from time to time, and she was acting like a different woman from the silly flirt who'd arrived on the train. Richard had shown what he really was, and Trilby was sick at heart thinking she could have been demented enough to think herself in love with him. Even Julie seemed to be having second thoughts. Richard might be handsome, but he was shallow and selfish.

"Because of him?" Thorn asked curtly, nodding toward Richard. "You aren't even going to be in the running when he gets his mind sorted out."

"I do know that," she said stiffly.

"Then face facts," he told her. "You and I slept together and you were a virgin. In my world, that means you marry me. We're doing the right thing to correct our mistake," he continued softly. "Doesn't that make up for it, a little?"

She lifted her wide, gray eyes to his. "This is no sudden decision on your part, Thorn. I have no idea if you planned what happened, even unconsciously. I have heard the rumors, you know."

"What rumors?" he asked slowly.

"That Los Santos has poisoned water holes here and on your holdings in Mexico and you need access to the water on our land," she said bravely. "Is marrying me not a solution to that problem?"

He nodded. "Yes, it is," he said honestly. "But you must realize that I want you. Even an innocent could hardly mistake my interest for greed."

"I do know that," she agreed. "It will mean that I can never go home again," she said, almost to herself. "I will have to stay with you." She buried her face in her hands. It was simply too much at once.

"Don't do that," he said angrily, wounded by her lack of enthusiasm for becoming his wife. It wasn't as if he asked every third woman to marry him. In fact, Sally was the only woman to whom he'd ever proposed. "It is hardly the end of the world because you have to marry me, Trilby."

"Is it not?"

His lean face set in unfamiliar lines as the insult registered. He wanted to remind her that she was as abandoned as any madam in his arms, but that would be unfair. His hands were tied now. She would marry him, but her heart still belonged to the Eastern man. How could he fight that? And more importantly, why did he want to? The question plagued him all the way home.

* * *

Lisa Morris was still in the infirmary two days later. She was better, but not quite well enough to leave. She would have to go to Mrs. Moye, and for that, she had not quite enough strength.

In the meanwhile, it was pleasant to lie and listen to a very irritable Todd Powell going about his household chores in the evening.

He grumbled as he managed to make a pot of stew. The meat was underdone and the vegetables were over-done, but the broth was at least properly seasoned. He brought a bowl of it to Lisa and wouldn't be satisfied until he spoon-fed her every drop of it.

She was too thin, he told her. In the flannel gown she wore, it was easy to tell that she had lost weight.

"Your husband sent word that he will not contest the divorce," he told her. "It appears that he intends to marry the woman in Douglas."

She nodded. "I'm not really surprised." She lay back against the pillows with a soft sigh. "It's for the best. We were little more than enemies long before I lost the baby."

He put the bowl and spoon aside and took her pulse. It was a bit fast, and he smiled at the evidence of how he affected her. He put the stethoscope around his neck and looped it up to his ears. "Cough," he instructed, sliding it under the bodice of the gown against her warm, soft skin.

She did, but the feel of his hand was making her giddy. She knew that her heart was going crazy, and that he could hear it. Her whole body clenched at the faintest brush of his fingers.

He lifted his head, suddenly aware of her nervousness.

He stared at her, but he didn't move his hand. Very slowly, almost experimentally, he moved his fingers away from the broad metal circle of the stethoscope and onto her bare breast.

She caught her breath audibly. But she didn't move. Or push at his hand. Or protest. Her eyes grew very wide and curious.

His lips parted. He stared intently into her eyes while he explored the soft curve of her breast, lingering on the sudden hardness of her nipple. He took it between his thumb and forefinger and caressed it very gently.

"Oh, my dear," he whispered roughly.

She was shaking. He couldn't help but notice it.

He withdrew the stethoscope and put it aside. His big hands went to the buttons of the flannel gown, tremulous as they hesitated there.

She put her own hands on top of them and pressed, very gently.

It took a few seconds, because he was clumsy in his need to see her, to touch her. He helped her to sit up and slowly pushed the gown down to her waist, careful not to hurt her where she was burned.

She sat there, enthralled, her eyes on her breasts as he traced them with just the tips of his big, square-tipped fingers.

She wasn't big, but she was firm and beautifully formed. It was erotic to watch Todd's hands, so gently caressing her.

"I never…enjoyed it…before," she whispered.

His eyes slid up to meet hers. "You are beautiful," he whispered. "So beautiful."

She felt the awe that was reflected in his soft eyes.

"Gently," he whispered. He eased her into the curve

of his arm and slowly bent to press his lips slowly, tenderly, to her swollen breasts, to the hard nipples. He suckled her, so gently, and his big hand cupped her, to hold her up to his hungry mouth.

Her hands, trembling, caught in his thick, straight hair and pulled. She made a helpless sound deep in her throat and shivered.

He laid her back on the pillows, feeding on her white, soft body for minutes that stretched like hours. She sighed and moaned under the heat of his mouth, giving herself to it with aching abandon.

His control became more precarious by the second. When he touched her soft thighs, he lost it.

She moaned harshly. But then she moved, just a little, just enough to encourage him. He searched her eyes for only an instant before his hard, hungry mouth bit into hers and he groaned as he touched her with complete intimacy.

She stiffened as she felt the stark bareness of him against her, the absence of fabric. She gasped.

His head lifted just a fraction from her lips. "Let me pleasure you," he whispered unsteadily. "I care for you... so much. Let me show you what it can be, what it should be."

She looked into his eyes, embarrassed. But all at once, she relaxed, giving in to the soft, slow caresses of his hands. She jerked and her face grew taut with fear and shock.

"Don't fight it, my dear," he whispered tenderly. "Oh, Lisa, don't fight me," he groaned as his hips moved down and he joined his body with exquisite tenderness to hers. He gasped at the stab of pleasure, at the first intimacy he'd allowed himself since his wife's death.

The tide of movement caught Lisa unawares and it was suddenly too late for protest. Curling waves of pleasure were emanating from the slow, stroking movement of his body. She caught at his broad shoulders, her eyes going blank, her lips parting as the tension began to build madly in her body. She'd never known these sensations, never felt as if white heat were kindling in her belly and ropes were dragging her apart with pleasure. She'd never felt this incredible fullness of possession, the expansion of her own body to accommodate it. The tension was so great that it made her panic.

"Todd!" she cried, frightened.

"Oh, yes," he whispered passionately. "Yes, yes, my darling, yes."

She arched her back and began to shudder rhythmically, tiny cries tearing out of her throat as she became nothing more than an ocean-tossed bit of flotsam, riding the crest of something far more powerful and savage than she'd ever dreamed it could be.

He was whispering in her ear, secret things, shocking things, his voice as deep and erotic as his touch. As she started up the spiral again, her last thought was that she had never known what life was until now....

Afterward he calmed her with soft words and tender caresses and held her gently while she slept. When she woke, she told herself that it had been a dream. She never mentioned it, nor did he. But when she left to move in with Mrs. Moye, she knew that when her divorce was final, she would not be long alone. And so did he.

Chapter Fourteen

Trilby couldn't talk to her mother about what had happened on the camping trip. She couldn't even talk to Sissy. Her conscience ate at her for several days, while her guests lounged around and made more work for her mother and herself. Only Sissy and Ben helped at all. Richard seemed to feel that service was his due, and Julie sulked in her room almost all the time.

Despite their joy at the news of their engagement that a strangely subdued Trilby and Thorn had given them, Jack and Mary Lang had been horrified at the news of the Mexican party attacking the young people in the mountains.

"This uncivilized place," he groaned to Mary. "I wish I'd never been so wild to come out here. Now we can't afford to go home, and it's my fault. What if Trilby and the others had been killed?"

"But they weren't, thanks to Thorn and that nice Apache man," Mary said gently. "Do stop worrying," she added, patting his arm. "It's all right now."

"Is it, though?" he wondered. "You know, there's

much talk of atrocities being committed all along the border. It reminds me of a powder keg, waiting for someone to light it."

"We're not very close to Douglas," Mary said. "I'm sure we'll be all right."

"I wish I were," he said, but he stopped worrying the point and conversation turned quite naturally to the engagement of Thorn and Trilby, about which both Mary and Jack were excited and pleased. "I must say, I never thought they'd do it," he added, grinning. "All that eternal fighting. But I daresay they'll make a go of it. It makes me proud that Trilby's done so well for herself."

Mary said, "I think Thorn has, too," and laughed at her husband's reddened face as he apologized somewhat sheepishly for undervaluing his own daughter.

Richard, Ben and Julie packed that same day in preparation for leaving the next morning.

"I really can't bear another day of this." Richard laughed apologetically. "The West just isn't my cup of tea. I long for civilized society."

"You are a snob, Richard." Sissy sighed. "Well, go if you must, but I won't miss Trilby's wedding."

"It was a rather rushed announcement, don't you think?" Richard queried.

"Thorn said that they'd planned it for a long time. They'd only decided while we were on the camping trip," Ben amended.

Richard was unpacified. "He's taking advantage of her. She should come back with us and get away from him while she can. She isn't suited to desert life."

"Any woman would be suited to life with a man like

Thorn, brother, dear." Sissy chuckled. "He'll take care of her; don't you worry."

"She was my girl first," Richard said sulkily.

"How silly, when you did nothing but flirt with Julie from the day we arrived," Sissy retorted softly, so that Julie, already packed and waiting in the living room, wouldn't overhear. "You pushed Trilby right into Thorn's arms, and I'm glad. He's twice the man you are."

Richard's face burned with rage. "I had better not hear of any assignations with that wretched Indian you fancy!" he told her.

"That wretched Indian saved your life," she reminded him. "As to my private affairs, you have no right to dictate them. I do not answer to you."

"Bah!"

"Don't forget to write. Tell Mother I'll come home after the wedding," she added gleefully, winking at Ben, who hid a smile.

"Mother will be furious!"

"No, she won't. She was in favor of my going to the university when you and Father snickered at the idea. I'll be an archaeologist one day, you wait and see."

"A woman's place is in the home," Richard said in their father's sternest voice.

"Perhaps it was. Not anymore. And once we all become educated, there'll be no keeping us at the stove all day."

"Oh, bother. Let's get packed, Ben. You can't argue with anything female," Richard said, with utter disgust.

Ben only shrugged, but the smile he gave his sister was warm and sincere.

Julie hardly spoke to anyone. She was a different woman going home, a sad shadow of her former self.

She looked at Richard with cold eyes now, as disgusted with him as Sissy and Trilby had been. But he was so thick that he didn't seem to notice.

At the station, Thorn managed to be on hand as Trilby said goodbye to the former man in her life.

He stood beside her, one arm loosely around her waist, while she shook hands politely with a gloomy Richard.

"I hope you'll be very happy, Trilby," he said stiffly, sparing a cold glance for Thorn. "Do keep in touch, won't you?"

"Oh, you'll have to come out and see us next year, when we're properly settled," Thorn said curtly. "I'll arrange another hunting trip."

"Well, yes, that would be nice," Richard replied. He held Trilby's hand a little too long for politeness and squeezed it. She'd passed beyond his reach. He was sorry that he hadn't been more forceful while there had been time. Julie had blinded him to Trilby. Now she belonged to this arch ruffian, and God knew what would become of her. "Goodbye, Trilby," he said gently. "I will miss you, you know."

She smiled through threatening tears. It wasn't sadness at losing Richard. It was the sense of letting go of the past. He was part of her childhood, her adolescence. It had always been Richard, her golden boy, in the depths of her heart. Now she was thoroughly disillusioned. Her dreams had been a silly girl's musings. Richard was nothing like her sweet image of him. She was letting go of all she'd thought she loved, replacing her dreams of love with marriage to a man who cared nothing for her beyond obtaining her father's water rights.

"Oh, my," she whispered tearfully.

Richard, conceited to the last, thought she was openly mourning his loss. He caught his breath and would have said something, but a sharp movement from Thorn and a look from jet black eyes made him back down.

"If ever you need me, I'll be within reach, Trilby," he said haughtily, and letting go of her hand, turned to stride toward the train.

Trilby could have laughed at that act of bravado, but she was too miserable. Her heart was breaking and she didn't care if Thorn saw. He'd trapped her.

He did see. But he couldn't find the right words to express what he felt. He wanted to apologize for backing her into a corner, and he wanted to throw young Richard off the train into a cactus thicket. Neither choice was practicable. It was obvious to him that Trilby loved Richard—and hated Thorn for making her love impossible.

He let her go roughly and moved away, his deft fingers rolling a cigarette while Trilby said her goodbyes to Ben and, stiffly, to Julie. Then the train was puffing away from the station and, minutes later, it was only a speck of smoke against the gray horizon.

It was cold in the wind, even for southern Arizona in December.

The wedding was held three weeks later, on another cool, dreary day. Mary and Jack had tried to talk Trilby and Thorn into waiting until the following spring to be wed, but neither of them would budge. Thorn was especially insistent about the date. Almost, Mary thought privately, as if he had some reason for hurrying. Of course, nothing could have happened out in the mountains. There were too many people to allow for indiscretion. Perhaps

it was only that Thorn loved Trilby and was afraid of
losing her to Richard. Yes, that had to be it. But…Rich-
ard had gone, along with a somber Julie and Ben, back
to Louisiana. So, why was Thorn so insistent?

The question went unanswered. Trilby stood in her
long white satin gown with a face no bride should have
shown on her wedding day, stiff and somber while she
parroted her vows like a sleepwalker. There was no joy
in either her posture or her face, and when an equally
stiff Thorn bent to kiss her, she gave him her cheek instead of her mouth.

The distance between them was stark. The reception
did nothing to lessen it, especially when Thorn's cousin
Curt came by to kiss the bride.

Trilby smiled at him, a gesture her husband had yet
to receive. "Thank you, Curt," she said softly.

"I'm really sorry for the way things began for you out
here," he said self-consciously. "I hope you and Thorn
will be happy. I really mean that."

"So do I," she managed.

Sissy stared after him curiously. "He's nice," she said.

"Yes, he is." She noticed that little Samantha looked
uneasy when Curt spoke to her, and that she quickly
went to her father's side. But Trilby was diverted by
Sissy and it went right out of her mind. She smiled at the
picture her friend made in pink ruffles and lace. "You
look very pretty," she said, noticing that Sissy had her
hair down for once.

"A certain tall gentleman likes my hair this way."
She sighed and glanced around them. "He isn't here,
of course. He's doing the polite thing and avoiding me.
Eventually I'll hear a flute sometime in the night, and
I'll creep out to stand inside his blanket while we talk

about ancient races and recite Shakespeare's sonnets to each other."

"You're not serious," Trilby exclaimed mischievously.

"Oh, but I am. It's so hopeless, Trilby," she said, the humor going into eclipse. "There's no future for us, but I can't stay away from him. Every second is precious; I have to go home tomorrow."

"You could come and stay with me," Trilby said, grasping at straws.

Sissy laughed mirthlessly. "On your honeymoon? Certainly I could." She grimaced. "Shame on you. What would Thorn say?"

"I don't care."

The other girl pressed her hands gently. "You aren't afraid of him, are you?" she asked solemnly. "I don't know much more than you do about it, but I'm a great reader. It won't hurt much, and then if you love a man, it's supposed to be very nice, despite what the older people tell you," she whispered conspiratorially.

Trilby flushed, because she knew too much already. She couldn't admit it. "I'm not afraid of him," she said, darting a glance toward her tall, dark-suited husband in a nearby group of well-wishers.

"Samantha is," Sissy noted, nodding toward the child. Samantha was standing all alone at the refreshment table, trying to look invisible. "I feel sorry for her. She's just like me at that age. You, too," she added, with a rueful smile at her friend. "Neither of us was particularly outgoing."

"I'll take good care of her," Trilby said, her heart warming as she watched the child. "She's had very little love. Her father isn't the sort of man who believes in affection."

"He might surprise you," Sissy said. "He seems very deep to me, a man who hides what he feels because he doesn't want to be hurt. He didn't have a happy marriage, did he?"

"Why, no, I don't believe he did."

Sissy nodded. "Well, this might be the best thing for both of you. Certainly you're better off with Thorn than you would have been with my brother, Trilby. I think you know it, too."

"Yes, I know it. Richard was such a big part of my life," she said slowly. "I suppose I wanted the past back so badly that I mixed it up with him."

"Certainly you're better off with Thorn. If Richard had even married you, he'd have left you at home while he chased other women. He can't even be faithful to a girlfriend. How would it be to have to put up with a man like that inside marriage?"

"It would have been terrible," Trilby confessed. "I thought I loved him once, you know," she said sadly. "It took this trip to convince me that I never did. Not really."

"You can learn to love Thorn. He's very much a man, you know," Sissy emphasized. "I don't imagine you'll have too many regrets."

"That remains to be seen." She put her hand through Sissy's arm and drew her to the punch bowl while she closed her mind to the night ahead. "Let's have some refreshments."

Later, Samantha came shyly up to Trilby, who knelt to be on a level with the child.

"I only wanted to say congratulations," Samantha

said in her quiet voice. "I'm glad you married my father. I hope you'll be very happy."

"I hope *you* will," Trilby said. "I want us to be friends."

"Will you have lots of babies, do you think?" the unsmiling child asked resignedly.

Trilby flushed. "We shan't talk about that now, all right?"

That produced a faint smile. "All right."

"We'll have lots of time to get to know each other. I'll try to be a friend to you, Samantha. Really, I will."

"Do you love my father, Miss Lang?" Samantha asked in a very wise tone. "I mean…Mother." She corrected herself stiffly.

"Wouldn't it be easier to just call me Trilby?" she asked the child, and neatly avoided answering her question.

"My father said that I have to call you Mother."

"Suppose we do that just in front of him, then," Trilby said softly, and smiled. "And when it's just the two of us, you may call me Trilby."

That brightened the dark young eyes. "All right, then."

Trilby laughed. "It will be our secret."

"Yes, indeed. Trilby, could you help me with my studies? I don't want to have to live with Uncle Curt and go to school in town," she said worriedly.

"I'm sure we can work something out," Trilby said. "I don't like the idea of having you in Douglas right now with all this border trouble. I'll talk to your father about it."

"I'm glad." She looked at Trilby with worried eyes. "I have to go home with Uncle Curt tonight. Must I?"

"I'm afraid so. Don't you like your uncle and aunt?"

Samantha closed up. "They're all right. I can come home tomorrow, they say."

Trilby started to relent until she remembered that tonight was her wedding night. Only she and Thorn knew that it wasn't going to be their first time alone together, but they could hardly advertise their indiscretion.

"Then, I'll see you tomorrow, won't I?" Trilby asked, and forced a smile.

Trilby and Thorn were kept busy saying goodbye to the guests until late. But inevitably they were alone together in the lamplit coziness of the living room with a small fire in the fireplace, sipping the last of the champagne.

After the guests had gone, Trilby had changed into a plain gray dress. She'd thought about putting on her night things, but she was too afraid that Thorn might misconstrue it as an invitation to her bed. That was the last thing she wanted right now.

He hadn't changed at all. He was wearing black trousers with a pristine white shirt and a black string tie. He'd removed his jacket, though, and already his lean fingers were unfastening the tie and shirt.

"I'm tired, are you?" he asked conversationally. "I didn't remember how wearing it was to get married."

That reminded her that it wasn't his first time to the altar. She studied the bubbles in her champagne glass. "Yes, it is wearing."

His eyes fell to the gracefully shaped glass in her hand. "Do you know why champagne glasses are shaped like that?" he asked suddenly.

She glanced at him and then studied the elegant glass. "Why, no. Why?"

He smiled faintly. "Are you certain you want to know?"

"Yes, of course," she replied quizzically.

He leaned a little forward, sensuously stroking the glass in his own hand. "They were modeled after a mold of Marie Antoinette's breasts," he said softly.

She dropped the glass. It wasn't the surprise of his answer so much as the way he was caressing his own glass and looking at Trilby's bosom.

He laughed softly at the visible evidence of her unease. He put down his own glass and got up. As he approached her, she saw the darkness glittering in his eyes, the faint sensual threat of his body.

She stood quickly. "I'd better clean this up," she began frantically.

But he scooped her up in his arms as if she had no weight. "Not until we've made love," he said huskily. He bent and began to kiss her, his mouth tasting of champagne and mint, his breath warm as it filled her mouth.

She wanted to protest, to fight, but his touch drugged her. She relented only seconds later and her arms slid shyly up to his neck. Her body trembled with delicious anticipation, remembering the last time and how glorious it had been, even in the cool damp of the tent on the hard ground. This time it would be in a warm bed with no possibility of interruptions, and they had all night.

"I've wanted you for so long, Trilby," he said unsteadily as he laid her gently on the spotless white coverlet of the bed. "You're all I dream about."

She lay there in the faint light from the kerosene lamp, her breasts rising and falling erratically as he began to remove his shirt. She was about to ask him to blow out the lamp when he pulled off the shirt and tossed it aside.

Her eyes found what her hands had long since learned about him, that he was hairy and muscular and very, very male. She was so fascinated with the lean muscle of his torso that she didn't even notice that he was unfastening his trousers.

When he began to ease them down, revealing the part of him that was all male, threateningly male, she stilled and her lips parted on a gasp.

"Now you know," he said in a softly menacing tone.

She averted her eyes, expecting amused laughter, but there was none. The rustle of fabric and the thud of heavy boots came to her ears, and then he was sitting beside her.

"The lamp, Thorn," she whispered frantically when his hands went to the fastening of her dress.

"I want it on, Trilby," he said very quietly. "I want you to see me. I want to see you, in this greatest of all intimacies."

"But…" She blushed furiously as he removed everything above her waist and eased her back down so that he could remove the rest of her underthings and slide the dress completely from her body, along with everything else.

She tried to cover herself, but his hands prevented her. After a few shocked, stifling seconds, she lay still while his eyes completed their rapt possession of her nudity.

"Thorn, please…" she began self-consciously.

"All my life, it's been in the dark," he said, his eyes on her breasts. "This time, I want to see it all, every second of it. I've never wanted anyone the way I want you." He bent and put his mouth to the very tip of her breast. He kissed it and suckled it and very quickly made it hard.

She caught her breath at the remembered pleasure.

Her hands nervously cradled his thick dark hair and she lay at his mercy, her eyes on the faint movements of his face as he experienced her.

His other hand ran slowly down her bare thighs and hips and over her flat stomach. Seconds drew into long, lazy minutes, and his mouth and hands grew more intrusive, more bold, like the noises that pulsed past Trilby's dry lips.

When she was completely responsive, he coaxed her hands to his own body and let her explore it, teaching her where to touch and how, so that his own pleasure grew at a pace with hers.

"It's…indecent!" she choked as he finally levered his body between her legs and caught her thighs to pull her sharply up into stark intimacy. Her eyes looked straight into his as he did it. She felt the jerk of his body in pleasure, and saw it, as well as the sudden spreading darkness of his eyes and the pulling of muscles in his sweat-dampened face.

"Yes," he choked. His eyes slowly went down the wide space he'd left between their bodies and found where they were slowly joining. "Look, Trilby," he whispered.

She did, automatically, and gasped as he stilled, letting her see the starkness of their intimacy. He looked up, meeting her shocked eyes. He held them, and slowly, with the motion of the summer wind in the trees, began to tease his way inside her welcoming body.

"It is beautiful," he whispered, searching her face as the pleasure bit into his body. "This, with you, is something far, far more profound than a lustful joining of bodies."

His unexpected tenderness touched her. She relaxed

as he furthered his possession, and her hands went up to cradle his face, caressing his hard mouth as he gasped for breath and began to shudder.

Her body, like his, was building to ecstasy. She shivered with every slow, deep movement. She didn't hide her eyes. She let him watch her. That seemed to heighten his pleasure, because he groaned now with every tender motion.

"Accept me," he breathed unsteadily. He moved suddenly into complete possession and buffeted her with sharp, quick darts of pleasure that lifted her off the mattress in her shaken frenzy.

She had no comprehension of anything then, except for the silken blast of color and heat and oblivion that left her crying out for what he could give her.

He fulfilled her. It was as simple, as profound, as that. He rolled away from her finally and lay on his back, staring at the ceiling while he came to grips with the fact that he loved her. Only love would explain the fever she kindled not only in his body but in his mind and heart, in his very soul. The way he possessed her had little to do with a fleeting need in his loins. This time had been even more incredible than the last. He could barely believe the pleasure of it.

Trilby lay beside him, open to his eyes, and forced herself to concentrate on trying to breathe. She felt languid now in the aftermath of pleasure, as if she were still a part of him. He looked at her, and she made no attempt to cover herself. She belonged to him now.

His eyes were slow and thorough, seeing all the places he'd touched her with his mouth and hands, seeing the red marks of pleasure that his devouring hunger had left on her.

"You will have bruises," he said quietly. "I'm sorry. I never meant to be so rough with you."

"At the last, it was—was hardly possible to be gentle," she said, and flushed. She averted her eyes.

"I gave you pleasure, did I not?" he asked quietly, reading her reply in the worsening color and faint sound she made. "Have you been taught that women are not supposed to enjoy intimacy with their husbands?"

"Yes," she confessed. "They say that only bad women had pleasure with a man."

"You're hardly a bad woman." He lifted her hand and kissed it gently. "Thank you for the pleasure you gave me."

"Thorn…"

He bent and kissed her eyelids closed. "Let me have you again," he whispered, slowly teasing his way down to her mouth.

"But it wouldn't be right!" she cried frantically.

"Why not?"

His mouth drew lazily over hers and, while she was trying to think up reasons, he slid back onto her body and possessed her with deft, sweet efficiency. By the time her mind actually began to work again, she was lying against him in the second, sated, aftermath.

"I never dreamed it could be so good," he said drowsily. He cradled her against him and pulled up the covers. "Sleep now, little one."

"My clothes," she protested.

He turned her face toward his just before he blew out the lamp and looked deeply into her eyes. "In the morning, we will want each other again, even more than we already have. It will be easier without the burden of clothing to remove."

She went scarlet and shivered faintly with anticipation.

"It is no sin to want to make love with me," he whispered, smiling. "God gave us pleasure to heighten the joy of marriage and the children it brings. Enjoy me, Trilby. Let me enjoy you. There's no shame in it."

She weakened, because she did want him very much. It wasn't quite reasonable. Surely part of her still resented the way Thorn had maneuvered her into marriage. But when he held her, all she knew was the seduction of her senses, her body. He was everything she wanted when he came within five feet of her.

With a little sigh, she snuggled close to him, laying her cheek on his broad, warm shoulder as she closed her eyes.

"Yes, that's it," he whispered. "Go to sleep. I've exhausted you, haven't I?"

She thought that it was the most wonderful exhaustion she'd ever known. She whispered it as he turned out the lamp and she drifted off.

Far from the Lang house, two figures stood in the confines of a blanket and watched the moon rise. One was tall and played a flute. The other was very feminine, her head on his chest while she enjoyed her last evening with the man she loved.

"What was that last song?" Sissy asked contentedly as he finished.

"Another in a long line of love songs," Naki murmured dryly. "We have an endless supply. Men are always trying to woo women into their wickiups to tend fires and cook and have babies for them."

Babies. She'd never have them, because children of

two races were unwelcome in the world. The thought made her sad.

"If I were an Apache woman, I could live with you," she said.

"I would have to pay several horses for you," he reminded her. "And your brother would never agree."

"My brother is a terrible man."

"Is your father like him?"

She sighed. "I'm afraid so. But my mother is like me. She's very much against the old ways. She thinks women should use their minds. She thinks we should be allowed to vote," she added, with a smile.

"Apaches are not allowed to vote," he replied, and laughed shortly. "It is our country, and we are denied suffrage."

"Many injustices need correction," she said.

"Indeed."

She stood quietly in his arms and there was peace between them for a long time. "I must leave tomorrow."

"A wise decision," he replied. "It grows more difficult for me to leave you when we part."

"It is difficult for me as well."

He traced her chin with his thumb and slowly pushed it up so that he could see her eyes in the dim light from the moon. "You would like to sleep with me, would you not?" he whispered.

"Yes," she replied honestly.

"And I with you." He sighed. "I wish that you were Apache."

"And I that you were white." She reached up and kissed the corner of his mouth. "Naki, you could come to Louisiana with me…."

He put his finger over her mouth. "Never speak my

name," he said. "It is a taboo among us. A name has power."

She smiled. "You are very superstitious."

"It is my heritage." He stroked her long hair. "I cannot leave here. Back East, I would be nothing more than a curiosity or an embarrassment. This is where I belong."

"I could stay," she said boldly.

"And live in a primitive shack on a reservation?" he asked sadly. "Where you would be treated like a disease? Many of my people hate whites."

She groaned. "Why does it have to be like this?"

His powerful shoulders lifted and fell. "Who can say?" he replied sadly. "We are of a kind, you and I. How we found our way each to the other, I do not know. But my life will be empty without you in it."

"And mine without you," she said huskily.

He bent to her lips, kissing her softly, with aching tenderness.

"Oh, not like that," she pleaded, tugging at his long, thick hair.

He untangled her fingers and clasped them warmly. "Just like that," he corrected. "So that we can part without any risk of stepping across the line of convention."

"I would risk anything—" she began.

"The child we made would pay our price," he reminded her. "And it would be a high one."

She desisted. "You're right, of course. Why are you always right?"

"Oh, because I am superior and brilliant."

She laughed and struck his chest playfully. "You are conceited."

"It is the inevitable result of having a beautiful and intelligent woman throw herself at me," he whispered.

She reached up and kissed him gently. "So it is." She pressed close then, determined not to give way to tears. Her heart felt as if it might break inside her.

Naki, sensitive to her emotions, felt that sadness echoed inside himself. Giving her up was the only sensible thing to do. That didn't make it easy. He'd never known what loneliness was before, even if he'd thought so when Conchita was killed. But he could taste it now. Life without this woman was going to hurt.

After a minute, he lifted the flute back to his lips. This time, the song he played was not a love song. Instead, it was one that his people traditionally played after the death of a loved one.

Chapter Fifteen

Sissy left by train the next day. She was tearful but composed. Thorn and Trilby had driven her to the station in his Ford and watched her depart. Naki had been nowhere in sight, but Trilby would have bet anything that he was somewhere close by.

In fact, he was. There was a rise not too far from the station; he was sitting his horse atop it, saying a quiet goodbye to the woman his heart wanted.

"Look! Isn't that an Indian?" one of the women in the coach asked excitedly, pointing.

"Yes," her male traveling companion said, with disinterest. "The place is crawling with them. Filthy, ignorant savages! It will be a better world when they're all wiped out!"

Sissy clutched her purse tightly to prevent an outburst. She detested that kind of blind ignorance, but it was rife in the world. This insulting man probably had no concept of the kind of person Naki was, no idea of the cultures that had existed here long before the first white men arrived on American soil. Someday, she promised herself, that would change. When people learned more about the Native Americans, they would learn to respect them.

Her eyes found the solitary figure on the painted horse far in the distance and she called him a silent goodbye. As he grew smaller and smaller, he became a crystalline blur in her tear-filled eyes. Finally he was visible only in Sissy's heart, a bright memory of love that would last her all her life.

Thorn drove Trilby back to the ranch and left her with Samantha while he changed back into his working garb. They were still not very comfortable together in the daylight, despite the sensual magic of the night before.

"I'll get to work, then," he said when he was in more comfortable garb. He clutched his Stetson in his hand and looked down at Trilby with a faintly impatient hunger. "I'll try to come home at noon," he said.

"That would be nice."

She wouldn't look at him. He tilted her face up to his with a lean, gentle hand. "Why do you persist in treating me like a stranger?" he said, and it was half query, half plea. "Do you mean to pretend that you didn't find heaven in my arms last night?"

Her expression wavered and she flushed. "That is hardly a fit topic for—for discussion," she stammered.

"But it is," he said gently. "We're married."

"Just the same…"

"Little prude," he said, with a soft sigh. "All right, keep your secrets. I'll have them all one day." His dark eyes narrowed as he towered over her. "You miss your friend, don't you?"

"Sissy and I have been friends for many years," she

replied. "I always thought that one day she'd be my sister-in-law."

The second the words were out she wished she could take them back. She put her hand to her mouth and felt sick all over as she saw the expression that came and went in Thorn's hard face.

"So it's the man you miss, not his sister. I should have known," he said bitterly. He turned away while he struggled with wounded pride and pain. After a minute, when he spoke, his voice was very composed. "Well, it seems that lust is no real substitute for love, even if I've been telling myself it could be." He glared down at Trilby and a faint sneer came to his hard lips. "Dream of your lost love, if you must, Trilby. It won't matter to me. Just don't whisper his name in my bed."

"That was foul, Thorn!"

"And I'll return the favor," he continued, mad and wanting to hurt. "I'll try not to whisper Sally's name when I lie in your arms. God knows, as sweet as you are, you're no substitute for her!"

He turned and walked away, leaving her with wounds that went soul deep. Incredible, she thought dizzily, not to know that she was in love with him until he as much as admitted that he was still in love with his first wife and was only using Trilby as a substitute for her in bed. She sat down heavily in a chair and moaned out loud.

Thorn had holdings in Mexico, and he was worried about them. The cavalry at Fort Huachuca had been ordered to the border late in November and a troop of the 8th Cavalry was camped in Douglas at the stockyards. Water holes were drying up and springs were lessening their flow. Thorn had mentioned being grateful to have access to Jack Lang's water for his thirsty cattle. He was also talking about cutting his losses and disposing of his Mexican holdings.

The Mexican revolutionists were trying to drive out the foreigners who owned most of their land. They didn't care if the investors, or *hacendados,* were kind or not, they only wanted Mexico to belong to her people again. The revolutionaries might think that attacking Thorn's hacienda in Mexico would force him out—there had been dozens of head of cattle run off, and horses as well. Two of his ranch workers in Mexico had been shot. Thorn hadn't told Trilby that, but Jorge had. As she lived on the ranch, Trilby learned more and more about Thorn's business, and Jorge was a walking encyclopedia of his deeds.

"He is so good to my people, señora," Jorge told her, with feeling. "He is *el jefe* to us, the *patrón.* He feeds the hungry and makes sure that there is a little land for our families to farm. When the government took away our land, we had not even a way to provide for our little children. Many people went to the cities to live, but there was no work and they had to beg for food." His face darkened. "I tell you, señora, the wind will sweep over Mexico and tear Díaz from his office. Madero will heal all wounds when he is in power, I know it!"

"For your people's sake, I hope so, Jorge," Trilby said quietly. "But if he is good to the people who work on his land in Mexico, why did Mexicans attack him?"

"It was the *Federales* and the *rurales,* señora," Jorge told her coldly. "The peasants who work for Díaz and his predators. They are our enemies. Murderers. *Matadores!*"

She blinked. "I thought a matador was a bullfighter."

"There is no Spanish word for bullfighter, señora," he explained patiently. "*Matador* means killer."

She shivered. "I see."

"Many of my people hate the Spanish and the Americans. They are all white men, you see, those who have power over us. But Madero, may the Holy Virgin bless him, has said that we will drive them all out of Mexico and take back our country that they have stolen from us. No longer will the wealthy gringo mine owners and industrialists make slaves of us."

"In Louisiana," Trilby said hesitantly, "there are farmers who work for wealthy men. They are called sharecroppers, because they work the other man's land for a share of the crop. But it always seems to work out so that the farmer only goes deeper in debt and never gets much for his labors."

"*Sí.*" Jorge nodded. "That is the way of things everywhere, is it not, that the poor are enslaved by the wealthy? They keep us hungry so that we must depend on them for *dinero.* But it will change. These…sharecroppers. Why do they not revolt, as we have, and shoot the wealthy landowners?"

Trilby tried to imagine an armed action like that in her home state and smiled faintly. "I don't suppose it would even occur to them," she said honestly. "I hope your countrymen gain their independence, Jorge."

"As I do, señora. So many have already died. And more will." His thin shoulders lifted and fell. "It is not right that men should have to kill and die for a little flour and beans."

For the rest of the day, she considered what Jorge had said. The newspapers were full of the escalating fighting in Mexico. Pascual Orozco, the leader of the insurgents in western Chihuahua, had called all patriotic Mexicans to arms against Díaz. Fighting in Chihuahua was fierce, and agents of the Mexican Northwestern Railroad were hard-pressed to find trainmen to even operate trains in the vicinity. Thousands of men, *insurrectos* and *Federales,* were poised to clash, and the border was under constant scrutiny from local troops of cavalry and infantry. Everyone was nervous.

Trilby was so caught up in her thoughts that Samantha had to ask her twice about Christmas preparations.

"Oh, we'll have a *nacimiento,* of course," Samantha said, speaking of the Mexican custom of a nativity scene of carved wood that was placed in the house during Christmas. "But I would love to have a Christmas tree. My mother always had a grand one, but I was never allowed to help decorate it. Could I help you?"

"Of course," Trilby said, smiling down at the child. It was the first gaiety, the first enthusiasm, that she'd ever noticed in the little girl.

They began the preparations for Christmas with subdued excitement, ignoring Thorn's irritated mumbling about the mess they were making as they prepared popcorn and cranberry chains and began to cut out colorful paper ornaments.

"As long as we don't tuck ornaments into your saddle and rig, I hardly think you have cause to complain," Trilby told him, with a straight face.

She was trying to tease, but Thorn had weathered too many emotional crises to be lighthearted. He backed away from any attempt Trilby made to come close, and she knew it.

"Do any of the men come for Christmas dinner?" Trilby asked, one further attempt to make conversation.

"Most of them have families and take the day off to spend it with them," he said. "Naki has no family, and he's a Christian, so I usually invite him to dinner."

"He's welcome."

"Except," he added, "that he took off into the mountains right after we married and nobody knows where he is."

Trilby was almost certain that the Apache's disappearance had something to do with Sissy. If she and Thorn had been more cordial, she'd have said so.

"If he comes back in time, you won't mind two savages at the table?" he asked dryly.

She flushed and didn't look up. "I've made a cake for dessert tonight," she said pleasantly, ignoring the sarcasm. "It's lemon."

"I won't be in for supper," he said.

When she and Samantha were alone again, Trilby allowed herself to regret the amount of time Thorn managed to spend away from the house these days. For a short time, she'd hoped they might become as close in the daylight as they had that one magical night they'd spent together since their marriage. But as time passed, it seemed less and less likely that anything would change for the better. He thought she was missing Richard. She'd let him, because of his taunt about Sally. Now she wondered if they weren't both disguising their true feelings to avoid being hurt, each by the other. She tried to approach him, but he backed away from her. He wouldn't speak of anything personal. She'd given up, not because she didn't care, but because it was so obvious that he desired nothing from her anymore. He didn't even want her, and he'd made it obvious.

Just the week before, a man and his pretty wife got lost and stopped by Los Santos for directions. Thorn's manner toward the woman had been very chivalrous and tender, and Trilby had been out of sorts for the rest of the day remembering it. He'd been like that toward her once, before Richard had arrived to destroy her hope of happiness.

Sissy had written. She mentioned the possibility of coming back with Professor McCollum's archaeology class later in the spring. She didn't mention Naki, but Trilby could read between the lines. That night Trilby and Thorn had shared his tent seemed so long ago. Her eyes grew sad as she considered the sudden distance between them.

Thorn had seen the sadness in Trilby's face and looked over her shoulder to see Sissy's beautiful, legible handwriting. Further down, there was a reference to Richard and a debutante he'd become infatuated with. He mistakenly thought that the lines about her former beau had made Trilby sad.

"So he's found someone new, has he? How sad for you, Trilby," he said coldly.

She went blank for a moment; then she realized what he was thinking. She looked up, furious. "Have you nothing better to do than taunt me?"

He cocked an eyebrow. "Forgive me. I'm sure you spend every day of your life comparing the Eastern fellow to me and wishing I could match up to him. Cold comfort, isn't it, my dear, that he has to depend on the charity of relatives for his livelihood?"

She blinked. "What do you mean?"

"He travels constantly from one manor house to the other out of choice? I believe Sissy said that her college education was going to be difficult for her people to manage because they were not well-off financially."

That had never occurred to Trilby. Yes, Richard did travel extensively, and always to the abode of some rich relative. She'd never thought of him as a parasite before, but Thorn obviously had.

She stiffened with pride. "Richard's manner of livelihood is his own business."

"Fortunately, you don't have to share it. How would you like being a burden on your relatives to keep up appearances?"

"I should hate it," she whispered huskily.

He nodded. "As would I. We are alike in that we both have too much pride." He bent suddenly and caught her hair around one lean hand, dragging her face back so that he could see it. In the back of his mind, it barely registered that she didn't protest. In fact, she seemed completely at his mercy for once. His eyes fell to her soft, parted lips. "What a waste," he breathed as he leaned over her and caught her mouth hungrily under his.

She whimpered with unexpected pleasure. It had been so long, so…long!

But when she moved closer, he let her go and stood up, his eyes mocking. "Do you miss him that much?" he demanded. "So much that even I can substitute for him? What a pity you didn't leave when he did."

She swallowed, her body trembling. "What a pity you seduced me!"

He considered that. He shook his head very slowly. "No, I won't agree with that. It was beautiful. The only regret I have is that a child didn't come of it."

She flushed and looked down at her lap. She toyed with her skirts. "I…would not have minded a child."

He hesitated. She was less withdrawn than she had been. For a moment, he almost believed that she was warming to him.

"I could give you a child, if you wanted me to," he said slowly, and then held his breath waiting for her to reply.

She bit her lower lip. The temptation was shattering. She wanted that, wanted a child of her own to hold, to love. But would it be fair, when she and Thorn barely spoke, when he obviously resented her very presence?

She looked up into watchful dark eyes. "You—you still love Sally," she said slowly, sadly. "I—I do not want a child born because you used me to substitute for her."

He caught his breath. She couldn't believe that! But she could, and did; he saw it in her face. He'd played his part too well.

"Is it that?" he asked. "Or is it because I'm not the Eastern dude?"

She opened her mouth to speak, to tell him the truth. Her eyes softened. But before she could get the words out, Samantha danced into the room with more colored paper, still a little shy around her father but quite at home with Trilby as she sat down beside the woman and began to chatter about decorations.

Thorn sighed heavily and left them there. He wondered for the rest of the day what Trilby might have told him.

"I like red, don't you, Trilby?" Samantha asked when he was gone, bringing Trilby's dizzy mind back to the task at hand. She put glue on the paper to make chains while Trilby cut out the pieces for her.

"I like it very much," Trilby replied. "It's colorful, like Christmas, isn't it?"

"Oh, yes." Samantha chewed on her lower lip and finally looked up at Trilby with troubled eyes. "Trilby, do you think Cousin Curt will come on Christmas Day?"

"I'm certain that he and your aunt will come if you want them to."

"No, I don't!" the child cried. "I don't want him to come! I don't want him here!"

Trilby's heart seemed to stop in her chest. She laid down the scissors. "But why, darling?"

The child's huge eyes brightened with tears. "Because she locked me in the pantry."

"I don't understand."

"I saw them kissing. My mama and Cousin Curt," Samantha said miserably. "They were in the bed and they hadn't any clothes on. I opened the door and my mama screamed at me and hit me, and then she locked me in the pantry! She made me stay there for a whole hour, Trilby, and there was a rat in the pantry!" The child shivered. "It bit me and I screamed, but she wouldn't let me out. See, look!" She pulled down her long stocking and showed the scar on her calf. Judging by the size of it, it must have been a bad bite.

"Oh, my dear," she said softly, and gathered the child into her arms. "My dear, I'm so sorry!"

Samantha wept her heart out. It was nice, for once, to have a grown person listen to her and hold her. She'd had so little affection from the grownups in her life.

"Didn't you tell your father?" Trilby asked when the tears slackened and she was drying them with her handkerchief.

"She said I mustn't," the child explained, with a sniff. "She said she'd do much worse than lock me in the pantry next time, and Cousin Curt was looking at me as if he disliked me very much. He still does. He asked me last time if I said anything to my father. He scares me." She wiped her eyes again. "I hate having to stay with Cousin Curt. I don't like him, and he doesn't like me, either. He's forever telling me not to dare tell my father what I saw."

"You never shall have to stay with him again," Trilby promised. "Not ever!"

"My father said—"

"Never mind what your father said," she replied. "I shall speak to him."

"But you can't tell him!" Samantha begged. "You can't! He loved my mommy, Trilby."

As he doesn't love me, Trilby thought, but she didn't say it. She lifted her chin. "Samantha…"

"You mustn't," the child persisted. "It's a secret."

Trilby's eyes went to the scar on the child's leg and she wondered how many other terrible punishments had been endured while Sally pleasured herself with her husband's cousin. Having experienced Thorn's mastery in bed, Trilby found it almost unbelievable that Sally could prefer another man.

"We won't speak of it again, then," she promised, and smiled. Samantha was too relieved to notice that Trilby hadn't promised not to tell Thorn.

And she did tell him, graphically, after dinner that night while they spent a few rare minutes alone in the living room. They had separate bedrooms and separate lives. They had so little contact that, despite their marriage, they might be strangers.

"You mustn't make her stay with him again," Trilby said quietly. "You do understand that now? She's really frightened of him, Thorn."

"I can't believe it," he said grimly. "To think that Sally and Curt would both betray me..." he said harshly. "No!"

"I'm sorry that you had to find it out like this," Trilby said, with quiet anguish, her hands folded primly in her lap. "But Samantha is afraid that you'll invite your cousin to Christmas dinner and she's afraid of him. She has a great, terrible scar on her leg from a rat bite she got in the pantry, Thorn."

"Rat bite!" He looked horrified.

"She screamed and your wife would not let her out," she said gently. "You never noticed the bite?"

"She showed me a bad cut. Sally said she fell and did it on a piece of tin," he said stiffly. "I had no idea!"

She felt guilty. He looked tormented, and he did love his child, even if he didn't show it very much. He'd loved Sally, too. Trilby was jealous of his first wife, but she wouldn't have told him about Sally unless she'd had to. It was for Samantha's sake. In a roundabout way, it also exonerated Trilby from the last breath of suspicion—if Thorn had harbored any that she'd ever been involved with Curt. No wonder Sally had lied to Thorn and accused Trilby of being the other woman in Curt's life!

"I don't know if anything else was done to Samantha," Trilby added reluctantly. "Forgive me, but it seems that if your wife was unfeeling enough to punish her by locking her in a pantry with rats—"

"Then she might have done other things," Thorn added for her. He stared down at the floor. "I've been blind."

"You only loved your wife. I would never have told you except that your daughter is so afraid of Curt."

"And I've left her there so much lately." He stood up, moving aimlessly around the room. He picked up the tintype of Sally and stared at it. "She was a beautiful woman. Samantha was never pretty enough to suit her. She hated the child, and me. I knew she was unhappy. But to take it out on her own little girl… It's heartless!"

"I wish I hadn't had to tell you," she said quietly.

"Samantha never said a word."

"She was afraid you wouldn't believe her," Trilby replied.

He grimaced. "Is she afraid of me, too?"

She went close to him, trying to ignore the message her senses were screaming at her. She had an aching impulse to reach up and kiss away his pain. "Thorn, you spend so little time with her," she said.

"She seems to prefer it that way," he said stiffly. "She acts as though I'm a stranger to her."

"But you are," she emphasized.

"A little girl needs a mother," he replied implacably. "She and I have nothing to talk about, no common ground."

Trilby didn't know how to proceed. He wouldn't listen. "Curt doesn't know that Samantha's said anything," she said.

"Don't expect me to keep any secrets, Trilby," he replied heatedly. "Damn him! He even let me suspect you, instead of telling me the truth. What would it have hurt then? She was dead."

"You loved her, didn't you?" she hedged.

"In my way, yes, I did," he said finally, refusing to elaborate further. His very manner forbade any further discussion. "I'll talk to Curt. Tell Samantha he won't be coming here again."

"You're fond of him."

"No man who is a man plays around with someone

else's wife." His voice was icy cold. "If it—it matters," he added hesitantly, "I'm sorry for the way I treated you. Sally told me— Well, you know what she told me. Obviously she was only trying to protect herself."

"I decided that for myself." She searched his hard face, sad for him now. "Sometimes women do crazy things, Thorn," she said. "It wouldn't mean that Sally didn't love you. Maybe she was looking for excitement."

"At the risk of losing her child, her husband, her reputation?" He laughed curtly. "I seem to have been living in a dreamworld. Are people ever what they seem?"

"I don't suppose they are," she said sadly, thinking of Richard and how madly she'd loved him, only to find him with feet of clay. She looked up at him. "Will you get me a tree?"

He didn't reply for a moment. Those soft gray eyes made his knees go weak. He loved the exquisite tenderness in them, the way her long lashes curled up from them. He found himself smiling wistfully. "What kind do you want?" he asked softly.

She tingled all over from the way he was looking at her. "Not a paloverde," she whispered.

"All right." He bent and brushed his mouth, very gently, against her forehead. "Don't worry. I'll take care of Curt."

He'd gone before she could tell him what kind of tree she wanted. He came back with a straggly piñon pine. It was a scruffy little thing, although the homemade decorations Trilby and Samantha put on it helped its homeliness.

Trilby baked and Samantha decorated confections and cakes. By Christmas Day, they had a delightful array of baked goods to give to the employees' families, as well as some to eat for themselves.

At the table, they all dressed in their Sunday best and Thorn carved the delicately browned turkey Trilby had made.

"Isn't it lovely, Father?" Samantha asked shyly. "I helped."

"You certainly did," Trilby agreed, smiling at her. "I couldn't have done it without you."

Thorn glanced at his daughter. She openly adored Trilby, who was gentle and kind and warm with her. All the things, in fact, that she wasn't with him. She'd avoided him since she'd made her soft confession. He wondered sometimes if he'd dreamed the two nights they'd had together.

It wouldn't do to look back, he told himself. She was missing her Richard, and he was trying to work himself into the grave to keep from going to her one dark night. It was difficult to keep his head.

He hadn't kept it with Curt. He'd found the man at home and knocked him down, to his wife's astonishment. He hadn't explained, hadn't said a word. But Curt knew; it was in his eyes. He hadn't retaliated. Thorn had left him lying on the floor without a word, and Curt didn't have to be told that his favorite relation would no longer welcome him at Los Santos.

But the hardest thing of all was coming face-to-face with what a fool he'd been. He'd never suspected Sally of infidelity, and all the time she'd been pushing him out of her bed, she'd been pulling Curt into it. The knowledge did something terrible to his ego, to his self-confidence. In the beginning, Sally had cared for him, as he had for her. Now he wondered if he could ever trust his own judgment again. Samantha had paid a high price for his blindness. He wondered if she ever blamed him for the pain she'd endured at her mother's hands. He wished he could ask her.

"Father, you're not eating," Samantha said shyly.

"What? No, I suppose I'm not." He tasted his turkey and smiled at Samantha. "It's very good."

"Thank you," Trilby murmured shyly.

He didn't reply. After they finished eating, he leaned back and rolled and lit a cigarette. "McCollum may come a little sooner than expected to do some digging," he said.

"Your archaeologist friend?" Trilby asked carefully.

"Yes. He'll be bringing a few students with him. They can stay in the bunkhouse."

"Is Sissy coming with the group?" Trilby asked. "She hasn't mentioned it in her letters, and she won't actually be in his class until January. Will he let her come anyway?"

"I don't know. We'll have to wait and see." He stared at her. "You liked him, didn't you?" he added, with a cold laugh. "He's civilized."

He got to his feet and smiled at Samantha on his way out.

Trilby looked up at him, but he didn't meet her eyes. He'd been a fool once already. He wasn't risking his heart again, not when she was sitting there pining for that damned blond fellow back East.

They opened their presents that evening. Trilby had made a lacy, ruffled yellow dress for Samantha, who adored it. For Thorn, there was a silk tie in a subdued blue paisley that she'd made by hand.

He, in turn, gave his daughter a new store-bought doll with blond hair, a china tea set, and a tiddleywinks game. He presented Trilby with a music box. That night they sat in the living room with the candles lit on the Christmas tree and were serenaded by several guitar-playing Mexican cowboys.

It was almost idyllic, except that Trilby missed her own family, where Christmas had been such a happy and boisterous affair with the extended family gathered all around back in New Orleans. By comparison, this was a sad and lonely affair. She telephoned her parents that night and it brightened her smile when they said they'd be over the next day to see them. At least it wouldn't be quite so lonely then.

Trilby wished them good-night at bedtime and carried the little music box to her room. It was round and made of wood, with a beautiful green and gold pattern on it. Inside it was a place to keep loose powder. She turned the key and listened with rapt delight to the Viennese waltz it played.

A rough knock at the door made her turn. Thorn came stiffly into the room, pausing just inside the door.

"I wanted to thank you for making Christmas so enjoyable for Samantha," he told her. "She hadn't had much in the way of attention for some time. She enjoyed tonight."

"So did I," she said quietly.

He had, too, but he couldn't admit that without giving away feelings he didn't want to admit he had. "I'll be away for a few days," he stated abruptly. "It's unavoidable. I have to go down into Mexico and make some arrangements about my holdings there. It's getting too dangerous to try to hold on to the hacienda."

"My parents and Teddy are coming over tomorrow," she said slowly. "You…won't stay just until then?"

"There's no point," he said curtly, thinking how difficult it would be to see Trilby laugh and smile with her people when she resembled a prisoner in his house.

Her eyes became dull and she looked everywhere except at him. "I see," she whispered. "I'll give them your best, then."

Her calm manner infuriated him. "You're so damned proper, Trilby!" he said through his teeth. "Just once, I'd love to see you snarling and spitting."

"I was raised to behave properly," she said defensively.

"Yes, like that anemic city boy you love," he replied coldly. "God knows what you saw in each other. You're both so proper that you probably couldn't even manage to make love. You'd be fumbling to get the lights out and undress in the dark, so that you wouldn't embarrass each other."

"At least he isn't a savage!" she cried.

His face hardened at the charge. "There are times when you don't mind that. In fact," he said harshly, "there are times when you love it!"

She picked up the music box and hurled it at him in a humiliated rage. It hit the wall and split open, falling noisily to the floor.

Her wide, tragic eyes stared at him out of a white face. "How dare you treat me like this?" she said, choking. "Like a common woman of the night!"

"God, how I wish you were," he spat out. "A lady of the evening has the advantage of being honest about what she feels and thinks and does. You're so starchy that no real man could get near you. Richard Bates was just your style, Trilby. I'm damned sorry that I lost my head and forced us into this marriage. I regret it more than you'll ever know."

He looked at the music box, lying there shattered. He'd shopped for it himself, tried to find something that Trilby would like, something that belonged to her world, her kind of life. And this was how she felt about a present he'd given her. It was trash to her. Nothing but trash.

With a violent kick, he sent it back into the wall, totally destroying it. He glanced at her with rage in his whole posture before he went out the door and slammed it behind him.

Trilby picked up the broken music box with cold, trembling hands and began to cry. It had been so beautiful, the kind of gift she'd never imagined a rough man like Thorn would ever give her. It had been a sensitive, thoughtful present, and she'd broken it beyond repair.

Until she saw it on the floor, she hadn't realized the care Thorn had taken with her present. Now she did, and she bitterly regretted the argument that had widened the distance between them. It looked as if there would never be a way to breach it.

Her parents and Teddy came over the next day, and she enjoyed their visit. But Thorn had left before dawn that morning, without a single word to her. Despite her pleasure in her family, she missed Thorn and it showed.

"He'll be back soon, darling," Mary Lang told her, smiling, unaware of her daughter's plight. "Are you happy?"

"Of course," Trilby said, smiling back. "Come on. Do let's have some coffee and I'll read you Sissy's last letter."

Chapter Sixteen

Thorn came back even more taciturn than when he'd left. Trilby apologized for the music box, but he hardly seemed to hear her, and after that he openly avoided her.

Trilby mourned what might have been. She often tried to gather enough courage to go to him and explain all that had happened, but she never could gather enough nerve. New Year's passed and winter came suddenly, blowing snow and freezing cold.

The fighting in Mexico was still fierce and more troops had been slung along the border. Two days before Christmas, insurgents had captured a train near Juárez, and the passengers had been marooned along the tracks. Bridges had been blown up and tracks dynamited, and rebels were preventing repairs. An engine and a car had been stolen at Guzman. *Insurrecto* chieftain Pascual Orozco had just seized a train in Chihuahua and noted that a hundred and fifty *insurrectos* had been killed.

With the beginning of February, a small detachment of soldiers was sent to San Bernardino to guard the border, and rumors were flying that Orozco was going to attack

Juárez. There were three rebel leaders now, all becoming quite well known to people around Douglas. There were Bracamento and Cabral, and best known locally one Arturo "Red" López, who spoke perfect English and often acted as interpreter. Col. José Blanco was right-hand man for the revolutionary forces in Chihuahua. He had had a rift with Orozco and was now the most talked-about overall leader in the rebel camps. It was rumored that several Americans were fighting with the rebels under López, and Thorn was certain that one of the men was Naki, who had vanished abruptly from the ranch after Sissy's departure. Trilby hoped he was wrong. It would kill Sissy if Naki were hurt.

They kept close to home, because incidents near the border became frightening now that twenty thousand U.S. troops had been ordered to patrol the entire border of Mexico from Texas to Arizona and the oceans at either end. It was the most extensive movement of troops and vessels of war ever assembled in time of peace in the United States. Rumors of war with Mexico were flying wildly, although President Taft had assured ailing President Díaz that the rumors were groundless. Nevertheless, despite the public announcement that the U.S. troops were performing "maneuvers" along the border, ranchers and townspeople alike were keeping loaded guns near to hand and saying their prayers. Church membership rose.

March brought more news of conflict. Trilby and Samantha busied themselves with sewing and cleaning, while Thorn worried over raids on his cattle, accounts and bookkeeping, and helped his men repair outbuildings in preparation for the coming spring planting and calving.

He'd already sold his Mexican land. But the situation in Agua Prieta suddenly exploded with the advent of an *insurrecto* force led by "Red" López at the gates of Agua Prieta, which was just over the border from Douglas. However, the rebels backed off and, almost simultaneously, there were reports that Madero was wounded in a fight in Chihuahua. Díaz invoked the death penalty against the lawless in Mexico in a last-ditch effort to suppress the rebellion.

Fifteen Americans had been captured at Casas Grandes, the newspaper announced, and they were feared shot following Díaz's threat to put all *insurrectos* to death. Thorn had cursed when he read the news and gone immediately to telephone as many prestigious people as he knew in Washington—and there were a few—to make inquiries. President Taft had asked Madero to inquire about the fate of the captives, but there was still no word about their identities.

McCollum had telephoned Thorn after the abortive Agua Prieta threat, and Thorn had persuaded him not to come until April, when the visit might be safer. Trilby was vaguely disappointed, because she'd hoped that Sissy might come with the group and the visit might make her life a little easier. Thorn was alternately hostile and sarcastic. They barely spoke at all, and never touched.

Trilby fell into a sad, silent routine and the happy sparkle left her eyes. She'd long since discovered that she wasn't pregnant. She was disappointed, but she knew it was for the best. Considering her relationship with Thorn, a child would have a difficult time of it. Thorn hadn't said a word when she told him. His face had been without expression at all, and if she was hoping for a reaction, she was disappointed. He hardly spoke to her after that, unless he had to.

Meanwhile she was gaining ground with Samantha. The child had a quick mind and she enjoyed her studies. Now that the weather was warmer, they sat on the porch swing on days when the wind was low and went over lessons.

In a way, it was one of the happiest times of Trilby's life. She was in control of the house and she had Samantha for company. There were times when she could forget for an hour that she'd once lain in Thorn's strong arms and thrilled to his kisses and his touch. These days, he never looked at her. He sometimes ate and slept in the bunkhouse during particularly bad times when the cattle had to be rounded up and branded and closely watched against rustlers.

During the winter, there had been fewer raids. But once spring began to lighten the paloverde trees and the grass, and the weather became hot, raids increased.

Certainly the army units stationed at Douglas had stepped up their patrols all along the border, and incidents of violence increased. Col. David Morris had kept a careful eye on the situation and was ready to back up the Douglas troops again if necessary.

Lisa Morris had obtained her divorce, and Dr. Powell now called on her regularly. There was no hint of impropriety. She never saw him alone. But Lisa knew very well how the doctor felt about her, and her delight in his company was obvious to Mrs. Moye.

"My divorce is final, you know," Lisa told Dr. Powell. She was oddly stiff with him these days.

Strange, when she'd been more intimate with him in some ways than she'd ever been with her husband.

"Yes, I know." He leaned back in his chair and stared at her bluntly. "Your husband apparently has plans to marry his woman in Douglas. At least, that's the talk around the post."

"I hope he will be happy with her," she said quietly.

"Has he been in touch with you?"

"Through his attorney," she replied. "Just to make it clear that he is willing to pay the fees, also. I thought that was kind."

"Considering the pain he's caused you, it was his due."

She noticed the anger in his deep voice and it made her feel warm inside. He hadn't mentioned the future, not once. She wondered if he might be having second thoughts; he was still very reticent, even after she'd deliberately and brazenly emphasized her newly single state.

"You know that I was married," he said. "That my wife and son were killed by Apaches."

"Yes."

He averted his eyes and ran his hat through his big, lean hands. "I have been dead inside for some time. I have not wanted…involvement."

She clasped her folded hands tightly. Her heart sank. She must have misread his intentions completely. "Of course," she said in a dull, softly wounded tone.

His shaggy head lifted, and the blue eyes that met hers were like lightning striking. "But I want it now," he said levelly. "I want it damned bad, madam!"

She flushed from the force of feeling that was in his

voice. Her wide eyes searched his in the static silence that followed the blunt declaration.

He got to his feet a little clumsily. "That could have been better said. I have no manners. I beg your pardon."

She stood up, too. "There is no need for that," she said, lifting her bright, happy eyes to his. "I am…delighted…that you—that you…"

He moved a little closer, wary of the open door and Mrs. Moye somewhere beyond it. The proprieties were always observed here.

"Oh, Lisa!" he said huskily, his fierce eyes worshiping her. "I want so much more than words. So much more!"

Her breath caught. She looked at him with trembling need, her eyes and face radiant with it, her legs trembling.

His hand crushed the brim of his khaki hat and he muttered something under his breath as he fought valiantly against the need to drag her into his arms and kiss her mouth until it was red and swollen. "I must go!" he said roughly. "I have to join the detachment in Douglas. You know there's been some trouble down there. We are wary of relaxing our guard."

She felt the hunger he couldn't hide, and she shifted her eyes to the wall. "Yes, I know. Oh, Todd, you will be careful?" she whispered worriedly, her eyes wide and troubled as they met his.

The soft query made him stiffen with pleasure. He looked suddenly wild. His face was livid with repressed desire. His blue eyes fastened on her bodice for so long that she felt her breasts swell. He saw the peaks forming and he groaned.

She quickly folded her arms over them, apprehensive.

He caught her hand in his and lifted it hungrily to his

mouth. "Yes. I will be careful. It is good of you to…concern yourself on my account. Good day…Mrs. Morris," he said in an unnaturally choked tone. None of this was what he wanted to say. Damn convention!

She was thinking the same thing. The half-open door inhibited her, too. She grimaced. "Good day, Captain Powell," she whispered miserably.

He gave her one long, last look and forced himself to leave her. The widow Moye didn't say a word, but the smile she gave a shaken Lisa was expressive.

April came. A warrant had been issued for "Red" López for an alleged killing in Fronteras, after charges had been made against him for disorderly conduct in Douglas by the Mexican Consul. But the local law-enforcement officers denied that López was drunk or disorderly and did not arrest him. Teddy read that and grinned. López was something of a hero to his young mind, and he eagerly read every word about the rebel captain that he could find, saving it up to tell Trilby whenever he saw her. It was Teddy who imparted the news that López was now known as "El Capitán," and was becoming a local legend. Thorn had met the man, but he rarely spoke of anything regarding the revolution. It made Trilby uneasy that he was so quiet on the subject, and she wondered just how much he knew that he hadn't told her. If only they could talk!

The archaeology students arrived the first week of April. They were a bright, happy bunch of young men. Trilby had hoped up until the last minute that Sissy would be coming with them, but McCollum and several young men got off the train by themselves in Douglas.

"I tried to get Miss Bates to come along," McCollum said in his jovial, gruff manner. "But the matter of a chaperon had to be addressed, and her mother felt that to have her travel in the company of so many single young men was improper. She did not protest the decision," he added, in case Trilby hadn't already gotten the idea.

So Sissy hadn't wanted to come. Presumably she knew that Naki wasn't going to back down an inch and she was doing what she thought was best for both of them. Trilby was sad just the same. She'd have loved spending some time with her friend. It would have been wonderful to have someone to talk to, now that she and Thorn had such a distance between them. Sissy didn't know about Naki's absence, or what they were beginning to suspect as the cause of it. There was no confirmation that he was down in Mexico, of course, but there was suspicion.

"I do have letters from Miss Bates and her brother for you," McCollum said, producing them with a smile. "She sends her love."

"How are they all?" Trilby asked, without being specific. She was all too aware of a terse, solemn Thorn standing just behind Craig McCollum.

"I believe that young Ben is thinking of coming back out here to seek his fortune as a cowboy." He laughed. "And Richard…" He hesitated, with a glance at Thorn.

"Go ahead. Tell her," Thorn invited grimly.

"He…uh…sent Trilby a letter."

"I'll see it, if you don't mind," Thorn replied.

"I mind," Trilby interjected, glaring at him. "It's my letter!"

"You're my wife," Thorn told her, his black eyes

glittering. "And I draw the line at love letters from other men!"

McCollum looked, and felt, uncomfortable. Bates had forced the letter onto him and he hadn't wanted to interfere. He had some inkling of how jealous Thorn was of his young wife. "I'll have to find it," he told Thorn. "It's packed."

"When we get to the house, then," Thorn said. He fought for composure, through the outrage he felt. Damn Richard!

Trilby was uncertain as to why Richard should be writing personal letters to her when he knew she was married. It disturbed her almost as much as Thorn's unreasonable anger. It wasn't as if she'd solicited the letter!

McCollum smiled apologetically at Trilby. "I'm an archaeologist, not a diplomat," he said. "I hope I haven't caused you any problems." He had dark eyes, with very long lashes, and a lean, rugged face. He was tall, like Thorn, but huskier.

"No, of course not," she said, dismissing her worries. "You study old things, don't you?" Trilby asked. "Like the skeletons of dinosaurs?"

McCollum groaned. "That's paleontology, not archaeology."

"He'll pitch you headfirst down a kiva if you say things like that to him," one of his bespectacled students interrupted, faintly amused. "He's very volatile for an educated man. Aren't you, Dr. McCollum, *sir?*"

"If you want to pass my course, Haskins, you'd better treat me with the proper respect," McCollum said jokingly. "Down on your knees, man, and beg forgiveness!"

Trilby began looking around rather pointedly, her hand shading her eyes.

"What are you looking for?" McCollum asked.

"Men with nets."

McCollum laughed. He had a deep, rich voice and it thundered around them pleasantly. "Touché. You have a sense of humor, Mrs. Vance. You need it, no doubt, to live with Thorn."

Thorn glared at him. "I have an even disposition."

McCollum nodded. "Like a rattlesnake planted head-first in a tar pit."

Trilby started laughing and couldn't stop. After a minute, Thorn muttered something about supervising the loading of the luggage.

"Here, I'll help you with that," McCollum volunteered, striding along with him.

"He's not so gruff when you get to know him," the student, Haskins, said, with a grin.

"I met him very briefly once before," Trilby said politely. "Is he married?"

"Widowed," Haskins said. "He has a son about twelve who stays with his sister most of the time. They don't really get along very well."

"Do you like him? Dr. McCollum, I mean."

"We all do," Haskins said. "He's very knowledgeable, and for all his brusque manner, he's a kind man." He gestured to some other well-dressed young men. "There's the rest of the group, Harry, Sid, Marty, and Darren. They're nice. We're all graduate students, you know, not freshmen. This archaeology course is just a refresher for most of us, and the emphasis this trip is going to be on some anthropological studies of the local Apaches— with a dash of digging in the old Hohokam ruins. Dr.

McCollum says we're going to be well rounded in anthropology and archaeology when he's finished with us!"

"Mr. Haskins, I don't doubt that a bit," she said, and smiled at him.

Chapter Seventeen

Trilby had hoped that she could get a quick look at what Richard had written before they got to Los Santos. But with McCollum and his students in the car with them, and several more in a hired car behind, it was impossible. And when they got to the ranch, even before Thorn saw his guests to their quarters, he demanded to see the letter.

McCollum made a silent apology to Trilby as he produced it from his valise and reluctantly handed it over. He muttered something about talking to Haskins and left the two of them alone.

"It's mine," Trilby protested.

Thorn looked right at her and opened it. "And you're mine," he said flatly. "I won't have other men writing to you while we're married."

The letter was very legible, full of regret and apology. Richard wrote that Trilby's face as he left haunted him. He wanted her to write to him so that he'd know she was all right. Having been married to a savage, and he emphasized the word, she might need a shoulder to cry on. His was broad, and she was welcome to it. He was deeply sorry for the way he'd treated her during his visit. In fact, he added, he was reconsidering his entire means of living. He was certain that he'd made a terrible mistake when he'd turned his back on Trilby.

Thorn felt sick all over. He handed the letter to Trilby with a steady hand and eyes that were cold and lifeless. "He sends his condolences for your predicament," he said curtly. "The knowledge that you've married a 'savage' like me is obviously weighing on his mind."

He turned and strode out of the room to find the archaeology students and get them settled, leaving Trilby alone.

She fingered the letter and stared at it without really seeing it. The look in Thorn's eyes had made her want to cry. She hadn't thought of him as a savage for a very long time, but he didn't know that. She hadn't managed to find enough nerve to tell him.

Later Dr. McCollum took his students out by automobile to do some digging in a site near the ranch. Pottery shards had been found there, and a few Folsom points— the fluted projectile points of the Paleo-Indians, the Ice Age hunters who preyed on the woolly mammoths and mastadons that had inhabited North America during the late Pleistocene time period—almost twelve thousand years ago. They were to stop by the Apache reservation on the way home to do some cultural research.

Trilby sat and worried about Thorn. He didn't know how she felt, but she hoped he cared about her. There was always hope. But sometimes hope needed a little help. She'd allowed things to rock along between Thorn and herself without trying to approach him. She'd thought she was doing the right thing, giving him time to come to grips with Sally and Curt's betrayal. Perhaps she'd been wrong to do that.

Her parents always went to town on Saturday, along with Teddy. She phoned while Thorn was out and persuaded them to take Samantha along, to get some new cloth for a dress.

"Do pick out something pretty, Samantha," Trilby told her. "Bright, remember, with flowers."

"I will, Trilby," the child said, and she smiled. She did a lot of that these days. She was even much more at ease with her father, who managed a little time at the end of each day to read her a story. That was the one feather in Trilby's cap, that she'd managed to bring father and daughter closer together and make a family environment for little Samantha. "Won't you be lonely?"

"Your father will be home for dinner soon," Trilby said. "I'll busy myself baking him a cake."

"He likes chocolate 'specially," Samantha said, with a tiny grin.

"And so does a little girl I know," Trilby murmured.

Samantha laughed and waved as she rode off with the Langs.

Trilby baked the cake. Then she changed into a pretty light blue dress with ruffles and lace, brushed her hair and left it loose, and put on some of her precious perfume.

When Thorn came in, he was tired. He'd been in a meeting with some other border landowners all morning. He looked different in a city suit. It lent him an unusual elegance.

"Are you going somewhere?" he asked when he saw Trilby sitting in the parlor with her needlework.

"Why, no," she said, smiling up at him. "Would you like something to drink?"

"A glass of iced tea would be nice."

She laid her needlework aside and went to get it while he sat wearily down on the sofa. He was just a little dusty from the ride home, and when she got back, he was brushing himself down.

"Thank you," he said formally. He took the glass of cold tea and drank half of it without taking a breath. "God, that's good."

Trilby took the brush from him and did his boots so that the black leather shone like glass. She paused there, with one soft hand on his knee.

He froze at the contact. She never touched him. It was always he who did the approaching, or had, until it became a chore to get past her resistance. It had been a long time since he'd had the nerve to touch Trilby and risk being rejected.

"I would like to ask you something," she said, looking up at him quietly.

"What do you want? A divorce?" he asked, with a mocking smile to conceal the sudden cold stillness inside him.

She looked away. "No. Not that."

He relaxed slowly. "What then?"

She hesitated. "You…might not want to."

He put the glass down and drew her close between his knees, coaxing her face up to his quiet, dark eyes. "What do you want, Trilby?"

Her soft lips parted with a nervous sigh. She searched his eyes hopefully. "Thorn, would you give me a child?"

He didn't react. Not one muscle moved in his face. "I beg your pardon?" he asked. His voice was deep and measured, but there was a strange note in it.

"I want to have a baby," she said before she lost all her courage. Her face flushed, but she looked at him bravely.

He let out the breath he'd been holding. His hands tightened on her arms. "I—I only know of one way to give you one," he said hesitantly.

She nodded.

"Does this sudden decision have anything to do with Bates's letter?" he asked, with cold menace.

"No, although I suppose you'll certainly think so," she replied, with resignation. "Richard is part of the past now. I am married to you and I do not believe in divorce."

"And you think having my child would improve our relationship?"

"Wouldn't it?" she replied, her eyes soft and steady on his hard face. "Oh, Thorn, wouldn't you really like another child? A son this time, perhaps?"

He wasn't breathing quite steadily. She was offering him heaven, but he didn't trust her. It was too soon after that damned letter.

"A baby…is a big step," he began.

"Yes." She reached up and looped her arms around his neck. She let her eyes fall to his hard, thin mouth and she looked at it until he began to yield to the pressure she exerted to bring his face down to hers. "Isn't this the way you like to kiss me?" she whispered, and put her open mouth on his.

He made a sound deep in his throat. It took only a few seconds to weaken his resolve and bring him to the brink

of madness. He gathered her up against him and kissed
her and kissed her—until the fever burned too high to
be quenched with kisses alone. He'd been starved for so
long that he could barely breathe while he kissed her.

With a harsh groan, he stood up, taking her with him.
He carried her down the hall and into his bedroom, closing and locking the door behind them.

The room was at the back of the house, and fairly dark
in the daylight. Trilby didn't notice. She was as fever-
ish as Thorn was, hungry for him, eager to feel his skin
against hers. By the time he had the clothes out of the
way, she was desperate for him.

They fell onto the coverlet, fiercely ardent as they
struggled to get even closer than skin to skin would
allow. Thorn covered her body with his and went into
her almost at once, his need so urgent that he was able
to hold back nothing.

He held her mouth in bondage while he buffeted her,
his voice hoarse as he groaned his pleasure past her lips,
his hands holding her hips still while he invaded the
sweet softness of her welcoming body.

She had no shame, no reservations. For once, she
matched him, as wild and abandoned as he was, and
just as anxious for fulfillment.

When it came, she cried out, her voice throbbing,
high-pitched, as she sobbed in violent ecstasy. She felt
and heard Thorn above her, giving into the same convulsive madness that had her imprisoned in its silky heat.

His taut muscles relaxed finally, and she felt his full
weight on her. He was trembling, as weak as she, but
his arms were still possessive.

She could never remember feeling anything that approached this fever of need. Her arms clung to his neck,

her body began to move again, insistent, helplessly seeking him.

"Please," she whispered hoarsely. She kissed him ardently, her body trembling as she felt the hunger begin again. "Please, Thorn, please, please, again!"

"Trilby, I can't."

"You must," she moaned, and sought his lips with her own. She moved under him rhythmically, her body as supple as quicksilver, her hips thrusting up against his in a sensual brush that accomplished a small miracle.

He gasped audibly at the sudden fierce arousal of his body that resulted from her movements.

"Yes," she whispered, arching up to invite a full, deep possession. She moaned as she felt the rough invasion, and her eyes looked into his, drowsy and sultry. She ran her hands down his flat belly and touched him, watching his face go ruddy with heat as he shivered.

"Make me pregnant," she said, choking. "Thorn!"

He cried out as the words penetrated his mind, his body, his very soul. He rolled over with her, capturing her mouth as his body began to move with hers. They went from one side of the bed to the other, touching in ways they never had, whispering hoarsely to each other, exploring with hands that grew bold and invasive and demanding.

It took a long time, and when they reached fulfillment, Thorn's shattered cry was a rough echo of Trilby's in the still room, a triumphant shout of victory over consciousness itself.

"You never answered me," he said a long time later, when his passion had cooled. "Was it because of Bates's letter?"

"It was because I want your child," she whispered. She turned, levering her body over him. Her swollen lips reached down to brush his. "You never made love to me like that before. Not even on our wedding night." Her face revealed hidden worry. "Thorn, you weren't thinking of—of Sally?"

He could have lied, but he didn't dare. Not now. "No," he said. "I was thinking of nothing except you and the pleasure you were giving me."

She relaxed against his cool, muscular body, uncaring that his eyes were on her bare, swollen breasts and her small waist and flaring hips.

She looked, too, discovering his maleness and power and strength.

"In broad daylight," he sighed ruefully.

"You watched me," she said huskily.

His face tautened. "I like watching you. Your eyes go black when you reach your peak. Black as diamonds."

She flushed at the memory of just how intimate it had been. At no time in her life had she felt more like a woman.

"Do you want to sleep in my bed from now on, like a proper wife?" he asked. "Or is procreation the only purpose you had this afternoon?"

She searched his eyes. "No, it wasn't the only purpose. I would like to sleep with you at night, Thorn."

He thanked God for miracles, but he didn't give away the delight she'd dealt him. His pride had taken a beating from her in the past. This time, he was going to play his cards close to his chest.

"I would like that as well," he said.

He rolled away from her and got up, keeping his back

to her as he found the clothes he'd hastily discarded and put them on.

She didn't rush to get into her own things. She lay, lazy and contented, and watched him dress, her hair haloed on the pillow around her head.

He noticed only when he was dressed that she wasn't. He turned and looked down at her pink and mauve body in exquisite disarray on his bed. He smiled slowly, with aching pleasure, as his eyes traced her.

"As much as you please my eyes, Mrs. Vance, it might be politic to get your things back on. I hear the sound of automobiles, which I expect means our guests are on their way back."

"Already!" She sat up. "But they only just left…"

"Hours ago."

She blushed at the realization of how long she'd spent in her husband's arms. "Oh."

"I'll head them off." He handed her things to her. His dark eyes swept over her face and body. "I want a child with you, Trilby," he said, deep velvet in his voice. "I can think of nothing that would please me more."

He bent and kissed her, softly. He lifted his head reluctantly and his eyes were somber, his face grim. "I wish that I were more of a gentleman and less a savage," he said quietly. "Perhaps you might be happier here then."

"Thorn, I don't—" she protested.

But voices echoed into the stillness, then the bang of an engine being disengaged, and Thorn turned to the door, impatient to spare Trilby any embarrassment. "Dress quickly," he told her over his shoulder. "I'll head them off."

Trilby did dress quickly, all thumbs, and through her

blushes, she made up the bed. She'd only just finished and started down the hall when McCollum came along, downtrodden and morose.

"What is it?" Trilby asked, sensing disaster.

"I've had some bad news. We stopped by the reservation," he said quietly. "It seems that the rumors were true. Thorn's friend Naki has gone over into Mexico to fight with the rebels."

Trilby straightened. None of them had heard anything of Naki for months, except Jorge, who mentioned something once about a rumor that he was with López. She'd never written to Sissy about it; she simply could not say that to Sissy.

"We had heard that he was in Mexico," she said slowly.

"I'm sorry to bring the news. It's very dangerous down there right now."

Indeed it was, and several rebels had been shot, some Americans among them if the rumors were true. She couldn't bear to think of Naki among them. She changed the disturbing subject. "Otherwise, how did your field-work go?"

That coaxed him back into a good mood. McCollum loved nothing better than to talk about his work. He expounded on it in great detail. Thorn joined them shortly thereafter, no hint of jealousy in his face as he found McCollum with Trilby. In fact, he looked very thoughtful and intense.

The next few days were fascinating ones for McCollum's graduate students as they divided their time between exploring the sites of the earliest Indian occupation and learning firsthand about daily life among the Apaches.

Thorn had urged caution, however, because down in Mexico some of the fiercest fighting of the revolution had been reported, and small towns switched hands almost daily from rebels to *Federales.* More dynamiting of railroads and bridges and even narrow trails had been reported. In addition, the Mexican War Department had placed an order in France for twenty million Mauser cartridges for immediate delivery.

McCollum took the situation seriously and allowed Thorn to send some cowboys along as escort when he went to the reservation. They waited in the hills for McCollum and his students to do their fieldwork.

"They're a fascinating people," Haskins remarked under his breath to Dr. McCollum when they were sharing a meal of meat and beans and tortillas with their host, a sub-chief of the tribe.

"Indeed," McCollum agreed, glancing at his other rapt students. "Not what you expected, are they, Mr. Greensboro?" he asked a tall, dark man.

"Not at all, sir," Greensboro replied. "I had expected a Stone Age group of people. They are not the ignorant savages I thought to find. Despite the belief in magic and the superstitions, they are an intelligent and proud people."

"Seen close up like this, most tribes are. They may not practice social customs in the manner we do, but they have much to tell us about survival in one of the harshest environments on earth."

"Why is the myth of ignorance perpetuated? It is easy to see that prejudice still abounds here in the West," Haskins remarked.

"Indeed, yes." McCollum belched to show his host that the meal had been enjoyable, scowling until the others got the idea and quickly followed suit. Then, with permission, he lit his pipe and smoked it while the others finished. "You can hardly expect centuries of prejudice to disappear because the century has turned over, Haskins. I'm afraid we shall have to live with it for many more years before civilized people become enlightened enough to accept and appreciate differences in other cultures."

"We do," Greensboro pointed out.

"Of course. But, then, we're intelligent." McCollum grinned. "Do belch again, Mr. Greensboro. You have our host worried. He thinks you don't like your food."

"Oh. Sorry." Greensboro produced a very satisfying belch.

"In the backwoods of the East, it is also considered good manners to belch after a meal," McCollum pointed out when he saw the faint unease on his students' faces. "And I'll remind you that despite the exquisite manners one finds in an Eastern parlor at teatime, among elite families there does exist the incredible custom of dressing young boys like little girls."

"But some Indian tribes have men who dress like women," Greensboro interjected. "They call them *berdache.*"

"Very good, Mr. Greensboro! You do occasionally listen when I lecture, then?"

Greensboro colored. "Of course, sir!"

"What is this lecture?" the sub-chief, who was keeping silent during the conversation, asked politely.

"It is the way we teach in college," McCollum told him. He said the Apache word for learning. "I teach anthropology as well as archaeology." And he went on to explain that as well.

"I see," the older man replied when he finished. He looked around at the students. "Do these young ones live in wickiups, as we do—" he indicated the lodge in which they sat "—and learn the ways of manhood as we teach our youth?"

"You mean, how to go without water in the desert by sucking pebbles and fasting to gain a vision or a spirit guide?" McCollum asked. "No. Not exactly. These men are learning how to appreciate other cultures and other ways of life, as well as learning about how early men lived. They will, in turn, teach others."

The sub-chief nodded. "This is good. We will learn about each other and there will be less—" he paused, searching for the wood "—hostility."

"We hope so," McCollum replied.

The sub-chief drew out the ceremonial pipe and, with a twinkle in his eyes, glanced at McCollum as he filled it. "Have you explained this custom to them?"

McCollum was uneasy about it. He knew of the use of peyote, but this was his host's home and he was required by ethics and custom not to refuse the hospitality. "Yes, I have," McCollum said, looking around with eyes that dared any of his students to make a disparaging remark.

"Not to worry, sir," Haskins said, with a twinkle in his bespectacled eyes. "We're troupers."

As he spoke, the sub-chief finished filling the pipe. He offered it to the four directions with a prayerful solemnity.

When the ritual was complete, the pipe was handed around the group, with everyone taking a puff. A ceremonial drink from a central container followed. The noxious liquid smelled even worse than it looked, but ritual demanded participation. Only a brief time later, there was a mad scramble for the flap that closed the wickiup, as the students and their professor barely made it to the undergrowth in time.

"Good medicine." The sub-chief chuckled as he, too, emptied the contents of his stomach. "It cleanses."

McCollum, who knew all too well—from studying Eastern Indians—about the noxious "black drink" that accompanied each meeting with white men, murmured a weak assent. His head was spinning and his stomach felt like all the fires of hell. "Good medicine," he agreed gamely.

Haskins thought he might die. He was offered a drink of water and took it eagerly, his face pale but still game.

"Congratulations," McCollum said under his breath. "You are now a man."

"Thank you so mu—"

The rest of the contents of his stomach came up.

The sub-chief was delighted at the fortitude of his guests. He opened up to them, then, detailing small facets of Apache life that even Naki hadn't shared with McCollum. He told them about the various sicknesses—bear sickness, coyote sickness—and how they were treated. He told them how the owl was feared, because the souls of the evil dead inhabited them at the moment of death. He told them about the casting out of disease and how to recognize a witch. These were very secret things, and only by promising to keep the knowledge secret were they allowed to hear it. McCollum respected the customs and confidences of his host and insisted that his students do the same.

"The mysticism is fascinating," Greensboro whispered as they followed the old man around the village.

"Don't ever make the mistake of criticizing the beliefs of people from other cultures," McCollum advised. "In most ancient cultures, illness and death are considered abnormal events that are caused by magic."

"Yes, I know," Haskins said knowledgeably. "I've read about some tragedies involving the breaking of tribal taboos by outsiders." He mentioned a massacre in a South American country connected with one.

"Such things happen," McCollum agreed. "A very dangerous thing, meddling in mysticism."

"Surely the Apaches aren't that hostile…?"

"They're very superstitious," McCollum replied. "They might not kill you, but you could undo all my hard work here. Don't jeopardize my research with any careless remarks. You don't have to agree with their customs to respect them."

"Of course, sir. Certainly I won't give offense."

"You're doing very well, Greensboro," McCollum added quietly. "Quite well. I think you have the makings of a superior archaeologist."

The young man colored with embarrassed delight. "Why, thank you, sir."

"You've never said that about *me,*" Haskins pointed out.

His thick blond eyebrows arched. "Do I look stupid, Haskins? You've made perfect scores on all my exams, and the dean tells me I'm in danger of losing my chair to you before you even graduate! My God, encouragement is the last thing you need!"

Everyone laughed, including Haskins.

Chapter Eighteen

Thorn and McCollum were subdued at the evening meal, and Trilby realized that it was because of what they'd learned today about Naki. Thorn had asked Jorge for any news from Mexico about the missing Apache. When pressed, the Mexican had reluctantly told McCollum that there was a rumor from some cousins in Mexico that Naki could be dead. No one knew.

Trilby didn't know how she was going to break the news to Sissy when she wrote to her next. The other girl's most recent letter had been heartrending, hungry for any news of Naki. Trilby had waited to answer it, hoping for something to ease Sissy's mind. She had, it seemed, waited in vain.

Trilby had a flash of insight as she realized how it would be if Thorn were fighting in Mexico and hadn't been heard from in months. She got sick to her stomach and had to sit down.

"What is it?" McCollum asked.

"Nothing," Trilby replied. But she felt hollow inside. The full force of what she felt for Thorn blossomed inside her. She'd always known that she cared for him, but she hadn't really known how much until now. He had become her world. If she lost him, wouldn't she feel exactly as Sissy would when she knew about Naki?

"Can I get you something?"

Thorn came through the doorway and scowled when he saw Trilby sitting down and a worried McCollum hovering over her. "What's wrong?" he asked quickly.

"Trilby was a little wobbly, that's all. I'll leave her in your hands."

Thorn knelt beside Trilby, his eyes almost on a level with hers because he was so tall. "Are you all right, sweetheart?" he asked gently.

She looked into his eyes and some of the terror vanished. She touched his face slowly, tracing his cheek down to his mouth. Impulsively she leaned forward and put her mouth softly to his.

He made a rough sound and jerked back.

"Oh, I—I am sorry," she faltered, embarrassed. Her hand dropped. "I didn't mean to—"

But he caught her hand and brought it back to his face. His other hand tangled suddenly in her hair, and she had a glimpse of blazing dark eyes before he jerked her face to his and kissed her with a passion that made her knees go weak.

His lean hands smoothed over her back. "I wasn't expecting that," he said heavily, with an odd laugh. "You don't usually touch me, Trilby."

She lifted her head and looked up into soft, quiet dark eyes. "I could, if you—if you like it."

His face went tense. "I like it, all right."

She reached up, her hands tracing his lean face slowly,

tenderly. "You're very handsome," she whispered. "And I like the way it feels when we kiss."

His breath darted through his nose in sharp jerks. "So do I." His eyes fastened on her mouth. "I would very much like to stretch you over the kitchen table and—"

"Oh, Thorn!" she moaned.

The sound of approaching footsteps brought back sanity. He moved her discreetly away from his powerful body and laughed unsteadily. "You take my breath away."

"How nice," she whispered impishly.

"Are you trying to drive me mad?" he groaned.

Her eyelashes fluttered. She was alive as never before, conscious of her power and his vulnerability. "Tit for tat," she whispered. "I can barely stand."

"Will you sleep with me tonight?"

She looked up. "Of course."

His cheekbones went ruddy with color, and there was something explosive in his dark eyes as McCollum paused at the doorway.

"Is everything all right?" he asked, aware of some odd undercurrents in the room.

"I'm quite all right. Really I am," Trilby told him. "It was just a dizzy spell. I get them from time to time. It's nothing serious."

"Are you sure?" Thorn asked worriedly.

She smiled into his dark eyes. "Oh, yes. I'm sure."

Trilby didn't want McCollum to tell Sissy about Naki. He promised that he would keep the confidence.

"I'm sorry about Naki," McCollum said wearily.

"So am I," Thorn agreed.

"He might still turn up, you know," McCollum added, smiling. "He's resourceful."

"He'll need to be." Thorn toyed with his fork and studied Trilby with eyes that grew quickly hungry. He'd kissed her last night until his mouth ached, but he didn't dare do more than that after the passionate loving they'd shared in the afternoon. So he'd cradled her against his heart under the covers and they'd held each other all night. This morning, there was a totally new relationship between them. She looked at him openly with warm, secretive eyes, and the looks he gave her back were darkly possessive. When his arm slid around her shoulders, she didn't draw away. She pressed close and laid her cheek against his chest. He could barely breathe for the utter delight he felt. For once, he didn't consider motives or causes. He pushed the specter of Richard Bates to the back of his mind and was determined to live for the moment.

Three days later, McCollum and his students boarded a train and left. They'd had plans to stay for two weeks, but McCollum was called back early. It was just as well, Thorn told Trilby, because the situation over in Agua Prieta had suddenly ignited again as projections of a rebel attack mounted. The Nacozari train, which came up from the mining camps in Sonora, had been boarded and delayed by "El Capitán" López at Fronteras. Their orders had been to take the train into Agua Prieta to attack, but there were women and Americans on the train, and López refused to put them at risk. The very controversial López's stock went up several points in Thorn's eyes after that.

No sooner were Trilby and Samantha and Thorn back

at Los Santos than a lone rider appeared on the horizon, riding hell-for-leather toward the house.

Trilby had taken Samantha inside. Thorn waited on the porch for the horseman, his keen eyes already having determined the visitor's identity.

"Naki!" he burst out when the other man dismounted at the steps. "Is it you?"

He had to ask, because the man wearing conventional cowboy clothing with boots and a gunbelt and a huge Mexican hat didn't look like Naki. He'd even cut his long hair. When he took off the hat, he looked like a highborn Spanish grandee, right down to the arrogance of his dark eyes and high-bridged straight nose.

"Yes, it's me," Naki said. He was half out of breath. "Where is she? They said you had McCollum and several students here. I hoped she might be among them. I rode all night to get here... Is she in the house?"

Thorn just stared at him, faintly horrified. "She's not here."

Naki stared back. "They said—"

"She didn't come," he replied. "Only McCollum and several male students. McCollum was told that you'd gone to fight for the Maderistas and that you hadn't been heard from. Jorge said you were missing in action and presumed dead."

He hesitated, his face grim. "Does Alexandra know? Has someone told her that I was dead?"

"No," Thorn said. "No, not yet. Trilby swore McCollum to secrecy."

Naki ran a lean hand over his forehead to wipe away the sweat. "I got embroiled in the fight. It seemed like a second chance, somehow, to help free an oppressed people. I've been riding with Colonel José de luz

Blanco's people, mostly with Red López, against the *Federales*. It's been hell. I was wounded in the shoulder and it took me a few weeks to get completely back on my feet, but I'm certainly not dead."

"Thank God," Thorn said.

Naki shrugged, fingering the reins. "Perhaps it's for the best that Alexandra didn't come," he said dully. "Blanco said that after the revolution, I could probably manage a ranch for one of the *hacendados* or even buy a place of my own. There isn't so much prejudice in Mexico, except against highborn Spaniards and whites." He looked up. "Unless I tell people I'm Apache, they don't know."

Thorn studied the other man quietly. "And how long do you think you can ignore your heritage, deny your ancestry?"

Naki groaned. He looked toward the horizon. "I can't. I'm proud of what I am. I don't try to hide it, even in Mexico, but there's so little prejudice among the rebels. All of us are misfits. After the revolution, if we win, it won't matter what race I am. Not in Mexico." He turned to Thorn. "I love her!"

The anguish in that deep voice touched Thorn's very soul. "I know," he said heavily. "But she wouldn't want you to sacrifice your heritage. She accepts you as you are. She loves you as you are."

Naki turned back toward him. "Thorn, I could never live back East. And despite what she thinks, the reservation would destroy her. The only common ground possible is Mexico."

"Mexico is in the throes of revolution."

"I noticed," the Apache said dryly.

"Come in and visit for a while, at least," Thorn said.

"You can tell us what's happening. Jorge is the only source we have for any news of the revolution."

Trilby, delighted to see that Thorn's friend was very much alive, set an extra place at the table, and Naki filled them in on the latest developments.

"Here in the north we have an able leader in Colonel Blanco, and there are others. There's a game fellow named Arturo López who leads a contingent. They call him Red. I'm with his group right now." He shook his head. "You can't believe the diversity of our men. I've seen French Foreign Legionnaires, Germans, Dutch, and plenty of cowboys from Texas and Arizona and New Mexico. Even some Eastern dudes, among them a Harvard graduate." He grinned, his teeth very white against his tan. "And rumor has it—" he leaned forward conspiratorially "—that there's an Apache Indian in the fight!"

"No!" Thorn exclaimed.

"Who would believe that?" Trilby teased, smiling. "Will Madero win?"

"Of course," Naki replied. "Even so, I doubt that he will remain in power very long. He has a kind heart, but it takes much more than that to lead a country. It takes ruthlessness."

After they ate, Thorn walked his friend out to the barn, where his horse had been fed and watered for the journey back.

"Are you sure you won't spend the night?" Thorn asked.

"I gave my word that I'd return by morning," came the reply. Naki hesitated. "I act as translator when López isn't available. I trust you to say nothing. There is a great battle in the offing. It would be wise to keep to the ranch for a while and go no nearer Douglas than this. I can say no more, and you must keep my confidence."

"I will. Thank you." Thorn didn't press the other man for information, but he wanted to. "What shall we tell Sissy when she writes?"

Naki hesitated. He finished saddling his horse and adjusted the cinch strap again. "Tell her nothing," he said finally, his face hard and resigned as he turned back to the other man. "Until the revolution is won or lost, it is best that she know nothing."

Thorn hesitated. Trilby had said that Sissy had sounded desperate for news in her last letter. Thinking Naki dead, she might very well do something drastic.

"I hope McCollum can keep his mouth shut if Sissy asks him about you," Thorn said heavily. "He means well, but women fluster him—especially upset women. What if he tells her the gossip about you?"

"I can almost see what you think," Naki remarked astutely. "But you underestimate Alexandra. I know how she feels, but she is too strong, too gritty, to take her own life. If someone tells her that I am no longer alive, she will survive the grief and be stronger for it. I know her."

"What if you're wrong?" Thorn asked. "Can you live with it?"

"Of course not," came the quiet reply. "But I'm not wrong. Eventually, if I can cope with life in Mexico, I will tell her myself and give her the choice. If I cannot, it is best that she believes me dead. For her own sake."

"In your place, I don't think I could be so noble," Thorn replied. "I'd kill for Trilby. I'd die for her."

"I know. Have you told her?"

Thorn laughed coldly. "She's still in love with that

Eastern fellow. She finds me acceptable now, but I don't have her heart."

"Don't lose hope," Naki told him. "The Eastern fellow isn't here. You are."

"I know. That's my ace." He shook hands with his friend. "Don't get your guts shot out."

"Don't sleep too soundly at night. You may have given up your Mexican lands, but your cattle are tempting to hungry men desperate to win a revolution. Keep both eyes open. Remember what I said about Douglas."

"I will. And thanks."

"De nada."

"Try to keep in touch, at least through Jorge's relatives, couldn't you?"

Naki sat astride the horse, looking elegant and right at home. "I'll do my best."

"Adios."

"Vaya con Dios," came the soft reply. Naki turned his horse and rode away, a lonely silhouette against the sky.

"But why won't he let us tell Sissy?" Trilby asked plaintively. "Doesn't he know that it will kill her to think he's dead?"

"He knows. It's for her sake that he doesn't want to raise her hopes, only to have them dashed. It's an incredible thing he's trying to do, Trilby—giving up his country for love of a woman."

"Imagine a man willing to do that for a mere female," she said softly, peeking up at him through her lashes.

He smiled slowly. Samantha had already been put to bed. The house was quiet and empty of noise, except for the unusually loud ticktock of the grandfather clock in the hall.

"I want you," he said softly.

Such plain speaking still had the power to frazzle Trilby's nerves and make her blush like a bride. "Thorn!"

"I know. I'm not quite civilized, am I?" he asked, moving close to her. He stopped when he was scant inches away, so close that she could feel the heat from his body, smell the tobacco and leather scent of his clothing. "I'm too rough and too Western for a gentlewoman like you."

"No, you aren't," she whispered, shivering. "I want you!"

Her breath swept heavily from her lungs. She looked up at his shocked face with eyes that grew heated with slow passion. Her hands went to the neck of her dress and she began to unfasten it without taking her eyes from Thorn's. She didn't stop until she had it open all the way down the front. And while he watched, she peeled everything down to her waist and stood there, bare breasted, breathing as if she'd been running.

"Oh, Trilby," he whispered reverently.

She reached up and took his face in her cold, nervous hands. She drew it gently toward her.

"My darling," he said under his breath, sliding his warm hands around her body to cradle her. "My darling."

Surely that was more than just passion in his deep voice! She yielded to the warm, moist touch of his lips as they explored her soft breasts, making the tips go hard and sensitive.

He picked her up, with his mouth completely covering

one soft breast, and walked quickly down the hall into their bedroom, pausing just long enough to lock the door.

He carried her in the darkness to the bed and began to remove her clothing, but her hand stayed him.

"Do you not want me?" he asked unsteadily, pausing.

"Light the lamp," she whispered. "I...want to watch you take me."

He groaned, fumbling for matches and almost upending the lamp in his haste to get it lit. He turned to her, shaking with passion, devouring her body with his eyes.

"Have I shocked you?" she whispered, propped on her elbows. "Am I—am I too forward?"

"No, you are not," he said huskily.

He went to her, his mouth ardent as it found her lips and roughly caressed it. "Seduce me," he breathed boldly against her ear as his hands went to the rest of the fastenings that secured her dress. "I will never taunt you with it, Trilby. Be as forward as you like. It delights me."

She moaned and gave way to her most outrageous impulses then, drowning in his masculinity and her own femininity. She touched him, whispered to him, adored him as she'd only ever dreamed of doing. He permitted her touch, encouraged it, his voice breaking as he told her what to do.

When he moved over her, she was so desperate for him that her voice sobbed with every deep motion of his body as she clung to him and arched her hips to his in welcome.

But he refused to be rushed. Each movement was calculated, deliberate, each kiss tender and soft and adoring. It was like no other time between them. His voice broke as he whispered to her that this possession was the deepest, most profound he'd ever shared with her.

Even as the words embarrassed, they excited. He whispered that as deep as he was within her, he wanted an even closer melding….

She cried out, because the words and the slow movement of his hips combined to produce a terrifying pinnacle of pleasure. She sobbed against his hard, warm mouth and wondered if she could survive the hot oblivion that actually cost her her consciousness for a few shuddering seconds.

When her eyes opened, Thorn's strained face was there. He had watched her all the way through it, gloried in her pleasure.

"You saw it…?" she whispered breathlessly.

"Yes. And now you will, Trilby," he whispered back, his jaw clenching as he began to move. "Watch. I'll let you… Watch, Trilby. Watch…watch…watch me!"

He cried out, and she did watch, fascinated, as his neck muscles went taut and his head went back, his mouth opening in a hoarse shout of ecstasy. His body shuddered so violently that she caught her breath. And then he relaxed and his weight was heavy on her body, shivering in the aftermath.

"Oh…my," she said unsteadily, cradling him.

"In the light," he murmured in exhaustion. "And your eyes on me, and mine on you. I never dreamed of it."

"Nor I." She held him possessively, protesting sharply when he sought to move. "Oh, no, please!" she whispered urgently.

He lifted his head and looked into her misty eyes. "It is not possible…."

"I know," she said softly, searching his face. "I only want to feel you…like this."

He smiled with such tenderness that her heart ached;

then his hands touched her face as he began to kiss it with soft wonder.

"It was me that you wanted, wasn't it?" she asked slowly.

"I could ask you the same question," he replied, lifting his head to look at her with solemnity. "Do you lie in my arms and think of the man you lost?"

"It would not be possible," she said after a minute. "Not when we lie together like this, in such intimacy."

He felt some of the tension go out of him. Under his body, hers was warm and soft, like silk. He traced her swollen mouth with a faintly unsteady hand. "With my seed deep inside you," he breathed reverently, watching her color.

"Yes," she replied, despite her shyness.

He bent and his mouth opened hers, probing delicately inside it. Within her, he stirred and began to swell. She made a sound, halfway between a whimper and a gasp.

"I am capable again," he whispered into her open mouth. "Are you?"

"Yes…yes! Thorn…please!"

He lifted and, as he moved down, he looked into her eyes. He thought, as the pleasure began to build all over again, that he saw eternity there….

Life was very good for the next few days. Thorn could barely keep himself away from Trilby, who was radiant and happy in ways that everyone noticed.

The only thing that marred their happiness was a note from Sissy, begging for any news that came of Naki. McCollum, it seemed, had been persuaded to tell her about Naki's disappearance and possible death. Sissy was upset and obviously terribly depressed. Trilby had wanted to write back and tell her the truth. But Thorn had convinced her that it wasn't Naki's wish. He didn't want Sissy to know. So she wrote her friend and pleaded with her not to give up hope. Even as she wrote it, she could feel the girl's terror and pain. It was the only blight on her own radiant happiness with her husband. Until the next morning, when that joy turned to anguish.

"I've never seen my girl look so radiant," Jack Lang remarked on one of his rare visits to the ranch the next day. He and Thorn were checking brands to make sure that none of Blackwater Springs's cattle had ventured onto Los Santos property. It was roundup and tempers were usually fraught—especially Thorn's. But this morning, he was even more testy and irritable than usual. He hardly spoke, and his eyes were as disturbed as his expression.

"Haven't you?" Thorn murmured in reply to Jack's remark, and felt cold inside. Trilby did look radiant, but only he knew what the reason might be, and it made him cold all over.

"Is there a particular reason for that radiance I saw in her face when we left the ranch this morning?" the older man probed gently.

Thorn's jaw clenched. "If you mean, is she pregnant," he said shortly, "that isn't why she was smiling."

"I would hardly have been so blunt," Jack said stiffly. "I hope that she is as content as she seems. You got off to a rocky start. Trilby had to change some old attitudes, you know. She was raised in a very genteel environment. It was difficult for her to adjust to life out here." He swept his hand across the vista before them.

"I think she manages very well," Thorn said. He didn't mention that something that had happened this very morning had terrified him. Their intimacy had been complete and almost painfully sweet. Thorn had never known such happiness. But even as he savored his wife and the joy she brought him, he had begun to brood over the past and the way he'd seduced her into marriage. He would never know if her reasons for marrying him, and staying with him, had any basis except for propriety's sake.

She was wild in his arms, wanton and abandoned, but she never spoke of love. Neither did he, despite the effort it cost him. He didn't dare let her know how much he loved her, for fear of giving her the ultimate weapon to use against him if things ever went bad between them again.

Now it seemed he had cause for his lack of trust. Bates had written to her. He'd seen the letter only this morning, where she must have left it lying on the hall table.

Richard Bates wrote of the great change in his mode of living. He was no longer traveling around Europe. In fact, he'd taken a job in the local bank. He groaned inwardly as he remembered what else the man had written, words that threatened to destroy his very soul.

"You're very quiet today," Jack remarked.

"He wrote to her. Bates, that is. He has taken a job in a bank."

"Dick? My God, a miracle."

Thorn looked at Jack Lang levelly. "Trilby loved him once. Does she still, do you think?"

Jack's face went ruddy. "What a hell of a question!"

"I have to know!" Thorn said roughly.

"Why don't you ask her?"

"Because she won't talk to me," he said heavily. "Not about that, at least. She won't speak of him."

"She was infatuated with him," Jack said after a minute. "I'm not sure it was ever more than that, really. Puppy love, don't you see?"

"I think that perhaps he didn't know how he felt about her until she married me," Thorn said. "If he discovered that he had feelings for her, perhaps he has changed his way of life in an attempt to make her see him as a better person."

"But Trilby's happy with you."

"She could be making the most of her situation," Thorn said stubbornly. He even thought privately that her ardor was almost exclusively a result of her desire for a child. She might think that a child would keep her content as she made a life for herself without the man she really loved.

"She must love you."

"Must she? Why?" Thorn asked, glancing at Jack. "I have considered offering her a divorce," he said, shocking his father-in-law speechless.

"A divorce? Why?"

"If she would be happier with Bates, how can I force her to stay with me?" he asked bitterly, hating the memory of seeing it, hating the words he'd read. Trilby had left it on the hall table, and he'd found it and read it. Afterward, he'd replaced it so that she wouldn't know, and he'd left the house without a word to her.

"What was in that letter, Thorn?" Jack asked worriedly.

Thorn smoothed his palms over the saddle horn and stared into space with an aching heart. "He said that he had a good job and excellent prospects. That he realized only too late how much he loved her. He wants her to leave me and marry him. He says that she will be much happier in her own environment, where she won't have to suffer deprivation with a…savage like me."

Chapter Nineteen

"Surely you're mistaken...?" Jack began.

"I'm not. I read the letter twice. She didn't tell me about it," he added. That was what had hurt most. "She didn't mention it at all."

"But she would hardly have left it in plain view if she had minded your seeing it," Jack protested.

"Wouldn't she? Perhaps she thought it was the kindest way to tell me that she wanted to leave."

That was possible. Jack was lost for words. Thorn was quite obviously crushed, despite the brave face he was putting on. He felt sorry for the man, for the first time in memory.

"I could speak to her," Jack offered.

"To what purpose? To tell her that divorce is unthinkable? I don't want a woman who endures me and romances over another man," he said stiffly. "I must let her go."

"I don't know what to say."

"Then say nothing, least of all to Trilby. We must

work this out ourselves," he said quietly. "I'll do whatever she wants. Her happiness is my only concern."

Jack stared at him. "I thought you didn't love her."

Thorn laughed hardly. "I would die for her," he said huskily.

The older man sighed softly. "I'm sorry."

"Yes. So am I." Thorn wheeled his horse. "We haven't much time," he added, glancing at the darkening sky. "We'd better hurry the men along."

Thorn tormented himself with painful thoughts all day. When he got home that evening, it was dark and the house was quiet. He tiptoed in to say good night to Samantha, but she was sound asleep. He stood looking down at her. His child. It seemed so long ago that Sally had presented him with a tiny red infant. He'd adored her, but Sally's attitude had prevented much contact with the child. Distance had separated them until Trilby had come here to live. Now, Samantha was no longer withdrawn and shy. She laughed and played like a happy child, and her pleasure in her father's company was very evident.

"She's asleep," Trilby said from the door.

He stiffened. "Yes, I know."

"Are you hungry? There's some soup that I've just reheated, and I made some bread to go with it."

"I am rather empty. Thank you," he said. But he didn't look at her. He took off his hat and tossed it onto the rack near the door, the spurs on his booted feet making sharp little jingling noises as he walked down the hall behind her toward the dining room.

Trilby felt his stiffness, his formality. It puzzled her. Then she remembered quite suddenly the letter she'd found lying on the hall table. Samantha had taken it from her dresser to ask if she could have the stamp for her collection—and then had forgotten it when she found Trilby taking a plate of cookies out of the oven.

By the time Samantha remembered again, and Trilby retrieved it, Thorn had long since left the house. She'd worried that he might have accidentally seen it. Now she was certain that her worst fears were confirmed.

She looked across the table at him, her hands clenched on the back of the ladder-back, cane-bottomed chair. "Thorn, you saw the letter, did you not?" she asked hesitantly.

He lifted an eyebrow, but not one muscle in his face moved. "Surely you meant for me to see it?" he asked. "Write to Bates if you like," he added, pulling out a chair and dropping into it. "It makes no difference to me... when your body responds so hungrily to mine in bed." He looked straight into her shocked eyes, his own darkly mocking as the raging pain and hurt inside him found utterance. "I do want your body, Trilby, and perhaps a son," he added, to complete the deception. "As long as I have you, Bates is welcome to your heart."

She went paper white. If it hadn't been for her grip on the chair, she might have fallen. "What?" she asked thinly.

"You heard me." He shook out the linen napkin and put it in his lap, then helped himself to a ladle of soup from the china bowl Trilby had set at his place. "Is there some butter for this bread?" he asked carelessly.

Trilby fetched it from the icebox, her hands shaking as she placed it on the table and removed the cloth that covered it. She almost dropped the butter knife before she managed to get it beside the dish.

"Thank you," he said. "Aren't you eating?"

"I had mine with Samantha. If you don't mind, could you leave the dishes in the sink when you're through? I'll deal with them in the morning."

He looked at her with veiled anger. "Will you still welcome me tonight, Trilby? Or is your head stuffed with romantic daydreams of Bates? I promise you, if you're asleep when I come to you, I won't have any qualms about waking you. He may want to marry you now, but you're my wife until I decide to send you away."

She stared at him as if he were a stranger. "You opened it," she exclaimed. She put a hand to her throat. "You read my letter."

"Yes, I read it," he said furiously. "Is that why you've been so generous in my arms, Trilby? Are you trying to sweeten me up so that I'll agree to a divorce?" He felt his temper slipping its bonds, and he couldn't stop it. "Damn you, how many other letters have there been before this one?"

"None," she said hurriedly. "None, Thorn, I swear!"

He got up, overturning the chair as he went around the table and took hold of her, his eyes blazing, his body taut and shivering with an excess of emotion. "By God, Trilby, you won't think of him tonight. I swear you won't!"

His mouth went down to cover hers, devouring it. He lifted her roughly from the floor and carried her down the hall, his lips clinging to hers, demanding, insistent with desperate passion.

Trilby tried to protest, but his strength was frightening. He carried her into their bedroom, locked the door, and threw her onto the bed.

"Bates thinks I'm a savage," he said, standing over her with a face like carved stone. "You've never thought of me any other way. Perhaps it's time I lived down to your low image of me."

And even as he finished speaking, he knelt over her, his hands determined, his eyes blazing with passion. Trilby's last thought was that he acted much more like a hurt and jealous lover than a man making the most of a second marriage.

First light came in through the lacy curtains, and Trilby opened her eyes with a grimace. There wasn't one tiny spot on her body that hadn't felt Thorn's hands and lips. Their passion had always been sweet and satisfying, but this morning she felt positively ravished, and she blushed remembering some of the things he'd done to her.

He might have meant to be brutal, but it hadn't been that way at all. He'd been totally abandoned when his powerful body had overwhelmed her.

The shameful thing was that she'd experienced the most powerful surge of pleasure he'd ever given her in the process. His anguish—and her need to appease it—had created a tension that had built to the point of madness before his violently thrusting body had exacted ecstasy for both of them. She remembered sobbing brokenly as she went over the edge, her entire body blazing with heat as completion made her mindless with the sweetest kind of anguish.

It had been that way for him, too. She knew it had. But once hadn't satisfied him. He'd taken her again and again, his passion endless, tireless, his voice breaking as he felt the world explode under them time and time again through the long night. Only when exhaustion made it impossible to go on any longer did he roll away from her, finally, to sleep. Trilby had drifted off immediately, her

nude body on top of the covers shamelessly as she slept.
She looked around the room, but Thorn was nowhere to
be seen. One of the wardrobes was standing just a little
ajar. And as she sat up, she noticed writing on a pad on
the table. She stared at it, wondering uneasily what she
was going to find there.

She couldn't know that Thorn had cursed himself
the minute he awoke that morning, long before she did,
and kept cursing himself as he dressed. His eyes swept
over Trilby's prone body and he saw the marks his fingers and mouth had left on her alabaster skin. Guilt, and
jealousy, and hopelessness, and anguished grief con-
sumed him. He'd shocked and shamed himself with his
abandon, his vulnerability. It had begun with temper—
and ended in a loss of control he'd never experienced
before in his life. He knew that a woman of her gentility
would—could—never forgive what he'd done to her in
the night. He could never forgive himself. She couldn't
help it if she loved someone else.

It was only that he wanted her love so much, he thought
miserably. He'd loved her endlessly, until his heart hurt
at just the sight of her. And now he knew the hopelessness of it. She loved Bates. She would never be happy
with him because Bates had finally admitted his love and
need of her. It would destroy their marriage.

The only honorable thing he could do now, to make
amends for his unacceptable behavior, was to let her
go—to send her back to the man she really loved. Yes,
he decided finally, with bitter resignation, that was the
only thing left to do.

He took some paper from the writing table and sat
down at the window, scribbling a few words on the

pristine white tablet. He read them over, signed his name, and with one long last look at Trilby, left the room.

He was taking the coward's way out, but he couldn't help it. The contempt and distaste he knew he would see on her face would have destroyed his manhood. He simply could not face her after what he'd done to her the night before….

"Good morning, señor," Jorge greeted him. "You are much earlier than usual." He frowned at the packed valise Thorn was carrying as he started toward the car. "Señor, you are going somewhere?"

"Yes. To Tucson. I'm going to look at some cattle I was contacted about last month."

"Those. *Sí.* But I understood that you had decided not to buy them…?"

Thorn glared at him from bloodshot eyes. "And now I have," he said curtly. "Come on. You'll have to drive me in to the station and bring the car back."

"*Sí,* señor." Jorge smiled in a conciliatory way. He knew the *patrón's* temper too well to risk provoking it.

"Look out for Mrs. Vance as long as she's here. I've already told her that she can leave Samantha with her people if she—if she needs to, for any reason."

Jorge frowned, puzzled. "Yes, señor."

"I'll be back in a few days." He cranked the car, put his valise in back, and waited for an uneasy Jorge to get in beside him before he drove away. He didn't look back. If he had, he was certain that he wouldn't have the strength to leave.

Trilby picked up the pad with trembling hands and read it. Her breath drew in painfully.

"I beg your forgiveness for last night," Thorn had written,

> even though what I did was unforgivable. The only
> amends I can make is to give you your freedom.
> You can leave Samantha with your parents. It will
> be all right. I have put some money on your vanity
> table so that you can buy a ticket home on the train.
> It will be easier if you divorce me. Tell your attor-
> ney that he may send me his bill. I deeply regret
> the pain I have caused you. I know that you will
> be happier with Bates than you have ever been
> with me.

It was signed with his black scrawl, and left starkly revealed where he'd put it.

Trilby sat down unsteadily in the chair he must have occupied while he wrote it. He was letting her go. He was sending her away. He thought she loved Richard, that she wanted to go!

She put her face in her hands and wept brokenly. Why hadn't she told him the truth? She loved him with all her heart. She hadn't been making the most of a bad situation. She stayed with him because he was her whole world. Nights in his arms were as close to heaven as she'd ever been. And yesterday, when the letter from Richard came, she'd just been out behind the house losing her breakfast for the third day in a row. She was almost certainly pregnant, and had apparently been that way for some weeks. It all added up; her fainting spells, her lack of appetite, her unusual fatigue.... She'd been so happy, so radiant. She'd started out to tell Thorn when her father had ridden up on his horse and prevented her.

The two men had ridden away. Trilby hadn't been upset, because she could tell Thorn when he came home. She was certain that he'd be pleased with her news. He spoke much less of Sally these days, and he was all tenderness and consideration in bed and out of it. She had begun to hope…

Why? Why had Richard suddenly decided to love her, just when she knew she cared nothing for him, when she loved her husband and was carrying his child? It was so unfair!

She got up and dressed, barely making it to the back porch before she lost the coffee she'd just swallowed. The thought of a long train trip to Louisiana was unpleasant and unwelcome. But Thorn's note had made it clear that he expected her to leave, wanted her to leave. He'd even gone away himself to make the break easier, giving her instructions about his daughter to ease her way.

She could stay in spite of the letter, she knew. She could refuse to go. But what if she did? He'd told her last night that what he felt for her was desire, not love. Even though he might regret his abandoned passion of the previous night, he was more than willing to let her get a divorce and go to Richard. If he loved her, surely he'd have fought to keep her. It wasn't Thorn's way to back off from a fight, to give up something he wanted without a struggle.

It was that thought that decided her to leave. She was convinced now that Thorn was telling her to leave. He was giving her away, like a gun he'd tired of using.

She dashed at the hot tears. Well, she had his child, she thought. It was some consolation to know that. He wouldn't know. She grimaced. She'd go away and have his child and he'd never know. Of course he would, she

thought miserably, because her parents would surely
know and tell him. She could hardly marry Richard,
either. She didn't love him at all.

With resignation, she went to pack. She could worry
about it all when she got back to Louisiana. She would
take Samantha to her parents on the pretext of shopping, she thought, working it out. Then, from the train
station she could telephone and let them know she was
leaving, at the last minute. That way, there would be no
danger that they might try to sway her. It was impossible to stay with Thorn, knowing that he felt nothing for
her except desire and perhaps pity. But she didn't really
know how she was going to manage without him. He'd
already become the center of her life.

It was Thursday the thirteenth of April, but it felt
more like Friday the thirteenth, she thought with black
humor. She had Jorge, more puzzled than ever when the
señora decided to leave on the heels of Señor Vance,
drive her to town. She didn't tell him they were going
to the train depot. She only said she was going to shop
and that Samantha must stay with Jack and Mary and
Teddy while she was away.

"I like Teddy," Samantha said brightly as they pulled
up at the Langs' front steps. "He's so nice to me."

"He's a nice boy," Trilby replied. She kissed Samantha' s cheek and gave her a long, sad look. "And you're
a nice girl. I do love you, Samantha."

"I love you, too, Trilby," the child said, frowning.
"You look very pale. Are you all right?"

"Certainly." She forced a smile to her tight lips. "Be
good for Grandma and Grandpa, won't you? I shouldn't
be too long."

Samantha got out of the car with Trilby and went into the house, but she was worried.

"Thank you for looking after her," Trilby told Mary.

"She's no trouble at all, you know. And Teddy adores her. Look."

Teddy was teaching Samantha how to play marbles, his voice excited and kind. Samantha was laughing at the way he squinted and stuck his tongue out when he shot the lone marble at the group of them.

"I'm glad they get along so well."

Mary frowned. "You look unwell," she said. "Shouldn't you sit down?"

"I'll be fine. I'm only going to buy some fabric for new summer dresses. Shall I get something for you?" she added to cover her retreat.

"No, dear. I'll go in myself and look, thank you just the same. You should have on a hat," she added.

"It's in the car," Trilby said. "I shouldn't be too long. I'll be back by dark."

"Good. Good. Drive carefully, Jorge!"

"*Sí*, señora." The small man grinned, holding his hat over his heart as he opened the door for Trilby. Thank goodness, she thought, her valises were in the floor-board, where Mary couldn't see them. Jorge had, though, and he frowned all the way to Douglas. Something very serious was going on. He could feel it in his bones.

Trilby hadn't wanted him to have to take her to the train, but the streetcars in Douglas didn't run all the way to the depot. She had no choice. The walk, in the heat and considering her condition, would have been intolerable. Odd how many people were in town, she thought absently, and how many soldiers were around. If she'd been less upset, she might have paid more attention to the industry that heralded trouble.

As she'd expected, when she told Jorge to drive to the train station, he was upset. But he didn't speak until she was standing on the platform with her luggage beside her, waiting for the porter. "Señora, you must not leave," he pleaded. "Señor Vance will be so unhappy."

"I don't believe he will, not at all," she said stiffly. "He told me to go," she added, almost choking on the words.

"But he adores you," he protested. "Señora, he speaks of you as if you are the moon in the night sky, with such tenderness and need. If he sent you away, it was in bad temper, which he will regret soon enough. You must not go!"

"I must, Jorge, you'll see—"

Neither of them had noticed the sudden proliferation of khaki uniforms and the assembling of many citizens on the streets. But the shouts and the sudden sound of gunfire froze them where they stood.

"Take cover!" a soldier yelled. "It's started!"

Trilby tried to ask what had started, but Jorge herded her into the train station and closed the door. The glass shattered at once, and little Jorge caught his chest and fell. He lay on his back, his eyes open and horrified, as blood began to stream from his shoulder.

"Jorge!" Trilby screamed.

She started toward him, but no sooner had she taken a step than a party of ragged, armed Mexicans stormed the door and surrounded the shocked passengers.

Rapid-fire Spanish echoed around her. One man grabbed her by the arm. Two other passengers were also pulled along, both elderly.

"You come with us and no get hurt," one of the men managed in heavily accented English. *"¡Rápidamente!"*

A terrified Trilby was pulled along with the men and dragged into a car that was brimming over with Mauser rifles and ammunition. Seconds later, it sped toward the Mexican border.

Belatedly she realized that the men, probably Maderistas with their supply of rifles, were trying to escape the U.S. Army unit, which was rushing toward them, with officers in a big touring car flanked by khaki-clad men on horseback.

Mercifully Trilby's condition protected her from the hail of gunfire and turmoil that followed the car across the border. She passed out.

When she came to, they were in Mexico. Fighting was heavy in Agua Prieta, with the *Federales* and the snappily uniformed Mexican government troops firing at the piecemeal army of Colonel de luz Blanco as it rode and drove through the streets on horses and in motor cars and hung from the sides of the train that had brought the first wave of rebels in from Nacozari and now sat unmoving on the tracks of Agua Prieta.

Gunfire exploded all around them. A cannon shot burst, and she saw a horrible mirage of dust and blood and, behind it, the sound of screams.

Trilby felt desperately ill. She'd been fighting the sickness since they'd led her onto the train and put her in this seat. She couldn't sit up. She lay with her head against the worn upholstered arm, swallowing again and again to try and keep the nausea down.

"Señora, I am deeply sorry," a tall Mexican apologized, pausing beside her worriedly. "These men who brought you here are sympathizers only, not part of my command. They took you prisoner in order to escape your government's soldiers and bring us weapons. But it is not the mark of a man to hold a woman as a shield. I am deeply sorry for your inconvenience. Your name?"

She didn't know if she should give it, but she was too weak to think. "Trilby Vance, Mrs. Thorn Vance. I feel unwell." She slumped again in the seat as nausea overwhelmed her.

"¡Dios!" The white-haired officer muttered under his breath. He stared at her curiously. "Señora Vance, you are unwell?"

"I—I am with child," she whispered, terrified.

His face changed. He swept off his hat. *"¡Ay de mi!"* he exclaimed. *"¡Juan! ¡Aqui, pronto!"*

A shorter man came running. *"¿Sí, mi general?"*

The officer spoke in Spanish that Trilby couldn't follow through her nausea and fear, but there was an immediate, respectful response in the soldier.

"I have told this man that he will protect you with his very life, señora," the general told her fervently. "Have no fear. You will not be harmed. You are safe aboard this train. You have my word."

She lay weakly trying to focus on his face. "Thank you, señor," she managed.

"Stay with her!"

"¡Si, mi general!"

Juan ran his hat through his hands. "Señora, can I get anything for you? Some water?"

"That would be very nice."

It was no sooner said than done. He rushed to fetch a canteen. Trilby didn't care how many men had drunk from it, she only cared that it was cold and wet and refreshing. She drank sparingly, all the same, afraid to upset her stomach even more. She dashed a few precious drops onto her lacy handkerchief and held it to her mouth before she handed the canteen back. Living in the desert had taught her the value of water.

"What is happening?" Trilby asked over the sharp report of gunfire as she looked out the window at the blur of beige and brown and blue fabric that was only just visible in the smoke from the guns and the dust that flew up around the automobiles and running feet.

"We are taking Agua Prieta," the man, Juan, said proudly. "We are driving the *Federales* out and claiming this city as our own. Red López, a countryman who sympathizes with our cause, is himself leading the charge."

"There are so many of the Federal troops...."

"There are many more of us, señora," he said proudly. "At last, we are in a position to demand what should have been ours in the beginning. No longer will these pigs take our land and homes away from us and make us slaves in our own country. It is they who will run now. But we will catch them, no matter how far they run."

She looked at the men around her with eyes that had never seen them and understood why they fought. They were farmers and herders, these people, not soldiers. But they had learned to fight because they were tired of foreigners making fortunes from their mineral and agricultural wealth and exploiting the native people to extract that wealth. They had families who were starving. They had homes unfit for animals, rented homes that did not even belong to them. Like the serfs of old England, they were owned along with the land they farmed, all to put money in the pockets of people who came from outside Mexico.

"I think that you must win this struggle," Trilby said, watching Juan.

"As do we, señora. I am certain—"

"Trilby!"

The voice was familiar. Trilby turned her head and there was Naki, astonished to see her sitting on the train his men had captured.

"Isn't it odd, how you keep turning up?" she asked weakly.

He knelt beside her, indistinguishable in his garb from the Mexican soldiers around her. "Are you all right? You haven't been hurt…?"

"My goodness, no," she said quickly, managing a smile. "Juan here has been assigned to die in my defense by a very pleasant officer. I have not been harmed. They appropriated me in Douglas as I was waiting for a train. They seem to have appropriated this one, but it isn't moving."

"Where is Thorn?" he asked, looking around.

Her face went stiff. "He is in Tucson," she said. "Buying cattle."

"Why are you here?"

"He has sent me away," she said shortly. "I am on my way back to Louisiana to divorce him."

"Divorce him?"

"Ah, but you cannot do that, señora," Juan said, shaking his head. He looked at Naki. "The señora is *embarazada,*" he said confidentially.

"You're what?" Naki burst out, with eyes as huge as saucers.

"Tell the entire world, why don't you?" Trilby said, with a hard glare at Juan. She colored fiercely.

"*Lo siento,* señora: you must not leave Señor Vance,"

Juan continued, unabashed. "A man must have his son, is it not true, señor?" he asked Naki.

Naki was getting over the shock, but slowly. He studied Trilby for a long moment. "Juan is right."

"You and Juan can both go and sit on a bullet," she said sharply. "You have no right to interfere with me. Thorn said to go, and I'm going!"

"Why did he tell you to go— Look out!"

He pulled her down in the seat as a bullet careened through the open window and hit the opposite wall with a ping.

"This is really not the ideal place for such a discussion, you know," Trilby protested.

"I must agree." Naki pulled the pistol from his holster. *"Juan, cuidado, sí?"*

"Sí!"

"Stay down," Naki told her. "I'll be back when I can."

"Who is winning?"

"Who can tell?" He grinned. "Apparently we are."

There was another loud boom and shouting as men and munitions were redeployed. Trilby couldn't make head or tail of what was going on outside, but she did notice that a number of Blanco's troops were foreigners. The revolution had drawn plenty of outside help from people who sympathized with Madero and his men. Since her brief captivity began, she'd seen a German, an ex–French Foreign Legionnaire, and an ex–Texas Ranger wielding guns on behalf of the peons. The excitement was contagious, too. The fastidious Miss Lang—who would once have abhorred surroundings like these with such savage men—was actually invigorated by the heat of battle.

As she watched wounded men being brought inside

the train, she suddenly recalled that poor Jorge had been hit in the exchange of gunfire in Douglas, and she agonized over his condition. She knew nothing of wounds. She could only pray for his safety and his recovery. At the moment, her own welfare and that of her child were of greatest concern to her, but she seemed safe with Juan mounting guard over her. And the train seemed bulletproof, at least partially.

The shooting was very rapid and close now, and Trilby put a soft hand on her stomach. She was alone here, despite Juan and Naki's presence to comfort her. Thorn was in Tucson. As the gunfire increased, she began to worry. If she were killed by some stray bullet—and, to her horror, one had already penetrated the coach and hit a soldier nearby—Thorn wouldn't know about it for days. Then she realized that she might never see him again in this life and tears sprang to her eyes. Why hadn't she told him to take his ultimatum and go to hell? She could be back in her kitchen making cookies for Samantha. Then she remembered: Samantha was at her parents' house. And nobody knew where Trilby was!

Chapter Twenty

Back at the Lang ranch, night came, but Trilby didn't return, and Jack and Mary Lang were worried. So was Samantha, who kept asking where her stepmother was.

"I'll make a telephone call," Jack said. He phoned Los Santos first, but the foreman's wife answered and said that she hadn't heard from either Trilby or Thorn. He hesitated only a minute before he contacted a friend at the Gadsden Hotel in Douglas.

When he came back, he was pale. He didn't say a word as he buckled on his gun belt and grabbed his hat.

"What is it?" Mary asked in a rush, glancing back toward the kitchen, where she'd left Samantha making biscuits.

"Two Mexican officers and Red López led a couple of a hundred *insurrectos* to attack the Federal garrison in Agua Prieta this afternoon," Jack said through his teeth. "There was gunfire in Douglas and several people were wounded...and a few were killed."

Mary's face went white. "Jack! Trilby was going to the dry-goods store!" Mary began.

"Was she? Didn't it strike you as rather odd that she would leave Samantha with us on a shopping trip when she planned to buy fabric for Samantha's dresses?"

"Yes, but—"

"Jorge would know where Thorn is, but he was with Trilby. He hasn't returned to the ranch. I phoned and was told by the foreman that Mr. Vance had gone to Tucson. It's a big town."

"Oh, dear," Mary said worriedly.

"Try not to worry," he said.

"Dad," Teddy called, coming into the room, "isn't Trilby back yet?"

"Not yet," Jack said. He forced himself to smile and act normal. He patted the boy's shoulder. "Not to worry. I'm just going into town. Trilby and Jorge might have had trouble with the automobile."

Neither of the adults believed that, but Teddy in his innocence accepted it. He smiled and went back to the kitchen to talk to Samantha while she worked.

It was worse than Jack had suspected. He reached Douglas to find half the town on the rooftops, looking across the border with binoculars. Soldiers were everywhere, along with reporters and ambulances and dust. Wounded people were being ferried by wagon and car to hospitals and makeshift clinics. Mexican and American women were caring for the wounded on both sides of the conflict. The fighting, Jack was told, had lasted for three hours. More fighting was expected.

"What's going on?" he asked a bystander.

"Hell broke loose in Agua Prieta today," the bystander replied. "Fighting's still going on, too. They say the Maderistas are holed up across the border and they've overwhelmed the *Federales*. We've heard that they're detaining some people who were on the Naco train, and there may be an American woman over there who was taken hostage by some of the local junta as they went over to help López. I say, this is exciting!"

Jack found it something less than that. "The American woman," he said quickly, "do they know who she is?"

"Someone on the platform at the depot, I believe. Yes, a young woman. Mr. Heard said she'd just purchased a ticket to go back East."

"Oh, my God," Jack groaned. He leaned against the post and went looking for the army commander.

"My daughter's being held by the rebels," he told the first officer he could find. "You must do something!"

"We are trying to negotiate, I assure you, but there's a break in communications and the gunfire hasn't let up," Jack was told by a lieutenant. "The small Federal contingent was caught by surprise. Two captains and twenty-nine of their men dynamited their way out of the garrison and rushed over the border to surrender to us. But there are several left, and we're trying to get them over here, too. The rebels have a machine gun over there and they're using it. It's a hell of a mess, sir."

Even as they spoke, a captain came up and sent the other officer after something to use as a flag of truce. He looked so single-minded that Jack didn't even approach him for assistance. A minute later, the captain was mounted and, with a civilian at his side, rode right over the border.

"The captain has already had to fire at some civilians to keep them from joining the rebels," the lieutenant said. "I strongly advise you to seek cover and stay out of the streets. Gunfire has rained across the border for hours now."

"But, my daughter…" Jack said huskily.

"If she's held by the *insurrectos,* you needn't worry too much," the man said confidentially. "These people have a great respect for women. They will not harm her. Once we get the *Federales* out, perhaps we can negotiate and get the hostages back."

Jack knew the reverence of Mexican men for most women, but Trilby was an American and they had reason to dislike foreigners. Besides that, if they beat back the *Federales* and celebrated on mescal, there was no telling what might happen. He wasn't convinced. He cursed himself for ever coming to Arizona in the first place and jeopardizing his daughter in this manner. What would Thorn say when he found out? And, moreover, why had Trilby come here to catch a train back East? Surely to God, it had something to do with that damnable letter of Bates's that Thorn had told him about. He promised himself that if he got Trilby back and safe, he was going to get a ticket to Louisiana himself—for the express purpose of shooting Richard Bates!

He moved off the street, horrified at the sudden turn of events.

Thorn spent a lonely night in Tucson drinking alone in his hotel room and blaming himself for what he'd done to Trilby. The next day, all desire to do business had left him. He sat and brooded and wondered how Trilby had received his quick note, if she'd already gone. Probably he'd find Samantha with the Langs and she'd be worried. That was all the excuse he needed to cut his trip short and go home.

No one was expecting him, so he got off the train at the small Blackwater Springs depot and hitched a ride home in a passing car. The news that he got from the man who'd given him the ride sent him straight for his car the minute he got to Los Santos. He drove hell-for-leather straight for the Lang place, where he'd told Trilby to go if there was trouble. He couldn't let her leave with hell breaking loose in Douglas. Perhaps it wasn't too late to stop her from leaving, he thought. If he told her the truth, there was just a slight chance that he might win her yet.

But when he arrived at the Lang ranch, he found Mary sitting on the porch with red-rimmed eyes. His heart almost stopped. He knew something had happened. Something terrible from the look of it.

He cut off the engine and leaped from his car, his hat in his lean hand as he took the steps two at a time.

"Thorn!" Mary exclaimed, rising from her chair. "Oh, Thorn, what a terrible homecoming for you!"

"Trilby," he said quickly. "She's gone…?"

"Jack telephoned and said he thinks she's been taken prisoner by some rebel sympathizers and taken over the border to Agua Prieta," Mary blurted out, watching the horror darken his eyes. "We can't get her back, or even find out if she's all right. Jorge was shot, and we don't know if he's going to live. He's at Calumet Hospital."

"Oh, my God," Thorn said heavily. His heart was racing wildly. Trilby, in the hands of the rebels. God only knew what could happen to her!

"Jack's in Douglas now, trying to get information from the army," she said. "Thorn, wait. Samantha's here…."

"Take care of her, please," he said through his teeth,

without breaking stride as he walked back to his car, grim-faced. "I'll be back when I can."

"Certainly I'll look after her, Thorn," Mary said wearily. "Do be careful. And if you find out anything, anything at all…"

"I'll be in touch."

He drove away, his mind whirling, full of fear. He didn't know what he was going to find in Douglas or how he was going to get Trilby back. He only knew that he must. His eyes, fastened on the horizon, were black as the fear that settled in his heart.

Lisa Morris had stood on the porch to watch the rest of Captain Powell's troops move out hurriedly toward Douglas from Fort Huachuca, the motorized column formidable as it passed the small town where she lived with Mrs. Moye. Captain Powell had stopped to speak to Lisa.

He stepped up on the porch, where Lisa stood alone in a pretty ruffled blue gingham dress, in the shadows of the wide eave.

"Must you go?" she asked involuntarily, her soft eyes worried, blushing a little as she recalled their intimacy.

"Of course," he said, his voice gentle. "Agua Prieta is under attack and we have been ordered to Douglas as a relief column, along with some others. This could be a very dangerous situation. And war, sadly, is a physician's milieu."

"I am so afraid for you, Todd!"

He shifted, uneasy with her. He wanted her now to the point of madness, but they'd been circumspect even so. He looked into her eyes and had to clench his teeth for control. Soon, soon, her divorce would be final and they could be together! Meanwhile, giving way to the madness would damage her reputation.

"I'll be careful." He searched her small face with quiet anguish, seeing his own hunger there. He reached out a huge hand and lightly touched her cheek. "I'm a tough old bird. I won't get myself killed now, when I have so much to live for!"

Her lower lip trembled. She'd had nightmares about losing him. Her body ached for the comfort of his, for the closeness.

His breath caught at the way she was looking at him. Propriety, restraint, and discretion all fled his grasp.

"My God, Lisa, when you look at me like that…" he said under his breath, and he reached for her.

He kissed her with passion and need and quiet desperation. She kissed him back, giving way to the need that had tormented her since they had been intimate. She gloried in the hard crush of his arms and the feel of his hard, rough mouth on her own. She throbbed and burned from his kiss, needing to feel his skin next to hers. It was a kind of madness, she thought dizzily, but she didn't care. All she cared about was the taste of Todd Powell's mouth and getting as much of it as she could before she had to let him go.

When he lifted his head, he was flushed and a little unsteady on his feet. "Here," he said huskily, holding her gently until she gained her balance. "You're as rocky as I am."

She couldn't smile. Her eyes adored him. Her mouth felt swollen and still hungry. "I'm dizzy!" she whispered in soft delight.

"And I," he replied. "It is no good my telling myself

all the reasons against it. No good whatsoever. I want you too badly."

She saw things in his eyes that he would probably never say. She saw desperate hunger and loneliness, respect and need. And behind it all, love that would sacrifice his own happiness in her best interests.

"I want you, too," she said honestly. "I love you so much, Todd. With all my heart!"

His eyes flashed. He seemed to have trouble breathing, and his face tautened like a drawn cord. "I want you for my wife. But I am…much older than you. I am a widower, and in the past I have been known to drink to excess."

"None of that matters."

He exhaled heavily. He took one of her small hands in his and grasped it warmly, tightly. "I will put away the bottle forever. I will do anything you ever ask of me."

She smiled at him very tenderly. "I know."

He straightened. "I am not a wealthy man, and I imagine that I shall not achieve any more in the way of rank."

"That does not matter, either."

He lifted her palm to his mouth and kissed it with shattering hunger. "I love you," he said unsteadily, forcing the words out. "More than my life. More than honor itself!"

She cradled his cheek against her hand, unbearably touched by his confession. She hadn't expected this upswell of emotion in him, despite his passion, and the emotion she read in his normally composed face made her feel humble.

"When will you marry me?" he asked.

"Whenever you like. I should think that May is a particularly fine month for a wedding," she added.

"May," he agreed. He drew back reluctantly and smiled jerkily. "May it is, then."

"You won't take risks, Todd?" she asked worriedly.

"No," he murmured dryly. His eyes caressed her face one more time. He turned and went down the steps with the sudden agility of a much younger man. He laughed as he got into the car and waved as he drove off. She watched until the column was nothing more than a puff of smoke in the distance.

Thorn raced through Douglas looking for Jack Lang. When he finally found his father-in-law, Jack was pleading with an official for a pass to get into Agua Prieta through the Federal troops.

"I can't give you that," the nervous young officer in charge groaned. "Mr. Lang, you ask the impossible! No pass I wrote would satisfy the *insurrectos.* They have deployed along the railroad track at the embankment all the way to the U.S. customhouse. They'll fire at anything that moves, in their present mood. Several Americans who were on the Nacozari train are being held; we don't know where. But the *Federales* have surrendered, and once the city is secure in the hands of the revolutionaries, I can almost assure you that the hostages will be released. Your daughter is probably among them and probably quite safe."

"Come on, Jack," Thorn said curtly. He didn't speak to the officer at all, pulling the older man along with him without a word until they reached the street. "That isn't the way."

He headed for the Mexican part of town, through the turmoil of machines and troops and onlookers, with Jack at his side.

"What are you going to do?" Jack asked.

"Get help. This is the only way to get through to Agua Prieta now. We'll never be able to walk across the border with those U.S. troops there."

"I know," Jack said grimly. "They've already shot at one man to keep him from going over. What if the rebels are holding her for ransom?" Jack groaned. "I haven't any cash with me!"

Thorn's hands fell to his sidearm. Grim-visaged, he didn't break stride. "I'll pay them off in lead."

"I know how you feel, man, but you mustn't endanger her!" the other man pleaded.

"I won't," Thorn promised. "But I'll get her out. I swear I will—no matter what it takes!"

There was silence as they made their way through the crowd. "She was leaving you, wasn't she?" Jack asked. "Over that damned Bates."

"Yes." Thorn's voice was hoarse, bitter. "And she can still go. But I'll have to get her out of Mexico first."

"I'm certain she doesn't love the man."

"And I'm certain that she does. It doesn't matter. The thing is to save her life," Thorn said heavily. "Pray God we aren't too late!"

While Thorn and Jack were trying to think of a way to get across the border, past the hair triggers of the rebel sentries, a rested and refreshed Trilby was learning how to treat gunshot wounds. She'd wrapped a sheet around her as a makeshift apron and she was watching the Mexican physician stitch a wound by kerosene lantern. She was duplicating his technique on yet another wounded man, following the instructions by proxy. She understood no Spanish, so Naki was translating for the small, friendly physician.

"This is ridiculous!" Naki protested. "You're not in any condition to do this sort of thing."

"Do be quiet," she murmured, nodding as the doctor demonstrated his tying-off technique and watched her repeat it on her very drunk and singing patient. "I think I'm doing very well."

"Will you be reasonable? You're jeopardizing your health!"

"You sound just like my husband," Trilby said, ignoring him. "I'm all right. I've had some water and a piece of bread and cheese and I feel much better. Naki, I actually think I'm getting quite good at this!" she said enthusiastically as she began to stitch another wound with the doctor's supervision.

"Thorn will kill me," Naki muttered.

"I'm none of Thorn's business," she returned. "I'm leaving him. Will you be quiet? This is very tricky. Do ask the doctor if I should make two stitches here...."

Naki threw up his hands.

It was maddening to have to wait, but Thorn and Jack had to send for Jorge's brother and it took some time to find him. Going over the border in the dark without assistance was suicide, and no help at all to Trilby. With the help of Jorge's brother and one of his cousins, Thorn and Jack Lang were able to don Mexican garb and slip across the border, just out of town, with a small group of rebels the next morning at daylight.

It had been hell, worrying through the night, hard on both men, especially on Thorn. The only thing that made it bearable was learning that Jorge had improved and seemed to be rallying. The Americans who had been captured on the train had long since been released, and Thorn had rushed out to see if Trilby was among them. As he'd feared, she wasn't. Their only recourse then had been to wait for dawn.

"We don't even know where to look for her," Jack protested as they climbed up the bank into the outskirts of Agua Prieta.

"Of course we do," Thorn said impatiently. "She'll still be on that damned train. There's no way they could have moved her or the others in all this gunfire."

"Well, you're right," Jack said, relieved. "Oh, dear God, I hope they haven't harmed her."

"If they have, they won't live to regret it," the Arizonan said grimly.

The very tone of his voice was menacing. Jack hoped the other man would restrain that violence until they could retrieve Trilby from her captors. Afterward, he thought angrily, he'd probably be capable of getting off a few rounds himself.

Music could be heard along with sporadic gunfire as they made their way into the city. Agua Prieta was no tiny border town. It was fully garrisoned and the government troops had been formidable. But almost at once it became apparent that the Maderistas had control of the city.

A relief column was said to be on the way from Fort Huachuca, with another two troops due to arrive within a day or so. But they could do little more than keep the border secure. Several sympathizers had tried to cross the border, and one of them had been winged in the shoulder by a soldier, which had the effect of stemming the enthusiasm of his fellows for the fight. They retreated. No Americans were allowed into Agua Prieta. That was why Thorn and Jack had been forced to resort to chicanery in Trilby's interests.

The train was motionless on its tracks. Some of the windows were lit. Thorn stared at it with narrowed eyes. Then, with a small laugh, he pulled out his pistol and checked it, spinning the cylinder before he reholstered it.

"Are you game, Jack?" he asked.

"Game as I'll ever be," came the quiet reply.

Thorn walked out into the light. He was challenged immediately by two men, but he replied to their challenge with the day's password. The guns were lowered. Jack gave a sigh of relief, because the men had been very nervous and quick on the trigger.

"Don't quit on me now," Thorn said, glancing at his companion. "They think we're sympathizers. Did you think I'd dare come across without knowing the password?"

"I was afraid we were goners. Is she in there?"

"They said she's with the doctor," Thorn replied worriedly. "Come on."

He gained the entrance to the train and stopped suddenly in the doorway with Jack at his elbow. There was an audible gasp.

Trilby was hovering over a badly wounded man with needle and thread while a small man directed her movements with the needle in what looked to be a killing wound. The patient was, however, very cheerful and obviously intoxicated, singing as they sewed him up.

"Trilby!" Thorn exclaimed.

She heard his deep voice and looked up. A shock of warmth and color animated her face until she remembered vividly the night he'd left her. She glared at him.

"Hello, Thorn. Hello, Father." She greeted them stiffly. "Fancy meeting you here."

"What are you doing?" Thorn demanded, aghast.

"I'm acting as assistant to this poor, harassed doctor. He can't sew up everyone at once, you know." She turned to Naki, who looked very self-conscious as he met Thorn's furious scowl. "Tell the doctor I must speak with my father. I'll only be a minute." She handed Naki the needle and suture and stripped off her bloody apron as she approached the men.

"Trilby, girl, are you all right?" Jack asked worriedly, and went forward to embrace her enthusiastically. "Oh, thank God, thank God! When I heard they'd taken hostages, I was so afraid. Your mother is beside herself, and so is Teddy."

"I'm fine, really, Father," she assured him. She was pale and worn, her hair in wisps around her harried face, but she was managing quite well. She wouldn't look at Thorn. It was much too embarrassing to meet his eyes and remember how they'd parted.

"I have to talk to you," Thorn said formally. He took her arm before she could protest and escorted her out onto the platform at the rear of the car, aware of Mexicans patrolling around the perimeter. No one paid them much attention, however, so it was as much privacy as they were likely to get.

"Yes? What do you want? I'm quite busy," she said haughtily, avoiding his eyes.

"Trilby, for God's sake, you're a prisoner in an enemy camp, not a doctor making a house call!"

"I am not a hostage. I am giving aid and assistance

where it is needed. When they release me, and they've promised that I can go whenever I like, I am going back to Louisiana. That is what you want, is it not?"

Thorn couldn't manage to speak at all. He made a rough sound under his breath and caught the iron railing in his lean hands. It was cold and sturdy against his skin. In the distance, a guitar was playing and a fire was burning over which men were cooking beans and coffee. He heard voices all around them.

"I am deeply sorry for what I did that last night we were together," he said formally. "I had no right."

"That is true."

He straightened. "At least they have not harmed you."

"It would not occur to them. They are *gentlemen,*" she added, stressing the word.

His high cheekbones flushed. He turned and looked directly down into her eyes. "And I'm not. I'm a savage," he said quietly. "I even proved it to you, didn't I, Trilby?" he added, with cold self-contempt. "If you're looking for genteel company, you won't ever find it with me. Bates is more your sort. Maybe he was right in the first place. Maybe you do belong with him."

She had no need to feel guilty, but she did. He looked torn apart.

She frowned slightly. She hadn't considered the motivation for his violent behavior all that much. She'd thought he might be jealous that another man wanted her. But this went beyond jealousy. There was more emotion in that lean face than she'd seen on it since they married. He was tired and there were deep lines in his lean cheeks. His eyes were bloodshot. In them was wounded resignation, and something more. Something deeper, much deeper, than she'd realized. He'd come all this way, risked being killed, to get to her. He was risking his life even now, gladly, just to be with her. It put things into perspective vividly, and at once, as she considered his motives.

She moved close to him and only then saw how her proximity reacted on him. He tensed all over. His face muscles drew up. His mouth compressed, as if he had to exercise a great deal of control not to show how she affected him.

"What's wrong, Thorn?" she asked quietly. "Surely I don't disturb you?"

She took a step closer, and he actually moved away, his face threatening.

"It's Bates you want, or have you forgotten?" he asked coldly. "I'm please to see that you're undamaged. I'll talk to López and get you out of here."

"Thorn," she called as he started back into the train.

He turned with one of those lightning moves that had once intimidated her. "Well?" he asked testily.

"You never once asked how I felt about Richard," she said, with dignity. "Or if I wanted to go to him. You didn't ask if I wanted a divorce."

"How could you not want one, for God's sake, after what I did to you?" he asked harshly.

The pain in his dark eyes was unbearable. She moved close again, looking up at him intently. "You made love to me," she said softly. "You were very passionate, but you were not cruel." She dropped her gaze to his chest. "You have never been cruel to me…in that way."

"I left bruises on you," he said, his voice throbbing with emotion. "I didn't have the courage to face you that next morning, don't you see? I couldn't bear to face you, so I ran!"

She gasped. The expression on his normally taciturn face made her knees week. Why had she never seen it before? That wasn't the look of a jealous or vindictive man. It was the look of a man who loved so intensely that it was killing him to lose her.

"Why...you love me!" she whispered, with sudden, stark realization.

Chapter Twenty-One

Thorn flinched at the accusation. He turned away, his eyes on the Mexicans grouped around the small cooking fire nearby, unseeing as he fought for control. He hadn't meant her to know. He didn't want to be vulnerable.

But he was, and now she knew it. She went to him in a daze. Her hands went out and caught his long, muscular arm. She drew it to her breasts and held it there, coaxing his eyes down to her rapt face.

"Is it so difficult to admit?" she asked.

His face went even harder, but his eyes lingered helplessly on her soft features. "You don't want me," he accused harshly. "You never did! I'm not cultured and soft like that Eastern fellow you're in love with."

"No, you aren't soft," she agreed, smiling up at his averted face gently, radiantly. "You're like your desert, Thorn, rock-hard and sometimes very harsh. But you're twice the man Richard ever was."

He'd averted his eyes, but that last remark brought them back. His face softened a little, and he looked as if he was hanging on every word.

"I couldn't admit it, but I really knew the day Richard kissed me, when Sissy and I were out looking for relics," she said matter-of-factly. "Because I felt nothing. Nothing at all. He held me and all I could think of was the way it felt to be in your arms."

His thin lips parted. He seemed to barely be breathing.

"How could you not know?" she asked huskily, staring up at him raptly. "I gave myself away a dozen times. Especially in intimacy, when I adored you so much that I had to have the lights on, so that I could see how much you wanted me."

His cheekbones went ruddy with color. "Did you?"

"Oh, yes," she whispered. "Even that last time," she added, blushing as her eyes fell to his chest. "Especially that last time, when you wanted me so desperately that you could hold back nothing. I thought that I would die, the pleasure was so terrible."

He felt shaky. His hand touched her cheek hesitantly, tracing its sweet curve. "I never meant to hurt you," he whispered unsteadily. "I was jealous and desperately afraid of losing you. I lost control."

"Yes." She moved close to him and impulsively slid her arms around him. She pressed herself to his powerful body and felt him shiver.

"Don't," he said, trying to move her away.

"It's all right," she whispered. "I'm trembling, too. Can't you feel it?"

He did. It only made his need worse. Unbearable. His lean hands caught her shoulders and bit in. "Trilby, I can't make you stay with me if you aren't happy. Bates loves you…."

"No, he doesn't. He loves himself. But I love you,"

she said, with total contentment. She lifted her eyes to his white face.

That was what she'd been saying all along, and he'd never realized it. He moaned softly and bent to kiss her eyelids shut. "Oh, God!" he whispered hoarsely.

"You truly didn't know, did you?" she asked, tightening her hold on him.

"No! How could I? You seemed to want me, but I thought you were only making the most of our marriage. And when you asked me for a child," he said unsteadily, "I thought you only wanted to make the best of a bad situation."

"I wanted to give you a child because I love you," she said, smiling against his broad chest. "Thorn," she whispered, caressing his chest softly. "I'm carrying your baby."

He was still. His body went rigid in her arms. "You are…what?" he asked, choking.

"I am with child," she repeated. There was no chance at all that she was making the most of a bad situation, he thought dazedly, not with that radiance in her face.

Then he remembered the night before he'd left for Tucson. He made a rough sound. "You are carrying my child…and I took you…like that?" He groaned, terrified. "My God, Trilby! My God, I could have hurt you so badly! And the baby…" He sounded frantic.

She soothed him, putting her hand over his mouth and caressing it, gentling him. "Thorn, it's all right. You didn't harm either of us. Listen to me, please. I'm all right."

He shook. Moisture stung his eyes. "Trilby, I'm sorry."

She pressed into his body, clinging. "I love you," she

said fervently. "And you love me. There is nothing to forgive. I hurt you, without meaning to. You were only trying to show me what you felt, but I didn't understand. Now I do. Thorn, you're my life!" she whispered.

He shuddered. His arms gathered her close and still he shuddered, washed in terror as he realized what he could have cost them both with his violent ardor.

"Oh, my darling," she said softly, "please don't be like this. I promise you, no harm came to me or to our child."

"Never again," he said, choking. "I'll never touch you like that again!"

"Yes, you will, when I'm properly fit again, because the way we are with each other is passionate and wild and glorious." She reached up and kissed his hard mouth hungrily. "I adore you," she breathed. "Adore you, worship you…"

Her soft kisses melted his pain. He gathered her up and kissed her slowly, until kissing was no longer enough. He groaned with the fever that throbbed inside him.

"Ahem."

The dry tone diverted them. They looked toward the doorway, where Naki was poised.

"Excuse me, but are you both deaf?"

Thorn frowned. As sanity returned, he heard sharp reports and there was suddenly a whizzing sound close by, followed by a hard thud.

"Do you hear that? Guns? *Firing* guns? Ricocheting bullets?" Naki prompted. "Pistols and rifles and that damned cannon they captured? If you both don't want to be impaled by a bullet, it might be a dandy idea to get in out of the line of fire."

"Why didn't you say something, damn it?" Thorn raged, herding Trilby into the car. "She's having a baby!"

"Yes, I know." Naki grinned. "Everyone knows. We've been taking turns guarding her. Juan over there thinks he's in love."

Thorn glared at the smiling little man. "He can go kiss his horse. She's mine."

"I'll tell him— Get down!"

He shoved them gently, urgently, to the floor as glass shattered all around them.

"I do believe," Naki murmured, with his lips inches from the floor, "that it's going to be a very long day."

It was. By afternoon, they were all worn out with nerves and lack of sleep. But the shooting had finally stopped, and according to the reports they were getting, a force of *Federales* was on its way to Agua Prieta. There would surely be more fighting soon. Hell was poised all around them, waiting for the chance to break loose.

She didn't know Red López on sight, but Juan pointed him out in the distance. She had expected the local hero of the revolution to be tall and handsome and dashing, like someone out of a dime novel. But he was rather ordinary-looking, with a ready smile for his men and an unhurried, polite manner when he was introduced later in the day to Trilby. Nobody could have looked less like an officer. But like so many of the rebel officers, he had a sharp mind and a sense of strategy and tactics. He was like a mosquito, biting and running, biting and running. His very elusiveness gave him an edge against the enemy.

The general who had first spoken with Trilby came back to speak to the small group of Americans shortly thereafter. "We must return you to *Los Estados Unidos,*" he told them. "But it will require caution, because your captain across the border has sworn to make prisoners of war of any *insurrectos* he catches on American soil. It is a dangerous situation."

Trilby smiled. "I find that I am getting used to danger, sir."

Thorn was so proud of her that he could barely contain himself. His gentle, sheltered Trilby had changed overnight, blossomed into a pioneer woman. He all but shook, just looking at her.

"My wife is with child," Thorn told the general, his voice deep and worried.

"As Juan said a moment ago," the general replied, sweeping off his hat to bow gallantly to Trilby. "*Felicidades,* señora," he added, with a smile. "And it will be my pleasure to escort you to the border."

"You are a gentleman, señor," she said, and smiled back.

"I will regret your loss, you know," he said surprisingly. "You have become one of my best medics. Who will take care of my poor men?"

"The hospitals across the border," Jack Lang volunteered. "There are makeshift clinics everywhere—and plenty of people to look after the wounded and dying. They'll take rebels, Federals, anyone."

The general nodded. "That is as it should be." He signaled to Juan, and, minutes later, after Trilby had wished the small doctor a gentle goodbye, they were on their way to the customhouse.

The general escorted them past the line of rebels along the embankment of the border under a flag of truce. The Mexican rebel general saluted the American army captain in charge there, who returned the salute with proper respect and walked back to his men. Jack Lang gave a sigh of relief.

"Thank God," he said. "American soil!"

"Yes," Thorn said, hugging Trilby close. "Thank God indeed. Naki, aren't you coming?" he asked when Naki stayed just over the line, watching the American officer approach.

The Apache shook his head with a slow smile. "I am becoming part of the revolution, my friend. My people lost their bid for freedom, but these people still have a chance. Many of us who are non-Mexicans are fighting for their cause. I cannot desert them now, when we are so close to claiming victory."

"But what about Sissy?" Trilby asked sadly.

Naki's face hardened. "Tell her nothing. Nothing at all."

"McCollum told her you were here," she said, with anguish. "She thinks you're dead!"

Naki's dark eyes closed and a shiver went through his tall body. "So be it, then," he said hoarsely. "It is for the best."

"She loves you."

Naki's eyes opened and in them was the purest hell Trilby had ever seen. "I know," he said fiercely. "How I know!"

"She would give up everything."

"As I would. As I have," Naki said quietly. He managed a grim smile. "When this is over, perhaps there will be a way."

Trilby didn't argue. She had no right to tell the man how to live his life. She hurt for him, for Sissy.

"Take care of yourself," Thorn told him. "Don't get killed down here."

"I promise to try. *Vaya con Dios.*"

"Yes. And you."

Naki waved and went back to join the others across the border, looking much more like a revolutionary soldier than a misplaced Apache.

Thorn, Jack, and Trilby continued on and were immediately surrounded by reporters and an angry American officer as they gained the American lines.

Thorn saw a way out and held up his hand. "Later, please," he said. "My wife is in a delicate condition. She feels faint and I must get her home."

That set the men, who were gentlemen, into a protective attitude, and Trilby was rushed to Jack Lang's car through the crowd.

"Did the greaser devils harm her?" one man blustered as they reached the car.

Trilby stopped dead and glared at the man. "They are Mexican rebel soldiers, not 'greasers.' Neither are they devils. In fact, my treatment at their hands was much more gentlemanly than it might be at the hands of any American man in the same situation, I daresay!"

The man cleared his throat and belatedly removed his hat.

"Idiot," Trilby said—loud enough for her voice to carry. She clasped Thorn's hand in hers as he closed the door behind them. "'Greasers,' indeed!"

Thorn glanced at Jack Lang and smiled indulgently. After promising the American officer as many details as he could remember once Trilby was safely home, they left town in a roar of yellow dust.

* * *

Agua Prieta belonged to the Maderistas for only a few days. Three of the rebel leaders surrendered to U.S. troops, and when a column of twelve thousand *Federales,* under the command of Col. Reynaldo Díaz, marched into Agua Prieta, they found the trenches deserted and the city looted. The siege was over. Fortunately for both nations, intervention and war were averted.

Shortly after the *Federales* retook Agua Prieta, two Maderista rebel officers, Francisco "Pancho" Villa and Pascual Orozco, led their forces against Juárez. Juárez fell, and Madero took office as president of Mexico. The rebels celebrated, and so did the others who had fought for Madero.

Red López died tragically not too long after the battle for Agua Prieta. It was noted in a newspaper story before the siege of Agua Prieta that while being interviewed he had given his bed to a reporter and slept on the floor. Possibly many of the unflattering things said about him were true, but Trilby, who had met him and heard about him from his own men, thought that he must have had some saving graces to inspire such devotion in his followers.

López was gone, but Orozco and Obregón and Villa and Zapata and many other rebel leaders were alive and heady with victory. The fiestas went on for days and days, even along the American side of the border. The first phase of the Mexican revolution ended on May 26, 1911, with the resignation and departure of Porfirio Díaz. Another election was held in November of the same year and Francisco Madero became president.

Trilby, rested and in the bosom of her family, was making a dress for Samantha and enjoying the renewal of her marriage. She and Thorn grew closer every day. There were no more doubts, no more sorrows. They loved, and their child ripened in Trilby's body as the days grew longer and hotter with the end of summer. There were no more secrets and no more uncertainties. When Thorn looked at his wife, the love in her eyes all but blinded him. He felt more like a king than a savage these days.

He told her so.

She laughed and reached up to kiss him tenderly. "The only savage thing about you, my darling, is the way you love me," she whispered. "And I hope that never changes."

He smiled against her welcoming lips. As he kissed her, he whispered back that it never would.

Jorge improved and came home to resume his duties at Los Santos. Sissy wrote regularly to Trilby, but her letters were sad and brief, and she never mentioned Naki. Nor did Trilby. There had been rumors, as there always were, that Naki had been one of the American rebel prisoners executed in Mexico. They had no word from him at Los Santos, and even Thorn had begun to believe he was really dead.

Fall came to Louisiana as well as Arizona. Alexandra Bates was sipping tea with her mother in the parlor when the maid announced a gentleman caller.

"That Harrow fellow again, I fear," Mrs. Bates said, with resignation and a wistful smile at Sissy. "We will have to have him shot, Sissy, or he won't go away. Well, show him in," she told the maid, who curtsied and went out. "Why does your father have to go off on these hunting trips and leave me to field your persistent suitors!"

Sissy smiled, but not with much enthusiasm. She was still mourning Naki. Over the months, her spirit had dwindled and she took little interest in anything. She had given up her studies, almost life itself. Richard had grown up, changed for the better, and had become engaged to a kind, sweet girl. Ben had gone to Texas, of all places, to become a Texas Ranger. Sissy was the only sibling still living at home. She wondered if she would ever be able to feel again. The Mr. Harrow to whom her mother referred was a widower who had taken a shine to Sissy, much against her wishes. She grew fatigued with finding ways to avoid him. She wanted only one man, and he was dead. She'd mourned him forever, it sometimes seemed.

Mrs. Bates greeted the caller before Sissy saw him. It was definitely not Mr. Harrow. This man was tall and elegantly dressed. He had a faintly Continental look, as a Frenchman would have, with black hair neatly cut and combed and eyes like liquid black pearls. He was incredibly handsome and refined, and the suit he wore was as immaculate as his highly polished black boots.

"Mrs. Bates?" he asked the elder woman, smiling. "I was told that I might find Alexandra here. Ah, yes. There you are!" he added, glancing past the older woman to where Sissy sat on the upholstered sofa.

Alexandra Bates, in her dark dress, sat and stared at him from a face that grew whiter and whiter, until not a drop of blood was left in it.

"Look out, she's going to faint!" Mrs. Bates exclaimed, shocked.

Naki leaped forward to catch her, his powerful body easily absorbing her weight. Her thinness tore at his heart.

He laid her gently on the sofa, and Mrs. Bates, fluttering, called for the maid and sent her for smelling salts.

"Oh, for goodness' sake, what's wrong with her?" Mrs. Bates moaned worriedly.

"Does she have these spells often?" Naki asked, his eyes clinging hungrily to Sissy's beloved, unconscious face.

"No. But she hasn't been the same since she came home from Arizona months ago. She's mourned that man…" She remembered that she had a guest, a stranger, and stopped speaking. She smiled. "It's of no importance. You haven't yet introduced yourself, young man."

"Haven't I?" he murmured absently, because she was stirring now. He possessed Alexandra's soft little hand and held it tightly. His fine dark eyes searched her face. "Sissy," he called gently.

She opened her eyes and they dilated. She shivered. "You're dead!" she whispered brokenly. "Naki, you're dead, you're dead!"

"No," he whispered tenderly, smiling. "How could I die and leave you behind?"

"Naki!" Her voice ripped with emotion. She held out her arms, and was lifted and cradled fiercely against his heart. His eyes closed. He rocked her, his arms enfolding her a little roughly as the months of loneliness boiled over, the emotion on his smooth features evident even to a blind woman, which Mrs. Bates quite definitely was not.

"Well," she said, clasping her hands before her as realization set in. She smiled. "I must say, young man, you are nothing like the mental picture I had of you."

He looked at her over Sissy's dark head with a soft,

slow smile. "I daresay you expected feathers and war paint?"

Mrs. Bates chuckled. "Exactly. Do you like tea?"

"With plenty of ice," he said, "if you please. Mexico is short of that particular commodity."

While Mrs. Bates left discreetly to supervise a tray for them, Naki helped Sissy into a sitting position and searched her radiant face warmly.

"I had a few close calls, but I'm all right. I've earned some land of my own, Alexandra. I bought a tract of it near Cancún," he said, without preamble. "It will be foreign to us both, I'm afraid, but we can live there in peace and without prejudice. I will always be Apache, and I have no intention of hiding my race or denying my pride in it. But heritage doesn't depend on geography. I can be an Apache in Mexico as well as I can in Arizona."

"You'd be giving up everything!" she protested weakly.

"Not quite," he replied quietly. "But the alternative is to either take you to the reservation, where you would suffer the prejudice, or try to live in a white world and suffer it myself. I think Mexico is our only choice." He searched her eyes hungrily. "You have to decide if sharing my life is worth giving up your home and your way of life."

Her eyes registered the enormity of what he was telling her. She smiled and went soft in his arms. "What a small thing to sacrifice, when I would gladly give up my life to stay with you," she said simply.

His eyes closed. It was profound, this feeling. More profound than anything he'd ever known. In his mind, he could picture Alexandra in his arms on tropical nights, the thunder and lightning crashing while he made himself master of her soft, virginal body. He shivered with the thought of the ecstasy they would share. He looked at her and thought that such a dream would be worth anything. Even, as she had said, life itself.

"Yes," he said huskily. "I feel just as deeply for you. Shall we risk it?"

She smiled and shook her head. "There will be no risk." She reached up and put her mouth hungrily against his.

"Even with love like this on both sides, it will not be easy." He tried to speak through her kisses.

She smiled and kissed him harder. "I want children after we're married," she said solemnly. She put her hand over his mouth when he began to protest. "I want lots and lots of children," she said again, each word measured and firm.

He sighed. "Alexandra, we have spoken of this mixing of races—"

"Which will go unnoticed in Mexico," she finished. She smiled. "And our children will be especially beautiful," she whispered, picturing them in her mind.

It was hard to argue with her. His hands framed her face and he smiled at her. "Beautiful children?" he breathed.

"Beautiful," she emphasized. "We'll tell them about their Apache heritage, and make them proud of it. And we'll love them so much," she said fervently, reaching up. "Almost as much as we love each other…"

He could find no argument with that. In the end, he began kissing her hungrily—and yielded with grace to the almost unbearable joy of a shared future.

* * *

Trilby and Thorn had a son late in the autumn, a handsome young man with his father's dark eyes and his mother's coloring. He was named Caleb, for his late paternal grandfather.

Naki and Sissy, on the other hand, had five children, all of whom favored their handsome and very successful father.

Richard Bates married his debutante, who loved him all her life, despite his tendency to stray.

Teddy Lang grew up to be sheriff of Cochise County, Arizona, and little Samantha Vance married a doctor in Douglas.

Ben Bates became a captain of the Texas Rangers.

Caleb Vance married a Spanish girl, ran for the United States Senate, and won.

As for Lisa Morris, she married her Captain Powell and surprised everyone by becoming pregnant the very next year.

Francisco "Pancho" Villa, who had become well known in revolutionary circles after the Battle of Juárez, meanwhile, was deserted by Madero, arrested, and placed in jail. He later escaped. In late November of 1911, Zapata rose against Madero. Orozco formed an army to oppose him and was defeated by Huerta, who had deposed Madero and had him put to death.

On March 6, 1913, in the night, Pancho Villa left El Paso and crossed the border into Mexico. He had with him eight men, nine rifles, five hundred rounds of ammunition, two pounds of coffee, two pounds of sugar, and a pound of salt. By 1914, he had raised an army, the Northern Division, and chased the *Federales* out of the capital city of Chihuahua and the state of Sonora. Several years after Trilby's experience, there would be a second, decisive battle for Agua Prieta, spearheaded by Pancho Villa on November 1, 1915—the first battle that Villa was to lose in the state of Sonora to the *Federales.*

Through the course of the revolution, despite his setbacks, Villa led charge after charge with his men and his cannon, *El Niño,* and was immortalized in a book by Harvard journalist John Reed, who rode with him. Among the foreigners who shared Villa's joys and defeats was an American who later had a grand career as a motion picture cowboy—a fellow by the name of Tom Mix.

Villa finally surrendered in 1920, three years after a new constitution was legislated that provided for land reform and nationalism. Zapata was killed in 1919, Villa was assassinated in 1923. The revolution was effectively over. Col. Alvaro Obregón became president of Mexico in 1921.

Despite the revolution, nothing really changed very much. There were reforms, yes, but influential foreign investors still controlled much of Mexico's wealth. The rural Mexican people still subsisted on meager wages. The only real change was the name of the man sitting in the president's chair.

Thorn and Trilby sat on their front porch several years after the first battle of Agua Prieta, watching the local aviator's biplane sail gracefully through the air in the early days of World War I in Europe.

"They say they'll be using those things in an air war overseas," he said, his fine dark eyes twinkling. "If I were a few years younger, I might try my hand at

aviation. Those planes seemed to work well enough for
Villa at the end of the revolution."

"The planes and *El Niño,*" she mused dryly.

He leaned back in the swing, sliding an easy arm
around her shoulders. Samantha had gone away to school
in the East, and young Caleb was out back with Teddy,
learning how to mend harnesses. And life was sweet.

"Do you ever miss the old life?" he asked suddenly,
glancing down at her. "Louisiana and cotillions and genteel company, I mean?"

She pressed her hand flat against his chest and laid
her cheek on his shoulder to stare up at him adoringly.
"No," she said simply.

"Not even a life without dust?" he persisted.

"I like dust. It's pretty. It goes well with my skin."
She traced his nose and smiled. "I love you," she whispered.

He sighed, appeased, and rested his cheek on her
hair. "You've changed."

"Oh, yes. I can shoot a gun and saddle a horse and
wield an ax," she replied jauntily. "Not to mention stitch-
ing wounds and participating in revolutions."

He chuckled. "And I do at least have a semblance of
party manners, so I won't embarrass Samantha when
she brings her young man home."

"You'd never embarrass any of us, least of all me, my
dear." She slid onto his lap and eased her head into the
crook of his arm. "But if you like, we can refresh your
memory on manners. For instance," she whispered, tugging his head down so that she could touch her warm
lips to his hard ones, "a gentleman always helps a lady
in distress."

Under her hand, his breathing increased, like his

heartbeat. Her ability to rouse him never weakened. "Are you in distress?" he asked.

"Oh, yes," she said fervently. "Great distress. Do you think you could assist me to the bedroom and help me to lie down?"

He chuckled wickedly. "I believe I might." He stood up, still holding her, and walked back into the deserted house. "I hope our son is very interested in mending harnesses."

"The door does have a lock," she whispered, laughing, and nibbled his ear as she clung to him.

He bent his head and kissed her back, smiling against her welcoming lips.

Overhead, the colorful biplane made a lazy loop in the sky and turned back toward Douglas, waggling its wings at two boys who stood watching it far out in the field. It sailed as if on angel's wings, a giant butterfly in the sun. And far below, on the winding road, the yellow dust blew on.

* * * * *

THE Essential COLLECTION

by Diana Palmer

YES! Please send me *The Essential Collection* by Diana Palmer. This collection will begin with 3 FREE BOOKS and 2 FREE GIFTS in my very first shipment—and more valuable free gifts will follow! My books will arrive in 8 monthly shipments until I have the entire 51-book *Essential Collection* by Diana Palmer. I will receive 2 free books in each shipment and I will pay just $4.49 U.S./$5.39 CDN for each of the other 4 books in each shipment, plus $2.99 for shipping and handling.* If I decide to keep the entire collection, I'll only have paid for 32 books because 19 books are free. I understand that accepting the 3 free books and gifts places me under no obligation to buy anything. I can always return a shipment and cancel at any time. My free books and gifts are mine to keep no matter what I decide.

279 HDK 9860   479 HDK 9860

Name	(PLEASE PRINT)	
Address		Apt. #
City	State/Prov.	Zip/Postal Code

Signature (if under 18, a parent or guardian must sign)

Mail to the **Reader Service:**

IN U.S.A.: P.O. Box 1867, Buffalo, NY 14240-1867
IN CANADA: P.O. Box 609, Fort Erie, Ontario L2A 5X3

* Terms and prices subject to change without notice. Prices do not include applicable taxes. Sales tax applicable in N.Y. Canadian residents will be charged applicable taxes. This offer is limited to one order per household. All orders subject to credit approval. Credit or debit balances in a customer's account(s) may be offset by any other outstanding balance owed by or to the customer. Please allow 4–6 weeks for delivery. Offer available while quantities last. Offer not available to Quebec residents.

ECDPBPA11